D1562025

LENINSKY PROSPEKT

Also by Katherine Bucknell

Canarino

LENINSKY PROSPEKT

KATHERINE BUCKNELL

FOURTH ESTATE • *London* and *New York*

First published in Great Britain in 2005 by Fourth Estate
A Division of HarperCollins*Publishers*
77–85 Fulham Palace Road
London W6 8JB
www.4thestate.com

1

A catalogue record for this book is
available from the British Library

ISBN 0 00 717867 0

Typeset in Bembo by Palimpsest Book Production Ltd,
Polmont, Stirlingshire

Printed in Great Britain by Clays Ltd, St Ives plc

For my mother and father
and
for Uncle Tom

LENINSKY PROSPEKT

Viktor was thinking about trees. He leaned back as far as he could and he saw brightness flash and move through his blindfold as the van heaved and tossed its way through whatever streets these were, and he imagined that he could see flickering translucent leaves turning and trembling in their thousands above him, layer upon soaring layer, spiralling up to the blue sky which he knew must lie beyond. It opened his head, what he could imagine today, with the continual changes in air, the thin real light and the ordinary city noises that he associated with Moscow and home. He resisted wondering exactly where he was or why he was being moved. Instead, he journeyed in his thoughts, along a rutted country road lined with white-trunked birch, their peeling bark showing black scored stripes and pink tree flesh among their chalky, breeze-twisted leaves. Beyond the birch, straight, taller firs with their sober-needled boughs marshalled the blue depths of the forest.

The road bent away in front until it was lost to view; he might make it hours still before he arrived at the little dacha, with its polished dark wood walls, its brick chimney, smoke twitching the nostrils, the chairs positioned on the veranda in the last patch of sun, his books and papers on the desk inside where he had left them, his pen still uncapped, the line to finish. Maybe she would be waiting outside, alert on the chair which she favoured, looking out for him. Or, no. Maybe she would be lying on the blowsy red sofa, by the desk, her feet up, reading a book, fidgeting with the splayed brown ends of her braids.

These were savoured images. For months, years, now, going over them and over them, Viktor had found he could make them more detailed, more real. He believed he could probably go on doing this for ever, but he had realized early on that he must be careful not to discover whether he was right. He must be careful not to find himself at the end of his resources. For instance, he tried not to find words for these images; whenever he had pencil and paper, he didn't write about them. Instead, he forced himself to begin making new images, new scenes to turn to, before he could tire of the ones he loved best. He kept his mind moving, fresh, alive, by planning poems but not writing them down until he had an idea for a new one, a better one. Like a cook, he was always preparing something for himself to look forward to, to indulge himself in, even though he had to cook without meat or even a carrot or an onion for his pot. The feeling of anticipation was deeply pleasurable to Viktor; the feeling of nostalgia was not. He never allowed himself to consider what he had lost. Regret weakened him.

And he never allowed himself to get close to her, close enough, say, to reach for her. He knew that when tenderness turned to appetite, he couldn't float his imagination over it, couldn't lift his mind out of the trap he was in, his body. He was better off with sentimentality, with pictures that he softened on purpose in order to comfort his heart. Physical desire was too hard a struggle.

With such disciplines, he had lasted a total of nearly five years in prison. Once, after the first four years, he had been released, shoved into the open: the clamouring, all-talking, over-bright reality where other people's trains of thought unpredictably crashed in on his. He had not been allowed back to the institute to continue his research, but a friend helped him get temporary work in the library there. The unregimented hours away from his inner life had made him fretful, as if he were starved of sleep. This, too, he had learned to cope with, but then his freedom hadn't lasted.

Since returning to prison, he had continually practised engaging with others – exchanging messages and making deals at exercise time, giving impromptu lectures, organizing work strikes, hunger strikes, writing letters of complaint, writing on the walls, until, often, he was put into solitary confinement. And he kept an image ready for freedom. It wasn't an image that he dared to explore at all; it was only a black dot, like a punctuation mark or a hole, which made his breath come shallow and sharp when he considered, even for the briefest second, that it existed. Still, he wouldn't allow himself to forget it was there: a possibility, hurtling towards him – liberation, confusion, a kind of death – the moment when he might again feel a certain kind of concern about the actions of others. He feared this moment pressing upon his thoughts more even than flesh, more than the likely slide into depravity that he along with all his fellow prisoners continually risked, through lack of choice, through bondage.

Today, he let himself drive his father's black Pobeda further than usual along the tree-lined road. He imagined that he had the windows rolled down, until the spreading twilight nipped at his black-haired forearm, muscular as it had once been, lying in the opening atop the car door. To make the trip last longer, he thought again about the leaves, the fractal intricacies of their countless edges, their intimate exchanging of breath with light, with air, as they ceaselessly moved and grew. He didn't think for a moment about where the van was actually taking him tonight.

October, 28, 1962. The tiered, red and gold glory of the crowded Bolshoi was prickling and rustling with tension, and the momentary hush before the start of the Sunday evening programme was suffused with almost liquid anxiety, as if everyone in the theatre was drowning in stage fright. Maybe tonight would be their last night on earth. They shrugged off their wraps, licked their reeds, flexed and stretched their calves, their metatarsals, their hopes. Audience, musicians, dancers in their separated spheres struggled to still themselves, to collect their shuddering thoughts, their gossiping fretful tongues, so they could engage one more time with the grandeur of civilization: why not lose themselves in ballet as the planet mutely spun through its final tilted rotation?

The conductor, his wasp-waisted, black uprightness just visible above the creamy, red-lipped orchestra pit, raised his arms over the fidgeting sea of preparation, pulled it towards him like a tide. His bent wrists, his curled fingers lightly commanded the disciplined glance of his musicians. The conductor was American. The musicians were Soviet, mostly Soviet the audience at his back. The hush fizzed and foamed, expanded to the point of pain, to bursting. Then, with a ruthless intake of breath, a brusque snap of his chin, the conductor simply began.

From the Russian strings and winds rose the Second Movement of Mendelssohn's 'Scottish' Symphony. The red and gold curtain parted, and on the stage American ballet dancers, dressed in kilts and tartan socks, skipped before the whirlwind, bar by measured bar, step by springing step, jaunty, death-defying. Ballet was their mother tongue, and everyone in the Bolshoi that night understood the music, the dance, the ritual of artist and audience.

The performance wrung tears of nostalgia and of rage from Nina Davenport, who bowed her teased and sprayed chestnut flip over her fists, dashed with blanched knuckles at the hollows underneath her mascaraed eyes. It seemed easy, beautiful, obvious – the years of mental and physical devotion flowering in lively complexity on this foreign stage.

Nina sat alone in the eighth row, one seat left of the left side aisle. Beside her was the only empty seat in the house; John Davenport was at the American Embassy. She cried for John, too, for his absence, for their newly married heartache of impatience, misunderstanding, lapse of conviction. She cried for unfinished mysteries, for the slow pulse of love smashed by anonymous brutality. And she cried for the pale, undying sylph on the stage, circled by the men of the corps de ballet so that, for a yearning instant, her lover couldn't reach her.

Nina tried to keep the wet of her tears off the wisps of paper crushed in her hands. As she dragged her eyes back to the stage, she dropped the papers onto her lap. They were the same colour as her white wool skirt but more fragile, wrinkled, translucent. The skirt was robust with workmanship, a thickly woven bouclé, soft as a cloud to touch, taut across her pressed-together caramel nylon knees. She felt hot in the matching short jacket, which she wore as she had been told to, with its three saucer-like gold buttons done all the way up to the stiff, stand-away collar. The beige silk lining whispered and slid against her skin as she fretted in her red velvet chair, smoothing the patch pockets of the skirt with the heels of her hands, with her pearl-pink painted fingernails.

She had ordered the suit in Paris the day she and John got off the boat from New York. 'There's nothing to wear in Moscow,' her mother had said fiercely, in her husky, smoke-abused voice, 'but that doesn't mean you won't need things.' She had given Nina twenty thousand dollars in cash.

'Start at Balenciaga, darling.' Mother's tone had been resigned, then she had sighed, indulgent, conspiratorial, 'Cristóbal has absolutely perfect taste. He'll get your eye in. And that way you'll be recognized for what you are by anyone who can tell. Nobody else matters. A diplomat's wife ought to be chic, especially in Europe. He has flair, a touch of flamenco, but he's never vulgar – he's a Roman Catholic, you see. And you'll like the colours he uses. From Goya's paintings, or maybe from an olive grove he remembers in the Spanish countryside. I know you don't give a damn about clothes, but you owe it to John, dear.'

Nina had felt impressed but not surprised by how much her mother had learned about such things in six years of restless, unaccompanied circling from Paris to New York, Buffalo to Palm Beach, while Nina struggled through Wellesley, languished behind the reception desk of a well-established, little-frequented Old Masters gallery on Madison Avenue, sat numb at a ballet, fell passionately in love. She had accepted the money in order to soothe her mother's distress over the fact that she was moving with John back to Russia. And maybe to soothe her own. As if clothes or even money could somehow protect Nina from whatever awesome, difficult experiences Russia was bound to offer her.

'I understand how you feel about John,' Nina's mother had said in another, earlier, conversation. 'Think how crazy I was about your poor father to follow him there when I was your age. My parents did everything to stop me. I didn't listen to them; naturally I thought my husband was far more exciting and important than Buffalo, New York or a sewing machine fortune that he had persuaded me no individual deserved to have or inherit when people everywhere were hungry. But I didn't know anything about Russia, or about life, for that matter. I had been totally spoiled by my upbringing. I had no idea what I was giving up. And then you came along.'

Mother had bitten her tongue on this, stopped short. 'Not you, dear. I don't mean you.' But somehow it had seemed as if she did mean Nina; she so often struck these clumsy, inadvertent blows, then tried to take them back. She had softened her voice, almost pleading, 'Nina, dear, after everything we've been through, I just can't understand why you and John want to do this. I can't believe the two of you think it's safe. I like John; at least I thought I liked John. But what kind of a man is he, that he would take you to Moscow, knowing everything about you as he does? Why is the State Department even allowing it, for God's sake? That's what I don't understand.'

Nina had been firm, confident, justified. 'Don't start on the what-kind-of-a-man thing, Mother. It's my decision. I'm perfectly happy to go back. John has told you he would give it up if I asked him to; you and I both know he means it. His job has absolutely nothing to do with what happened to you and Dad.'

But it had given her another fit of inward trembling. All the while, she had known what her mother was remembering, what her mother had hoped in America to forget once and for all: the ZAGS office near Gorky Street hit by a German incendiary bomb in 1943, every single document in the building burned to cinders, buckets of sand poured on the flames to no avail by the night-time fire brigades, rain transforming official records into sodden mounds of indecipherable, tar-coloured debris – births, deaths, marriages obliterated. On Nina's new registration, her mother had written: Born 1937, Buffalo, New York. Afterwards, she had taken Nina straight to the park and begun teaching her to say she was six years old, not four.

Her parents had fought bitterly over her. Their rage still bellowed at Nina down the years.

'It's her only chance. You can't do anything for us now.'

'Are you crazy? You've put her in inconceivable danger – all of us! She's a true Soviet, why put this mark against her? How could I even *be* her father if she was born in 1937? You were still in Greenwich Village most of 1937, and I hadn't seen you for at least a year! Besides that, how the hell will you explain how tiny she is?'

'Nobody left in Moscow has enough to eat. All the children have stopped growing.'

'What about the doctor?'

'I'll find a new doctor. Lots of people go privately. I can get the money. I have plenty of translating work at the Foreign Ministry.'

'If she's six, she needs to start school next year.'

'She can do it. She's a smart little girl. I know how to get her ready; I'm a teacher now, after all. Everything around us is in complete chaos anyway. The children who were evacuated have been coming back in mobs. Who will notice?'

And so they had chanced it, on the basis of chaos, counting on bureaucratic inefficiency, gnawing their fingernails to blood when each new year, each new challenge in Nina's childish life brought a new set of anxieties.

When Nina and her mother had arrived in the USA on Soviet passports in 1956, the US passport office in Washington, DC, had been eager to accept whatever statements they offered. Why would they want to undermine Nina's right to be an American citizen, her right to hold an American passport? Her father had been dead for three years, but both her parents were American; nobody doubted that. There was already a cable in Nina's file about her interview at the embassy in Moscow; it was necessary only to confirm certain details. No record of Nina's birth could be traced, so Aunt Josephine came from Buffalo to swear to it, a rambling, engaging, cunning swear.

'The weather was so appalling that winter, and Dr Ainsworth was getting old. He must have been way past retirement age. A home birth, in the middle of the night, and then getting out in the snow to file papers? He just wasn't very professional that way. He was really more of a family friend. And the truth is,' here, as Aunt Josephine had later told it to Nina, to Mother, she came over all trusting, confidential, 'you see, the truth is, my sister wasn't *married*. My hunch is that Dr Ainsworth was making some old-fashioned attempt to spare embarrassment – leaving the details to the discretion of the family. We were prominent locally, after all. Not that anyone was trying to pretend it had never happened, but maybe just – fudging things a little. My sister left for Russia as soon as she was strong enough, to join the baby's father. She put the baby on her own passport of course, and then all those documents were confiscated over there. Naturally, our parents destroyed everything to do with my sister, they were so distressed. They're dead now, and that house has been sold, and Dr Ainsworth is dead, too, and his office closed years ago.'

Thus, it had been established firmly, once and for all. But Mother knew, Aunt Josephine knew, Nina knew, John knew. And at a small, sequestered bank in upstate New York, there had been an enormous pile of money building up quietly during the years Mother was away. Nina's grandparents hadn't wished to expunge their daughter from memory at all. On the contrary, they had left her a fortune in hopes of luring her home.

Eventually, Nina's mother had stopped trying to persuade Nina to wait out John's Moscow tour in Buffalo or in New York.

'I can't go back and sit in that gallery on Madison Avenue all day, Mother. It never meant anything to me, no matter how much I love paintings, drawings. Where could it lead? I want to be with my husband. I need to be.'

She and her mother had silently begun to pretend that Moscow would be Europe: parties, museums, opera and ballet, a desirable post for a young American wife. A post that called for a spectacular wardrobe, because that seemed to be the only preparation they could make.

The trunks and suitcases had already been jammed when the Davenports left Washington; the cartons of books, linen, kitchen and cleaning supplies, toilet paper, were sealed. So in Paris, between fittings and pilgrimages to the Opéra, the Louvre, the Sainte Chapelle, Nina bought another trunk from Louis Vuitton and began to fill its sleek emptiness with the finest personal items she could find, make-up and stockings and belts and scarves and gloves and shoes and fly-away silk nightgowns and chemises and armour-weight girdles that she believed could stop a bullet at close range. Last of all she had packed the beautifully hand-sewn clothes when they were ready. It had seemed like a lifetime's trousseau, assembled as if she might never be able to visit such shops and such craftsmen again. Some of it she had never even worn, and already the lifetime was running out. Hers and the world's, ticking away in the agitated, overcast, windy October twilight. Soon, unexpectedly soon.

The tears burned inside her straight, broad nose and around the rims of her wide, blue, ruined eyes. She felt the nuclear panic again, like a black wave rising, smoking at her, and the exhausted sensation of trying to quell it. She straightened her neck from the top of her spine as she had so often watched the dancers do lately, squinted hard at the stage. She considered that there was probably no one in the Bolshoi tonight who remained unaware that the rivalry between the Soviet Union and the United States had finally reached a cosmic stare-down over the missiles which Khrushchev had positioned in Cuba during September and early October. In some half-conscious, continually patrolling corner of her mind, Nina pictured him wherever he might be – closeted with the Presidium, pacing his dining-room floor, on his way to watch a travelling Bulgarian show – shaking his cruelly belittled fist, scowling pugnaciously at President Kennedy, his accidental nemesis. Both sides were now spitting into the abyss, she thought, the whistling nothingness beyond Armageddon.

It's worse, being in the audience, she decided. The dancers can at least dance. Being forced to stand by, to take it, whatever comes – you almost wish it would just goddamn happen and be over with. Khrushchev goes on giving orders, writing letters; the president holds meetings, makes speeches. As if they've narrowed down the whole universe to just the two of them. And they can't even talk to each other. Don't speak each other's language. Still she couldn't believe it. She couldn't conceive of it.

She longed pathetically for the fear-free ebullience of the New York City Ballet's opening night at the Bolshoi two and a half weeks ago. And she remembered from the opening programme the ballet called *Agon*. Contest. Struggle. It sums up everything, she thought; it might as well have been a prophecy. She stared at *Scotch Symphony* but what she saw now was the endless blue-lit set of *Agon*, without floor without walls, the plain modern leotards and tights. It had begun with wit, with saucy, twisting shoulders and hips – sophisticated, playful; but then a darkness, an undertow of mistiming, anxious syncopations had set in, bodies moving perfectly out of time, on top of the beat, before it, beside it, with deliberate mismatched precision; the swing of a leg kicking off the swing of some other leg, catapulting it further, so that the energy escalated, towards the limit of control. In the pas de deux, the guarded pride of the rooted, muscular black dancer, the haughty energy of the ballerina. The tension that had built between them was more than sex, more than race; it was every tension, every conflict epitomized, acted out. They and the others, gladiators, had issued challenge upon reckless challenge, dare upon bodily dare, raising the ante to impossible heights of technical virtuosity, chancing the edge of doom. Even now, Nina heard Stravinsky's bright, hectic music above Mendelssohn's; even now she saw those dancers and that dance.

October 6, 1962. The New York City Ballet arrived at Sheremetyevo Airport like a glamour bomb, an explosion of self-confident, long-limbed physical beauty, spreading and undulating past the green-clad border guards towards the truck-mounted floodlights, official photographers, grim-faced journalists, and ubiquitous, grey-suited, hummingbird-eyed officers of the KGB.

Sixty-odd pairs of perfectly muscled legs sauntered and flickered with restrained braggadocio over the colourless airport floors and past the drab bureaucratic demands of official paperwork, washed hair coiffed and swishing, perfectly fitting suits barely aeroplane creased, eyes glowing under false lashes, pastel-coloured vanity cases professionally gripped.

In the vanguard, George Balanchine, fifty-eight years old, slim, hawk-faced, spruce in cowboy shirt and string tie, stepped warily upon the Russian soil he had last trod when he was only twenty. He had been master for many years of his own ballet company, and his bearing consummately revealed that he felt himself master, too, of his own destiny. This tour to the Soviet Union was not, for him, a homecoming. He flaunted his American passport in his hand; he inflated his chest inside his Wild West costume. He would not easily submit to any nonsense of Soviet political choreography.

The dancers were greeted with nearly rampant curiosity tempered by puritanical suspicion and self-defensive disdain. Above the chatter and shouting in Russian and in English, Balanchine heard, 'Welcome to the home of classical ballet, Mr Balanchine!'

Coolly, he threw back, 'America is now the home of the classical ballet.'

The exchange with the press revealed nothing especially personal, nothing to suggest how Balanchine felt about his hurried, unremarked departure for Berlin on July 4, 1924, about his further emigration to America a decade later, about the deaths during his absence of his bon vivant composer father, his pretty, uncomplaining mother, his mild older sister who had not been gifted enough to become a ballerina. He had not seen them since 1918, the year in which he had turned fourteen. Instead the interview established that the tour of eight weeks would proceed from Moscow to the Kirov in Leningrad – where Balanchine himself had trained as a dancer – to Kiev, to Tbilisi – his boyhood home in Georgia – then finally to Baku; that a group of dancers from the Bolshoi, the twin element in this great cosmopolitan moment of cultural openness, had already taken to the stage in New York throughout the month of September and had been received with ecstatic acclaim.

From the mêlée burst Balanchine's younger, shorter, only brother, also a composer, Andrei Balanchivadze.

Balanchine cried out, 'Andryusha, it's you!' embracing him warmly. The official Soviet cameras flashed and popped. Then Balanchine somehow interposed his American passport and the cameras stopped.

Nina Davenport stood waiting with the representatives of the US State Department. Now it was her turn to be introduced, not to Balanchine himself, but to a clutch of young women dancers trailing along at the rear of the group.

'I'd make a friend of Mrs Davenport if I were you, ladies, and I'm sure you won't find it hard to do, either.' Fred Wentz, the newly arrived Special Officer representing the International Cultural Exchange Program of the US Government, had his large hand on Nina's small back, offering her up. His deep, Alabaman voice was honeyed with official enthusiasm. 'She is just what you need in this town, a native Muscovite. She really knows what goes on. She can answer all your questions', he lowered his voice, flirtatious, taunting, 'and tell you what not to ask.' Then more soberly, 'The official Soviet interpreters can be a little – formal. So Mrs Davenport has generously offered to spend as much time with you as you like. I understand she loves what you do. And, in my humble opinion,' grinning again, 'she's pretty enough to dance with you, too.' He ducked his head down to one side, casting a playful look at the ballerinas' legs, then at Nina's legs, equally slim, almost as shapely. 'I'm sure I'm going to love what you do, myself. Anything at all.'

There was a silence as his voice died. The ballerinas all dropped their eyes demurely to the floor and Nina felt herself blushing in irritation at the Special Cultural Officer. She forced a smile.

'I danced when I was a girl,' she admitted in her fluty, change-able voice. She cleared her throat, started again on a lower note, nodding benevolently, 'But I didn't have the stamina for a pro-fessional career – let alone the talent. And I don't think, Mr Wentz, that you can tell a lot about a dancer just by looking at her legs.' She tried not to sound prim; she made it more of a sportsman-like sally. But even so, she felt the bulldog will of her mother rise in her inexplicably, along with her mother's upstate New York reluctance to move the lips when talking, so that her voice came out all through her nose, awkward, ugly, somehow dismissive, not what she intended.

Wentz was a big man, solid. Underneath his loose-flapping, grey plaid suit, he held his shoulders wide, his chest expanded, so that his whole body seemed to be smiling, inviting attention. His gold hair curled just a little, as if with mischief. He continued to play up, crinkle-eyed, 'Well, I can certainly tell that I might like to look over my schedule and see how much time *I* can free up for tour-guiding and hand-holding over the next few weeks.'

There was a splurge of giggles from a bowed head in the depths of the bevy, and then giggles all around.

They are so young, Nina thought. Babies, some of them. The girls began to look up, prattling, smiling, rosy, and she took their hands one by one to shake them, '*Dobro pozhalovat*'. Welcome,' she said again and again, feeling the weightless, dry poise of their fingers in hers, their shy friendliness. And she said the Russian words with her tongue and her teeth, tasting them like morsels of food, like a whole meal she was hungry for.

At the back of the little group she saw one or two older faces, and she recognized in the features and the names as they were introduced that several of the girls had their mothers with them, chaperoning. That's dedication, she thought. But she felt nothing good about the mothers. A chaperone's role is to prevent, to restrain. Nina disliked restraint. A young girl wants to make up her own mind, she reflected. Why shouldn't she? How late she stays up, what she eats, how she fixes her hair, how loudly she laughs if there are boys nearby. The mothers looked tired, frowning, impossibly dumpy beside their glowing offspring; they were dressed to inspire hesitation in bulky, dark wool coats, one colour, one size, no shape.

Nina glanced at Wentz, wondering if the mothers were necessary. If mothers were ever necessary. Then suddenly she felt confused about her own role. A made-up job, she thought, to keep me busy, shepherding the younger women dancers. She felt overwhelmed with embarrassment. What do they need me for? Why am I here? All dressed up in a bright blue dress and jacket ensemble from Balenciaga, mink pillbox hat, brown gloves. This is – fake. I'm really not old enough to look after anyone, to stand alongside mothers. She wondered whether John had pressured somebody at the embassy to let her join in so that she could pretend to have something to do. It seemed that the professional embassy staff, the ballet company itself, and the Russians, had already provided enough chaperones and interpreters.

And just at that moment, as if to prove it, one of the official Soviet interpreters, a woman, approached to be introduced, with a cat-like smile which silently asserted, Nina thought, I know what you all would like to do, and I know how I will stop you.

I know how I will make you do what *I* want you to do. Highly trained, ambitious, in her single-breasted charcoal suit, her single-minded composure, the official interpreter would guide the dancers around Moscow, would engage and control them, would mark their every word and their every movement, their every passing interest. She would look after them perfectly. And she would report on them in full detail every day.

Nina stepped back. She did not want to be noticed, to be observed, not even in an official public place. She had been followed almost constantly since she and John had arrived in August. It felt odd to be thrown, now, into competition with someone reporting to the KGB. Some of the Americans at the embassy laughed off their minders, but Nina knew how minders could squeeze the soul, shut it down, just by watching, just by telling. She felt more and more impatient to leave the airport, this place of coming and going, passports, papers, entry and exit. It created in her a burning anxiety.

As they made their way to the buses waiting in the dark outside, Nina, head down, abashed, fell into step with a silent, brown-haired girl.

'Can I help with that stuff?'

The girl was tiny. She had a monster fur coat slung over one arm, a big square make-up case hanging from her hand, and an enormous sack-like handbag over her other shoulder. She grimaced and tilted her head, friendly. 'Thanks. It's OK.'

But Nina thought she could see the childlike forearm trembling with strain in its thin camel cardigan sleeve.

'Oh, come on. Please let me,' she said casually, and she took the make-up case in both hands, pausing for the girl to unclench and unstick her fingers from the handle. It must weigh thirty or forty pounds, Nina thought, hefting it up before her in both arms as they followed the meandering line through the airport doors and collected on the pavement beside three smoke-belching buses.

'You're Alice, is that right?'

'Uh-hm.' Alice nodded, accepting Nina's attention reservedly. She was pale, pretty enough, but without much contrast in her colouring, as if someone had wiped away any drama along with her stage make-up. And she kept her eyes hidden.

They climbed aboard the second bus and pushed towards the back, piling their laps high like everyone else's.

After a few minutes, Alice said quietly, 'I was all ready for them to search my stuff at the airport. They didn't even open my suitcase.'

Nina glanced around, then leaned near. 'They'll do it later, at the hotel,' she said, 'when you're out.'

'What?' Alice was startled, hugged her things closer.

'You probably won't even be able to tell. They won't take anything. Unless you brought cigarettes or stockings to give away and you leave some right on top for them.'

After another silence, in which she seemed to be considering this, Alice asked, 'So how can you be a native Muscovite, or whatever he said?'

'I know.' Nina nodded sympathetically.

Alice glanced at her sideways, brown-grey eyebrows raised in question.

'My parents were both American. They brought me here as a tiny child.'

'To – the embassy – or something?'

'Well, no.' Nina gathered her strength for the explanation. 'My father wasn't in the embassy. Actually, he gave up his American citizenship. So anything to do with the embassy – wouldn't have been –' she felt constrained, picking her words, '– possible.'

'I don't get it.'

'People don't,' Nina said, 'Americans don't.' Again, she glanced around. There was nobody especially near them who wasn't already talking, fully engaged. Black, massed trees flashed past the windows. 'My father was pretty radical for America.' She lowered her voice. 'A communist, is what I mean. We came here because this is where he wanted to live, what he believed in. He wasn't comfortable in America. He was – involved – in – the labour movement. I mean he wrote articles, gave speeches, explaining to workers where their interests really lay, encouraging them to stick up for themselves, band together, whatever. It was all before I was born. Or you for that matter. The world is a different place now. And America is different.'

She waved a hand as if she could rub it out, the past. Then she went on positively, bouncing the words out like a list of points, like an argument for her father's beliefs, 'The Soviet Union was his dream; he came here as royalty – not an approved Soviet word, but, still, in the beginning that's what he was. He was an engineer, which they needed here. He helped build the Metro – the Moscow subway system. You'll ride on it, maybe. And he talked my mother into – joining him. We lived just off Gorky Street, in Maly Gnezdnikovsky Lane.

There was a silence. Alice unwrapped her arms from her belongings, leaned back a little, and said, 'Good grief. You sound so American. I mean – you must have been there? The government must have let you in?'

Nina laughed, 'What? America? Of course they let me in – and my mother. Getting out of here was the hard part. But we were allowed to go –' Her voice let her down. She swallowed the word, tried again, '– home, a few years after my father died. So I went to college in America and then worked in New York for a while. All my friends are over there. Who knows why the Soviets have let me come back again.'

'Really?' At last Nina got a look at Alice's eyes – brown, amazed, unguarded.

'I'm just kidding.' She tapped Alice's forearm with two fingertips, ever so lightly, smiling. 'I mean, I know why. It's because of my husband. He *is* at the embassy. It figures, doesn't it, that I would marry someone obsessed with Russia, the Russian language, the Soviet Union? So they let me come back in with him. American diplomats are privileged privileged privileged.

Anyway it's only for a few years this time.' Nina's voice was joking, offhand, but suddenly she found she couldn't hold Alice's simple, curious gaze, and she had to look away.

From across the aisle, a tall, bony girl dropped her bag on the floor beside them. It made a loud, slapping thud.

'God, I'm sick of that thing.' She lifted her shoulders in her tightly fitting, light blue and white plaid wool suit jacket, circled them, stretched her arms delicately, beautifully, touched the smooth French twist of her hair, as if adjusting a pin, then looked around under her thatch of waved blonde bangs to check who was watching her. She smiled at Nina. Nina smiled back.

'Hi, Patrice,' said Alice, wagging her head familiarly. And then to Nina, 'Patrice and I room together, unless my husband comes.'

'You're married? You seem –'

'Young?' asked Alice.

Nina shrugged, conceding.

'I'm twenty-one. Plus, I have a baby boy at home.'

'Wow,' Nina said, her voice lifting in surprise. 'A baby?'

'Nearly killed me to leave him.' Alice whispered, 'Mr B. can't stand it – babies and ballerinas.' Now it was Alice who looked around to see who was listening. 'But I'm not a nun, you know. I'm as strong as ever, stronger. Everyone's different, that's all. A ballet career doesn't last, no matter what you give up for it. So, who knows?' She shrugged. 'Anyway, I'm not the only one; look at Allegra Kent. She dances with even more guts now than before, and Mr B. knows nothing scares her, not him, not her body. She gives off heat like a bonfire.' Alice blushed ever so slightly.

Nina was silenced, ruminating on the toughness that could dance professionally, talk so boldly, and yet needed a baby. Was a baby something you could leave thousands of miles away? she wondered. Alice didn't match any picture Nina had of a ballerina. Nor did she match anything Nina had come across at Wellesley, where the girls had been generally brainy and genteel, voluptuous, lazy, strong, and nice-smelling. Amateurs – willing, well-trained, eager to please. Both of these young American dancers, with their crisp, maidenly manners, their spindly, self-conscious physical aplomb, their seemingly reckless commitment to their vocation, made her sting with uncertainty. A sense of something she had forgotten – or misunderstood. They affected her almost like some kind of personal rebuke.

Nina had spent hours watching ballet during the last six years. In New York, even when she was at Wellesley, she got hold of tickets, dragged her mother, dragged John, went alone. She used to explain to them that ballet was, for her, the most immediate, the only way to think about life, to understand all that had happened to her, to make sense of who she had been and what she was becoming – Russian, American. But she knew that the hours in darkened auditoriums had also been an anaesthetic, a form of hypnosis. The ballet carried her back to something purely physical, impersonal: joy she knew she had felt in girlhood – music, movement, the excitement of wordless grace. She didn't think about the dancers onstage as real people; she lost herself in the full, concrete experience – what they did, what they made. Sometimes she watched in staring blankness, thoughtless, content.

When she and John became engaged to get married, she went less and less – not much at all after the wedding, until Paris and Moscow. Now, talking to Alice and Patrice, she began to think for the first time in years of what she had known about dancers when she had been a student at the Bolshoi training school. All at once, unexpectedly aching with it, she remembered edgy, single-minded devotion to teachers, ferocious, permanent silence, determination cloaked in meekness and hardened by constant work. Of course, they had been much younger, she and her classmates at the Bolshoi, and they had not had – any will of their own. They hadn't needed it. Everything was decided for them. Nina had been taught that ballerinas needed no will. She had even come to believe it could only be a danger to them. But Alice clearly possessed plenty, and probably Patrice, too.

She bestirred herself. 'If you two are rooming together, you might want to bear in mind that it's wise to —'

Both girls leaned towards her with such alertness that Nina abruptly stopped talking, bridled uncomfortably. She deliberately didn't look around her; she dropped her eyes to Alice's green vanity case and her own gloved hands still gripping the strap on it. This wasn't the place, she was thinking, to be giving out advice about conducting private conversations. But where was the place? She didn't want to act as though it was some big drama.

So she went on in a low voice, eyes down, 'I guess you've already been advised to just keep it kind of bland when you're talking in your hotel room. Don't mention specific names of anyone you meet. I mean names of — Russians. If you're even allowed to meet any.'

She turned her head a little towards Alice, and then the other way, towards Patrice; the girls' eyes were wide, intent. They wanted to know; they'd been waiting to hear. And yet Nina could feel her own face flushing. She cursed her lack of subtlety, her heavy feeling of alarm. How was this done, she wondered, the duenna role, the gracious, light-handed introduction to local customs?

But then she wondered, What's gracious about electronic eavesdropping? There's no good way to introduce that, she thought. It has no charm whatsoever. And how could you tell such open, unaccustomed faces these sinister truths? It seemed impossible, looking at their dimpled attentiveness, that anyone would need or want to monitor the private conversations of Alice and Patrice anyway. But innocence could be such a danger; maybe not to them, but to someone. And Nina saw in their solemn anticipation, in Alice's deep-pulling brown gaze, in Patrice's menthol stare, the little tongues of fear flickering, the restless adrenaline that liquefies the eye, and she heard in their throats the tiny inbreaths of excitement. She was familiar with these signs.

After all, there must be plenty of infighting and backstabbing in the company, she reassured herself. They didn't get this far by being ninnies, by being kind.

'It's not a big deal,' she said. 'I wouldn't worry about it.' She wanted them to cope with Moscow, to like it. But the girls fell quiet. Were they taking her advice to heart? Or were they struck dumb with anxiety? Give them something lighter, Nina thought to herself, give them a titbit of pleasure now.

She looked past Alice, out the window into the populous, electrified Moscow night. 'Look, there's the river. We're nearly at the hotel. Wait till you see it!'

Suddenly it loomed up over them, the Ukraina, Stalin's pale, uncanny skyscraper, a tower of raw-hewn geometry poised on the river bank, its lower floors like colossal insect legs elbowing the dropping sweep of lawn and ringed by listless, flood-lit Ukrainian poplars.

John was late coming home that night, so Nina left the uncooked veal chops out on the wooden drop-leaf table in the kitchenette and washed her hair. What was the point of another supper getting cold? The charmless, roomy apartment on the eighth floor of the staring modern block on Leninsky Prospekt seemed to have an endless supply of hot water. She just about filled the narrow bath and lolled in it, wetting and soaping her hair.

At moments like these, when she was unfocused, alone, memories batted at her like moths, slight, powder-winged, urgent. In America she had made it her habit to brush them away, swat them down with resolve, even crush them; but as the days passed in Moscow, growing shorter and darker into the autumn, there were little memories, twilight-coloured, grey or brown, mere sensations once put to sleep, with which she felt she might be safe enough. In her solitary, undisciplined existence, they even offered a kind of companionship, and she felt inclined to accommodate them, to hold up the light of her attention so as to draw them to her, lure them into the palm of her hand where she might study them. They came in no apparent order, yet Nina sensed there was some way to assemble them, to pin them down, which might help her to be more at ease with herself in her new circumstances.

Now, for instance, as she lay in the miraculous convenience of her bath, she tentatively recalled that her father's apartment in Maly Gnezdnikovsky Lane had never seemed to have any hot water at all when she was growing up. It had never seemed warm, either – an old house, stucco, badly insulated. The heat bled out at the windows and probably through the roof – the wind-rattled, iron-sheeted roof which leaked rust down the outside walls when the snow melted, when it rained. From these practical considerations, her thoughts crept cautiously on to others more vivid, more enveloping: how sometimes the whole house had seemed to sag with wet, the splintered, tilting staircase, soft under your tread as you climbed, smelling of darkness, rot. How winter had always felt like a cruel tonic, abrasive, reassuring, the dank walls going hard and clean with the shock of ice in the air, the shock right inside your chest.

Then came one of the pinpricks of insight – sharp, conclusive – that, really, Nina was after, that fixed something in place: Mother made the cold her excuse not to be home, Nina thought. She never complained, but she used to say it was warmer at the school where she worked, or at the library, a museum, a lecture, even at a film if there was money. At least, Nina nodded to herself, I don't remember any complaining. Mother just went out. But waiting for her to button her coat was – oh, God. Dad and I held our breaths or something. She buttoned it like murder.

Nina plunged her hair back under the bath water, holding her breath even now, remembering. She felt her ribcage expand; she floated and bobbed, half-submerged. I'm not going to struggle with that rubber hose, she thought, stroking the red-brown weed of her hair free of suds under the water. She immersed herself a little deeper; she didn't struggle back towards the present.

Whenever she was going to take me with her, Mother breathed snorts while we hunted for my mittens. Accusing me. We racketed up and down the echoing, wood-floored hall, slipped our hands inside felt boots, under cushions, folded back the musty corners of rugs, searching. That must have been when I was pretty small. I can still feel the anger up around her head, around her heart, like a dark halo, an aura. Did I lose my mittens every time? Or did Mother forget how young I really was, forget that she had taken away two years of my childhood so that we could pretend I was born in America?

Somehow I know that Mother thought Dad could have gotten them to turn up the heat in the apartment if he had made more of a big deal about being a registered invalid. Maybe turn up lots of other things, too. Dad wasn't like that, and Mother was perfectly aware that he wasn't. I never heard her say anything out loud; at least if I did hear, I can't remember the words. But she left Dad alone. Maybe that was worse than complaining.

Nina sighed with the pleasure of her bath. She could make the comparison; she could see how lucky she was. It must have been a nightmare. Devastating. At first, Mother might have been able to believe that whatever Moscow was like, it would get better. Because people do believe things like that. And maybe it was comfortable enough. Maybe in the beginning they were warm. Before I was born.

Twenty years though, she mused. No money. No way to get out. Christ.

She considered how many trips her mother had made to the dentist lately, in Buffalo, in Manhattan. It was because of Russia, those trips to the dentist. How it ravaged your teeth, your very bones.

Obviously Mother had lost interest years and years ago in anything she couldn't actually see. She stopped believing in love, marriage, babies, any of it. That's why she tried to scare the hell out of me. What does she live for now? Every morning she gets out of her lace-canopied bed, dresses with meticulous care, sees to the house, her cook, her plans. She doesn't need to work, not for money. But she has such a challenge before her, such a task; she has to gather to herself everything she is entitled to. She has to wear her clothes, use her wealth, feel the existence, the benefit, of all her possessions; she has to reassure herself that everything is there, that she controls it, that nobody will try to stop her. It's an obsession, an illness. Like a child with too many toys, exhausted by his own greedy rota, his obligation to use each one. Where's the freedom in that? wondered Nina. What's the point? Trying to have her childhood back, play for ever with no consequences.

Like a bright, black movement inside Nina's head, somewhere behind her closed eyes as she lay supine, almost afloat, the crude, long-ago elevator dropped to the floor of the rough-walled shaft. Freighted with consequences. She imagined the maiming, heavy smack reverberating. Then silence, clods of earth skittering. As if her father were dead, gone. No cry, no groan in the cavernous tunnel.

Oh God, Mother's bitterness. Somehow, silently, blaming everyone around her for the ruin of her life, the smell of darkness on the stairs, the house rancid with disappointment, with sorrow.

At least Dad didn't have to fight in the war. We were never separated. That can't have been official sympathy, the State letting us care for him?

It wasn't just Dad's accident. It was everything. The whole dream, the whole idea. And it's still going on, and I still don't understand it. Nina thought with bewilderment, with intense frustration, about the city that lay eight floors below her – a remote, impenetrable scene. I might as well be a prisoner in a tower, not allowed down because I'm an American. Then the image reversed itself, height becoming depth, towers becoming shafts, so that she felt the metropolis soar and sink to stupendous distances, and its vast constructed, mechanized features seemed to have no reality at their centre, no human fleshly life. Yes, she thought, sometimes I felt as if Dad had left me underground, in the dark, in the maze of unfinished tunnels – here and there a station I recognized, a ray of light, even parts that looked beautiful. But so much that Dad believed he was building, taking part in, he just never explained to me. The socialist state. I needed a map, a blueprint. I don't even know exactly where he was when the accident happened; I only know vaguely when – 1940. What was he trying for? Where was it all supposed to lead? He seemed – content.

After she drained the bath, Nina made herself clean it, dry it, polish the chrome fittings with a soft cloth. Yelena Petrovna won't even know I've taken a bath, she grunted to herself, rubbing. Fine. It satisfied Nina to flummox the maid, to cover her tracks. Why supply any clues at all? Nina wondered. We always used to clean the bath for Professor Szabo and his wife. She cringed, recollecting their forced crepuscular intimacy – Madame Szabo's grey-shadowed, diabetic skin, Professor Szabo's broad, flapping bottom. And she felt as though she could hear her father's tired, persistent assertion, 'They compactified others much more harshly than us. With us they've been generous.' But housing two invalids at the top of a long, narrow flight of stairs? Where was the generosity in that? Dad needed help just to climb in and out of the bath tub.

Nina couldn't recall a time when they hadn't shared that apartment; Mother used to say, 'Two rooms were perfectly OK without a baby.' So – the Szabos must have known exactly how old I was, and they never told anyone. Why were they made to share an apartment anyway, a professor at Stalin's Industrial Academy? Though it must have been the biggest one in the building – high ceilings, the bathroom.

They were witty, the Szabos. And they spoke English with us. That should have won Mother over. Dad would have had no one at all to keep him company, nor would Madame Szabo in her dim, semi-blind world. Madame Szabo took trouble over Dad, fussed in the kitchen for tea, waddled about with his ashtrays, accepted certain confidences. And Professor Szabo made it a point of honour to compete with Dad to do my math homework, as if they were colleagues discussing work, some matter affecting the foundation of socialism. These were gallantries, courtesies, human kindnesses.

I never seemed to catch up at school though, no matter how much they helped me. When we finished, they would give me chocolate. Mother said, 'The poor woman can't have it, so she gives it to you to cheer herself up. Honestly, Nina.' Honestly what? Nina wondered. She flung another handful of water around the inside of the tub to rinse it again. I was too old for chocolate? Would get too fat to dance? Or something about being weak, being drawn in. Dependent. Implicated. Because Mother wanted us to keep to ourselves, keep a difference, a distance. In that apartment? They weren't even Russian anyway, the Szabos. They were Hungarian. And usefully well-connected in Moscow, generous, with no children of their own to strive for.

Dad would have – what – thrown himself in more? Not just winking at me to eat the chocolate when Mother wasn't there, but participating in – everything. Life, Soviet life. It's just that – he couldn't.

And Nina thought, The kindest thing Professor Szabo did was slaving over bits of Tchaikovsky on his violin. Fast, tricky passages, so that I could do steps for Dad. It must have looked awful, kicking the walls, tipping over laughing. Dad loved it. Especially when Masha was allowed back from the Bolshoi school with me, and we took turns showing off, pretending we didn't feel smug with the praise, telling them all they were too easy to please, that they had no idea how our teachers would have scorned such foolishness, sent us back to the barre, given us eight of this, sixteen of that. We boasted of how strict school was, its huge demands, which we loved.

Fair, wiry Masha. She was entirely the colour of a raw almond, her skin, her hair, pale white-yellow all over. And from inside the perfect eggshell of her face, her eyes glowed out like uncanny lights, startling blue, serene. Nothing fazed her; she was never tired, never worried. And she looked exactly as she was, unblemished, innocent. Dad liked to call her my best friend, because he wanted me to have a friend like that. She and I would never have voiced such an embarrassing thing. We hardly spoke to each other at all.

Masha was accepted into the class for girls of ten when she was only nine; I was only eight, but she never knew that she was the older one. 1947 – everything so disorganized after the war that they were glad to have any strong bodies at all. We were too young to sweat even, had no smell to one another, might as well have been kittens, with limbs like air, of lightness, deftness, covered in feathery invisible hairs. Our friendship was all about holding hands. Always partners, always the same height; from year to year we must have grown at the same rate. Wordless, intense, upright, inseparable.

Where is Masha now? Nina wondered. Why haven't I noticed her at the Bolshoi? Not even in the corps? She must have given up, too, in the end.

Amidst these recollections, Nina knew perfectly well that really she was polishing the taps because she had nothing else to do. In her few months back in Moscow, she had committed herself as vigorously as possible to the smallest domestic chores just in order to make the minutes pass. She hated to be still, hated to wait, had never seen the point of leisure. Last week, she had spent a whole morning hanging four Chagall lithographs above the blue living-room sofa. She had bought them in Paris with guilty sums of her mother's money, paid for the simple frames, justified the purchase as making up part of her wardrobe in some other sense, the wardrobe of a diplomat's apartment, where he might entertain.

These are images which matter to me, she had thought, taking them from their cardboard wrappings in Leninsky Prospekt, methodically polishing the glass. Not Old Masters. These show something of what I longed for when I sometimes used to long for Russia. There was the angel-faced, clown-trousered artist, carrying his village house in one hand, his palette in the other, as if he could recreate his forsaken beginnings, the babushka crying out for him on the doorstep, a peasant self perched out of her sight on the warm chimney pot. They aren't real, these images, Nina had observed to herself. They don't exist. But they are true. And I recognize them. An émigré's daydream, his fantasy. An idyll because it is lost.

There were the lovers, big-eyed and blessed like icons, beside the sacred, fabulous tree, flush with leaves, with songbirds. There the maiden offering her bouquet, the best of herself, to the courtly, horned violinist, beseeching his beastly self-absorption as he danced his gay dance. There the poet at peace on the bowered breast of his uneasy beloved, the intense red sun so strong, so close.

Hesitantly, with two of the prints hung and two still leaning against the sofa, she had sidled off to the shelves where her books were stacked side by side with John's, mingled casually, indiscriminately. From among the Russian-language ones, she had taken down a thin brown volume, desiccated, alarmingly creased, powdered with dust, saying to herself, 'It's only a book.' She hadn't opened it in five years. Was it dangerous to have it here in Moscow? she wondered. Camouflaged among the rows of other books?

On the loose endpapers, there was no printed title, no list of contents, only the name of the author, Viktor Derzhavin, and at the bottom of another page, Moscow, 1954. But Viktor had written in his dense, emphatic hand, '*Sylvan Philosophies*. For dearest Nina. 23 October 1956. V.N.D.'

They were short lyric poems, twenty of them, about the woods and the changing seasons – chopping up a dead tree, finding a path through the snow, fetching water from a stream, damming the stream to make a pool for bathing, building a fire of fallen leaves, sparrows scattering and rising when a raven drops among them, a spring that arrives unbearably late. At the start of each poem, Viktor had written in the revealing, satirical titles which had eventually gotten him into so much trouble: 'Revolution', 'Pioneer', 'Virgin Lands', 'KGB', 'Ghosts', 'Thaw'.

For Nina, October 23 had not been about the start of an uprising in Hungary, but about visiting Viktor on Granovsky Street, in one of the massive old reddish stone buildings there. His father's big, warm apartment had honey-coloured parquet floors, brocade-draped windows, heavy, pale wood furniture tinkling with crystal-hung candelabra and glowing with shaded brass lamps. There in Viktor's room – strewn with open books, heavily marked papers, heaped ashtrays, up a step at the end of a long, book-lined cor-ridor – he had read the little book to her, pausing as he came to the end of each poem to write out its title, ceremoniously, in silence. Hardly any words passed between them that day apart from the words of the poems. He had been excited, intense, grey eyes alight, urging the verses on her, and she had felt a crystalline energy of attention between them, the sensation of being drawn up out of her body into the excitement of the images, the little explosions of sound.

Yet his unmade bed had waited behind her all the time, and she had listened rigid with the certainty that soon he would touch her, touch her face, her hair, any part of her at all. By the time he did, they had to hurry. Viktor's father would be returning; she was expected at home. And it had seemed to her like something fumbled, something that created an appetite rather than slaked it.

Leaning against the bookcase in Leninsky Prospekt, studying the slight, brown book spread open in the palm of her hand, Nina had thought, I felt he had written each poem for me, to trans-port me to the woods; I felt transported. And then the prick of clarity, Of course, he must have written them all before he even met me; they were just what he had to offer that day. She had stared at the stately Cyrillic script, the cheap paper, and heard Viktor announcing in his triumphant way, from deep in his throat, as if with his heart and soul and even some part of his guts, that he would recite the titles out loud the next time he read the poems publicly: 'You inspire me to this.' She had shut the book, finished hanging the Chagalls.

On another long, lonely morning, Nina had tacked black and white photographs to the wall in the kitchenette. The wedding party. Her two roommates from Wellesley – Jean and Barbara – and John's little sister in tightly sashed, full-skirted, watered silk dresses with close-fitting, scoop-neck bodices and little cap sleeves. Christmas wreathes on their hair, of stephanotis, holly with berries, ivy. The dresses had been soft crimson, the sashes apple green. Not quite Christmas, Mother had suggested, the colours should be more subtle than that. John's brother and Nina's five first cousins in tailcoats and striped morning trousers, all tall, all dark, their faces soft-fleshed, smiling in the winter sunshine. The girls had been too cold for pictures outdoors, but the boys had stood it with shouts, horseplay, frosty breath in front of the rugged grey stone walls of the Episcopal church.

The wedding had sealed Nina's American identity. And there it was, on the wall in front of her eyes, a second life that also now seemed to have slipped just out of her reach, under glass – the family she had longed for in childhood, the much confided-in girlfriends she would once have feared to tell things to, the holes in her education filled by American history, French philosophy, twentieth-century avant-garde culture, by freedom, by long hours of hard work. It was a strange flip-flop of fate: falling in love with John, she had ceased to think much about Russia. She had been entirely certain that she could settle down with John anywhere. And yet, studying the photographs while she had arranged them on the wall last week, it had crossed her mind that, from the very beginning, she had somehow expected John to bring her back to Moscow. She had resigned herself to it long before they had talked of marriage – an unavoidable destiny; she loved him no matter what he asked of her, no matter where he wanted to take her.

Wasn't that partly why I felt so absolutely sure about him? Because I knew he cared about Russia? I must have known it was a journey we would have to make. Not so soon, though; I did that for John. And she thought, Chagall shows that – about love. How it makes such a display of perfection, how it wants to disregard darkness, difficulty, even guilt. Her eye fell again on the girl in the print, alone in her wakefulness, startled.

Nina had told herself, as she laboriously tapped in the pin-like brass nails with the heel of her loafer, that she ought to go and buy a hammer because she would probably need one again for something else anyway and that it would make her little home seem real, seem permanent – having a hammer. The errand could use up a whole morning. But no sane American would stand in an interminable line to buy a tenth-rate Russian hammer anyway. She could manage fine with the heel of the loafer. With this logic, she had pretended to disguise her true feelings from herself: that something in her was not settling down to this Russian sojourn, was already packing up and preparing to leave. After all, if she didn't want to *buy* a hammer, she could easily have borrowed one, from the General Services Office at the embassy or, even better, from a neighbour. But if she had borrowed a hammer, she would have had to spend a few minutes chatting. And there would have been the next visit, when she returned the hammer, offered an invitation to come for coffee, try out her cake. That was how it should have begun, her life as an embassy wife, cultivating a niche in the small, involving, warm-hearted expatriate community.

Nina was finding it difficult to face the central challenge of her new life, being an American embassy wife. The other wives were so friendly, so inquisitive. They asked all about where she had lived as a child; they wanted her to take them shopping in some authentic Muscovite market away from the central places, or drive out of town together to hunt for mushrooms, boletuses with their white legs and brown caps, growing on moss pads in the woods since late August. Nina couldn't bring herself to do it. It had seemed easy sometimes to reveal to Jean, even to Barbara, this or that about her old Moscow life; her Wellesley friends had never pressed her. But now that she was here, there seemed to be so much more of her past, so much she was unsure of, and the embassy wives seemed too interested, pushy almost. How could any one of them – resourceful, cheerful Americans – possibly understand who she was, what she was? She had found she couldn't explain herself to anyone just now. It was practically illegal to try. Sometimes even John didn't seem to understand her all that well. And everything that she tried to make herself do felt somehow artificial. No matter where she went in Moscow, she was almost all imposter. What if she came across someone she recognized? If that were to happen, she needed to be alone. Everyone at the embassy knew how dangerous it could be for Russians to be seen meeting with foreigners. She hardly knew whether she would feel able to signal some acknowledgement, whether she would say little, or nothing at all. But she dreaded giving the impression of flaunting new American friends, of preferring them.

So she hid from the other wives, went out only when she knew she wouldn't meet them, and she felt painfully cut off. She found it hard to think realistically about what she wanted, what she had expected. Something that didn't exist any more, or that she could never really get at, the scenes in Chagall's prints, an old shattered life. Without really admitting it to herself, she was biding her time, going through the motions of embassy wife, waiting. Maybe she would be herself again only in America. The thought made her feel impatient, fretful. Sometimes it felt like an almost unbearable tension.

As she tied her quilted, raspberry silk bathrobe around her waist, she heard the front door open.

'Nina?' he boomed with friendly urgency. 'Sorry I'm so late. Did you eat already?' His voice was big, sweet, civil, rolling low and strong from his chest.

She felt herself soften inwardly with relief. It eased everything, John coming home. It was completely dependable. He lit up the apartment with life and purpose, made the straitened hours seem balmy, enchanted, rich. Now she wished she had braised the veal chops already and left them warm for him on the edge of the stove.

She opened the bathroom door, smiling, swathed in warm wet air on the threshold, and he put his stiff, cold raincoat arms around her, kissed her, took off his dripping fedora so that, closing her eyes, she felt first the thin hard hat brim knock against her forehead, then the light brightening around them both as he dropped the hat on the floor, then his grip so muscular that it seemed at odds with his office clothing, his professional demeanour.

How weird, she thought, as she swayed towards him with her contented heart, that he carries a briefcase, knows how to read. And she had often thought this before about John, that the accessories of modern life were beside the point with him, that he was a roving magnetic field, hot energy, barely contained by his lanky physique; that the uniform of adult duty and conventional public tasks couldn't conceal the natural boy, mostly coursing blood and febrile enthusiasms, on the brink of running wild. His gift with languages, for instance, didn't seem to be the result of bookish inclination. It had nothing to do with all those years at Dartmouth, at Columbia. It was just an expression of his instinctive chemistry with all mankind. He seemed to feel someone else's speech from underneath his skin, to sense what was trying to pass back and forth in the words; he learned the book side afterwards, as if to check whether his gut was right, his articulate gut. Nina thought that language was really a sport for him, something that he had picked up through natural athletic gifts, observing it, getting it, joining in the game.

'Yum,' he smacked his lips at her. 'There's a tender morsel to warm a working man's belly. Or tender damsel is maybe more the phrase. You smell like a newly washed pullover. You're not drowning yourself in there in that bath, Nina? Slashing your wrists over my protracted absence?' He turned her wrists over and held them up to the light from the bathroom door, lightly mocking, then kissed them by turns. 'Survived another day of Soviet solitude?' She felt the rough of his upper lip against the blue veins of her wrist; his bleached hazel eyes glowed under their shaggy, slanted brows, filled the doorway, warmed her chest.

'I'm OK, John,' Nina laughed. 'Thanks for asking. The ballet dancers arrived today, you know. So that was fun. Well – interesting anyway. Certainly took up plenty of time, waiting at the airport, going to the hotel with them. Though who knows what help they really need from me. And the airport kind of gives me the creeps – getting in, getting out, the frontier thing.'

She freed one of her hands and reached down to pick up his hat, then pulled him back along the hall towards the kitchenette. John dragged playfully against her weight, then gave in and followed, shrugging off his coat to hook it over one of the pegs on the wall as they passed. It dripped a little on the linoleum floor.

'How'd you get them to include me, John?' There was tension in her voice, and she tried to conceal it with busyness. He watched her rummage through a basket of clean laundry for a dish towel, press the folded towel carefully against the wet felt of his hat, then walk back to the hall to dry the floor under his coat.

At last, looking around the doorframe, he said, 'Don't be silly, Nina. What American embassy wife speaks mother-tongue Russian, trained at the Bolshoi, and is a Wellesley graduate on top of all that? They leaped at the chance.'

She interrupted him, embarrassed, trying to be light-hearted, 'Russian is really not my mother tongue, John. You know you're exaggerating. Mother would do anything to avoid speaking Russian, and there weren't even many Russians living in our building.'

But John went on with his flattery, courting her with his eyes, 'To me, you seem most yourself when you speak Russian. Enchanting, passionate, bracingly coherent.'

She wagged a blushing finger at his nonsense, and he grinned. 'Nina, you just don't realize how over-awing this town can be.

You've never had to do it as a real outsider, a stranger. What they know how to do is dance. They aren't supposed to be linguists or diplomats. They'll be able to relax and have a little fun with you along to show them around and explain things. Just be a friend. Frankly, we all have a lot on our minds at the office right now, and I know the ambassador feels reassured having you with that group. It's a serious business, this tour. A showcase. And you should speak up, too, if anything doesn't seem right.'

He stopped suddenly, looked around warily, as if there were presences floating above them on the ceiling, listeners. 'What am I saying? This isn't the office.'

Nina laughed. 'You're still OK, I'd say – just. But wait. I'm about to start banging a few pots and pans. I couldn't bring myself to cook supper without you.'

And she set to, clanging a black cast-iron frying pan, a shiny aluminium saucepan, a lid. She chopped an onion, sizzled it in butter, opened a can of chicken broth from Stockman's in Finland, ran cold water over a small bunch of beets and rolled up her soft pink sleeves to scrub the dirt from the voluptuous red-purple curves.

'Aren't these gorgeous?' she said as she tossed the beets into the saucepan to steam them. 'I got them from a babushka outside the Metro. Everything else is already starting to look shrivelled. It's going to be a long winter. Just you wait.'

Then she smiled at John because she knew these bitter little comments of hers worried him. She knew he wondered every single day what he had done bringing his new wife back to the USSR, wondered whether she would make it. She gave him a loopy, lips-together grin and clowned for him a little, shuffling her feet, waving her wooden spoon gaily like a flag, tipping her head coquettishly from side to side. 'I promise to do something about my hair right after supper, John,' she said sweetly, pulling the wet, heavy strands away from her face. 'I must look like a madwoman.'

Now John laughed, just a little. 'Do you want some Scotch?' He was reaching for the bottle on the wooden shelves above the table.

'Love some.'

He poured them each a drink, and they clinked their glasses, just barely, almost stealthily, near the rim, as if they were sharing a secret. They had reached a moment which they reached most evenings alone together when they felt a confident harmony with one another and with their nearly year-old marriage, a harmony which drowned out everything else. They both knew perfectly well how it had come about that they were here together in Russia, of all difficult places; they knew they belonged together, that they had no choice. They had talked about it often, the fact that the love sensation was still bigger than any other sensation either one of them could lay claim to ever having felt. Everything else had to fall in line with that. They would say things to each other like, A whole lifetime isn't enough time to spend with you. And they understood the meaning of what they were saying, meant it. The newness, the feeling of desperation, was still kindling between them; they were happy, but they were not yet satisfied; married, but still trying somehow to catch hold of each other entirely. When they were alone together, they forgot about everything else. They were building a private world for themselves.

John took off his dark grey suit jacket, loosened his dull blue, paisley tie, settled his long bony frame awkwardly at the little wooden table. 'Your hair's fine all mangled,' he said. 'I love it however.' Then he put his fingers in his own close-cut, light brown hair and rubbed it hard, grinning. 'See mine? Madwoman's spouse. Let's just have a nice supper and go to bed. You can fix your hair tomorrow.'

Nina lifted her glass, toasting his appearance. 'Very attractive.' And she smiled down at him, sipping, stirring, lifting lids, peering under them. 'What's keeping you at that office so much, anyway?'

But John held a finger in the air, alert, reminding her to take care what she said.

She turned on the radio, then the water in the sink, and threw open the window above it, letting the wind and rain blow in along with the faint blare of street noises from far below.

'Have to clear the smoke out,' she said brightly. She went back to the stove, checked again under all the lids, then walked to the table and perched on John's lap, laying her head on his chest with her ear beside his mouth.

He plucked at her wet hair without saying anything until she rolled her head around and looked him in the eye.

'You're making me burn the beets.'

He laughed, just a sniffing laugh, and murmured very quietly, 'Oh, sweetheart – letters, teletypes. We meet, we talk, we translate, we explain. God knows if anyone hears or even listens. Khrushchev never stops thinking about how to get our troops out of West Berlin, and the president is never going to abandon the West Germans. It's much more interesting here at home, since you are so pretty and, at present, so vulnerably *déshabillée*.' He twitched the lapel of her bathrobe, as if to look inside, and she trapped his hand and pressed it flat, helpless, against her breast.

John leaned closer, sealed his lips against Nina's ear to say something more, then instead took the curling top edge of her ear between his teeth and bit it so that she suddenly sat up. They both laughed.

She gathered her robe around her, stood up with exaggerated, mocking caution, kissed his forehead crisply and said, 'I'm going to give you supper straight from the stove. Do you mind? No serving dishes?'

'Of course I don't mind.' He picked up his glass of Scotch and drained it.

As she lifted the meat onto the plates, ladled the sauce, fished for beets, John muttered, 'The thing about democracy is of course that everything gets dropped for these damned mid-term elections.'

Then suddenly, he spoke up loudly, lifting his chin, and called out tauntingly to the walls and to the ceiling, 'You hear that? It's not such a perfect system, Western democracy.'

Nina put his plate in front of him, amused, stepping back to let him rant. But he wrapped a long arm around her light, bundled torso, pulled her close, and went on in a loud whisper, 'A few pretty loud-mouthed Republicans have been sounding off about how the president should be more aggressive on Cuba. Nobody likes the fact that the Russians have been shipping military equipment in there all summer, but the Cubans are entitled to defend themselves. And the president's so busy dealing with that kind of criticism that he really doesn't listen to anything else. All his time and energy just now is aimed at making sure his side stays in power; forget foreign relations.'

Nina leaned down and whispered back, 'It can't be any different in this country, my dearest. Just because there are no elections doesn't mean people don't have to fight and compromise to hold onto power. Everyone struggles to stay in power.'

'You are so damned smart, Nina. Yup. So maybe that explains why our Russian friends are being so sympathetic to the president's plight. They've promised, on the quiet, to just lay off until after the November elections, especially on Berlin.' He shrugged a little, in mild surprise. 'The president will give them another summit if they don't stir things up.'

Nina took a step towards the stove, reached for her plate, and brought it around opposite him. 'Sympathetic – just to be nice?' It made no sense to her at all, a sympathetic Russian leader. She raised her eyebrows cynically. 'You're kidding, aren't you?'

There was a pause, and then she leaned right across the table, her thick bathrobe almost touching the food on her plate. With a babyish pout, her lips pushed out as if to be kissed, she crooned very low, 'Don't let your fetching American sense of fairplay and your boyish idealism blind you to the Soviet character – or to human nature, for that matter. If the Soviets think the president is seriously preoccupied, they'll find some way to take advantage of it. And by the way, I'm not any smarter than you are, dearest. I'm just far less of a gentleman.'

John started to smile, but then looked startled, thoughtful. Silently he lifted a forkful of food to his mouth. For a few moments the only sounds in the room were the strains of a crackling, turgid symphony barely audible over the radio, the water running into the sink, and the tinkling knocks of their cutlery against the china. They glanced at each other from time to time as they chewed, then down at their plates, cutting, spearing. Suddenly, the window banged closed.

They both jumped with alarm, chastened by the frankness of their conversation. They knew they shouldn't talk in the apartment about anything political. The trouble was that Nina loved it so much, and was so hungry for conversation of real substance, that John couldn't bear to keep things from her. And she was astute in such unexpected, convincing ways that he couldn't resist finding out her opinions. He felt that whatever views she had, belonged to him, that he ought to know them all, that they were a valuable resource, that they shouldn't go to waste. He hardly realized the extent to which he was continuously at work trying to master and make use of her Russianness.

They went on eyeing each other dubiously, anxiously, as they cleaned their plates. Finally, they broke out in grim laughter.

Nina said, slowly, quietly, 'Our guys were in here sweeping for bugs again just yesterday. I know they miss things, but maybe . . .' She puckered her lips, twitched them about like a rabbit's quick nose, nervous, as if she might smell a listening device or do away with it by magic.

'We didn't say anything we shouldn't have.' Even if they had, they couldn't take it back now. They had to brazen it out.

'So tell me about George Balanchine,' John finally said with a shrug.

Nina got up, latched the window, turned off the water.

'Well,' she began, with a lilt of self-deprecation, hands plunged in her pockets as she stood in the middle of the floor, 'I didn't get to meet him personally. Not yet anyway. A real scene at the airport. A lot of press and – all the usual onlookers.' She said this with sarcastic emphasis, not mentioning the KGB or any elements of the State propaganda machine. 'And he was interviewed in very pointed fashion, to elicit certain – newsworthy answers. But after all, he's a Russian. They want to look upon him as one of their own, and from what I could see, he knew exactly what he was doing. One of the reporters called out, "Welcome to the home of classical ballet," and he said, "America is now the home of classical ballet." Incredibly bold, as if it all belonged to him, the whole tradition, and he had just taken it all with him when he left. I think his work will make the Bolshoi stuff look fat and dull, romantic, old-fashioned. The Russians'll be stunned.' She paused, her eyes sparkling. 'You remember when you went with me in New York?'

'Not in the way *you* remember, Nines. It was beautiful, but I had no idea why.'

'Well, it's the speed, the decisiveness, the musicality, and the – the inventiveness. It's so original, so complex.' She was breathless with it, springing a little on the balls of her feet. 'Even I was gagging with boredom the last time we went to the Bolshoi; there are only so many times you can watch a swan die.'

John grinned with pleasure at her knowledge, at her relish, at her untrickableness.

Nina rushed on, confident he was appreciating that she could dish it out. 'He understands the music as a musician, you see, so it's almost as if he – I don't know – plays the dancers instead of playing the keys on a piano or the instruments in the orchestra. There's usually not much story or acting out. And it moves fast fast fast. It's unbelievably demanding for the ballerinas – who are the centre of *everything*. The men are just there to hold them up, to show them off. Balanchine's crazy about ballerinas. You'll see.'

'But it was the Kirov, eh, where Nureyev danced?' Half lazily, John shifted ground to the one thing he thought he understood about ballet dancers: their wish to leave the Soviet Union if they could.

'Nureyev went straight to Balanchine when he defected to the West. But that's what I mean about men. Nureyev's too much of a star. In Balanchine's troop, everyone is supposed to be the same, all on equal footing. He doesn't want stars, especially not men – not men like Nureyev anyway.'

'Sounds pretty communist to me,' John remarked diffidently.

Nina nodded. 'I know. But it's something pre- all that, some older ideal. It's certainly Russian just as much as it's American. Maybe more. He's very religious, Balanchine, Russian Orthodox. And how he is about ballerinas is – well – mystical.'

She fell quiet for a moment, a little self-conscious about her high-flown talk; then, shaking herself, she began to clear the table. When she had all the dishes in the sink, she crept a quick, questioning look around at John, checking to see whether he'd had enough of her obsession with ballet, whether he was just humouring her. There was no one else she could talk to as she could talk to him, and she didn't want to use him up.

But he smiled at her warmly, so she started afresh, in a gossipy, confidential tone, making it juicy for him, 'Balanchine has an incredibly interesting personal life, you know. He marries his ballerinas, at shocking ages, really young, one after another.' She took a breath, slowed down a little. 'But the one he's married to now caught polio, and so she's paralysed from the waist down. Can you imagine anything worse, for a ballerina? And she was a star. Or she was going to be. He left her in New York in a wheelchair.'

'That's rough. God.' John yawned, linked his hands behind his head, leaned back in his chair just enough to lift the two front legs off the floor. His loosened tie forked haphazardly over the white cotton expanse of his chest; his shirtsleeves hung deep and loose under his long skinny arms.

'What would you do if that happened to me?'

'If – what?' The chair legs snapped down onto the linoleum.

'If I became paralysed?' She was staring into the plate she was rinsing, her hair down around her face like a rough russet curtain.

'That's an awful question. I don't even want to think about it.'

'But what would you do?' Now she turned towards him, drying the plate, shaking her hair back, then dipping her face down towards his so that he couldn't avoid her eyes.

'Nina, you are not paralysed. I have no idea what I would do.' John spread his arms high up in the air, bewildered, smiling.

'Would you stay with me?' Her eyes bore into him with their unsmirched, unrelenting blueness.

'Of course I'd stay with you, but . . .' he stopped himself. What was this all about, he wondered, this sudden whimsical comparison with a ballerina he had never even heard of before? 'Are you serious, Nina? It's a huge question. I don't have an answer ready. I've never had to think about this.'

'But what about, "In sickness and in health"?'

'Nina, why crank things up in such a crazy way? Of course I've promised you that. You've promised me the same thing. But let's give ourselves some time before we start in on ultimate tests. I like to think that I'd pass the test, but I don't want to wallow in imaginary problems ahead of time.' As he spoke, he reached for the knot of his tie, pried it loose with a long decisive index finger, snapped it off his neck, and hung it over the back of his chair. All the while, he held her look, quizzing, concerned.

She turned back to the sink. 'Leaving someone you love, when they can't move, can't go with you. It's completely awful.' Her voice was flat, empty.

'Jeez. You are having a bad time, aren't you, sweetheart? I am so sorry. Is this about your father?'

'Oh, God. I don't know.'

He got up and put his arms around her from behind, and she started to scrub at the frying pan.

'Can't you wash the dishes tomorrow morning?' he said. 'Let's go to bed.'

'The dishes and also my hair?'

'But you have all day. That's what you always tell me.'

'Actually, though, I don't.' Her voice was impatient. 'I'm a chaperone and guide, now. Remember? You've got me a so-called job.' There was a sour edge, too, but John ignored it.

He pulled her around away from the sink, leaning down to her mouth. 'You are a beautiful chaperone and a beautiful guide and I can't resist you.'

She pulled free after one long, swooning kiss.

'Nina, come on. It's not as if the KGB's going to come in and check to see whether you've washed the dishes. We can do as we like.'

She scowled at him. 'You know I don't care about the dishes, John. Why can't you understand me, listen to me, humour me? If you really love me, don't do this to me. Just leave me alone.' And she shoved him backwards, away from the sink, away from her.

'Do what to you, Nina? What's going on? Now I can't even touch you?'

She didn't answer.

John scratched his head, irritated, mystified. Then he said, slowly and carefully, 'You know, all day long, I concentrate just as hard as I can on finding some common ground between these two monumentally complex nations. I agonize over all the finer points of the Soviet Union, Mother Russia – how to understand her, interpret her, translate her, how to explain to her the needs and the views of the government of the United States. It's pretty formal, pretty high stakes, pretty unpredictable. And what gets me through is you. Honestly.'

She seemed to pay no attention at all as he spoke, and he became impatient, and raised his voice a little. 'Sometimes lately you have seemed just as enigmatic, just as opaque, just as unyielding as this whole damn country. What I think is that you are right and that it is going to be a very long winter – where you are, the ice is already on the ponds. How can you be so cold? So unreasonably cold.'

Now Nina turned her back altogether; they both knew she felt wounded. 'I am not cold,' she muttered without conviction. 'I don't feel cold at all towards you. You know that. I adore you. I wait all day for you with unbearable anticipation. I feel faint when I finally see you.' Still she kept her eyes down, eking her words out with girlish shyness, halting but determined, as if she had planned her speech. 'But I know you'll get me into that bedroom and start on the baby thing again. And I don't want a baby. It kills me to tell you. It makes me angry with us both. And I'm saying it now before you get me weak at the knees and make me think differently. I *cannot* have a baby here, John. I can't bear the thought of it. You have got to take my side, you have got to sympathize with me about this.'

'Sympathize? What – just to be nice?'

Nina grinned at his joke, swallowing her anger for a moment, caught out. 'But *you* are a gentleman, John. Yes. Just to be nice.'

'Nina, all I want is to come home to something easy, direct, immediate. And something – physical. I know you understand that. We don't need diplomacy here. We don't need to negotiate. Do we?'

She rinsed the frying pan and laid it on the draining board. 'I'll come to bed,' she said guardedly, 'if that's what you want. But I don't want a child, John. I don't know how to make it any more clear to you. Not while we are living here in Moscow. It's not a question of negotiating or pleading. I can't do it. I won't do it.' She snapped out the last words like stamping her foot, but then she paused, lowered her voice, invited his concern with a tender look. 'What if there was some problem about its American citizenship? What if we couldn't get the baby out? Or what if suddenly *I* couldn't get out? If you had to leave us? It scares me to death. I can hardly breathe when I think about it.'

'Honey, you and I are both American citizens. And we both have diplomatic passports. You know you don't have to worry about all this stuff. Anyway, if you got pregnant, you could leave. The baby could be born on US soil, in Buffalo. I'll send you home to your mother.'

'No!' She was shocked by his suggestion. 'No, no, no.' She grabbed the ends of the belt on her bathrobe, cinched it tight, flounced away from him across the little room even as she proclaimed, 'I want to be with you. You and only you. I am never going home to my mother. I won't be separated from you. Never. It's bad enough when you're at the embassy all day. Besides, once the child was born, I'd have to come back here with it anyway. And I couldn't do that, either. As long as we live in Russia, I need to be light on my feet, ready to move, able to fly at a moment's notice. I can't be burdened down with a child. It nearly killed my mother, John. And frankly, it nearly killed me: I *was* the child who was holding her back, who was keeping her here, exposing her to suffering, want, manipulation, fear, heartbreak. She could have left before the war if it hadn't been for me. Because of me, she delayed and then it was too late.'

John was silent. Nina's relationship with her mother was an unfathomable, tortured area, full of love, hate, generosity and selfishness in the most irrational welter. He accepted that maybe Nina could not go home to her mother ever again — why should a married woman want to do such a thing, anyway? He could see that it smacked of failure, loss of independence. And yet he felt swamped by the practical considerations; how could he take responsibility for the happiness, minute by minute, of this woman he loved and had taken away from her chosen homeland? How could he address her increasingly difficult state of mind, so unexpected? She didn't seem to be the inspired, resilient woman he had married.

At the office, there was plenty of talk about adjustment, settling in, newlyweds, loneliness. He had been encouraged to treat it as a normal, temporary feature of his own job, handling Nina, being attentive to her moods, to her resistance. But he sensed that to Nina, Moscow was a metaphysical experience, swallowing her alive. And he knew the office vocabulary was useless to describe what was happening to her.

There was something inside Nina, something burning, some lit, primitive energy that he couldn't understand. It wasn't that she had fooled him; on the contrary, she sometimes treated him to breathtaking, even hurtful outbursts of honesty, stunning revelations. But there was a depth of passion in her that he had not yet plumbed. He could remember the first few times he had met her, the way she used to avert her eyes, as if she were too shy to look at him straight, and she would flex her feet, rising onto her toes, as if she might lift into the air. Her blue eyes were dark-flecked, pixelated, her small face square-cheeked, square-jawed, the fine bones seeming almost to show through the taut-stretched, white skin; later he discovered that if he ducked down and held her look, he could feel the flash and strength of her so intensely that he had to avert his own eyes. Her vitality dazzled him; it was irresistible, unpredictable. He had believed, still believed, that if he held her eyes, her arms, firmly enough, cradled her soul, steadied her, it would gradually come out, and he would be able to see it, engage with it – the ferment. But he knew that he had not yet gotten to the bottom of her. Her feverish, evanescent restlessness.

He didn't agree with Nina about the baby. He wasn't about to tell her now, but he himself had come to the conclusion that a baby would make them both happy. Certainly it was something they had wanted before the assignment to Moscow had come up. They had daydreamed aloud about it in the most sentimental terms. Still, who was he to force something on this woman, so brilliant, so beautiful, so sure of herself and yet so skittish, even if he did think it might stop her feeling lonely when he was at work?

She looked at him, standing off, gripping the sash of her robe, when he wanted her beside him, as one with him. What did she expect of him? Could he actually provide it? Happiness? Were husbands supposed to be able to deliver that? He had wanted to give her everything her heart desired. It wasn't working. I was insane to bring her here, and she was more insane to want to come. She was so certain, so positive that I could get her in. And that was all we focused on. It was what I wanted, so she made it her business to want the same thing.

John could remember the anxiety of getting Nina's visa to enter the USSR, how he had anguished over giving up the assignment, made up his mind that she was worth any sacrifice, that if she couldn't get in, there would be another job somewhere else. Too bad if he couldn't use his Russian, he would wait. There had been day upon day of interviews for both of them. But the paperwork had gone through without a hitch. We let ourselves be tricked by that, he realized, by the official OK. All along, I was expecting someone to tell us we couldn't go. Waiting to be told no, that the risk was absurd. But nobody tried to stop us, apart from Nina's mother. Nobody interfered. Then again, we were the only ones who knew the truth about Nina's place of birth; why would anyone else suggest it was an obstacle? When the papers came, we opened a bottle of champagne; we looked on it as a victory – getting away with it. After that, I never let myself pause to imagine what difficulties there might be once Nina was here. I just pictured how happily she would take to a familiar city, how it would be a lark for her.

Finally he said, solemn, reluctant, 'OK. Well. No baby. I agree. All precautions in place, then.'

'You've said that before, too, haven't you?' She was accusing him of something. He felt confused by her unexpectedly strident tone.

'I want to trust you,' she almost shouted. She was back at the sink, slapping at the dirty dishwater, whacking dishes with a cloth. 'But it all gets so – impossible. Heated. You never are as careful as you say. Condoms, all this stuff, it's so unbeautiful, so distracting. I know how you feel about it. I feel the same. It's one thing we intended to be free of once we were married, isn't it? And I am no good at resisting anything, at stopping you or even slowing you down. And they are listening to us, John. I can't talk. I can't tell you what I feel. What I want. They are in *bed* with us and I'm not sure you even care! Even that doesn't stop you.'

John went deep painful red. And his voice came out tipped with rage. 'We don't have to discuss this any more, Nina. Not that I think the KGB bothers to listen to drunken domestic quarrels. Our guys wouldn't. Who can afford the resources? We're not teenagers. And I'm not such a cad. Don't lay all the blame at my door. I don't think that's fair. You're the one who's shouting, if you're so worried about being overheard. And you've got methods of contraception you haven't even bothered to take out of the box. What about that diaphragm you've made so much fun of? All you've shown me is soul-destroying lingerie from Paris.'

Now she was crying, but she tried not to let him see. She knew it was true, that she was blaming him more than was fair. Ever since he had brought her to Moscow, she had tended to blame him more and more for everything. She had forgotten how to take responsibility for herself. There were no avenues for it; she had no choices. She felt boxed in, suspended.

'They do listen!' she said with a feeling of pathetic self-righteousness. 'They think they know just when people will let their guard down. And anyway I'm sure they're bored out of their minds, so it's like – it's like – pornography to them – which you can't get here.' Her voice trailed away querulously. 'This is a – very – puritanical society. You know the joke – Khrushchev's joke – everyone repeats – there IS no sex in the Soviet Union. The atmosphere here is not – natural. It affects people in the weirdest ways. It makes them – sick.'

'Oh, Christ, Nina. You're talking nuts. Where do you get this stuff? Just stop.' There was disgust in his voice, and a kind of horror. She was right for all he knew, but he couldn't let these ideas into his head. He didn't want to start thinking like this. He was already afraid that what she had said might never leave him now; he felt it spreading in him, like a disease.

'I don't think tonight's the night anyway, Nina,' he growled as she stood there with her tears dropping into the sink, ignored. 'Frankly, I feel chilled to the core. But maybe that's what you're trying for. You'll be perfectly safe from sex and babymaking. I'll sleep on the sofa.'

October 9. Nina slipped into the Bolshoi through the stage door in Petrovka Street. The guard was a woman, stocky, formidable. As she lurched forward on her stool, studying Nina's face, her neat, expensive suit, her Russian-language paperwork, her photograph and her name, then straining over the list of foreigners, outsiders, Nina felt from her a deep familiar chemistry: resentment reacting with benevolence. There on the threshold, the custodial instinct to keep Nina out was mingling with and giving way to a motherly instinct to take Nina in. Nina was moved so powerfully by this chemistry that she nearly spoke up with the truth, Yes, you're right. You do know me. You watched over my other, girlish life, my years of training. I was one of the cosseted brood, a dancing bird in *Cinderella,* the Breadcrumb Fairy in *Sleeping Beauty*, a stick-legged hopeful at the yearly graduation show.

But the fact is, Nina realized, my American identity works like a disguise, a mask. The guard could never recognize me now, in my American Embassy role, not without a great deal of persuading and explaining. And Nina didn't ask for it, the recognition which she knew might feel warm if it were simple and wholehearted but which might feel painful if it were uncertain or even angry. Anyway, her name was on the list; she was expected.

As she climbed the tiled stairs, sooty diamonds of red set with black and yellow, she thought she could hear piano music from the ballet room, a leaping yowl, all tempo and cowboy boot heels –' Red River Valley', 'Goodnight Ladies' – starting, stopping. She crept up the half-flight and looked around the door, catching sight of attitudes at the barre: stretched, scattered bodies layered with wraps of wool at the ankle, below the hip; a curve of lower back exposed in the mottled shine of the wide, heavily framed mirror, studied, straightened; and one slender wreath of arms carried in front like an enormous platter of air, delicate, steel-bound, nowhere to put it down on the pale, rippling floorboards.

An urgent, slim, black-clad woman pressed by her with a clip-board, approached a splay-footed girl who sat on a broken chair cracking away at the soles of her silky shoes. An old fear darted at Nina, that she herself would not be called. Silly, she thought, turning away.

All along the pipe-slung hallways, there was a pressure of hurry and focus, brusque commands, hushed intensity. The atmosphere encased her like a uniform; she knew this discipline, felt beck-oned, pulled in.

Nobody noticed her as she emerged under the stairs to the prop room at the back of the enormous set-strewn stage. She crept past the lighting control board and the prompter's station towards the dim revelation of the auditorium. She could just see the rows of polished dark wooden armchairs and the rising circles of creamy, gold-embossed boxes facing her, shabby-looking without their occupants, the red velvet seats worn and unevenly faded. Five or six people were sitting in the front row on the far side of the stage. Press, thought Nina.

Near her, she heard a piping complaint. 'The thing is Danny, it makes me feel like I'm going to land right on my face.' Nina didn't look around.

Then came a low, reassuring reply. 'What you need to realize is how well it makes you work. From the minute you come onstage, nothing is neutral. Even when you stand still on this raked floor, you're in motion because you're working against gravity all the time. It won't let you be dead; it won't let you give no energy. It's very exciting. That practice stage upstairs has the same rake, you know. And you were fine. Take it slower for now. Think about footwork, but don't overcompensate because at a certain point you have to just throw yourself into it. You'll get so used to it, you won't be able to land or take off on the flat stage when we get home, I promise you. Watch the boys jump. We all love it, because the rake launches us so high.'

Still the needy whine continued, 'I know it's just confidence. But, God, when I have to go upstage, I'm completely exhausted.'

'Yeah. Upstage is hard work. It's because – well, upstage is up. But Mr B. will make all your big moves go downstage for you. Just wait.' Then, 'Look – he wants you back now. Go on.'

And the small troubled figure swung herself around into the light, strode hip-to-hip across the stage, toe shoes knocking the steep wooden pitch with hollow defiance, head bowed to receive guidance. Nina realized it was Alice.

Balanchine was like sparks popping at the dancers, gesture and flash, chin up, thin as a wraith, a few disjointed words, and then a conflagration of silent, hot scrutiny, his eyes energizing them. Even where she stood in the shadows at the side of the stage, Nina could feel his concentration wax when he fell silent, and she could feel the desire of the dancers to be seen by him, to be watched. She knew, as if by telepathy, that they moved only to elucidate some idea he wanted to convey through them, and she could tell by their hypnotized eyes, their somnolent obedience, that they moved in the way that he told them to move even if they didn't understand what the idea was. She thought to herself, They just believe his idea will come to them through their bodies once their bodies have mastered it. And they let that happen, accept they are a vehicle. She wanted to make fun of it, itched at this informal exposure of such seriousness, but she couldn't. She thought their willingness was sublime.

She crept a little further downstage, and suddenly she was looking into the orchestra pit, another world of activity: slouching, slack-haired Soviet musicians leafing through scores, marking, counting bars, questioning the American conductors by means of interpreters, tapping on this or that passage with articulate fingers, heavy-nailed, nicotine-stained, emphatic. And Nina thought, What can they possibly make of it all, Tchaikovsky, Stravinsky, 'On Top of Old Smokey'? She wanted them to like it, then felt her want to be absurd; they were professionals, after all. They would play it regardless. Nevertheless, she wondered.

Now there was an uproar behind her, offstage. Nina heard Russian and English being shouted back and forth, with no resolution and, she sensed, no comprehension. Something beyond impatience had overtaken the stage workers; she detected defensive anger, loutish panic, Russians cursing one another, '*Khvatit*! *Idit'e k chortu*!' That's enough! Now you've really gotten to me! Go to hell! It was not their fault. They had no idea where the trucks were, it was not their job to know. Some higher authority was to blame. Nothing could be done now; it should not have been expected of them to begin with; they would take no responsibility. It was far too late.

And an American voice, a woman, hoarse, definite, outrageous, 'They're deliberately sabotaging the tour. How could this happen by mistake? Everyone knows why we're here! And we open tonight. They don't want us? Fine. Who do they think we are doing this for? We never treated the Bolshoi like this in New York. This is crap.'

Oh, great, Nina thought. And she glanced across at the little clutch of reporters from *Izvestia, Literaturnaya Gazeta*, the illustrated magazine *Ogonyok*, Radio Moscow, and even *The New York Times*. Their faces were turned towards the argument, but she couldn't tell if they could hear.

Someone grabbed her elbow, saying, 'You're the embassy person, can't you find out where the damn scenery and costumes are? How can they lose truckloads of stuff? Sets, props, everything. One of our own stage managers is lost with it, too! We're running out of goddamn time.'

Nina spun around, certain there must be someone else here who should take charge of such a matter, the Special Officer for the Cultural Exchange Program, some big-voiced man. But she soon found herself inside a ring of burly, dirty Soviet stage hands, persuading a livid deputy stage manager to telephone the Palace of Congresses in the Kremlin, where the ballet was to move after the opening performances.

'Maybe the trucks went there by mistake,' she urged. 'It's perfectly understandable. And if they aren't there, you better place a call to Vienna and find out how long ago they left after the last performance there. Or if you want, I'll telephone the operator at the American Embassy,' Nina sounded sweet-voiced, pliant, 'and ask her to make the call to Austria.'

The stage manager was visibly pricked by Nina's resourcefulness. He looked around at his crew; they were silent now, arms folded or linked behind their necks, with blank stares or eyes on the floor. He repeated Nina's own remark that the mistake was perfectly understandable. He was no longer shouting, but he carefully refused to let her take charge. If the crisis was not entirely his responsibility, then maybe he could help to resolve it after all. He would go to the telephone. He raised both hands, wrists bent back, palms horizontal, signalling patience, and announced that the trucks would be found and that everyone should calm down.

As he turned to leave, a costume mistress demanded, 'So what did he say? What have they done with it all?'

'He'll find out,' Nina sighed, putting her hand on the woman's plump, insistent forearm. 'He will. The staff here is a little nervous.' She half smiled, half grimaced, trying to explain. 'They're not sure what to expect, any more than any of you. Obviously, everyone is – excited – about tonight, but being excited isn't a sensation they can necessarily enjoy. It's – probably pretty scary. They have to be – suspicious. It's habitual. They can't help it. I wouldn't assume anyone has lost things on purpose. Nobody would risk such a thing.' She lowered her voice a little, hoping for sympathy. 'The trouble is that even though he doesn't speak English, he sensed he was being accused of that – of deliberate provocation – if you can forgive me for being so frank.'

The costume mistress bristled, but only slightly. 'Well, we can't dance without costumes. Maybe without scenery. There's plenty of it around to borrow. But to come all this way – Mr B. will sew costumes himself if he has to. It won't be the first time. But I can tell you, he has no time for that.'

'Yes,' Nina said. She couldn't think of anything else to add. She understood both sides too well. Feebly she muttered, 'Let's hope the stage manager is efficient on the telephone. Time is obviously vital now.'

She thought of going to the embassy all the same, while they were waiting. But she pictured the chain of telephone calls that might result, and she decided it would only take longer if somebody had to field a diplomatic request; they wouldn't be able to concentrate on finding the trucks. And of course, the fear ingredient would be increased, and then nobody would be able to concentrate at all. The whole system might seize up.

A man now broke in on her thoughts, gently haranguing, in a soft, nasal monotone that reminded Nina of the seen-it-all streets of Manhattan, 'At least the kids have practice clothes. Half of the ballets, that's about what they wear anyway. These bastards won't even put up a black backdrop for me. Can you at least get them to do that?'

Nina held back another sigh. She looked him in the eye, saw tension and pleading there, pink-rimmed, overworked, with wrinkled dry skin around the edges. 'I can try. But wait until the stage manager comes back. Give him a chance.'

And for this she got a friendly, silent tip-up of the chin. The man reached for a pack of cigarettes in his pocket. 'I'll take a break,' he said, feeling the pack. 'Don't disappear on me.'

Nina wandered back to watch the dancers again. One of the ballerinas had a sore foot. Balanchine was waving his hands at her, scowling.

'If that hurts, don't do it. Like this.'

He stepped in close to the ballerina, assumed her posture, raised

56

his eyebrows and half-closed his eyes in an expression of yearning nobility, then demonstrated a combination by which he seemed as if magically to glide backwards using only one foot. Afterwards, he looked at the ballerina, waiting, smouldering with the thrill of his solution. In the silence, she copied him.

'So. Just so,' he said, nodding fiercely. 'It's better for you. And first you rest.'

Then he clapped his hands three times, looked around the stage, and threw his eyes into the air, all the way to the back of the theatre. Behind him, dancers scurried, stood up, began to assemble. He rubbed his hands together, as if with appetite, and walked away.

The orchestra now began to play, and it seemed to Nina like a miracle that the dancers began to dance without Balanchine among them. She sensed him there, still, at the centre of their group.

For a while, she was lost, watching. Then, from nowhere, Alice was beside her whispering, 'Luckily Mr B. can make it up as he goes along. Two of the kids got hit by a trolley car the day after we opened in Hamburg. Everything had to be changed.'

Nina looked around, stunned. 'A trolley car?'

'It was bad. But they're going to be OK. Honestly. They both ache like hell.' Then Alice ran her hands over her tightly smoothed-back dark hair and sighed. 'It's good for me, in a way, I'm getting lots of parts. I've never danced so much. But, God, I miss my little boy! He's only one and a half. Have you got children?'

Nina felt intensely embarrassed by this question, not only because she had managed during her visits to the Bolshoi to forget at last the horrible scene she had had with John, but also because in her role of chaperone she felt she should be more experienced than the dancers. Clearly, she was not more experienced than Alice and she wasn't much older.

All Nina said was, 'Not yet.'

And Alice whispered on, friendly, 'Children change everything, that's the thing. Anyone who says otherwise is lying. See that girl?'

She leaned close in the shadows, her cheek brushing Nina's so that Nina could feel the light sweat on it, smell the fragrant layer of cold cream surfacing with the heat of Alice's skin.

Alice was pointing to a coltish ballerina, big-eyed, young, with hair swinging from a knot at the top of her head. The girl had one endless leg flung up onto the black iron stair rail beside one of the entrances to the back of the stage; she reached along it towards her arched foot, demi-pliéd, rose again.

'That girl,' Alice confided, 'learned a whole brand-new ballet overnight because the ballerina Mr B. choreographed it on got pregnant and her doctor suddenly ordered her to lie down. And now that girl will be a star. All of a sudden Mr B. has noticed her. And she is totally unpregnant, that girl. A maiden.' Alice giggled. 'If you know what I mean.'

Nina giggled, too; she couldn't help it. Alice surprised her. The giggle didn't feel malicious; it felt realistic, practical, accurate. To Nina, Alice seemed delightfully unfettered, brave.

And then Alice said, 'A tour like this, with everyone on top of each other night and day, is pretty much nothing but love affairs. The windows of the bus were steaming up when we left Vienna.'

Again they giggled.

'So why isn't *everyone* pregnant?' asked Nina.

'Good question. Maybe they are?' Then Alice abandoned her smart-alecky tone and said soberly, 'But you know, sometimes I think ballerinas just aren't that fertile. I mean, we miss our periods half the time anyway. Some girls are on the pill, but it makes you fat is the thing.'

'Well, so does being pregnant.' Nina laughed again, but she no longer felt light of heart. Suddenly, she felt afraid, assaulted by her obsessive private anxieties which she couldn't share with Alice. It made her conscious that she was pretending to be friendly, trying, because she envied Alice's candour about personal matters, her apparent freedom, for a girlish chumminess that she had never really been that good at.

Nina had thought constantly about the pill since arriving in Moscow, wishing she had asked her doctor for a lifetime's supply before she left Washington. But in Washington, she hadn't foreseen not wanting a baby. And since arriving in Moscow, she hadn't been able to bring herself to inquire about the pill with the embassy doctor. It wasn't that she feared he might disapprove. Although that was part of it. It was also that she didn't want to risk the disappointment if he told her he couldn't supply it, couldn't lay hands on it. And above all, she feared the further loss of her privacy: the doctor knowing, the doctor judging, the doctor reporting to someone else about her most intimate life. It was natural to feel embarrassed, but she felt more than that; she felt as if wanting birth control might cast doubt on her character, as if it revealed something overly sophisticated, libertine, decadent in her appetites – wanting sex but not wanting a baby. Pleasure for its own sake.

She had considered going out to Finland to a doctor, but she thought a medical visit abroad would alarm John. Anyway, it was melodramatic. Everyone would ask why she needed to see a Finnish doctor. Her minders wouldn't ask her directly, but they would ask someone, and they would probably find out.

So she had become paralysed about birth control, about sex. She felt the world intruding, watching, conferring, as she had often felt in her girlhood, teachers at the Bolshoi discussing her physique, medical officers examining her, her own mother puritanically accusing her about boys, loudly consulting the Szabos after her father's death, reviling Nina's lack of self-control, her vulgar appetites. What was it they all needed to know about her – the spies, the eavesdroppers? And she was trying to clutch a veil around her person, around her body, to hide something precious, her shyness, a sense of delicacy. Lately it had felt almost as if her married state had been taken away from her, society's permission to embark on an adult relationship, to feel and do anything, everything, in complete privacy, without hesitation, without guilt.

In the silence that fell between her and Alice now, Nina sensed there was a possibility of nearer friendship. She chewed her lower lip; Alice watched the dancers onstage, silently critiquing, memorizing. Nina began to want to reach for the possibility. Alice's easy banter was seductive. Could I launch myself like that, copy her? Find out? Her lip curled with self-disdain. Posing. Faking. And she thought, I'm just a middle-class housewife. She's a dancer, an artist. There's an allowance for however it is that Alice might misstep, surprise, even shock, as long as she's not onstage. She's supposed to be — bohemian. I'm supposed to get it all perfect. I'm not a debutante in Russia. What she ended up telling herself was that Alice would be leaving Moscow in just a few weeks anyway, so what was the point of becoming friends? Although she knew full well that Alice's certain departure was the very reason she felt safe with her.

Just then the stage manager came up to Nina, pulled her back into the wings, spoke jovially in Russian.

'Everything is found,' he said, 'you will be glad to know. The men are bringing up the trunks now, to the wardrobe. Go look in the elevator. You'll see it's completely full with big metal boxes. But you should help direct — boys' side, girls' side — if you don't want to waste any more time. The writing is all English. Only one of these guys from the USA speaks Russian. It's laughable for us.'

Nina looked around for the costume mistress, saying, 'I'll get someone to come right away. Was it all at the Kremlin?'

'Not at all. Don't be silly. It came straight to the Bolshoi, just as it should. The drivers were held up at the Polish border and also at the Czech border. As if on purpose. How should I know why? Maybe the Poles and the Czechs want to wreck our relations. It wouldn't surprise me. Anyway, the border guards look through everything for security. And these trucks are carrying a lot of things. Mountains.'

As Nina started through the door, he added smugly, with a broad smile, 'By the way, I've requested extra ironers. More women are coming now. You Americans will be pleased how hard they work.'

By the time Nina arrived at the opening night party at the American ambassador's residence, Spaso House, she felt winded with tiredness. She took John's arm as they climbed the broad, shallow steps from the vestibule, and she leaned on it more and more heavily as people pressed and darted around them in the receiving line.

'What did you think, dear?' asked the ambassador's wife, reaching for Nina's hand, pulling her along with professional insistence to greet the ambassador, to keep the line moving through the soaring pillared entry into the main salon. 'You're our expert.'

Nina tried to smile. She ought to have a remark prepared; she was familiar with the instant of greeting at the second pillar. Ambassador Kohler and his wife, Phyllis, both small, unimposing, always received by the second pillar. And they were kind, these two childless Midwesterners, gentle and homey with the embassy staff.

Out tumbled, 'Beautiful.' That was all Nina could manage. She repeated it, hopelessly, 'Beautiful.' It didn't begin to describe what she had seen that night at the Bolshoi, what she had felt, the tumult of awe, the ecstatic pleasure.

It didn't even describe the ostentatious splendour of Spaso House on a night like tonight: the pre-revolutionary palace ablaze with light from countless sconces and hanging fixtures and from the stupendous crystal and gold chandelier festooned with gem-cut beads, orbited by candles, and suspended like a celestial apparition in the three-storey dome of the eighty-foot salon.

Nina let go of John's arm to shake hands, and she drifted alone to the round, marble-topped table centred under the chandelier. She tried to collect herself. The carpet, with its rich circular pattern, red, black, blue, spun away on all sides towards the endless weave of the blond parquet, dizzying, and so she lifted her eyes to the turquoise-and-gold-embossed vault of the ceiling and the balconied loggia of the first floor beneath it. Still she felt bewildered, hurried. Her heart, or maybe it was her lungs, felt tight and dark, congested with a faint sense of alarm.

I'm just not used to so much company all day and so much talking and arguing, she told herself. Did I ever even sit down? Not until the performance; and by then I was so overexcited that it was more like anguish than joy. Tomorrow will be easier. Tomorrow I can relax a little.

I need something to eat, she thought, something to ballast myself. There was a bad taste in her mouth, nausea rising in her nose like a chemical odour.

On she floated to the dark-panelled state dining room. The light and the noise seemed to drop away in the distance. A little group strolled ahead of her, right through the dining room into the ballroom beyond as she came in, so that she was alone. The elaborate curtains hanging down around the open doors, the gleaming, wood-lined walls, the grandiose fireplace with its mantel upon mantel supported on great twisted columns of wood reaching higher than her head, seemed to hold the world at bay. She felt insulated, soothed.

The long dining table had been pulled to the end of the room in front of the fireplace and its flanking glass-doored display cabinets. There were three big vases of bronze chrysanthemums standing in a row on the table. Nina studied them ruefully. The good wives, the sociable ones, will have arranged those flowers, she thought. And I wasn't here. Then she thought, But I *was* helping. Trying to help.

The chairs with their yellow satin seats and backs were lined up against the walls. Can I sit down now? she wondered, sinking wearily onto one.

A waiter rushed through with a tray of drinks, suddenly stopping when he saw her, bending to offer one.

'By the way, madam,' he said in soft, careful English, 'you will have supper in the ballroom when the ballet arrives.'

Nina thanked him in Russian, '*Spasibo*.' But when he smiled at her friendly gesture, she felt an inexplicable wrench of sorrow. It was the way he leaned down to her, the patience with which he paused. She had to look away from his warm, solicitous eyes, his obvious concern.

She couldn't face vodka, champagne. She took a glass of ice water, and nodded, keeping her eyes down until he was gone.

You're completely pathetic, she told herself, sipping it. Then she made herself get up from her chair and put the glass on the table. She smoothed the stiff green silk zibeline of her sleeveless Givenchy cocktail dress and went on into the bland modern ballroom.

The rows of tables draped in heavy white cloth were stacked with crested blue and gold-rimmed plates and lined with bow-legged silver frames waiting for chafing dishes to be set in them. Beside a row of napkins folded like bishops' mitres, cutlery protruding from inside, Nina found baskets of bread already set out. She helped herself.

The first soft, white American roll made her feel famished; she looked around her, took another furtively, then swung full-circle and leaned boldly against the table as she chewed.

She felt better after the second roll and ventured back towards the party.

The rooms were filling up, throbbing and swaying. The crowd swelled around the ambassador in slow bunches whenever someone important arrived, the Soviet minister for culture, the Soviet foreign minister, the British ambassador, and Nina watched a few familiar visitors slipping by without shaking the ambassador's hand. They made off quickly around the corners to the music room and the small green dining room where they couldn't easily be seen. She admired their daring; at a party like this, a Russian could lose his watchful companions and mingle freely, privately, for a few precious moments. Some had concerns which might be regarded as professional; others were seriously interested in the food. But everyone knew that the opportunities were brief, chancy.

When Balanchine came in, the receiving line broke down in chaos. Guests who had been glad-handed through now surged back against the flow to congratulate and praise him. But he moved deftly forward, leaving plenty of their attention to the ancient Bolshoi ballerina Elizaveta Pavlovna Gerdt who was escorting him. He was soon surrounded by American and Soviet press in a space he instinctively created for himself in the middle of the main salon. One of the aides standing near the ambassador to mouth names in his ear broke away to join Balanchine's group, making it somehow official.

Nina sensed a hearty, authentic excitement in the air. A few of the ballerinas came in still holding armfuls of bouquets. Had someone advised them to do this charming, inconvenient thing? she wondered. Or had they been offered nowhere to leave the flowers, no vases, no water? She felt the energy of their upright, strong-footed beauty filling the room, and she went to help them, as if she were now joining in with a performance. She signalled to a waiter, and together they made great show of relieving the girls of their flattering burdens, raising the flowers high in the air, bearing them off to a basement pantry to be kept fresh in cold water until the end of the evening.

When Nina came back she was smiling happily and went in search of a drink from the bar set up on a table in the music room.

'It *was* a terrific success, though,' Fred Wentz was saying to a tall, imposing man with a monumental, cadaverous face and close-cropped dark hair. 'If you think the applause was reticent, you have to bear in mind it was mostly official Moscow in the audience tonight. They are bureaucrats, civil servants, heads of various unions and labour organizations. They are not the ballet lovers. They attend because it's a great state occasion and the tickets are given to them as a reward, a form of recognition.' He dropped his voice. 'The point is, they *have* to attend, whether they want to or not.'

'No reaction at all for *Serenade*,' the man grunted. His voice was Yankee, cultured, clipped.

'Have you met Nina Davenport?' Wentz asked, half turning towards her, pulling her into the conversation as she stepped back from the bar with her icy Scotch tilting in her hands.

The tall man nodded at her with faint recognition, his tan eyes electric, watchful behind horn-rimmed eyeglasses.

She said, 'I was hanging around the theatre, trying to help find the sets.'

'Oh, yes. Thank God,' he replied, with a tone of dry impatience that conveyed Olympian disdain for the amateur uselessness of the personnel in charge of costumes and sets.

It struck Nina as comical, but she restrained a burbling laugh.

Then he held out his gigantic hand, and hers was lost in its bone-cracking grip. 'Lincoln Kirstein.'

Her eyes widened in excitement. 'Oh! Mr Balanchine's – partner. What an honour.'

He pressed his lips together and stared at her solemnly.

So Nina continued, 'But it's true, you know, what Mr Wentz was just saying. The party officials and workers who were there tonight are a stolid bunch. There's a mania here for ballet, for art generally. Very articulate and informed. The Soviet audience will have no trouble at all appreciating the New York City Ballet and Mr Balanchine's work. Really. They are primed for it – starved, even.'

Nina felt Kirstein's eyes leave hers and rove over her shoulder; her earnestness felt superfluous, embarrassing. His lips in repose had the shape of a sneer, of doubt; he wasn't listening. She stopped talking as the rotund figure of a powerful Soviet ballet critic inserted himself into their group just beside her, nodding, sweating a little, gripping a tiny glass of vodka in his fist.

But now Kirstein asked her in a stentorian voice, 'Starved?'

Nina shrugged, reluctant to explain herself in front of the critic. She said demurely, awkwardly, 'It will be interesting to see how a broader Russian audience responds − to − to − so many new combinations, such an unfamiliar choreographic vocabulary. I think they'll see right away that there is meaning even in Balanchine's "plotless" ballets. The Russian audience is − very special.'

Kirstein's eyes flickered from her face to the critic's and back again until Wentz bestirred himself to make introductions all around.

The critic preened and smoothed back his thick, oily hair. Then he remarked in sonorous, archly cultivated English, 'I understand Mr Balanchine chooses to ignore the Soviet request to remove *Prodigal Son* from upcoming programmes. May we suppose he clings to this old-fashioned and narrow-minded religious narrative because it reveals something of personal importance about how he feels on returning to his own fatherland?'

Nina was struck by the suggestiveness of this question, but it was offered with numbing pomposity, and the agenda she recognized behind it warned her not to respond.

There was a silence.

At last, Kirstein, with a formal little bow of his head, a large, precise finger adjusting his eyeglasses, slowly said, 'Fascinating question. I wouldn't care to reply for Mr Balanchine. It's a good ballet. Overly ingenious in places; deeply moving − the vulnerability of the son at the end, his shame finally covered by the father's cloak. The father implacable. I've always felt pleased Mr Balanchine agreed to revive it. At one time he didn't believe in reviving anything, only in moving forward. The past doesn't appear to interest him; *now* is what interests him, now and what is still to come. The language of ballet is a breath, a memory, and soon looks out of fashion. There's Prokofiev's music, of course − a Russian who *did* return.'

This produced another silence. Nina bit her lip, sensing that

Kirstein meant them all to reflect on Prokofiev's artistic dehydration, his death, exhausted by official disapproval, on the exact same day as Stalin's.

Kirstein added under his breath, almost as if turning it over in his mind, 'One would have thought music and dance less susceptible to state control than literature, but perhaps not.'

Wentz, with uncharacteristic nervousness, ventured, 'You're a poet, aren't you, sir?'

'Not an important one,' growled Kirstein, dismissing himself, 'but I admire poetry. If I could read Russian, I'd like to read Mandelstam, Akhmatova, Tsvetaeva, Pasternak, Derzhavin – do you recommend others?'

Nina felt moisture springing on her forehead, underneath her arms; she tried desperately to concentrate on what should come next in such a conversation. Who else belonged on this list? But none of the group seemed to find Kirstein's remarks at all normal. Nobody answered him.

The critic gave a weird half smile, then said caustically, as if nobody had mentioned poetry at all, 'The ballet seems to have a story, at least.'

Wentz burst out noisily, 'Spectacular jumps, too, doesn't it? That's what I've heard.'

They all laughed with relief.

Kirstein indulged Wentz's boyish enthusiasm. 'Yes, in the beginning there are a few.'

The critic, sly-eyed, avoiding Nina's gaze, remarked to Wentz under his breath, 'Wait until you see the *pas de deux* with the Siren. Licensed carnality, staggering.'

Wentz winked at Nina. 'So who's the Siren? Is she here tonight?' he asked and looked around optimistically.

Following his eyes, Nina caught sight of all their vivacious backs moving and trembling in the huge gilded mirror on the wall behind Wentz. For a moment, she watched their sparring, their sniffing, their strained mutual effort to please and be pleased, and then she saw that the mirror also reflected another mirror hanging on the wall immediately behind her. Their little group was endlessly repeated in smaller and smaller panes of glass as if through a crystal tunnel or a kaleidoscope. She could even see the entrance to the state dining room behind her to her left; if he looked, Wentz could probably see the entrance to the grand salon from the front hall, behind him and around the corner to his right.

It's like a dance studio, Nina thought, perfect for watching and being watched. Two dancers loped past behind her, a man and a woman, like upright gazelles, exotic in colourful party clothes, their long hair decorative as plumes, their bodies musical, moody. They were talking excitedly, full of the brilliance of opening night. Nina studied the back of her own dress, its wide straps interlacing as a bow between her shoulder blades, emerald green in the underbrush of dark suits and drab Soviet evening wear; she opened her shoulders a little, loosened her arms, faced the critic, faced Kirstein, as they finally ceased to shake with willed pseudo-mirth.

Then she nervily started in, 'Balanchine's father died years ago, didn't he? He must feel a little guilty about that. Or sad anyway.'

She felt eyes lock onto her, and went on defiantly, 'After all, he never had a chance to say goodbye, did he? That leaves a wound that never really heals. But if he included *Prodigal Son* as a gesture to his fatherland – well, it's only an act of courtesy. He doesn't mean to apologize for anything he's done. You can tell that simply by watching the way he walks. In his own life story, it's the father who is ruined anyway, not the son. And it's not as if he plans to stay here, is it? It would be sheer sentimentality to imagine otherwise.' Her voice was clear, ringing, steady.

There was another silence before the critic remarked appraisingly, 'You are a psychologist, Mrs Davenport.'

Nina decided to accept this as a compliment despite feeling it was not intended to be one. 'Thank you,' she smiled.

'As a young dancer, at the Maryinsky, Mr Balanchine enrolled at the Conservatory of Music just across the street from the theatre.

So he studied piano and composing, too,' said Kirstein, catching each of their eyes by turn and smoothly shifting the direction of the conversation, just as if he were a conductor bringing in the first violins, then the seconds, with a new, more predictable, more soothing theme. 'What really intrigues him is the music,' Kirstein continued, 'that's what Mr Balanchine's trying to express.'

But Wentz bounded along in yet another direction. 'Speaking of music, I guess you all know that Stravinsky is in Russia now, too? Chairman Khrushchev will receive him later this week to congratulate him on his eightieth birthday.'

And then Wentz abruptly reached between Nina and the critic, grabbing another grey-suited American, pulling him with his companions into their circle. 'Tom, say hello. I've just been telling our friends that Stravinsky is here this week, too. It's an incredible time for our two nations. Friendly, exciting. Don't you think?'

Nina was smiling so hard that her cheeks were starting to ache, and she nodded and smiled some more as they were all now once again introduced.

Tom Phipps had arrived not long before the Davenports to help prepare for the September visit of the US Secretary of Agriculture. He was still here, working alongside the young assistant agricultural attaché at the embassy, Rodney Carlson. Carlson was dark, floppy-haired, skinny, and wore eyeglasses with frames so black and heavy that they threw his eyes into shadow.

With Phipps and Carlson was an upright, red-haired Russian, grey at the temples, balding, Colonel Oleg Penkovsky. Penkovsky said in good enough English that he was a member of the State Committee for the Coordination of Scientific Research Work.

The greetings were formal, superficial; Nina's eyes drifted to the mirror again, and she had the half-conscious sense that someone else's eyes flickered away. She scanned the reflected crowd, and for a moment she couldn't help but see herself as the centre of something, her green dress washed like a bit of seaweed or like a splinter of bright broken glass by the rolling surge of partygoers.

Her little circle seemed to spread and mingle indistinguishably with the next circle as a body leaned this way or that, talking, listening, in an endless shifting chain of energy, social appetite, interconnections all around the room. Then her eyes did meet someone else's, pale, rimless, in a fleshy blur of face. She turned around, summoning a smile out of courtesy, but still she saw only broad backs behind her.

It made her feel wobbly, hot, once again desperate to sit down. And as she swayed a little on her stiletto heels, she noticed John all the way across the room, looking straight at her from his height, like a beacon, familiar, unobscured. She couldn't read his expression, he was too far away. Nevertheless, she felt reassured, as if he had telegraphed encouragement, concern. He's the one who's entitled to have an eye on me, she thought.

John pressed towards her through the shifting, roaring rooms thinking, Nina's in the thick of it, jeez. Surrounded by goddamned spooks. I'm positive Carlson's one, attaching himself to that Russian technocrat, Penkovsky, pretending he's not trying to. A pretty woman offers them such an easy excuse to congregate; why don't they use somebody else's wife for that, or a ballerina even.

Nearby he noticed Alex Davison, the fair-haired, full-lipped young air force attaché in his thick round eyeglasses framed with translucent flesh-pink plastic; he was chatting earnestly to two stalwart Russian bureaucrats, clean-shaven, arctic-eyed, featureless. Davison gestured enthusiastically towards the dining room and ballroom, inviting his Russian acquaintances to eat; he put an encouraging hand on a strapping back. How could the Russians resist? John wondered. But one of them shook his head, smiling, wagging two fingers towards the floor where he stood, as if to say, Meet me here.

So they're not letting Penkovsky out of their sight anyway. None of them, John concluded.

He considered Wentz; he considered Phipps. Latching on to Balanchine's impresario, as if they were actually interested in ballet.

Lincoln Kirstein, thought John, there is one deep guy. Maybe too deep to plumb. Could he be one?

But Nina's for real; she's there for the beauty. He smiled with pleasure. She'll be giving them all a load of her candour, including that Russian ballet know-it-all. If only we could all read Nina in *Pravda* tomorrow. I don't want to miss this conversation, he thought. And she deserves to be rescued by now.

But as he set out across the floor, someone grabbed his elbow, pulled him back towards the ambassador.

Nina saw John stoop, turn away, move off. I'm handling it fine on my own, she told herself. Another hour or so. All I really need to do is hold up this dress. The dress can practically do it without me. But she longed to be near John.

Wentz drawled to Kirstein, 'You'll have to forgive these philistines. Rodney's expertise is in fertilizers and corn production.' Wentz's accent seemed to Nina to grow more southern when he mentioned farming. 'I may be the only one who's done any homework. I know all about Stravinsky, our *other* Russian exile – who wrote the music for your third ballet tonight, *Agon*, hey? But you have to admit, it was pretty hard to make sense of *that*.' And he gave a belly laugh, elbowing the Soviet critic in the ribs, acting the hillbilly.

This elicited a round of pedagogy from Kirstein, which was delivered with a thin pretence of caring whether it was under-stood. 'I'm sure you know that Mr Stravinsky composed *Agon* partly by what's called serial method – using a sequence of twelve tones – a new technique for him. And the choreography is also organized around the idea of twelve – twelve dancers, twelve movements, dividing into twos and threes and fours, duos, trios and quartets. The timings are exactly projected in minutes and seconds. It's exquisitely made. Spare, undecorated.'

Wentz seemed positively buoyant at the news. 'Well, isn't that something! It sounds like rocket science on stage!'

Again, naïve enthusiasm won the day, and there was much laughter and more ribbing.

The Russian critic remarked, half-smirking, competitive, 'We have our own Soviet ballet of the space age. Konstantin Sergeyev, of the Kirov, has made *Distant Planet* in honour of our hero Gagarin's flight – and with Gagarin we truly were first, long before John Glenn. But, you see, our ballerinas are not trained to count bars in the way of the West – ours dance with the soul, with the spirit. Dance is not a science for us, mechanistic, nuclear; it is an art. It transcends the physical, from within, even.'

Nina thought that Penkovsky, with his fine, bulbous nose, the soft cleft in his chin, his pouting mouth, looked tense. Why couldn't he, too, find rocket science amusing? His eyes were gentle, heavy-browed, hooded, but there seemed to be something the matter with them, some watering and redness, scum he kept wiping at, and for a moment Nina wondered if he was actually weeping. Really, Nina thought, Penkovksy seemed hardly able to stand still, as if his clothes itched, as if he might be in pain. He constantly glanced at Carlson, then glanced away, swivelling his whole head, even his shoulders, around behind his gaze, as if it were hard for him to see anything unless he looked directly at it.

A waiter passed and Wentz whirled around, lifting glasses from the tray. 'Who can hold another vodka?' Only the ballet critic accepted one, so Wentz drank the other himself, crying, '*Vashe zdorovye!*' and lifting his glass.

With his eye resting coldly on the critic, Kirstein continued, 'I believe *Agon* was inspired by some French Baroque dances. In fact, the dances are named on the score. So, as well as the ballistic feeling you have noted,' he tipped his massive head towards Wentz, 'there is also something from the Renaissance, and you can hear it perfectly clearly, a sound of clarions. Or sometimes you can almost imagine there is a lute playing. Picture a courtly tournament, with dancing rather than fighting. The dancers are the knights – competing, showing off. They have no regard for risk. They pretend it's easy, daring each other into one-upmanship, brinksmanship.'

Wentz smiled bashfully. 'You lost me there, sir. My goodness.' Then he turned to Nina, who unexpectedly found his look rather too direct, fresh even, so that she dropped her eyes. 'Maybe you understand that, Mrs Davenport, being a dancer yourself?'

Before she could reply, Penkovsky intoned in a tired voice, 'Come now, Mr Wentz. To anyone who follows the relations of our two governments, that interesting analysis should sound perfectly familiar.'

His voice gave Nina a chill, he seemed to speak from a depth of unhappiness, rage even, intense, suppressed. As she studied him, he looked away, perspiring, sweeping his head and shoulders all around the party as if he were searching for something, some hole in his existence, some gap through which he might slip.

Across the room, the American ambassador was at last circulating among his guests. John Davenport was still at his side.

'Your wife's a real pro, Davenport. She's turned herself out very attractively, and just look at her making friends for us. Good for her. That's what it's all about.'

As they watched, Fred Wentz gave the Russian ballet critic a hearty slap on the back and pulled away from the group, gesturing in the air, one finger up, laughing, admonishing. John couldn't hear anything but answering laughter. Then Wentz turned to Nina, leaned down close to her, whispered something. John saw him touch Nina's bare shoulder casually, confidently with his left hand before Wentz drifted off with Tom Phipps.

John pressed his lips together, the skin puckering out all around them in aggravation. Then he noticed that Phipps, thick-necked, muscular, almost immediately gravitated back towards Nina's group. Phipps's bullet-shaped skull showed pink-fleshed under his crew cut. He stood alone, his feet not quite flat on the floor, as if he might take another step, closer or further; his hands frisked his pockets, hunting for something, a pack of cigarettes.

What are they waiting for? John wondered. What are they expecting?

Phipps is definitely watching. And those two Russians are watching. And Davison, too.

He fell into step again with the ambassador who said, 'I'll go into supper with Balanchine and the director of the Bolshoi. Maybe you'd like to join your wife? Be sure she tells the dancers to eat all they can here where there's plenty of food, would you?'

'Fine, sir.'

As John turned back to look for Nina in the music room where he had just seen her, he nearly bumped into Wentz who remarked confidentially, 'Your wife is certainly in possession of subtle opinions, isn't she? How'd she get in with this whole ballet crowd?'

He found himself taken aback, not wanting to reply, but he said with grudging courtesy, 'She danced herself. I thought you knew that. Had to quit when she was fifteen or so. Got injured. She loves the ballet scene, though, and I think – well – they can just tell she loves it, the dancers, that's all.'

John wasn't sure what he thought about Fred Wentz. At the office, he'd heard that Wentz had once been a career Foreign Service officer and had served a tour of duty in Russia towards the end of the 1950s. According to rumour, Wentz had been sent home for handing out copies of *Dr Zhivago* on the Moscow-Leningrad overnight train. Not that the Russians had ever found out or would even have complained much; it was supposedly Wentz's own boasting that had gotten him into trouble. He was making Russian friends, talked openly and loudly of getting them other banned books, of how much he hated the interference with their right to know things. So he had left the State Department and gone to work in New York, for a big philanthropic foundation – Ford or Mellon or Rockefeller – handing out money instead of books, somebody else's money, to the arts, culture, education. He had set up some programme to bring foreign students into the US, graduates, on the theory that they would take American ideals back abroad with them – if they ever went back.

It wasn't entirely clear to John how Wentz had gotten himself picked to return to Moscow for the ballet tour. Nor how he'd snagged his apartment above the consular section in the embassy, an apartment which had stood empty all summer before he arrived, while longer-serving embassy staff who deserved to be comfortable there had been billeted in the bachelor quarters in America House on Kropotkinskaya Embankment. How could Wentz be CIA if he'd been sent home once already for showing poor judgement? Surely that would have blown any chance of advancement on the intelligence side? Maybe he traded on connections, Harvard, his southern pedigree. Kirstein was Harvard, too; maybe Kirstein had asked for Wentz. But resentment aside, John could see that Wentz had certain gifts – wit, urbanity, lightness of touch. He didn't seem to be much of a typical southerner, his name, for instance, and the fact that he had settled in Manhattan. The flamboyance, the extravagant manners, the farmboy's grinning awe hardly concealed Wentz's intellect; but they made it gracious, bearable. Wentz clearly wasn't surprised by much, and his Russian was still damn good.

'I'm after an informal introduction to one of those pairs of legs.' Wentz's confession was accompanied by a disarming flush. 'The greetings at the airport weren't exactly intimate. Will Mrs Davenport do that for me, do you think? Even though I'm only an American?'

John laughed, unbending a little. 'Have you been nice to her?'

'I think so.' Wentz made a face between a twinkle and a leer. 'I sure could be nicer, though.'

'None of that, you bastard.' John curled his hand into a loose fist and slapped it sideways against the inside of Wentz's biceps. '*I'll* be nice to my wife,' he said, letting go of his jealousy as they joked about it. 'You be nice to a ballerina. Let's get Nina to find you one who isn't married, OK? She's here somewhere. And I think she must know all of them by now.'

But Nina was nowhere to be found. John walked with skilled speed through all the rooms, Wentz sticking eagerly at his side;

they eyed the ballerinas, but they spoke to no one. When they ended up back in front of the second pillar, between the flights of stairs leading up to the loggia and down to the vestibule, all John could think to say was, 'She'll turn up.'

Just then, the powder-room door opened onto the landing and Nina burst out of it. When she saw them, she looked dismayed, went red, turned around and went back into the powder room, slamming the door behind her.

'She was mighty glad to see you,' said Wentz drily, raising his eyebrows. But then he smiled in a friendly, dismissive way.

'Who the hell knows what that was all about,' John said, planting his feet, crossing his arms. 'Maybe she realized she hadn't put herself together again just right. Let's give her another minute.'

'As long as you don't think she's trying to lose you on purpose? My French friends always tell me that a man should give his wife scope.' This was roguish, half taunting.

'But we're not French, are we, Wentz?' John tried not to take Wentz seriously. He mixed in a little sarcasm of his own. 'I hope you're not taking advice from the French ambassador on women? The one who managed to get himself seduced by the so-called wife of a KGB officer? Or are you referring to that poor military attaché who shot himself last summer when the KGB threatened to go public with the photos of him and *his* Russian girlfriend? From what I hear, most of them are only interested in the men supplied by the KGB anyway. The French are pretty good at making themselves targets for blackmail, huh?'

Wentz dropped his eyes. 'I just don't want to embarrass your wife by hanging around outside the bathroom door all night, Davenport.' He stepped away quickly down the stairs to the vestibule, peered around the corner at the coats silently hanging there, the attendant at the great wooden doors. But then he came back, restless, drifting along the red-carpeted hall towards the party.

John stood his ground, watching, waiting, then hit again, testy. 'Maybe you're the one who's embarrassed, Wentz?'

Wentz laughed. 'OK. But I'm not *that* embarrassed. I want to meet a ballerina and I can wait.'

Just then, Tom Phipps appeared through the columned entry to the salon. When he saw the pair of them staring leaden-eyed at the powder-room door, he seemed to John to rein himself in. Then he remarked with a kink of frustration in his voice, 'C'mon, guys. You both know how much trouble I've taken to get that powder room redecorated. If you hang around outside the damn door, the guests are going to be too shy to use it.'

Getting no response, he came up very close to John, and spoke softly, with forced nonchalance, 'And damn if I didn't leave my matches in there.' He slapped at the pockets of his jacket and then his trousers as he approached the powder-room door.

John said frostily, 'My wife's in there. And that's why I'm waiting out here.'

'So what the hell's your wife up to in there?' Phipps sounded genuinely annoyed.

John remained silent. His pupils swelled and shrank in their green-brown irises. His nostrils flared. What the hell was up with Phipps? And then it dawned on him that Phipps was using the bathroom for something, that he must be trying to exchange messages with a Russian.

'Lay off, Tom,' said Wentz, sounding bored. 'We're just hoping to meet some of the ballerinas, and she knows them all. It's nothing complicated. Unless you aim to make it so.'

John was bewildered by Nina's behaviour, and he felt irritated by his own uncertainty. He spoke up in a kind of husky whisper, defending her nonetheless, 'I'm not sure whether you are trying to imply anything in particular, Phipps, but I wish you wouldn't ruin the evening for her. Or for me, in fact. My wife really loves the ballet – and the music. She's been looking forward to all this in a way you can hardly imagine.'

The powder-room door opened and Nina came out, white-faced, her eyes huge, washed-out.

'God, I'm sorry,' she said. 'My stomach's just a little upset.'

John could see sweat shining through her newly freshened make-up; her hair had gone flat and dark at the temples.

'Are you feeling OK?' he asked.

'Well, I – I'm better now. Sorry. Can we –? Let's go back to the party. We must be missing out on supper.'

'Wentz wants to meet a ballerina, honey. What do you think?'

Nina smiled. 'So he told me. And I promised to introduce him. But don't get your hopes up,' she tossed at Wentz, 'they go to bed early, these girls. They are pretty serious about their work.'

She led the way back into the main salon.

Over the next few days, Nina accompanied the New York City Ballet dancers everywhere, and she became increasingly caught up in the excitement of their growing success. She attended their performances every night, watched Balanchine's daily company class, went on with them to rehearsals after lunch.

The bulky, unsmiling women manning the tiny blond-wood desks where they held the room keys at the entry to each long corridor in the Ukraina grew bored with her zealous arguments about the needs of the American ballerinas and began to let her pass with just a frown of recognition.

For all its size and splendour, the Ukraina was turning out to be mostly an imposing façade. The doorknob came off in Patrice's hand the first time she went into the bathroom; Nina had to call the matron from the hall desk to unlock the door and let Patrice out. The neat beds with their spooled headboards and silky-looking coverlets were narrow and hard; the coverlets were sticky Soviet nylon; there were no blankets at all. Alice told Nina they were piling their coats on top of themselves to keep warm in the small hours.

The hotel dining rooms – large, well appointed, sedate, a little gloomy – were equally sham. Grandiose calligraphy offered a choice of delicacies, *zakuski* of pickled cucumber, pickled mushrooms, beetroot, or *kolbasa*, smoked sturgeon, Stroganoff and *kasha*, chicken Kiev, dumplings, pies, sweet and savoury *pirozhki*. But the menus represented only a collective longing for such fare. The meals were repeatedly the same, soups and small rectangular slices of aromatic, dense Russian bread. Usually there were also meagre, brownish slices of what seemed to be mutton lying under a thick layer of yellow aspic, and *kolety*, meat patties of mysterious origin. But the girls couldn't bring themselves to eat these.

One day, late, racing after the other dancers, Nina, Alice and Patrice leaped into an unattended elevator, and Patrice, flailing, pressed a button with nothing on it. When Alice slid back the squealing doors on the unnumbered floor, it proved to be a hidden workplace, bristling with electric wires, recording machines, KGB technicians. The girls were pushed back inside the elevator with their mouths still open in surprise. Nina had warned them that someone might overhear anything they said in their rooms, but to see the size of it, the routine if it, the institutionalization of it, so mundanely exposed, was still a shock to all three of them. After that, whenever Nina and Alice and Patrice sat chatting on the twin beds or around the well-waxed oval table in the suite's snug little living room, they took to joking about indiscreet remarks, 'You're on the air,' because they now knew for certain why they could adjust the volume of the radio on the bedside table but could not switch it off.

With their official Soviet guides, the dancers went en masse to visit Lenin's Tomb, Red Square, St Basil's Cathedral, the Kremlin Museums. One clear morning they drove up to the Lenin Hills, underneath the needle-topped skyscraper of Stalin's new Moscow University, for the view of the city. Beyond the yellow October woods, beyond the river, stadium, sports palaces, softly coloured, undulating in the mist of nature and the smog of industry, lay the patchwork of timber and stucco, stone and steel – houses, palaces, apartments, power plants, roads, bridges – distressed by snow, by cold, by Moscow's own self-lacerating, shadowed vitality.

As they gazed, strolled about, took photographs, Danny was approached by two uniformed police who suddenly snatched his camera, escorted him by both firmly gripped elbows to their car, and drove off with him down the Vorobyev Highway.

'What the hell?' cried Alice, gesturing towards the air where he had just stood beside her in his dark blue ski jacket. She squinted at the short, sharp-edged little grey Lada as it sped away with Danny's wavy brown head visible as a smudge in the rear window.

A crescendo of dismay spread through the group.

'Get back in the bus,' Nina commanded. 'Get everyone back into the bus.' She ran to their guides, amazed that none of the KGB minders dragging around everywhere with the dancers had intervened in this summary arrest. It seemed they hadn't even noticed.

'Well, by the way,' said one, puffing out his cheeks with air, blowing in unconcern, 'it's a local precinct. They have their own job to do. Comrade Chairman Khrushchev's own house is just down the hill, there.'

'It was his camera,' Nina shouted. Her voice was panicked, pitched high; she felt viscous, suffocating helplessness rising in her like an oily, choking tide. The quagmire of absurdity could drown them all; it was entirely possible, right here in broad daylight. 'They were saying he took a picture of soldiers over there, a few minutes ago, out the window of the bus.' And she waved her arms down the hill to the right. 'It was by mistake. I'm sure he didn't even see the soldiers.'

'Well, of course, he shouldn't take such pictures; why should he need photographs of our military arrangements? You have the vista here especially for tourists.' The voice was lazy, condescending, smug.

'Oh, Christ,' Nina said under her breath, gasping. Then collecting herself, she shouted at him in righteous anger. 'You have to find out where they've taken him and get him released! Obviously he'll give them the film!'

And that's exactly what happened. But it took hours, numerous telephone calls, endless pleading, until Danny was finally handed over to a full-fledged miniature delegation comprised of a Soviet Foreign Ministry official, an American Embassy official, a representative from the New York City Ballet, and Nina — at the local police station. He came out flattened by fear, the panache faded from his bright, grey-flannel eyes, his chiselled features vague and splotchy. In the embassy car on the way back to the Ukraina, it became clear that he had accidentally photographed an anti-aircraft installation; Americans, even diplomats, were getting thrown out of Russia all the time for collecting information on defence installations. Danny missed that night's performance and rattled the company. But it wasn't long before he recovered his spirits.

The next day, at the Palace of Congresses, Nina was curled up on the stairs below the stage, reading. Danny and Patrice and another boy were stretching on the railings above her, and Nina could hear Danny repeating the story, now a tall tale, of his arrest and questioning by the KGB.

Something inside her flipped. She raged up the stairs and laid into him, 'Danny, you goddamn idiot. Shut up! Just shut up! You are so lucky that episode turned out to be nothing. Brag about it when you get back to America. Don't brag about it here where I or *any* Russian can hear you!'

Danny and the others were speechless. They just stared at her.

And then Patrice prissily said, 'Nina, you know, you really are not a *member* of this company. You don't have to spend every single second with us. And you certainly shouldn't be eavesdropping.'

No rebuke could have stung Nina more. It made her wince. But her fury was unabated, and she launched a reply.

'Why don't you read this,' she shouted, 'and go ahead and try to look after yourselves. Nobody can look after anybody in this country. It can't be done.'

She threw what she had been reading at their feet, a sheaf of flimsy typed pages stapled together.

They looked down at it, nonplussed, then looked back at her. There was a long silence.

Danny was the first to relent. He bent down and picked up the typescript, smoothed the pages, glancing at it, then held it out to Nina, taking a step towards her so that she had to accept it.

'We don't read Russian, Nina. Which is why, obviously, we need your help. And thank God you were there yesterday. I hope I told you that I am sincerely grateful.'

On this, he executed a dramatic, deep bow, arms gracefully extended, as if for a curtain call. His face as he stood up again was contrite, with no hint of mockery.

'So tell us,' he went on. 'I'm just trying to burn off some steam, you know, by making fun of what happened. It's just my way.'

Nina didn't reply.

Quietly, petulantly, Patrice asked, 'What's the typescript, Nina? Come on.'

Nina wiped away a tear. 'I don't like police,' she said apologetically, a crack in her voice. 'Nothing good ever happens in Russia when the police are involved.'

She stiffened, troubled by the sensation that she had been indiscreet in telling them about the typescript, and troubled by another, older sensation, lost yet omnipresent somewhere inside her, that she might always be putting someone else in danger by her forthrightness, by her lack of guile. She took a breath, tipped her head, and narrowed her eyes coldly. 'The typescript's a story being passed around the embassy. The editor of a magazine here wants to publish it. He's well connected. Maybe he'll be given permission. But I shouldn't be talking about it.' Now her voice was hard again, almost dismissive.

In America, Nina had peeled away restraint slowly, cautiously at first, then with relief, and finally jubilation; she found it painful now to button her lips as every Soviet child was taught to do. From her frustration was born a perverse, impatient impulse to express herself too freely, as if to test her strength, to assert her Americanness, her right to speak out.

She beat the papers against her thighs in a slow, rocking rhythm, lifting and dropping both arms, her eyes and mouth down-curved with sorrow, then burst out in a hoarse whisper, 'The story's about one day in a prison camp in Siberia – it would break your heart to read it. And it's about a *good* day. A day when the prisoner manages to enjoy his work, gets enough to eat, isn't sadistically punished. People in this country are sent to these forced labour camps for nothing. *Nothing.* And they die there. Maybe they hold the wrong opinion. Maybe not even that. Americans don't pay much attention, even though it's been reported in the papers in the West. But nobody here has been allowed to tell such things in print.'

Nina steadied herself, stood up a little, a veneer of calm returning, and she said casually, in a voice which seemed to acknowledge her excess of feeling and to invite understanding, 'I was very upset by what happened to you, Danny, and then reading this story – It's – It's the way the prisoner *takes* it, how hard he works, despite everything. The work he's *forced* to do, but which he somehow makes a choice of, as if he were free anyway, to choose – to choose to do it well anyhow.'

Patrice half raised her eyes from the floor to glance at Danny, then rolled them towards the other boy, but the boys stood still, solemn, hiding their scepticism from Nina, about what she was saying.

Nina could feel their uncertainty, their wish to get away. She leaned towards Patrice and said with sudden renewed passion, 'They really count on that here. It's all anybody really has – to choose work. As if work could save you. It's the same for dancers, you know.' She challenged them with it, bullying, angry. 'You should have seen someone like Ulanova dance. We used to have tickets to all the matinées, the kids at the Bolshoi school. I saw her. And this tiny repertoire she was confined to, an old woman dancing roles for a young girl, Juliet, Giselle. She had pared her life down to nothing – nothing but the dancing. And within the dancing, she had pared her gesture down to nothing. The economy, the simplicity – was breathtaking. But really, she was like someone starved of life.'

Nina's jittery, unpredictable voice grated and caught; she had to clear her throat with an ugly cough, force out her words like heavy phlegm, like rocks falling on the others, bruising their attention. 'You know what? Ulanova had just about no food at all when she trained in Leningrad during the war. Boy was she determined to keep her head down. She accepted what the State offered without complaint because she knew she could only expect worse; she could not expect better. She was like a nun of dance – even though she married. Oh, and she had a dog, too. But that was it. No children. Only her career. She would come in and practise alone for hours when all the dancers had the day off. Even though she was the biggest star. And when she was too old to dance, teaching, teaching, teaching; judging this or that competition; running the theatre, running the school.'

Finally Danny broke in, 'That's not so tragic, Nina. Come on. That's any dancer's life. We all work like that. Everyone knows the sacrifices. Physical pain, exhaustion. And everyone knows that's not what you think about when you are on stage. On stage, you know it's worth it. I saw Ulanova when she was on tour. We all did. A little old-fashioned maybe, but not tragic. And she seemed pretty well-fed, actually. Nobody had put her on a strict diet!'

Nina couldn't stop. 'Compared to you, the dancers here might as well be prisoners. They never have anything new, no control over what they dance. They go stale with the limitation, the repetition. It just wears them down. That's why someone like Nureyev would take his life in his hands and leave his homeland. There was nothing here to nourish him, nothing to grow with. But of course, he's one of the great ones. He's lucky.'

'Whoa, Nina!' Danny smiled, jokily held up his palms signalling stop. 'We've all *definitely* been advised not to talk about him. I'll just pretend I didn't even hear you.'

Then he took her gently by the shoulders, still smiling, and gave her a tender squeeze. He could tell – as some people could about Nina – that there was something in her that needed reassurance. And he handled her as he would handle any ballerina, with a dose of his physical solidity, his practised, professional, grounded strength, which to a skittish thoroughbred unfailingly conveyed, I can hold you, I can lift you, I know how you feel, I know how you will move. Just dance.

October 14. But the anger stayed with Nina, festering. The next morning when she woke up, she felt as though she had a hangover from the emotion of her outburst, and she lay in bed, queasy, reluctant.

'Do I get you back any time soon?' John asked dozily beside her. 'Or are you going to run away with this circus?'

Nina smiled, not moving. She knew from his mild tone of voice, from his unceremonious return to their bed, that he was offering her whatever she needed. But neither of them knew what it was that she did need. The ground seemed to be breaking up under her feet. It felt unbearably bitter to her, so recently so happy and now with nothing she could tell him, nothing for sure.

'You seem pretty tired, sweetheart.' His voice was kind. 'I guess it's all – sort of a strain? The excitement? They really get you on edge, don't they, these dancers?'

'Well, getting arrested! Wouldn't that get anyone on edge?'

They both laughed now, but only a murmur of laughter. And John sat up. Before he leaned down to kiss her, he made a definite space between their bodies, indicating his intention to move away rather than closer to her. He really was not sure how she felt, and he was determined not to offer any physical imposition. This was his new decorum, side by side, without push, without pull. He placed a dry, gentle kiss on her forehead then stood up and started opening drawers to find clothes.

'Seriously, Nina. It seems like you're operating on just adrenaline.'

'I've got no right to be this tired,' Nina said, 'I'm not doing any of the real work – the dancing.' Beneath the covers she untwisted her nightgown from around her hips, then rolled onto John's pillow, nestled on her side in his interrupted smell there.

'Dancing's not the only thing that makes people tired, Nina. You've been slaving over this visit. Give yourself some credit.'

'Can't. It's my Soviet past. It just won't let me.' She offered it as a witticism. But there was something dark about it. They both paused a moment.

And then, lying on her side, looking away from him, she said in a throaty tremolo, 'It's coming after me in the night, darling. Dreams. Nightmares.' Her voice went flat, matter-of-fact. 'No, that's not right – because I'm awake actually. Not sleeping at all, I'm so restless. So – God –' She tried to burrow deeper into the pillows, to get to some place there which had once felt like heaven, a certainty, something allowed, unpunctuated bliss. 'Everything is getting stirred up. Stuff that I'd forgotten – or – put away. Bolshoi memories. The year my father died. Then when I hurt myself. Old moth-eaten stuff. I dreamed I'd lost my passport. I guess that *was* a nightmare. God! I don't want to think about it all again. It *is* my Soviet past. Past. It's *past*.'

'Good girl.' And he kissed her again, but disengaging now, rushed. 'I'm sorry I have to go in on a Sunday morning. I'm only a lazy American, and I've got more work than I can cope with just now. I'll try to make it tonight, though. But maybe – well, just don't count on me.'

After John had left for the office, Nina lay in bed brooding. She knew it was making her ill, the struggle to keep certain things down, forgotten. Certain things which were too painful to think about. She got up to dress, felt overcome, ran into the bathroom, retched just as she had done at Spaso House on the opening night. Then she crawled back to bed, quivering, sweaty, in a turmoil of night thoughts.

More and more it was the camps. Their dark horror. The reality had been beyond her imagining, until she read that typescript. Now it seemed to be burned into her brain, her eyes, her heart.

She couldn't stop thinking about it, fearing it. The suffering. That was not a fate you could leave people to and cheerfully move on with your separate, chosen life elsewhere. Where were the friends she had left behind? Could they be mixing mortar, laying slag-blocks for a power plant in Siberian cold? Frostbitten, half-starved, scraping a bowl of porridge with a bread-crust spoon, scheming and fighting for an extra mouthful? Sleeping with hook-toothed bedbugs, with murderers.

I let those police snatch Danny from under my nose. I should have noticed what Danny was doing. I should have warned him.

There had been men, watching, waiting, outside the university lecture hall in Hertzen Street, that dolorous winter evening when her truant teenage life had been smashed, her brilliant band scattered. Those men hadn't been students, they hadn't been teachers. They certainly hadn't been interested in poetry. I knew when I crossed to the doors, proudly ignored them as they leaned against the pillars, among the frail trees, faking idleness, in the twilight. What did they want of us? They would have to speak up, make themselves interesting, worthwhile. Thugs.

Inside, all the way up the splendid, galleried stairs, I heard their shoes, skiffing and slapping on the broad stone treads behind me. They chose the opposite flight where the stairs divided at the landing under the portraits, and they watched from the red marble colonnade as if they belonged to the night gathering above the skylight, their hands in their black leather pockets beside the white statue, while we pressed, beloved, excited, with outbursts of greetings, into the hall.

The desks and chairs were groaning with people crammed on them, on laps. Coats and pullovers were piled on the floor, faces were flushed, itchy-looking in the overheated room.

'I've lied to my mother again!' Nina could remember her casual, embarrassed boast, her forced, giddy laugh, dragging a strand of hair back from her eyes, the habitual gesture to still all that nerve. 'Lucky she didn't come with me!'

89

'I'll look for you afterwards.' From Viktor's banter, she had sieved out the one thing she needed to hear.

And then, believing time was riches they could squander, shrugging, playing it cool, she had answered, 'Otherwise tomorrow. At the dacha. Because everyone else will want you, and I might even leave early, to keep her happy.'

Not expecting otherwise, despite the tension spiralling around them. Everyone smiling.

I lay in bed waiting, Nina thought, just like this, sick with it – I was so sure that he would come to Maly Gnezdnikovsky Lane, downstairs to the archway, the vaulted dark. I relied on it, childishly, took it as if he was deliberately breaking a promise, something personal because we had – a physical commitment, private. Which nobody else could possibly understand. Her recollections grew hectic, defensive. How could I have been so unprepared, so innocent?

It had been somehow the same with Masha. The dry familiar hand snatched from mine as we stood in the back row of thirteen-year-olds, not long on point. Masha taken to the front, in the big rehearsal room, and they stood her on a chair, or on what – a table? She's going to have a big role in something. I felt so excited for her, only a little jealous. Craning to see, smiling because we were taught to smile. What was the teacher saying? Why was Masha's face crumpling like paper, an ugly red patch, wet with confusion, disbelief, pleading?

What was happening? Some punishment? I knew she hadn't done anything wrong. Of course not.

Masha's father had been arrested. What was the reason? Nina couldn't hear. Did anyone know? Masha's father worked in a military town near the Urals, that was all Nina knew, a scientist. There had been some disaster, a reversal to the progress of socialism. Somehow, they were blaming it on Masha, *vreditelsvo*, sabotage.

But Nina could see that Masha didn't know anything about

what had happened. Nobody had told her. And the teachers knew perfectly well that Masha was blameless. Why weren't they wiping away her tears, embracing her? It enraged Nina, so that she pushed up onto her toes, ready to cry out from the back of the room, to go to Masha. She restrained herself only with great difficulty. Don't make it worse for her, wait until she looks at you. Wait until you hear the whole story. It's all a mistake. It will be sorted out as soon as Masha explains.

But Masha only went on crying.

And then it came around the rows like a blight, preying on the children, changing them for ever. Implicating them, corrupting them, making each of them complicit.

Did Masha tell you about her father? Did she tell you? Did she say she was sorry for his mistakes? Why did she hide this from us all the time? the teachers were asking. Nobody knew why Masha had concealed it. The children in front of Nina were saying Masha had done it on purpose. Masha was not a conscientious Young Pioneer. She thought she was better than the others. She was vain about being a class ahead for her age; she didn't work as hard, didn't earn her position. Nina knew that Masha worked harder than anyone else in the class, even though everything came easily to her, more easily than to all the gifted others. They are just jealous, Nina had thought.

Nina had felt it coming closer, the question and answer, the blight, and she feared it beyond comprehension. She wanted to run to Masha, drag her from the room, take her somewhere safe, take her home. I'm lucky to have Masha as my friend, she had thought. I've had to work to be worthy of her, to keep up with her. But Nina had been afraid.

She had leaned down to her shoes, as if she could hide somehow, bent double to the floor. One ribbon was sewn on badly, in a rush the night before, and she had looked at it, desperate, rubbed the clumsy pink stitches, picked with her fingernail at the loose knot anchoring the thread, tugged at the ribbon, so that the whole thing had unravelled, come free in her hand and the heel of the shoe flopped down hard on the floor with a slapping sound. Everyone turned towards her as she stood up, crimsoning, and she had covered her face with both hands. She had pulled the shoe from her foot, run from the room, hopping and stumbling over the long hard toe of the other shoe that was still on, ribbons trailing behind her on the floor.

Sobbing in the changing room, she had hated herself, hated her teachers. Sensed weakness, betrayal all around her.

I remember I wanted to tell Dad. I wanted him to explain to me what had happened. But not in front of the Szabos, not in the apartment. Instead, I went out with Mother to the second-hand shop, the Komissiony, on the Arbat where she liked to go see what they had, and I ended up telling her. I was too frightened to look at her face, but I could feel her expression, stern, impatient, pent up. I thought she was angry with me because that's how she always was. She only said, 'You're a smart girl, Nina.'

What did she mean? That I should be able by myself to understand what had happened to Masha? That she didn't want me to ask her any more questions? Did she mean, Figure it out for yourself?

Or did she mean that I had done the right thing, running out of the room? Maybe she was trying to offer me some kind of praise. But what I had done didn't feel right to me.

On the way home, Mother had brought it up again. 'Don't tell your father. He's scared enough.' This was her idea of kindness. But Dad died before he could explain it to me. I still needed to find out what had happened, what I should have done. I realized that far too late.

And what would happen to me now, if they found out at the Bolshoi school how old I was? That had worried me all the time. Because I knew I had been cheating somehow.

It was more than three years before I saw Masha again. Her father was rehabilitated after Stalin died; she was invited back to the Bolshoi. We all pretended that nothing had happened.

But everything had changed. Masha and I were no longer in the same classes. I was way ahead. She had lost her chance of becoming a star. There were only awkward glances in the corridors. Once she whispered, 'I knew you wouldn't denounce me, Nina. You did the right thing.'

Nina found it excruciating to recall that now.

I knew that I was the one who had benefited from her downfall. I was given all the opportunities that had once been given to her, the lavish, sickening attention. The injustice was unbearable. I wanted to tell Masha that Dad had died. That I was suffering, too. But it wasn't enough. What difference would that make to Masha? So I didn't even answer her, didn't accept her forgiveness. Didn't apologize. Masha turned away. Of course she turned away.

After that, I felt more mixed up than ever. Still the craving ambition, to please the teachers, to be noticed. But no joy in moving, in showing how I could. Every success took something more from Masha.

Even now, Nina could see Masha's simple eyes, wordlessly believing in her, willing her to be the best.

That was only the beginning, Nina thought, as she lay in her bed. Feeling all wrong at the Bolshoi, feeling that my shoes didn't fit, that the ribbons would never stay laced, never hold.

You're a smart girl, Nina. That's what Mother had said again on the way to the embassy, on the way to America. Getting me out. Making me safe, whether or not I wanted safety.

And Mother didn't have a clue, Nina thought, that those friends she took me from understood what had happened to me. They were the ones who could tell me what was really going on. They knew all the things that I wanted to find out.

I need to tell John all these things again, Nina thought. Talk it through with him now that we are actually here. She felt scared at the thought, but she knew how well he would understand. It was not something she could write a letter about, not something she now wanted to tell Jean or Barbara at all.

She dragged herself up, looked at her watch. I'll have to catch up with the company at class, she thought. The bus will have left the hotel already.

October 17. By Wednesday morning, Nina decided that she had to consult a doctor. She hadn't had her period since before Paris. Heavenly, light-hearted, indulging Paris, two months ago. She could no longer pretend it was only vague distress, the worry of moving, a change of diet. She felt all wrong. And she felt increasingly desperate, as if she might even be on the edge of some kind of nervous collapse. She was determined to see a Soviet doctor. She told herself that it was the only way to guard her privacy, worth any danger. She avoided reflecting on the fact that she was finding it harder and harder to abide behind the curtain of glass that seemed to divide her from the once familiar city of Moscow around her, and from the friends who pressed more and more insistently on her thoughts.

The doctor she had in mind was Felix Belov, who had befriended and cared for her in the beginning of 1954 when she fell and hurt herself during a practice on the Bolshoi stage. The last time she had seen him, just before she left Moscow, Felix had been still only a student, on the verge of qualifying. Nina felt certain that she could find him in the orthopaedic department at the Morozov Children's Hospital in Dobrininsky Lane. She tried to assure herself that a doctor wouldn't be at risk of criticism, of arrest, because a doctor was too necessary to society; still, she took elaborate precautions to make her way to Felix in secrecy.

She dressed with sober sentimentality in wrecked clothes saved lovingly from college, a long-sleeved white cotton blouse with a round collar, a grey-brown wool skirt falling straight and loose below her knees, a worn Shetland cardigan that didn't quite match

95

the colour of the skirt. Then she lugged on brown wool tights and flat, heavy-heeled brown leather shoes. Over this she piled a bulky mouse-coloured duffle coat and a dark blue wool hat of John's to hide her brilliant brown hair. Her skirt bunched against her legs as she snugged the coat around herself to do up the toggles, and the hem hung down and showed unevenly below the coat. Into her canvas shopping satchel, with her money and her keys, she stuffed a light brown kerchief. Despite the glow of her skin and eyes, she looked convincingly unfashionable. As she studied herself in the mirror, she thought she also looked a little stockier, matronly, plausibly Soviet.

It wasn't far at all to Dobrininsky Lane, a few minutes' walk, but Nina made an odd journey of it. She went into the Metro at the newly opened station in Oktyabrskaya Square, travelled across the river to Park Kultury, then changed and travelled back in to the Lenin Library in the centre of town. She strolled to Arbatskaya, casually, looking at the architecture, venturing into one or two shops where she studied the goods in boxes and measured the length of the bored, somnambulant queues as if she might join one. There outside the Metro was a bookseller's stall, long-haired readers standing thick around it in suits, ties, eyeglasses, heads bowed in devotion over the wares. She kept clear of it. Approaching her old neighbourhood, jumpy, she passed vending machines dispensing mineral water; their striped awnings seemed summery, fluttery, threatened by October. She turned back past the Tchaikovsky Conservatory and the old university buildings. Not once did she look behind her to see if she was being followed. She had been making it a point of honour to ignore her minders; today was not the day she would change her habit.

Eventually she circled all the way back again, across the park, Aleksandrovsky Sad, walked up to the Metro at Revolyutsii Square, and travelled to Novokuznetskaya, where she got out and walked to the Tretyakov Gallery. She went into the lobby and talked to the old lady about admittance, saying she might like to bring a group of friends on another day. Then, looking at her watch, murmuring something about the stove and her lunch, she rushed out and began to walk rapidly home towards Leninsky Prospekt. She was sure now that she was being followed, because she surprised her blue-overcoat-clad minder on the pavement right outside the gallery, but just as she was beginning to think he would never tire or grow bored with her pointless wanderings, she saw his unmistakeably similar relief enter a telephone booth two blocks ahead of her across the street on the right. As the door shut behind him, Nina saw the back of his head through the glass.

He won't look at me, he won't risk eye contact, she thought. He'll wait until I walk past. The one behind must have entered another phone booth, to place his signalling call. Yes, I saw it, Taksofon, a block or two back. She was certain.

OK, it's for real, she told herself, clenching her teeth. She held her breath, turned into the next small street on her left and walked as fast as she could to the corner before turning left again. Long strides, she told herself, easy ones; you always walk like this, you enjoy it. She was sweating with fear; the sliding hot drops under her arms surprised her, slick bugs racing down her flesh, inside her clothes. She feigned relaxation, a strolling posture, reminded herself to breathe, to carry her head high.

Occasionally in the past, she had lost her minders. But she had never done it deliberately. She had presumed on such days that they made an assessment that her movements were leading nowhere, or simply that her minders were lazy. Now at last, as she turned another corner, to the right, she allowed herself to look back. They'll return to the gallery, she thought, and the old lady there will tell them that I went home to eat. They'll probably find Yelena Petrovna there at the apartment, but maybe they'll think it's their own mistake. So they'll play it down, try to hide it.

She delved into her satchel and took out the brown kerchief, yanking off John's blue hat as she walked. Unless they recognize me in this kerchief, she thought. Then they'll realize I've lost them on purpose.

The second time she looked back there was still no one. As she turned right again, circling the block, she took off her coat, turned it inside out to the reversible blue lining, and put it back on. She struggled with her satchel, the coat sleeves, but she didn't stop walking.

Brown coat, blue hat, she said to herself in Russian, imagining how their voices might sound describing her to passersby as she had been dressed before. Dismissive, gruff, like the KGB agent who had done nothing to help Danny at the overlook on the Vorobyev Highway. What do they really care, she thought? And her cynicism made her feel bold.

If anyone noticed her going into the children's hospital, perhaps they would think her visit was of no particular importance. A child of a friend she might be inquiring about, or just a mistake. Perhaps no one would suspect she was a foreigner.

She was overdressed for the temperate autumn weather, perspiring heavily now with the exercise, apprehensive as she tried not to hurry up the few shallow steps, as she refrained from looking around. She took in only the well-remembered, low-built, red stucco façade, the staring white window frames cracked and darkened with mould, the pretty, rambling wings tilting and slumping under sodden, weed-sprouting roofs.

To the attendant she said brusquely, 'I'm just going back one more time,' lifting her satchel in the air significantly as if it contained something important, curative, specifically asked for – magical chicken soup or a prosthetic limb that all staff members had been told would need to be attached the instant she could deliver it.

The nearer she drew to Felix, the more Nina felt afraid at her impetuous journey. She was a grown woman, married, rich, a foreigner. But she had a problem which needed to be solved, and she had ceased to be able to think about anything else. She yearned for relief, for respite, like someone yearning for home; it could only be Felix. She meant him no harm.

Nina had not shed a tear when her father died; she had not allowed herself to. But she had cried for weeks over the ligaments and tendons around her anklebones. She had had a reputation as a hard worker, so when, after five days, despite excruciating sessions with the Bolshoi masseuse, she still couldn't walk, let alone take class, her mother had inserted herself into the medical section of the school, pleading, arguing, demanding, until paperwork was done, and Nina packed off by chauffeured Volga to be seen by a paediatric orthopaedic specialist.

Now, as she ploughed along the hospital hallways, she kept her head down, met no one's glance. It's just as it was, she thought; all exactly the same. She saw the chipped white tiles lining the walls, the babies playing on the dusty floors, heard the mothers clucking somewhere above their hairless, carefree heads. On a gurney lay a bruise-eyed child under dingy sheets, thin, asleep; at the gurney's head, partly within Nina's gaze, waited strong knees, heavily shod feet, folded work-worn hands, as the mother stood or sat there, pretending not to pray. And the smell. Nina could remember the smell of her own mother's fretful, impatient agitation mixed with carbolic acid, urine, bleach.

There had been the high-sided, cast-iron bathtub in the centre of the black and white marble floor, and her tears of distress as the matron, tough, enormous, had stripped off her clothes, ordered her into the tub, poured water over her. 'Wash yourself,' she had commanded, as if the damaged leg was the result of disease, of germs. And Nina had shivered with fear, with cold, with shame at her nakedness. She hated the monstrous hands, the flinty eyes, the disregard for her modesty, her dignity. Her mother was nowhere, sent away. Her clothes were replaced by an itchy, in-adequate gown.

On the ward, there had been five beds, high and hard, made of nickel, painted flesh colour and the paint scarred away to nothing. During the first night, the girl beside Nina had died – of blood poisoning from stepping on a nail. Nobody could believe how fast it had happened, not the doctors, not the silent, cold-faced nurses who had stared at Nina as if they disapproved of her hobbled vitality, her fat, black-purple ankle enthroned on a bowl of ice chips.

What was this place of ruined feet? Nina had wondered. Of falling? Falling by the wayside. She had felt so relieved when the girl's body was lifted from the bed, rolled away. And she had felt guilty at her own relief, suffocated. That night, she dreamed that Masha lay in the empty bed beside hers. That Masha's father was nearby, watching, angry.

During the day, the sun had streamed in through the colossal windows which soared to the height of the ceiling; she and the other children had sweated helplessly in their stiffly laundered sheets, enervated, stunned. She looked over from time to time at Masha's bed. Empty still.

Nina's emotional condition had not been recognized, not dis-cussed, until Felix came along on the rounds with his seniors. Why was she confined to bed? he had wondered.

'I fell,' she had replied simply. 'I jumped, and I fell and twisted my ankle when I landed.' She half lifted the tightly strapped leg. Maybe it was my shoe, which let me down. Maybe the ribbons . . .

'Three of the ligaments, possibly even four,' Felix had mur-mured, lingering over her notes. 'And the long peroneus tendon ruptured. Perhaps a hairline crack in the fibula. Torn muscle sheath, as well. A slow therapy to get you back on point. They push you hard, with those young muscles, eh, so much so soon? You should eat more!' He had smiled. 'And your spirits? How do they come to be so badly damaged?'

Nina had been so taken aback that she had nonsensically replied,

'*Cinderella.*' It was the ballet she had been rehearsing, the part of a dancing bird. She had known from the heat in her chest that if she didn't answer Felix, she would begin to cry.

Felix had gone on smiling, then nodded as if he understood.

So she had added, 'We're taught to heed her tale, to wait to be chosen.'

'You weren't chosen to jump?'

'Not Cinderella's jumps,' Nina had admitted, dropping her eyes.

'Well, you might wait for ever. So you had an accident, nobody's fault,' he had said cheerfully. And she had thought then about her dead father, about his accident – nobody's fault.

Nina pressed through a set of swinging doors which thunked on their hinges. A white-coated doctor and two nurses were wrestling with squid-like tubes swaying from a gruesome metal hook on a pole. A tiny body lay hidden among them, inert, its feet just lifting the sheet at their elbows.

There was a sign, Orthopaedic Medicine, and she went through the next set of swinging doors, making a breeze so that one of the nurses looked up automatically, sensing emergency in Nina's speed, but then the nurse looked down again at the absorbing life under her hands.

On the other side of the swinging doors, Nina stopped. She saw the door she was looking for. A little sign on it said, Dr Felix Belov. Her heart beat in her throat with the speed of her walk, with fear. She thought, I can't go through that door. It's like going back in time. Irreversible. Then right away, she took a breath, knocked lightly, and pushed through into the tiny room.

A slight, fair-haired man of about thirty in metal-rimmed eyeglasses and a white coat looked up at her across a high table where he stood writing in a brown folder. More folders were stacked high all around him. He looked mildly inquiring, myopic, as if he were about to ask, 'Are you looking for someone?' or perhaps, 'Are you lost?' But he remained silent.

His pale eyes glowed dark, swelled with emotion, then faded

behind his eyeglasses. A pulse showed at his colourless temple. Still he remained silent.

Nina waited, every thought pushed out of her head by throbs of blood.

At last Felix said, 'I am seeing a ghost.' But he gave no sign of welcome. He was terrifyingly calm.

Nina felt ashamed, at her weakness, at her need. Here she was returning from the West, with all her privilege, all her luck, all her fantastic freedom, to beg help from a man who, she could not help feeling as she stood before him now, was living real life. She was putting him in danger; she had no right. She began to expect angry words, to be sent flying. She hung her head.

Felix came around the table, went to the door, closed it silently without looking out into the hall. Then he stepped closer, put a finger under Nina's chin and lifted her face, studying it as if professionally for symptoms.

'I thought I would not see you again.' It seemed to be a clinical observation. She had been discharged; he had not expected her to be unwell, to require further attention. His manner disguised a depth of concern that she knew he would never express.

Nina felt tears welling. She blinked them back, fixing her eyes patiently on the ceiling, away from his eyes as he examined her.

'Still grieving, are you?' he asked kindly.

This made her laugh, and then sob.

At last, Felix gently embraced her, saying, 'Compose yourself, Nina.'

His stethoscope pressed against her uncomfortably, and she pulled away, trying to fish it out from between them.

'The ribs are sore?' Felix asked in a tone of sympathetic investigation, checking as ever for injury, for pain.

'Oh, no.' She felt embarrassed, laughed again, more heartily. But she knew she might not have much time, so she plunged in. 'I – I think I'm pregnant. You have to help me get rid of it. Please.'

Now Felix stepped back, surprised. But immediately he collected himself.

'You are dancing again?'

'No, no. That's not the reason, Felix.' Nina found she still could not meet his mild, watery eyes.

'Well – I thought you had – settled – on another life. Away from Moscow. Away – altogether.' His tone reflected not only perplexity about her emigration, but also, Nina thought, suspicion, and perhaps indignation about this visit.

'Felix, I'm married. To an American diplomat. And so I can't do anything without the whole embassy knowing.'

For a moment, Nina saw on his face the enormity of what she had done; he failed to conceal it from her. His eyes widened in alarm. 'Diplomat?' he mouthed.

Of course Felix could be arrested. She admitted it to herself. Anyone could. Espionage.

Then he rolled his eyes sadly, fatalistically. Why had she been idealistic enough to imagine she might find freedom in America? he seemed to be implying. No society was better than any other, no life any better, whatever hopes one might have.

'You think they won't know that you have come here?' His voice was only a murmur, but Nina saw his hands lifting and falling against the white of his coat, against his thighs.

She wanted to find their old way of talking, their groove of youthful sarcasm, defiance. 'They certainly won't know *why* I've come,' she remarked acidly. This stood between them as a joke. It earned a smile from Felix; she smiled back. 'Can you examine me, tell me if I am pregnant?'

'It's not my speciality,' he shrugged. But then, without hesitation, Felix began lifting the stacks of brown files from the table and placing them on the floor. 'You must remove your underclothes,' he said curtly. 'Don't take off your skirt. I can't lock the door.' Then he patted the table, indicating that Nina should climb onto it.

In his small room, on his squeaky, dilapidated table, the procedure was embarrassing. Neither of them spoke as he touched her, guided her limbs with his hands, moved her expertly this way and that, eyes lowered. When in the past he had manipulated her legs, it was, for instance, *à la seconde*, to consider the play of her hip joints, the strength, the flexibility, of her legs, of her spine.

He was quick, businesslike, rolled her gently away then pulled down her skirt, turning his back.

'I am quite sure you are pregnant,' he said evenly as he opened a tall cabinet against the wall and reached inside, 'but if you want one hundred per cent, you must urinate into this jar and I will send it for analysis.'

Nina took the jar from his hand, waiting for him to tell her where to go with it, but Felix turned his back on her again, folded his arms, leaned against the table.

'Should I –?' she faltered, realizing. 'Just here?'

'Here.' He didn't turn around.

She crouched on the floor by his table, blushing for the noise she made.

'How will I get the analysis to you?'

'I'll – come back.' Nina was red-faced, feeling a hot drip of urine run down one finger. There was no cloth, no paper anywhere in sight. She stood up, put the slippery jar on the table and said, 'I've made kind of a mess. I'm sorry.'

Felix took a breath and said firmly, as if to forbid her, 'Nina, it will surely be noticed if you come back here.'

She didn't reply, struggling with her underwear, shuffling her tights on. But once she was ready, she stood and faced him. They looked each other in the eye.

'Please. I want you to arrange for an abortion.' She said it forcibly, almost heatedly, like starting an argument. She was that unsure of her ground.

It was a long moment before Felix answered. 'Why are you

coming to me for this? This is not what I do.' His patience was taut, fluttered.

'I thought you might do it without asking why. I thought, in memory of our – student days, that there was a bond between us still – always. Is an abortion so hard to come by?'

Felix crossed his arms, drew himself up, and said with incandescent simplicity, 'One has to consider carefully what one risks one's career for – perhaps one's life. To prevent a life? I'm not so sure. This is important to you, but is it important to anyone else?'

Nina pressed her lips together hard. It was a criticism from her girlhood, that she was selfish, that she had no feeling for the collective. She knew she hadn't changed so much in America, indulged by choices, by lack of fear; she had always had in her this streak of wilfulness, of self-importance. How could she feel entitled to ask this of a friend, to ask something for herself, at his expense?

Or was there something in Felix that offered? That always offered? That wanted her to make demands of him? Felix could sense her confusion. He went on, plaintively, apologetically. 'It's been six years, Nina. What do I know of you now? Why don't you want this child? Who is the father?'

Again, she felt like a schoolgirl, now forced to confess some petty crime. 'My husband. My American husband – at the embassy.'

'And – you don't love your American husband?'

She wanted to speak to Felix as her equal, as her peer. Why did he take this fatherly tone with her? They had been friends. Had she been so wayward? Was her life so childish?

'Yes, I love him. But I – won't cope – can't – with a child now, not here, not in Russia. Have you got children, Felix?'

He looked surprised. Something like embarrassment crossed his face. 'I live by myself.'

And at this Nina felt able to admit, with reluctance, 'It's – I'm terrified, Felix. I can't do it. I'm falling apart.'

Felix considered her in silence. At last he said, 'I see.' It was like a sigh, uncomplaining, world-weary. Then, in a more practical tone, he went on, 'When you come back, I will tell you where to go. I will arrange it.'

Nina couldn't tell whether Felix acquiesced out of understanding or out of the sense of commitment to old ties of which she herself had reminded him. She wanted to think that he could understand exactly how she felt about the pregnancy, the nuance of anxiety and scruple, the burden she had felt herself to be as a child, her mother's claustrophobia and restlessness visited on her like a disease of which she still wasn't cured. Understanding would have absolved her of so much; and now she felt she wanted his absolution just as much as she wanted to be free of the pregnancy. She knew he was capable of it, or once had been capable.

But their meeting seemed to be over. Felix looked towards his folders, reached behind him for the doorknob.

Nina said, very quietly, 'What about Viktor?'

Felix grew still, steely-eyed. He stepped back against the door, leaning on it. There was something hostile in his face, mistrustful or angry.

'Viktor was released about two years ago,' he said in a hard voice. Then lifting his brows, nodding his pale head, shrugging, 'But . . . Viktor would not stop. And now – I don't know exactly. I can't say.' Whatever she wanted, he would not give it.

Nina waited.

Coldly, Felix stared at her; finally he recounted a few facts. 'He was arrested again. October. Almost exactly one year ago. You know that there were mass poetry readings at Mayakovsky Square? Broken up for the Twenty-second Party Congress. Snowploughs were used to clear the crowd, the leaders were picked up, beaten, threatened, then let go so they could be arrested all over again. Afterwards Viktor was involved in something right outside the Kremlin, the Lenin Library, a reading that attracted even the party delegates, well lubricated by their hard work, friendly at first. Because of that came a clamp-down. There were trials earlier this year.' It was as if he were chastising her, expecting that she had not bothered to follow such events.

But she nodded, solemn. 'Something appeared in the papers in the West – Jews sentenced to long prison terms in Moscow and in Leningrad –'

He cut her off. 'That's not it at all. The West always sees such things as a move against the Jews, as anti-Semitism, but it's not just ethnic, not just racial; it's much worse than that. It's terror against us all, repressing through fear – still the despot state. Khrushchev is afraid of his own thaw, as if Stalin will rise from the grave to take his revenge – last year they removed Stalin's corpse from Lenin's mausoleum, threw it in a hole in the ground and sealed it under with concrete. In the dead of night.'

He checked himself. 'At the trials, a few brave souls insisted that by Soviet law, the sentences had to be pronounced in public. It was a great victory, the open court. Because who ever takes note of the law? Still, they were found guilty, "Anti-Soviet Agitation and Propaganda".'

'So . . . ?' she ventured. 'A victory?'

There was silence. Felix left her to draw her own conclusion. He would not help her; she had to go the bitter route by herself, if she really wanted to know.

She said, 'I guess I had persuaded myself that Viktor was dead.'

At this, he suddenly took pity on her. Emphatically he said, 'Viktor is not dead.' It was as if Felix himself couldn't bear the thought of Viktor being dead; he had to correct her for both their sakes. But then he spoke more cautiously, more equivocally: 'I don't believe Viktor is dead. At the time that he learned you had gone to the West, he made a life decision.'

Now, they exchanged a long, aching look. It grew sorrowful, unbearable. They had known each other well, the three of them; they could hardly pretend otherwise.

'It wasn't because of me, Felix.'

He shrugged. He let it pass without argument.

And then he opened the door.

Nina felt his hand tremble against her back as he urged her out into the hallway.

She kept her eyes on the floor. She saw nothing, hurrying along, blind with tears.

All six thousand seats were taken in the Palace of Congresses that night, and the crowd was wild with enthusiasm, bursting out in fits of applause during *Scotch Symphony* and *Concerto Barocco*. At the interval, many in the audience leaped to their feet even while the gossamer counterpoint of arms and legs still welled up, playful, tenacious, from the pulsing fugue of the violins. Then, as the last note sounded, some of them stampeded to the exits. The glistening ballerinas, their black petals of skirt trembling on their long pink thighs, bowed to the backs streaming up the gangways, along the balconies, up the stairs, out of the vast, wood-lined modern hall.

'However much they love the ballet, they obviously love the cheap caviar and sausages more. Look at them go for it!' John was laughing up at Nina as they rode the glass-walled escalators to the banquet hall on the top floor, trying to hold their ground against a juggernaut of sharp, assertive elbows and shoulders over-taking them from below.

There were seven in their party from the embassy, the ambas-sador's wife, Fred Wentz, Tom Phipps, and Peter and Helen Semler, another young State Department couple recently arrived from the States with three baby daughters. It was a familiar joke, the food laid on by the State for important cultural occasions, and they all found the situation amusing.

All except Nina, who earnestly defended the Soviet hustle. 'Muscovites make fun of provincial greed, too, but these people really can't afford to be blasé like you; some of them haven't eaten properly in their lives. They hardly ever see the delicacies we get at the embassy; in fact, they hardly ever see the sort of food we just leave on our plates day after day and throw out.'

John looked taken aback, and he said gently, 'Of course, you're right, darling. We all know it. Thank God there's such a good reason for the treat.'

He guided Nina away from the rest of their group to the decimated buffet tables in the sunken centre of the bland, low-ceilinged room. But she wrinkled her nose at the remnants and shook her head.

'Don't tell me you feel too guilty to eat?' he asked in a frustrated undertone. 'There's plenty.'

She had the grace to laugh. 'God, I'm so self-righteous! What a depressing date. I'm just – not hungry. I'll cheer up. Honestly.'

'Do you want to go down to the little buffet behind the atrium? You always enjoy the palm trees.'

'You think I need a rest cure, huh? The sanatorium?' She reached up and put her hands flat against the lapels of his jacket, raising an eyebrow, pulling one of her faces. Then she noticed that the diamond on her engagement ring had swung around underneath her left hand so that it looked like she was wearing two gold bands, a double pledge. With her right hand, she fiddled the engagement ring upright, leaning against John ever so slightly on her left forearm and her left elbow. He tipped his head forward, straining his eyes down to watch.

In the artificial light, the diamond flashed its white familiar promise; they both saw it. And they both recalled the perfect moment when they had wordlessly agreed that the best way to protect the secret vitality of their relationship was to hide it behind conventional, outward appearances that everyone else was accustomed to and could easily accept and applaud – engagement, marriage. What could the diamond mean now? Was it something they themselves could depend on when the moment seemed far less clear? A mere symbol of commitment?

Nina rested both palms against John's chest again, and they looked at each other with certainty, half smiling. 'It's OK,' Nina said. 'Things aren't that bleak. Let's stay here with the others.'

Just then, Wentz came up behind them, and Nina turned towards him, friendly, catching John's right hand with her left for a moment, then letting it drop. 'What have you done with poor Mrs Kohler? I mean – I'm sure Mr Phipps can find her some food, but he seems a little short on small talk. Or is she with the Semlers? She likes them.'

Her bright tone wavered, died away. She went on nonetheless, as if to erase the impression of her earlier outburst. 'Shouldn't we be filling her in on the opera tunes coming up? Donizetti and Bellini? Maybe you've seen *La Sonnambula*, Mr Wentz? I never have, actually.' But she knew that it sounded forced, and she was unexpectedly overwhelmed by a sensation of melancholy. The melancholy pressed down on her so hard that she couldn't concentrate on what was happening around her, couldn't laugh, couldn't forget herself.

Wentz looked at her in silence, nodding, as if he sensed something was not quite right. Nina felt uncomfortable; he had this directness, continually implying something, although she didn't know what. He wasn't fresh exactly; she could have dealt more easily with that. But he seemed too knowing, as if her thoughts were transparent to him.

She just said, smiling weakly, 'The thing is, I don't feel great tonight. I'm really tired. Burning the candle, and – so forth.'

'I know the feeling,' Wentz said in his familiar way.

It was just short of insolence, she thought, sly, drawling. Or as if he owned her in some way, had a stake in her. And she wanted to deny it, to push him away, require more respect from him, decorum. She wanted to say, You can't possibly know what I am really thinking about.

Through the whole of *Donizetti Variations*, Nina drifted in and out of a reverie, half dozing, fretting. She wasn't certain of the extent to which the pregnancy was making her nauseous, but she felt that she was losing control of her thoughts. She obsessively reviewed her visit to Felix, going over and over each detail rather than really seeing the ballet. Again and again she considered whether she had been followed, whether anyone had been waiting for her when she emerged from the hospital. Again and again she reflected upon Felix's coolness towards her. Why did it come back to her so much more vividly than his warmth, his efficiency, his firm decision to help her? She had to remind herself of nearly everything except his moments of fear, of intense anger. And of his initial reluctance to acknowledge her at all. She planned how she would make her way back to the hospital, what day she would go, what route she would take, pondered whether she would incorporate a visit to the Tretyakov Gallery with Alice and Patrice and Danny in hopes of throwing her minders off the track, or whether it was safest to go alone.

Beneath her thoughts about Felix lay another darker train of anguished chaos to do with Viktor, and she struggled bitterly with herself to keep it at bay. But the more she fought to concentrate her mind on the final ballet, *La Sonnambula*, the more it seemed as though the figures on the stage were somehow coming from inside her own head. There was the manly poet, dressed in the white of his innocence, left alone at the ball. And now the spectral maiden haunting him. Why didn't the maiden wake up when the poet pursued her? Why didn't she hear him, respond to him? The coquette returned too soon, devilish in her red and black flounce of a dress, wet-looking with shine as if with desire. A chill went through Nina as she watched the poet die by the host's hand, the hand of privilege, authority, retribution – the unjustified hand. She could hardly hold up her head to look at the poet's dead body lying there. It's too late, she thought, as the maiden reappeared; he's the one who can't respond now. But as the slight, filmy figure bore away the impossibly heavy corpse, she wondered, Was that what the maiden really wanted to begin with?

And then, weirdly relieved, she thought, Perhaps the maiden is death. And that's how she sets the poet free.

Again, she daydreamed, nearly dozed, started with sudden anxiety. And the close-packed crowd, stirring with excitement in the semi-darkness, faintly sweating as the auditorium grew hotter, more airless, broke in on her dream like a disruptive force, an energy too stimulating, too disturbing. The crowd seemed to be more and more physically committed to the dancers, seemed to be forming a bond with them too passionate to make sense. It was frightening to Nina. She felt as if the crowd had become greedy to possess what was on the stage. Wanted a more and more intense involvement, to eat it up, consume it.

They were like the crowd which had listened to Viktor read his poems the night he was arrested, the crowd which had wanted to own Viktor, which had gone wild for him, which had somehow, as it had seemed to Nina, swallowed him alive into its maw. And tonight she couldn't stop the crowd from getting inside her, from shaking down her self-possession. Her head was crawling with the crowd's numerousness, its heat, its forcefulness, the intensity of its imagination and desire.

Now there was ferocious applause and the crowd began to stamp, chanting, 'Balanchine, Balanchine, Balanchine!'

The ballet's over, Nina told herself. You'll get out any minute now. Through the lobby and out into the air. She recited it to herself as if she could thereby escape sooner. Over the footbridge to the Manezh, home in the dark red Saab parked near there. She pictured the key fitting into the lock of the Saab, the door swinging open with a creak.

But the crowd went on shouting. The frenzy built and rolled around the endless layered platforms of seats above her, behind her. She felt for John's hand, but he was clapping with everyone else; she touched his thigh, then withdrew her tentative fingers.

Now some twitching of the curtain persuaded the crowd that Balanchine would not appear, and from the belly of the room, a fresh cry began: 'Villella, Villella, Villella!' Then they tried, '*Encore, Encore!*' and '*Bis, Bis!*' Nina found it almost unbearable.

She could not see, in the orchestra pit, the conductor's signal for the orchestra to turn back their scores; nor could she see Balanchine in the wings coldly nod to Edward Villella to go ahead and repeat his sequence from *Donizetti Variations.*

Balanchine's expression might have revealed to her his disdain for the encore, even though he was now allowing it. Perhaps what Balanchine was thinking at the moment was that an artist should never be satisfied, should never rest on what has already been achieved. Encores are repetition. He might have been thinking, Don't stop here, don't gloat and luxuriate; it's a trap, success. What does the crowd know? He might have been thinking, What else, what more shall we try for?

When Villella came back out onto the stage and began to dance, Nina didn't see Villella himself at all. She saw Viktor, wild-haired, with his huge grey eyes, huge nose, dark overhanging brow, and a few flimsy papers in the hefty big mitt of his hand. She remembered how she used to feel so absorbed by Viktor's presence, how it never even occurred to her that anyone else was in the room with them. In those days, she had thought she was the only audience that mattered to Viktor. But of course, after he was gone, she had realized how wrong she had been. As if he had left her alone in an enormous crowd, and she mattered to no one at all.

In Vladimir Prison, one hundred miles east of Moscow, where he had languished for eight months, Viktor Derzhavin still had an audience, and he still knew how to excite it to protest.

He leaned down to the reeking latrine in his cell and called into the darkness. Then he bent his ear closer to the filth, listening for a reply. There was never only one reply; everybody was party to the primitive plumbing system, nearly dry, flushed with

113

at most only one bucketful of water a day from each cell. Anyone who cared to could join in the yelling. Viktor heard calls coming back to him, impatient, barking. The first voice, maybe the second, might carry some articulate message. But quickly the sound built to irrational reverberations of rage, hatred, relief. Unloading into the latrines. One thing or the other, Viktor thought blackly, it's really the same, all shit.

He could tell the difference when someone who wanted peace and quiet to sleep in took the trouble to yell, 'Shut up, you fuckers!' But objections just added to the noise, to the theatre of echoes that screamed and rampaged absurdly around the clapped-out pipes.

His own cellmates never grumbled; there was no point. It was easier to believe in Viktor than to oppose him. Living with him was a career in itself, something to do. Now one of them banged on the heating element with his tin cup. Just a few taps, getting louder. He used the prisoner's Morse code, tapping out the first question anyone might ask in solitary confinement if he managed to make contact with someone else through a wall: Who are you? This was to impress Viktor, an admirer's joke. Solitary was rare; not everyone could boast knowledge of it. Gradually a crescendo of taps crashed back towards them, until the din was unspeakable. Viktor and his cellmates smiled at one another in satisfaction and the building roared and boiled around them, criminals and politicals alike. The guards were up; Viktor could feel the floor move with their rhythmic running. The noise had gotten to them; they were forced to investigate, to quell it. He bathed his brain in the waves of sound, pictured the shifting parabolas, their heights and widths, and how the parabolas would all, no matter how unique, soon flatten out.

He pitied the guards, condemned to their own hell of prison life. Just now, they would have been getting ready to pace the corridors through the night when even the prisoners were allowed to sleep. But Viktor couldn't leave the guards be. They were the exposed rock face of the State, at least from where he was situated; they had to be worked at, chipped away at. Viktor couldn't allow anything anywhere near him to settle, to solidify, to become easy, familiar, habitual, not for himself, not for his jailers. His tenacity was not just a clinging tenacity, not just a passive mode of surviving; he pricked himself to move forward all the time, to think of the future, of what was to come next; that was his discipline.

He knew how easy it might be to shut down on the world, to lose himself in his thoughts altogether. It was what his mother had often lovingly chastised him for, the indulged only child, never disturbed at his play, never obliged to break off concentration to fight for a soldier, a block, a piece of track for his train. Never accompanied in his maverick bivouacs in the forest, where he built houses, forts, entire settlements to rule and revel in alone. That was how, solving equations until dawn in his remote, untidy room at the end of the corridor in his parents' apartment, he had managed to ignore the knocking at the door, his father's raised voice, his mother's tearful disdain the night she was taken away by Riumin. He had only gradually woken up to the fact that she was never coming back, and since then he had never really slept again. He had learned to watch his father closely, pried into his father's affairs, his worries, forced his way into his father's confidence, and even looked stealthily through his father's papers. He refused to accept the ignorance that was supposed to keep the next generation safe, because he knew it would not.

And in prison, Viktor required of himself that he try something new, increase his velocity, redouble his defiance with each day that passed. He had to astonish his jailers. To make them afraid, if possible, of what they were doing; to make it more difficult, more expensive, less rewarding, more unpleasant. It was a simple problem of acceleration; it required the continual input of energy. He would devote his life to it; he knew that he had more energy than most. There wasn't much room for creativity and manoeuvre in prison routine; still, no opportunity to test it, disturb it, destabilize it, could be allowed to go unexplored, no tiny fissure unworked. He looked constantly for avenues the authorities had not foreseen, had not foreclosed, had not yet made illegal.

Now, as he listened to the guards running, Viktor tried to quantify what he had achieved – how many sets of boots, how many feet had been forced into motion? Was it six or eight? Naturally, the guards punished Viktor whenever he gave them an excuse, when he made their lives miserable. He tried to avoid being identified as a kingpin or as any more of a troublemaker than anyone else. He shared power and information with whomever would let him, which was partly what kept him strong. He lived by the conviction that generosity ennobles; he believed it was the opposite of fear. He had admired generosity in his father, his mother, in a handful of friends, Felix Belov, for instance; and he had seen fear make dwarves of practically everyone else, shrunken, grotesque. Some of the other prisoners protected Viktor, partly because he could alleviate their boredom and restlessness with his transfixing talk. He could recite whole books, much verse, by heart. Also, Viktor had beautiful manners of which he occasionally still made use.

He took his biggest risk when he used his precious pencil and paper to write letters of complaint about prison regulations that were being broken by officials in charge, the more senior the officials, the better. He always had to fear he might then have his pencil and paper taken away. Still, he had to write the letters. As many as possible, one complaint to a letter. He seldom wrote personal letters, to friends outside. His mother was dead; he felt that letters to anyone else, even his father, might endanger them and reveal weakness in himself. It was hardly necessary to be in contact; in fact, it was draining, wondering when news might come, fond words. Information that Viktor needed sometimes came to him unsolicited, from people he had never met, marked by the use of a phrase from one of his own poems.

Typically, Viktor persuaded other prisoners to sign his letters of complaint, but while he was writing them, he felt authentically himself, playing the game of voices, the game of words. With words, he was stronger, more versatile than any official; he would never tire in words, as he would never tire in numbers, not even in the face of the most monumental, the most intricate absurdities. He had time on his hands, and therefore he had time on his side. By law, the letters had to be answered within three days or forwarded on with an explanation; a bureaucrat who missed a three-day deadline would be criticized, maybe even lose bonus pay. So Viktor loaded the system with the maximum level of complaint, overloaded it, circulated as much paperwork as possible. Such was his means of making some slight impression on the bureaucrats who detained him.

But it was, personally, a serious risk. He depended on private study, thinking, writing, to sustain his spirit. He knew perfectly well that this was his point of vulnerability, and he constantly strived to free himself of material needs in this respect. He had long since begun to transfer his work, slowly, continuously, from real paper to the inside of his head, and he held it there accumulating, entirely safe from any inspection, confiscation, search, frisking, disinfection. He believed that the mind is a stronghold, however fragile. And if he often feared that his treasures might slip from his memory, break up, be lost for ever, more often, he counted them up, his treasures, gloating over how many he had managed to create and to store away during the time he had served.

When he copied books by others out into his own notebooks, it was partly in case the books were confiscated, but also as a way of committing them to memory along with his own writing. He tried to read as much as possible when he was allowed to have books, for he knew that the value of such reading would be proved in the use he could make of it over time. And also he looked for different kinds of problems that were simple in the stating, complex

117

in the solving, which could absorb many hours. Often he was not allowed books, sometimes for long periods. And then he consumed his mental library cautiously, sparingly, stopping to play chess with himself between paragraphs, between pages. In such periods, he worked so hard to reduce his appetite for books that it made him almost ill afterwards to read them, to feed off the words of others. His own words, his own thoughts, were the only reliable ones.

Maybe tonight wasn't going to be a lucky one for Viktor. As he counted the booted footsteps of the guards, he discerned purpose in their tread – two pairs now in the corridor below. There was a new stoolie in the cell directly underneath his; everybody knew that he was a stoolie and nobody was talking to him, so the stoolie in any case was getting desperate for something to report. It was obvious to some at least that Viktor was the originator of the latrine riot, the composer of tonight's music. So Viktor took his writing tablet from his pocket and slipped it, for safe-keeping, through a narrow hole in the underside of his mattress. It was a new tablet, page upon virgin page, which he had received during exercise today in exchange for passing a message about a sale of knife blades, tobacco. Working it with both hands from the top and bottom of the mattress at the same time, Viktor moved the tablet gradually away from the little hole into the lumpy, bug-infested wadding. All the while, he kept his back to the cell door, blocking the light, blocking a view of what he was doing. His cellmates paid no attention at all.

The guards came for him just before he lay down to sleep. They wouldn't throw him into solitary after a cosy night's snooze and a strengthening if shitty breakfast; they'd throw him in now, tired out. Let him soak his feet in the standing, icy water covering the floor, then let him slump all night on the stone bench. The bench was too hard, too narrow, too cold, for sleeping.

There was still plenty of shouting going on as Viktor was manhandled along the clammy, shuddering hallways. And new sounds flowed out in reaction to his punishment, muffled taunts, whistles, wave upon wave of rustling rivalry, curiosity, sympathy. Viktor knew that his charisma could only be enhanced by the patina of further barbarism, filth, starvation, now being crudely slapped onto him by his captors; solitary would brighten his aura. In the moments that he was being hunted, identified, singled out, and then moved by the guards, every inmate in the prison could palpably experience the conflict between prisoner and jailer. Viktor knew that he had to take advantage of his few moments of heightened stature to make his penalty worthwhile; this was his chance, on the threshold of such awesome suffering, to remind them all of their own conflict with the State. He was still plenty strong enough now to show defiance; it was an expensive opportunity, but he used it to the full. His bearing – chest thrown wide, hips thrust forward, lilting with fight – was like an outcry, his natural size a refusal to submit. He made it plain to everyone around him that all his titanic energy, his powerful intellect, his education, his personal cultivation and discipline, were directed against the Soviet system, its institutions, its rules, its lies.

Accelerate unrest among the others, he repeated to himself. Friction produces heat. That's what I'll have to warm myself with.

Then, as he watched the plume of his breath spread in the cold air of the isolator, he thought, This will be the first of five nights, or maybe ten. The uncertainty was always hard to deal with. He wrapped himself in his arms, kneading his shoulders, his biceps, encouraging his reluctant, downhearted blood. Ten was a lot to prepare for, almost too many; but Viktor knew that if he prepared for five and he was wrong, it could kill him. He decided to draw back from thinking about it.

He directed all his anger at the single light bulb, willing it to shatter. It would stay fucking glaringly lit no matter how long he was in for. Hard to sleep, nearly impossible to dream.

Once the door was locked and the bootfalls faded, Viktor took a stub of pencil from the crack in his bum. Its warm, cheesy smell felt like companionship, a bodily sensation to be inside of, something to experience. He began writing a poem on the wall of the cell, trying not to scrape the chapped skin of his fingers on the rough, furred cement. If the raw skin opened, if it bled, it might never heal; it could fester, and it would hurt. Viktor wasn't interested in illness, real or feigned; he wasn't interested in introducing germs under the skin to induce infection that could take him to the infirmary.

The pencil wobbled and jumped, making uneven, intermittent marks. He was writing about his belief that a nation which imprisons and kills its citizens simply in order to control them will have to imprison and kill them in greater and greater numbers, and even so must eventually spawn citizens who will refuse to be controlled. It was just as clear, he thought, as any problem in mathematics. It had taken, he reckoned, three generations; it was the task of his generation to refuse to be subdued. They had grown up surrounded by poverty, suffering, and fear; they were accustomed to irrational authority. Everything was already at risk; what more had they to lose? Truly it didn't matter whether he himself, Viktor, could survive the struggle; the struggle was going to happen anyway. It was inevitable. Let's say, it was even guaranteed by biology, by Darwin's theory of evolution; the human race adapts to find food, to reproduce. The human race will move on. Eventually the Soviet Union will be a union of ghosts, of the dead.

Viktor had written the poem in his head some time ago; tonight it was the poem he decided he wanted to write down. It would make no difference if the guards came and took his pencil away; it would make no difference if they made him wash the wall or if they painted over the poem. It was hardly legible anyway. He would always have the poem in his head. He would write it down again some place else, another time. Or he would recite it, tell it to others, again and again, to anyone who would listen, inside prison or out, until they, too, could repeat it. He'd always go on writing, spreading his word, whenever he had the chance. *Samizdat.*

October 19. It was not really morning yet on Friday when the American ambassador summoned some of his staff back to the embassy on Tchaikovsky Prospekt.

Practically everyone went with the security officer up to the eavesdrop-proof Plexiglas bubble on the tenth floor and left the offices deserted.

Downstairs, one trusted Foreign Service secretary yawned under the fluorescent light, trying not to think of her bed, the pale blue quilt thrown back, still warm, the nearly fresh loaf of bread she had been saving to slice for toast, the eggs there had been no time to fry. Now she couldn't even get coffee, which she badly needed. She fluffed her teased hair with her fingertips, digging in at the roots, pinching, pulling the strands gently upwards. Need to roll it up fresh tonight, she thought disgustedly. Wash it first. After I eat the darn eggs. She pictured the smooth off-balanced ovals on their weighty, fragile sides on the table beside her two-ring burner; they tipped and rocked, a blur of palest brown-white, cracking against each other, spinning towards the table edge, smash-able.

Then she sat up, realizing her eyes had shut. Tom Phipps was standing in front of her desk.

'I didn't hear you come in,' she said, half apologizing, half accusing.

'So what's up?' he asked her brightly.

'What do you mean?' she demanded, sleepy, protective.

'Well, all the coats. Everyone's in, I guess? Kind of early. And then – they've all disappeared?'

'Depends who you think "everyone" is. You're here kind of early yourself, huh?'

'Don't forget I'm sharing with Wentz, right here in the embassy annexe.'

'Well, that's not really anything I'd be aware of.' She rubbed her eyes, keeping them lowered, demure, blushed a little. 'It's pretty early in the morning, so I –'

'I heard the phone ring. Heard him leaving. He's got quite the personal life. In and out at all hours.' Phipps grinned suggestively.

'Well, this is nothing personal, I can assure you of that. He's upstairs with the rest of them, in the bubble. The ambassador, the whole political section, the air force attaché, the naval attaché, you name it. I don't know how they can breathe in there. And nobody's had any breakfast.'

But inside the bubble they weren't feeling hungry. Stunned, punch-drunk, at the nightmare they were waking up to.

John Davenport had been up all night with the ambassador, the deputy chief of mission, the first secretary, and a few others, helping to exchange coded messages with Washington, where some of their interlocutors had now finally gone to bed. Tense, nicotine-faced, in dirty, wilted collars, they were taking it in solemn turns to explain to their colleagues that on Tuesday morning, October 16, President Kennedy had been informed by the CIA that a U2 spy plane had photographed Russian nuclear missiles being positioned in Cuba.

The deputy chief of mission narrowed his eyes, spread his hands in the air, and said truculently, 'Launch pads, erectors, missile trailers and tents, control bunkers, you name it – our intelligence guys can identify this stuff, and they are sure that's what it is.'

Davenport was standing behind the deputy chief of mission's chair, hands folded on the back of it, hunching a little, leaning.

The ambassador spoke up, thin-lipped: 'You all know the Russians have assured us over and over again that they have not been sending offensive weapons to Cuba. But we are now forced to accept the fact that the Russians are just plain lying. They have even lied to the president – in person, in the White House. I can tell you that the president is shocked and, also, that he is absolutely furious.'

Davenport pulled himself upright sighing, not just with the tiredness of a night away from his bed, but with the deep exhaustion of disillusionment and bewilderment which came from discovering that no matter how well you knew the language and no matter how intimately you engaged with your diplomatic counterparts, you might not have the slightest understanding of what was really going on inside their heads. He believed in his skills, his intuition, and he believed in his handful of Soviet acquaintances. Everybody in the country couldn't be a liar, he thought; but there seemed to be a hell of a lot of lying around. Where did it start, where did it stop? How high, how low, did the lying go?

He didn't understand lying; he didn't do it himself, didn't know how it worked, and he hardly saw what purpose it could ever serve. Davenport thought that words were for getting as near to the truth as possible. Words in themselves were already opaque, changeable, so it was a lifetime's task to nail them down to reality, to make them work for you, to squeeze clarity from them across cultural frontiers. He knew that he had a gift for the task; he was well aware that he could sometimes tell what someone was trying to say just by watching, by reading lips, eyes, expression. Even if he didn't speak the language. He was devoted to it – to the task of understanding. So he felt shipwrecked by the turn of events these last few days. What was the point of embassies and diplomacy, if people, important people, leaders, were going to lie about big, crucial, world-ending matters? He hadn't forgotten what Nina had told him about Khrushchev, but he was a long way off understanding the reasons that she was proving to be right.

In fact, he was still struggling to assimilate the recent sequence of events, even as he was now called upon to repeat some of it out loud. 'Yesterday afternoon,' he began, scratching the back of his head with one long puzzled arm, roaming the floor like a lost man, the other hand in a trouser pocket, 'Foreign Minister Gromyko and the new Soviet ambassador to Washington, Anatoly Dobrynin, met with the president in the Oval Office, and Mr Gromyko *again* assured the president that the USSR would not be supplying offensive weapons to Cuba. Any weapons would be solely defensive, only to help repel attack. He even offered platitudes like Cuba wants peaceful coexistence with the US, and the USSR wants to supply bread to prevent hunger in Cuba. But at the very same time that Mr Gromyko and Ambassador Dobrynin were there in the room with the president telling him – well, frankly, telling him this load of *crap* –' his feet paused, and he lifted both hands in the air, palms upward, expostulating, 'The president actually had the photographs with him, right in his desk drawer. The photographs showing the nuclear missiles in Cuba which the Soviets say are not there.'

Davenport wondered, as he had wondered several times during the long night, what Gromyko's face had looked like while he was lying to the president; had the lie been obvious on his face? Or was Gromyko lying with his heart, with his whole being? How else could you succeed in lying, was what Davenport was thinking, unless you half believed it yourself? Unless you tricked yourself, too. That must be how it was done.

'It's beyond audacious,' said the ambassador, 'it's insulting. I know just how the president feels. I spent three goddamned hours with Premier Khrushchev on Tuesday, and what did he tell me but how mad he was at the Cubans for announcing this supposed fishing port the Soviets have agreed to build them; Premier Khrushchev claims he wanted them to wait and announce it after our elections. He wouldn't do *anything* to embarrass the president during the election campaign. According to him, the fishing port is entirely non-military. The man was wreathed in smiles.' The ambassador's voice was quiet but toxic with sarcasm. 'He did say he'd be attending the UN in November to make a speech, so maybe he's not planning to blow us all up before that.' And then under his breath he added, 'However badly the president wants to get Castro out of Cuba, I don't think you'd ever catch him muddying his own diplomatic channels with deliberate lies and ruining years of work. It's this underground, devious mentality that is just impossible for all of us.'

They were all sitting close together, perched on chair arms, table tops, leaning over typewriters, and their reactions gradually rippled around the room as through one body, a murmur of amazement, outrage, confusion, building up, resonating. These were men who believed in doing business with the Soviet Union, in talking to Russia. They had staked their claim on it. They had assured their friends at home, their countrymen, that they could get to grips with Russia, that they could work with the Soviets. And they had persuaded themselves they could, too. They were in up to their necks, over their heads. They were more than five hundred miles from the nearest border, with their wives, their children. The capriciousness of their hosts was beyond understanding. It was terrifying.

Somebody said, 'Oh, shit, shit, *shit*. Those bullshit sons of bitches. All those goddamned Russian ships going out from Odessa. They were loading them at night! That's why they've been turning off the goddamned street lights – as if they needed to repair them. As if there was some power problem!'

Wentz threw his arms in the air and let out a cynical guffaw. 'The balls of these guys. What the hell are they trying to prove?'

Davenport thought, Why is Wentz here?

The ambassador banged the flat of his hand on the table. 'Let's move ahead here,' he announced grimly.

But the way ahead was entirely unclear.

The deputy chief of mission shrugged and said, with his eyes on the table top, lips sceptically puckered, 'Well, we just don't know what the Russians are up to at all, and we have no reliable private channel to get better information. Georgi Bolshakov, the chief of the Washington Bureau of *TASS* who some of you know is also a colonel in the KGB, has been a whispering tennis partner to half the administration, but obviously he's been supplying misinformation for months now. Maybe he doesn't even know he's doing it. This new ambassador, Dobrynin, speaks perfect English, but either he's a liar like Gromyko, or else he's not being given accurate information by his own goddamned government. I don't know which is worse. Anyway, he's been insisting to the president's brother – I mean Robert Kennedy, the attorney general – that there are no missiles in Cuba.'

He sat back and looked at the ambassador. 'Sir?'

The ambassador tipped his head in assent, expressionless. Then he spoke with cautious intensity, like a father warning his children and hoping that a warning might be enough, trying not to scare them, thinking maybe nothing would actually go wrong in the end. 'I have to tell you that the president regards this as a very serious situation. And so do I. The most recent photographs show—' He looked at Davenport. 'Give me the details again, John?'

Davenport reached in through shoulders and picked up some notes lying on the table in front of the deputy chief of mission. 'The photographs show sixteen or possibly thirty-two missiles with a range of over one thousand miles. And they've now also identified a site for SS-5s; those can travel over two thousand miles. The CIA analysts can tell that the missiles are being pointed at American cities, and they estimate that within a few minutes of firing, eighty million Americans would die. There are more ships coming in every day bringing troops and equipment. Bombers are being unpacked, too, Il-28s.'

He paused and looked at the ambassador who went on, 'Our joint chiefs of staff are calling for immediate military intervention. They want air strikes to put the missiles out of commission. They're getting ready to bomb the missile sites on October 23 – that's Tuesday. Our military has been preparing for trouble since August, so you better believe they are set to go.'

The ambassador shifted in his seat. 'The president, naturally, is cautious because he has to fear –' and now he glanced around to see if his brood was paying attention, '– we all have to fear, gentlemen – a Russian counterattack, either from Cuba or in Berlin. And after that –' he cleared his throat, moved his tongue to moisten it, 'after that – everywhere. We are talking about the real possibility of all-out nuclear war.'

Now he waited a moment. The bubble was silent; there would have been nothing to eavesdrop for. Nobody moved.

Could he cheer them up? the ambassador wondered. Should he try? 'There are other options being discussed.' His tone became lighter, administrative, as he started to run through the list. 'The president has created an Executive Committee of the National Security Council, and they are meeting daily at the White House to decide how to proceed. I get the impression people are discussing this non-stop. Right through the night at the State Department, for instance. There's a view we should maybe talk directly to the Soviets here and ask them what the hell they think they are doing, but the president doesn't want them finding out how much we already know because we lose the advantage of surprise. We understand that the secretary of defense and the attorney general favour a naval blockade of Cuba to stop more weapons going in. But that won't get rid of the missiles which are already there.' His voice dwindled. It came off as lacklustre, the list of other options, he thought. And it was hopelessly short, almost non existent.

Now he just filled in the obvious. 'This is all highly confidential; at the moment, only a handful of people know what you've just heard. As far as we are aware, the Russians have no idea that we've realized what they're up to. The president said absolutely nothing about the missiles to Gromyko yesterday afternoon. Obviously, if any of you has any insights or any more information, we need to know.'

Still, the room was silent. A black, leaden weight of breathlessness fell upon each of them, isolating them from one another in their incredulity, their lurching fear.

The ambassador pushed back his chair, stood up slowly. They began to exchange looks, wary, flicking their eyes only, holding their seats, testing their fear against what they could see on one another's faces. Letting the situation become real. Still, nobody spoke; every possible remark seemed too trivial.

The door opened, and at almost exactly the same instant, somebody sneezed.

'*Gesundheit*,' said the ambassador. And then there was a sudden burbling hubbub, a need for fresh air, a smoke, breakfast, the john. Everyone was talking and moving at once, pressing out into the halls as if they could resolve the crisis by getting at this working day early, with vigour.

Davenport was thinking he needed to shut them all up; he called through the doorway, 'Loose lips, guys. Put a rag in it.'

He felt someone take his arm, just above the elbow. The ambassador was pulling him back into the bubble.

'Jeez, what's happening now, sir?' Davenport wanted it to be something small, something funny or personal. The meeting had been all sweat; mentally he'd been getting ready for it all night, and he needed to break stride for an instant so the pressure would lift off his head, unclamp from his chest.

The ambassador looked up at him with an angry expression, unexpected, alarming. Davenport stood as if to attention, sensing punishment, sensing he'd made some grave mistake.

'What the hell is your wife getting up to, John? I've just been told she went off and met with some suspected subversive or something, some reformed anti-Soviet agitator, the day before yesterday and the Russians are upset about it. *What* is going on?'

John could hardly take in the question. 'I've got no idea what you're talking about, sir.'

'This is obviously not a good time for messing around and getting adventurous – socially or in any other way. Nina's been given a big role on the cultural side, and she seemed to be making a good contribution with the ballet. I thought she had better judgement; at least that's what you've led me – all of us – to believe.'

John's face was swelling, glistening with rage. He felt betrayed, overwhelmed. Who was she, this woman the ambassador was talking about? Who was this woman who couldn't be relied on? He had nothing to say.

The ambassador went on rebuking him. 'I don't have time for any bullshit now that we have these missiles in Cuba and lies flying around – big important lies. I don't have any Russians I can trust for a favour, like turning a blind eye on eccentric behaviour on the part of someone who's a little unhappy or unsettled. To them, when it involves one of their own citizens, it's espionage. You know that. Make it stop, or I'm sending her home. And watch out, John, because I don't want the Russians telling me I have to send you home, too. I need your help – everyone needs it right now. Obviously.'

But Nina didn't seem the least bit unhappy or unsettled when John arrived home towards the end of the afternoon. He was tense, brittle, desperate for sleep; she was pretty well in command of herself, calmer, he thought, than she had seemed for several weeks.

She knew right away that something was wrong. She took his hand and said with tender sympathy, 'Can we walk over in the park, Novy Sad, before you lie down? Are you too tired?'

This was her invitation to talk away from professional ears, and in his exhaustion, John's first impulse was to tell her what was going on in Cuba. It wouldn't surprise her at all; he knew that. But it would scare her just as much as it had scared everyone in the office. What was the point of that, he wondered, if she was happy at the moment? It would be harder for her to deal with than for him; she was so much alone.

What they really needed to talk about was the other thing.

And John realized he would rather have talked about the missiles. All the way back downstairs, crushed into the tiny elevator with Nina and the elevator lady, he had a queasy feeling, an unaccountable sensation of confusion. He took Nina's hand as they crossed into the park and started down the hill. The flame-coloured trees drooped with damp, their black-edged leaves uselessly clinging as the light began to fade, the temperature to drop. There was a warm tang of smoke in the air from the piles of leaves burning, but the path was slimy, and he glanced protectively at Nina's feet, surprised to see she was wearing stalwart leather shoes and thick tights.

'So that's how you dress for winter here?' he said in a teasing voice, pointing at her tights.

'Sexy, aren't they?' she laughed. 'But it gets so cold you just don't care. I walked a lot today,' she added.

'Where to?'

'You were gone so early,' she said, as if this was an answer.

It made John feel that he should be completely direct with her. 'Nina, who was it you went to see earlier this week? Did you know it was some unacceptable type, someone at odds with the regime? There's been an informal complaint to the ambassador about it, and he laid into me. He acted as though you'd done it on purpose – like you knew, or should have known, that it would cause trouble.'

Nina took her hand from John's, her eyes forward, walking. 'Oh, come on. You guys are Americans –' her voice cracked, wavered and dropped like an adolescent boy's '– like me. You should be on the side of people who don't just lie down and take it. And even if you aren't on their side, since when is friendship supposed to be ideologically correct?'

Obviously it was true, John realized. She had been to see someone. He looked sideways at Nina, hardly able to see her face in the gloom. There was a tension playing over her jaw, fury, he thought, at being interfered with. She hated having her judgement questioned, her opinions. How had she ever coped, growing up here?

'Of course you're right, Nina, but you're being naïve. And I think you know it. We're here on sufferance, really. We have to be straighter than straight. And if this person is a good friend, you know you ought to stay away anyhow. You'll only attract the wrong kind of attention to him – or her.'

'Oh, for Christ's sake!' She threw her arms in the air as if in irritation, pressing ahead of him on the path, trying to conceal her distress. She knew she had put Felix in danger; it was unbearable to be reminded. 'I can't organize my life around what some bunch of diplomats thinks is acceptable behaviour. I don't want you and the ambassador deciding how I can spend my time, who I can be friends with, fobbing me off with those ballerinas in your welcome-wagon deal. Spying on me when I take a break from it.'

It made John angry. 'Nina, I think you're a little out of line. The problem is the KGB, not us. There are serious – terrifying – issues at play just now. I know it makes you feel that I'm being condescending when I tell you I can't say what the issues are, but that's how it is. This is not just about socializing and being free to express yourself. This is real-life stuff, and there are scary military aspects that are threatening – well – threatening a large number of people.' He swallowed the end of his sentence, self-conscious about dangling hints at her, aware that he never succeeded in keeping things back from her, was never as strict as he should be about confidential matters.

But Nina didn't seize upon it, didn't press him for more information as she so often did. She seemed to be too upset. She spoke in a brutish undertone, as if she didn't care whether he could hear her. 'You don't think I understand real danger, growing up in the Soviet Union, where innocent people disappeared in the night all through my girlhood? Where my crippled father waited and *waited* for it in his chair until he just died of the fear?'

Now it was John's turn to swear. 'Oh, Christ.' He was determined not to tell her about the missiles; in fact, he was starting to feel tense about things he had told her in the past which he should have kept to himself. But he knew they couldn't have anything like a helpful conversation when he was holding back secrets so awful that they made Nina's concerns seem to him to be utterly beside the point.

'Who was it that you went to see, anyway, Nina?' He spoke to her back.

'John, I'm sorry about what's happened. I didn't mean to get you – or anyone – into trouble. Moscow has changed, you know, since I left. It's freer, more open. I thought it would be OK. I – made a mistake. Maybe I've lost the habit of being careful, and maybe I've even confused things with – home, with America.' She lowered her voice, adopted a bored, methodical rhythm, paced out her words with her feet. 'I was interviewed to death about growing up here, and I never kept it a secret that some of my friends were pretty radical. You know perfectly well who they were. I've told you all about them, though I guess it's a while ago and maybe you've forgotten. I've been wanting desperately for us to talk it all through again; I need to. After I had to leave the Bolshoi, that was my – wild phase. You can understand that. You of all people. You used to understand everything about me.'

She was a half-step ahead of him on the path; she paused and waited for him, put a hand on his forearm, confiding, gentle. 'Ballet was a hell of a lot of discipline and hard work, and I had mixed feelings about giving it up. Looking back, I'd say – well, for one thing, I went boy crazy.' Her eyes rolled up towards his, sidelong, unsure. 'For me, it wasn't the least bit political. It was all emotional, all hormones and romance. Poets, intellectuals – they had all the glamour. OK, I was my father's daughter, attracted to the opposite side – any opposite side. But teenagers are like that all over the world.' She stopped talking, as if she had asked a question that John was now supposed to answer, or as if she needed affirmation.

But John said nothing. He was recollecting old conversations, troubled late-night confidences about lost student companions, Russian soulmates. And it took him aback, because he recognized at once that he had never considered these vanished friends of Nina's as complete individuals. Russia had had an unreal, subjective quality for him then; it had been a country of the imagination, a place where he had never physically been, and which he had tried to understand through literature, through language, through Nina. She had been pulse-quickeningly real, but her friends might as well have been characters in one of Nabokov's stories in *The New Yorker*, Russians of the diaspora, scattered by the winds of revolution. But of course, John thought with chagrin, they weren't even born then. He felt surprised and a little alarmed to discover these friends now coming to life, as if butterflies in a collection, captured, pinned, could suddenly unfreeze from their taxonomic perfection and begin to fly around the room.

I understood so well how Nina *felt*, John thought to himself, that I didn't really hear what she said, didn't listen to what she told me. So much love, so much sympathy I directed towards her, and yet this strange inattentiveness, a failure to read all the clues. It's so obvious, he thought. Her friends aren't imaginary, they're not literary, they're not in the past. They are here with us, present. It's just that I have never met them. Still, he thought with a certain sternness, a certain strictness, she's made a mistake, a poor decision, going to see this person. And he sensed she was only just beginning to explain herself.

In response to John's silence, Nina's voice grew more earnest. 'My friends then were older than me, John. And more serious about their ideas. More serious about injustice. They got into trouble – arrested, sent to prison – and because of that I lost touch with them; actually I don't even know all the details. For Christ's sake, I was nineteen –' she laughed crudely, as if she were jeering at herself, 'well, only seventeen – when I left Russia. They were what was cool, like the beatnik scene at home in the States, you know? My mother was appalled by it, terrified. But, listen, what

134

my friends were trying for, John, that scene, turned out to be nothing compared with the life I found in America, the freedom, the possibility. I saw right away that my father had got everything wrong – deciding to come here. Much as I loved him. I don't kid myself about that.'

She was answering him fully with her mood – mournful, regretful – but only in part with her words. She still hadn't given him a name.

John fished for what he sensed beneath the surface. 'So you went to see an old boyfriend? And that's why you didn't tell me? That's why you've been so – in such – an upheaval lately?'

She didn't answer, just walked along, swinging her arms at her sides.

It all made sense to him as he said it, and he felt things clearing a little. But, at the same time, he unexpectedly felt a new, personal discomfort about his wife. It spread like inward bruising. He might not have called it jealousy, but he was beginning to wonder about her past in a way that he had never wondered before. His thoughts were agitated by a sexual anger which had been playing between them for several weeks, and which he sensed he might at last be getting the measure of.

They walked more and more slowly; the silence between them was dark, potent. And the intimate humiliation and hurt growing inside him blended with the doom-laden atmosphere of his long night and day in the office, so that he felt, in his sleep-starved state, as if the fate of the world was concentrating in him and in his evidently failing relationship with his wife. He sensed some real ending, unlooked for, the end of everything, drawing near. Could the whole universe crack right here, between the two of them?

Then Nina laughed. 'He was never my boyfriend, John. I promise you!' She spoke as from the planet of the everyday.

John had no idea what to make of it, tried to draw back from the portentousness of his own frame of mind. I'm tired, he told himself. But there's so much Nina doesn't know. And then he thought, Yet, in a way, she knows much more than me. She knows what I want to know. And what she doesn't know, about the missiles, I wish I didn't know either.

Her voice came smiling at him, fresh, breezy. 'He was one of my doctors. He's a gifted, overworked, paediatric orthopaedic surgeon. John, he's the one who took care of me when I hurt my ankle. He made friends with me, is the thing. Which was probably what I needed most of all.' Then the freshness went from her voice as she seemed almost to trip over the subject of her father. 'When my father died, I didn't let myself feel it. I didn't let myself feel anything at all because that was what I had to do to get through it. At least that's what I thought. This doctor was the one who saw it – all the grieving I had never done. So – he became very important to me.' She delivered the last as a challenge, daring John to disapprove.

'Why did you visit him *now*, Nina?' He asked it tragically, at a loss before the weight of such a friendship, her right to it.

Nina's impulse was to tell John the truth. That was what he was pleading to hear. But he wouldn't like it, an abortion; she knew he wouldn't like it at all. There would be more fighting, unbearable conflict. Inside her head, she heard her mother saying, You're a smart girl, Nina, and she thought, I can duck this.

So she answered John without emotion, as if it were unimportant. 'I would have visited him sooner, but it took a long time to find out where he was working.'

'Well, how did you find out?' There was a sudden alertness in John's tone; he wanted to make her cough up, tell him exactly. He could feel her evading him somehow; he didn't understand it, but he could feel it.

'OK. OK.' Suddenly, she seemed to be giving in. She stopped in the middle of the path and turned towards him. In the dark, he couldn't see her eyes.

Nina concentrated on stating things that were true.

'Actually, I remembered where he worked, John. I was just guessing he'd still be there. But honestly, I haven't been in touch with him, nor with any other old friends. I promise you. I've been strict with myself about that. And as for why I went now – I can't say.' There was a little silence, then a rush of explanation. 'I mean, I don't really know. Maybe it's just being around the ballerinas. It's been hard for me. I love it, but it's stirred me up inside. There are chances I wish I had had, and – it all reminded me of the Bolshoi days – I guess that made me want to see Felix.'

'Felix?'

If she had been guarding the name before, she now gave it up deliberately. 'He's called Felix Belov, the man I visited, my friend. It was on Wednesday. Believe me, John, he was never my boyfriend – ever. Maybe he introduced me to people – that's another story.' He felt her offering the last remark as a tease, but her coyness fell flat with him. There was still something in Nina's voice that didn't sound right, volatility that she pretended to ignore, too much re-assurance, faked lightness of heart. And he thought she was using the dark to cover herself, to play some game, to hide. He was too tired to be certain, and all the time in the back of his mind was the unimaginable possibility that the world might be about to end. We need to be able to be straight with each other, was what John kept thinking. This whole situation is so much more urgent than Nina realizes. He wanted her to be his, heart and soul, in this very instant. She wasn't giving that. And he couldn't tell her why he wanted it so badly.

She reached for his hand. 'Let's go back. You should sleep.'

He didn't move, so she tugged on him a little.

This was the thing about their relationship; they could read each other if they were both willing. Even when there was dis-sembling, an awful lot was perfectly clear. If she wanted to pretend not to know how he felt just now, then she could pretend. And things would maybe get worse between them, more perverse, from there.

He didn't give in, so Nina stopped pulling. She tried to be conciliatory; she offered something she had been hoping he wouldn't ask for. 'If you don't want me to see him, it makes me sad, but I can accept it.' She paused, still holding his hand, stepped closer, circled his long, narrow torso, his slippery water-resistant coat, with her arms, breathed against him and said very quietly, 'You're being silly, sweetheart. You'd like him. I know that sounds corny, but you would. If the ambassador doesn't want me to see him, OK. But, honestly, I don't think it will threaten national security.'

'You can't see him again, Nina. If you do, you'll be sent home.' His voice was petulant, punishing her, and he sensed her anger returning; her body went rigid against him, she stepped back, delicately snorting.

They turned by silent mutual assent to walk home, and she added in a raw tone, grating, from the bottom of her throat, 'Felix – the friend I saw on Wednesday – will never be able to leave the Soviet Union. He has no options. So it's a *real* struggle for him, the struggle I – dabbled in. It's hard for me not to feel ashamed – as if I've run away from the one real challenge life has ever offered me. Real opposition, real political commitment.'

At first, John didn't answer her. He was thinking that he had had no idea just how different Nina was from the girls he had grown up with, he had had no idea how much of her was hidden, until he brought her to Moscow. In Buffalo, at Wellesley, in New York, in Washington, she had seemed shy, intelligent, sensitive, a little high-strung. Where did this iron voice come from? Her gravelly outrage?

'Oh, come on. That's not the only real challenge life ever offered you,' he said, refraining from pointing out that Nina's life had been one enormous challenge after another. And he felt that if only there were enough time, he could know her still, could find out who she was. He needed more time, time to be able to feel his way towards her. Trying for a casual tone, he said, 'And what

138

about being married to me? Doesn't that count as some kind of challenge? Being my wife?'

She merely quipped back, 'I don't find that hard, darling. Apart from the fact that you've brought me here to Moscow.'

He wondered if she meant it. By now, he thought he could only find out by going to bed with her, having everything out between them physically. It was long overdue.

But as they walked back up the hill in the smoky, sweet-smelling dark, he felt the desolation of deceiving and being deceived like some dark, heavy liquid entering his mouth, dragging his lips open, downward, in loose despair, unswallowable, flooding his teeth and throat. He thought he might drown in woe, separated from her, unable to reach her. Gagging on sorrow. And even that he couldn't even tell her, couldn't reveal.

October 20. On Saturday evening, Nina was already dressed for the ballet when John telephoned from the embassy to say he might not be able to make the performance.

'The ambassador is having dinner with Frol Kozlov, Khrushchev's number two, and there are still other things to deal with here, so I'm going to have to stay for a while. Go ahead without me. You'll still enjoy it, won't you, sweetheart?'

'Not as much.' She tried not to sound disappointed. 'But of course I'll go. What on earth can you be doing that's more important than taking your wife to see *Prodigal Son*?'

John was silent for a moment, so that Nina thought he was reconsidering and might join her after all. But she had it wrong, and his brusque reply took her by surprise. 'It's nothing to do with us, Nina. Don't worry about us – or – anything. Don't worry about *anything*.'

After she put down the phone, she stood in the dim little hallway wondering what John had been referring to. He had hung up too quickly for her to ask him to explain. Did he mean he wasn't being kept at the office to sort out some further misunderstanding about her visit to Felix? Or did he mean he wasn't staying at the office purposely to avoid spending his Saturday night with the woman who just now was making him unhappy? And if he had meant the latter, then it was obvious to Nina that, in fact, he *was* trying to avoid her.

She was heartsick and confused. The baby fear had engulfed her. Her sole objective was to get rid of it, to get past this obstacle without being discovered. She couldn't think clearly about anything else. She kept telling herself that once she had dealt with the baby, she'd be out in the open again, without any more need for deception, for constrained behaviour. She'd be strong, whole, beyond criticism, morally unimpeachable, capable of joy and affection. But first she had to commit this – this act that had become like a crime because it involved secrecy, risk, lying, betrayal. She wanted it behind her. She didn't want to think about it any more. She refused to consider the difficult truth that, baby or not, she would still be in Russia, that her inner strife was long-rooted, had many tendrils.

Now, for a moment, she couldn't help pausing on the worry, But what if John finds out? She believed that she wasn't really afraid of being caught for any other reason. She couldn't imagine the look on his face – she wasn't sure how he would feel, how much he would care. It was an area in him she couldn't fathom. In his sexual self, Nina thought, John is possessive, greedy; he makes assumptions. It was part of what she was attracted to, his decisive ownership of her – confident, even arrogant, ownership, but insightful, accurate. But with a baby? She didn't want him dictating to her. She didn't want him deciding.

Is it possible that John would never forgive me if he found out I had gotten rid of the baby behind his back? Could he care more about a baby than about me? I don't believe that. But if I believe he would care more about me, that he would forgive me sooner or later, then why can't I tell him sooner? Why can't I tell him now? I should tell him now, get his sympathy, his help.

He'd never let me go to a Soviet clinic, she thought. He'd insist on involving the embassy doctor, or make me go abroad.

And then she decided, with impatience, with a sense of real disappointment, He doesn't understand. He will never understand. And that's why I'm doing this. I have to. And she told herself, A Russian man understands this differently, as a practical matter, without false sentiment. She summoned to mind the abrupt, unquestioning way in which Felix had examined her, agreed to arrange things. She didn't summon to mind Felix's objections, his questions.

Nor did she admit to herself the possibility that the baby had now become an excuse for her to see Felix again, if she dared. She preferred not to reflect too explicitly on how much she longed to talk to Felix, and to ask Felix more about Viktor. So she cradled her secret excuse, the problem of the baby.

You're a smart girl, Nina, she told herself. John won't find out.

Then she clipped on her round, mother-of-pearl-and-gold earrings, adjusted her mink hat with the tips of her fingers, carefully, as if it were a bowl full of liquid which might slosh on her, took her mink coat from the bedroom cupboard, and went out to the elevator carrying the coat over her arms. It was too hot to put the coat on inside the apartment.

'Evidently, the president has flown back to the White House from a campaign speech in the Midwest; he's saying he has an upper respiratory infection. In fact, he's meeting with the ExComm this afternoon – Washington afternoon – right now.' The ambassador sat forward in his chair, intense, drawn.

The lights buzzed a little over his head, flickered; nobody noticed. Every face in the bubble was still, mouths down turned, obstinate with concentration. The air was stale with smoke, fear-sweat, tired worry.

'I got nothing from Kozlov tonight,' he conceded. 'He was only interested in the food and the booze. Hard not to call the man rude; he got nasty drunk.' He looked at the deputy chief of mission, the first secretary, then offered, shrugging, 'To me, he's a pig.'

Dry-mouthed, matter-of-fact, Davenport reported from his position behind the ambassador's chair: 'The president's getting ready to address the nation on Sunday night, or maybe Monday. Word is he'll go for the naval blockade and insist that the missiles are removed. He doesn't want to attack Cuba. He wants to give Mr Khrushchev time to come to his senses. A lot of government officials are being brought in to this now, and it may leak to the press even before the president makes his speech. The Organization of American States will support the blockade; likewise De Gaulle and Chancellor Adenauer of West Germany. US forces are on alert all around the world. Four tactical squadrons are ready to strike Cuba by air, and troops will be on the move tonight from Texas to Georgia, then from there to Florida.'

The ambassador sighed, rested his chin in his hands for a moment, then sat up, fortifying his voice. 'Let's continue to have resources here around the clock. Take turns getting some rest. We all need to be ready – everybody here in the embassy. Besides that, you need to think about how to get your families ready. Don't do anything obvious until after the president's address, because it will give the game away. I have a wife; together we have a cat. Otherwise, you are my family, and I hope we will all get out of this somehow.'

It was only about a second before anger overtook the group. They aired it in mutters and then in tense barks and clipped demands.

'This is insane!'

'This is one fucking step too far!'

'What the hell are the Russkies up to?'

Fred Wentz took it upon himself to insist that Khrushchev was only posturing. 'This is all about Berlin again,' he shouted into the building uproar. 'It's about Berlin, and it's about Europe. Khrushchev's just trying to get traction in the same old dispute. Jockeying for position. He wants our troops out of Berlin, and he's tried everything else he can think of. Of course he wants to get his missiles closer to us.'

Davenport leaned down and shook his finger in Wentz's face. 'I'll tell you what else he wants. He wants our Jupiter missiles out of Turkey, and probably even Italy. He doesn't like them poking him in the goddamn eye. What does he care about Cuba?'

A young political staff officer sitting next to Wentz asked quietly,

'But why *wouldn't* Khrushchev support the revolution in Cuba? We've had them embargoed since February, we've been pushing them out of the OAS, and we've been staging these huge military exercises in the area as if we're planning another invasion. I've heard sabotage rumours, too, like contaminating the sugar crop, plane-loads of anti-Castro leaflets being dropped . . . ?'

Nobody answered him.

Davenport cried out to the ceiling and the walls, as if Washington might be able to hear him, 'We don't need those missiles in Turkey anyway, do we? Can't we launch from our nuclear submarines?'

And the naval attaché, hardly moving his lips, grunted, 'The missiles in Turkey are obsolete; everybody in the administration knows that. Khrushchev probably knows it, too.'

The room fell quiet, and Wentz muttered reflectively, 'Hell of a lot of pressure on Khrushchev right now, if you think about it. The East Germans want a peace treaty, the Chinese are accusing him of betraying Lenin and Marx by criticizing Stalin and courting the West; his military is mad as hell about the huge cuts he's made. And then he's got violent industrial riots all over the map, Kiev, Riga, Chelyabinsk, Novocherkassk, and pretty widespread agricultural problems. You hear wild rumours – grain rotting because there are no roads to truck it over, cattle starving to death, people living outside Leningrad and Moscow eating horse meat. This Cuba thing just stinks of desperation.'

Then he went on in a cheerful, big, smart-alecky tone, 'I think Mr Khrushchev is overreaching himself. No matter how this comes out, he's going to regret it. Either we all end up dead or he loses face big time with his so-called colleagues in the Presidium. Some of those hardliners are much worse than the Republicans at home.'

Davenport felt annoyed by Wentz's lightness of heart. But the man is no fool, he mused. He knows all kinds of things. Maybe something in him is undeveloped, John thought, maybe he has no deeper emotions, no real sense of fear.

John heard the others laughing at Wentz. 'No matter how this comes out,' somebody repeated, aping Wentz's southern accent. And around the table, they slouched, breathed, let go of the furrows between their brows.

Wentz pushed back his chair, sidled over to John, leaned in close, smiled a private smile. 'In case it's my last chance, I'm going to hang around by that stage door tonight until Patrice comes out. I hope I'm not too late. If I can't elicit favours under this kind of pressure – well – I never will. Wish me luck.' And he was gone.

The warmth of this confidential remark felt like a blow. John knew he should be flattered by Wentz's friendliness, but he bitterly resented the contrast between Wentz's natural appetite for a girl he hardly knew, and his own estrangement from Nina. And Nina was the one who had introduced Wentz to Patrice.

Everything seemed all wrong to John. He was the loser in this chaotic excitement; he was out of the last bit of life going around on this black, forbidding night. Wentz wouldn't have to come back to the office until morning; John knew that he himself would probably be here long beyond then.

October 21. But John did get home before dawn. He crawled into bed beside Nina and fell into a deep sleep just in time to be woken up by the telephone.

The ringing struck him through with fear, and he struggled to sit up, raging, haunted, in a kind of narcotic exhaustion, the sheets clinging to his limbs as the cold sweat started.

'John, I know it's Sunday, but would you mind bringing your wife to the embassy? Now, I mean. Right away.'

'Wentz?'

'We'll talk when you get here.'

'What about Patrice?'

Wentz laughed. 'What about her?' Then he hung up.

John fell back on the mattress, rubbed his face.

Nina murmured through her hair, 'What's going on with Wentz and Patrice?' She yawned, rolled against John.

'I don't know. It seemed like they had a date last night. But maybe not. He wants us to meet him at the embassy.'

'Me?'

'Yes.' Lying on his back with his hands covering his face, John shrugged. 'Don't ask me.' Then he sat up again, groaning a little.

'Is this about Patrice?' Nina asked self-consciously. 'Or is it about me?'

'Don't get all upset, Nina. It must be something about the dancers, if Wentz – Wentz . . .' His voice faded as he turned and looked at her strained face lying against her pillow. 'Look, I won't let them send you home – unless you –?' His heart pounded with suspicion, and it was painful in his exhaustion to be reminded again of Friday's doubts. But he was certain at least that he could see in Nina's anxious blue eyes a straightforward neediness. She's afraid, he thought. But of what? Has she picked up on my fears, my absence, my preoccupation, without even knowing why? Or is she afraid of being deported? It made a turbulence in his ears, like wind.

We have to hurry, he thought. Wentz said, Right away.

The wind in his ears howled and rang, and his gut clenched and worked. I don't want to be separated from my wife, he thought. We're right in the middle of − something. Of a sort of emotional mess that isn't − characteristic of us, that needs − time. It needs plenty of time.

Somehow, John felt sure that Nina was relying on him, that she was appealing for his strength, for his understanding. He wanted to kiss her.

Instead he said, 'Nina, I'm on your side.'

All she said was, 'And I'm on yours. Whatever side that is.'

Their clattery little Saab sailed over the glinting river and rollicked through the still, Sunday-morning streets, slithering on trolley rails, bouncing over hewn stone pavements.

Nina and John were silent.

It was as if, all the way to the embassy, they were on the verge of giving in to one another, of starting a heart-to-heart talk that would never stop. Neither one of them doubted that the other was keeping something back; neither was ready to break the deadlock. Every time John changed gears, leaned towards her a little as he worked the stick, Nina thought he would turn his head, clear his throat, start to explain. As he drove, she watched his profile, studied his beard coming in like pale thorns over his bony jaw, noticed how he occasionally squinted his clear green-brown eyes, trying to see, trying to concentrate despite his lengthening string of sleepless nights.

And Nina wondered all over again how he would take it, in his wrung-out state, if she announced that she was having an abortion.

Maybe he would see that, for her, there was no choice. Maybe he would just accept it.

Then, as she moistened her lips to begin, she thought, But how unfair to tell him now, when he's been made vulnerable by tiredness, by the worry I've brought on us both, by whatever this is at the office all the time. It will seem manipulative, and afterwards, when the pressure is off, he might resent it. So she settled herself back in her seat, several times in succession, without speaking, looked out the window as they passed along Park Kultury, Smolenskaya.

You can figure it out by yourself, she thought. He's got enough on his mind.

At the embassy, Wentz greeted them like an undertaker, speaking quietly, eyes downcast, gripping their hands in both of his, gently, warmly, for a very long time.

'I'm going to take Nina into the bubble, John. Can you wait here, please?'

Nina turned to John, doe-eyed, questioning, and she thought he reeled backwards physically, that maybe he would even fall, so she reached up for his shoulders, held them firmly and said with casual decision, 'It'll be fine. Have a catnap in your office, why don't you, darling? You're a zombie.'

Then she took Wentz's arm, and they walked away quickly behind the silent security officer.

For a moment, John's face stung with amazement. But then he thought, Good. Perfect. Wentz is the right one to talk to her. Better than me. He got sent home himself, and he knows exactly how it feels. John vowed to himself that he wouldn't labour this episode. He would leave the two of them to their meeting and he would ask no questions. It's Nina's business, Wentz's business. After all, Wentz is her boss in a way. What she needs is room to breathe, a little more scope, her own resources. Instead of relying on me. This is better for both of us.

★　★　★

Nina was surprised and even a little disappointed to see that the bubble appeared to be an ordinary office room: big wooden tables, a few desks, typewriters, books, a Teletype machine.

She was more surprised to see Tom Phipps there, evidently waiting for her and for Wentz. He nodded as they came in.

'Tom will take a few notes for us.'

'OK.' It made her tentative, alert. She was trying to imagine what they would ask her, how to answer without doing any harm to herself or anyone else, and without lying. It was a scene she felt she had played before, last spring, when she had been interviewed in a nondescript house in Alexandria, Virginia, by three nameless bureaucrats who had seemed to have the power to decide whether or not she would be allowed to return to Russia with John.

'Strange you have all these typewriters in here,' she remarked, awkwardly trying to make conversation.

'The Soviets listen for everything,' said Phipps, gruff, professional. 'We don't like them to know how much typing we're doing. And we certainly don't want them working out a technique for deciphering it.'

Wentz rubbed his big hands together. 'So, Mrs Davenport –'

Nina raised her eyebrows cynically, humorously. 'I thought we were friends? What happened to Nina?'

He made no reply, just pulled out a chair for her and gestured with one hand. 'Please sit down.'

She shrugged, feeling deflated, and collapsed in the chair, eyes on the floor.

'The view around the embassy,' Wentz said in a cool monotone, standing over her, 'is that you are a liability to your husband's career because of your past life in Russia. I understand you've been reprimanded by the ambassador for dropping in on an old friend?'

Nina felt an inward jolt of embarrassment, but she didn't look up, and she didn't say anything. She covered her burning cheeks with the palms of her hands, waiting for the rest of her scolding.

Wentz kept on in a strange, uncadenced drawl. 'As a matter of fact, Tom Phipps and I have been waiting for you to get back in touch with your old friends – Nina.'

Still she looked at the floor. Where is this going? she wondered. A long, slow humiliation? Waiting for me to get back in touch with my friends? Waiting for the inevitable screw-up that will bury my husband, the weak link, the poor, lonely wife, the unreliable female.

But Wentz's voice grew warmer, more southern. 'In case anyone has made you feel bad for jeopardizing your husband's position, let me reassure you that when John Davenport applied for Moscow, we arranged to have his folder reach the top of the pile the minute we realized what a resource we would have in you. He's a gifted officer. But a wife who's a native – that's a rare commodity in the USSR. Nonexistent. To nobody's surprise, the Russians love your devotion to the culture scene and in particular to the ballet. Frankly, Mrs – frankly, Nina – until your visit to the children's hospital last week, we thought they were even going to give up following you around – you'd done nothing but act like an attractive, sociable embassy wife.'

'Who is "we"?' Nina demanded, suddenly impatient with the confusing mixture of praise and blame. She looked up and caught a flash of life from Wentz's eyes, and she thought, Let's get on with this. Let's talk straight.

But he kept to his methodical, indirect plod, smiling blandly. '"We" are the representatives of the US Government in this embassy – nobody in particular – the professional staff supporting the ambassador's mission here.'

'Oh, for Christ's sake,' Nina said. She crossed her legs, tugged her skirt down fiercely, pulled her calves in underneath her chair as if to hide their loveliness. 'You know what I mean. You're supposed to be the Special Officer representing the International Cultural Exchange Program and Mr Phipps is – what – a Special Agricultural Attaché, isn't he? This is obviously not about ballet or about the corn crop. I think you should tell me what "Special" means.'

Wentz looked at her for a moment. Nina didn't look away. She half rolled her eyes, lifted her eyebrows, daring him.

'"Special" just means temporary. Neither one of us is on the staff here at the embassy. The Soviets are pretty strict on staff numbers. But the workload's big lately, so whatever needs doing, we turn a hand to it. Mr Phipps is one hell of a typist; I'm not kidding you.' Wentz chuckled.

'Ballet, music, art − it's all part of the culture, the intellectual life. The White House is very interested in culture − in cultural freedom. So am I. It's one thing I have always cared about personally. The right to express yourself, to have new ideas, different ones. Freedom of expression gives a better balance to any society. Artists and intellectuals in this country survive under duress, if they survive at all. They could do with some nurturing. My guess is you would agree with that?'

Nina felt a little quiver in her throat as Wentz eyed her. She didn't even want him to see her swallow, she clenched the muscles in her neck, sucked saliva.

'Things seem to have been getting a little better under this regime,' he went on, 'but it's an uncertain business, Mrs − Nina. And we don't know as much about it as we would like to. So, when it came to our attention that you had begun to make contact with old friends, that you would − understandably − like to see them again, it seemed we could all help each other out.'

Wentz glanced at Phipps sitting silently behind Nina and occasionally noting something down, then he droned on, explaining, pleading, almost as if she were hard of hearing or simple-minded. 'We'd like to know more about your friends, Nina. I'm sure you are aware how dangerous it would be for them if we tried to make contact. It's dangerous for them even when *you* make contact. I'll be candid and tell you that your doctor friend has already had a visit from the KGB − as a result of your dropping by to see him.'

Nina snapped to attention; she couldn't stop herself. And Wentz visibly registered her alarm; he nodded and then looked vaguely satisfied. Her fear for Felix, for what she might have exposed him to, hung between them as an acknowledgement. Now they both knew they were talking about something real, not about supposition and conjecture.

As if to offer her a bit of comfort, Wentz said in a friendly voice, a little mocking in the over-familiar way that Nina recognized as some other persona he reserved for socializing, for parties, 'He was very quick-witted, your doctor friend. He told the KGB that you were pregnant and that you didn't want your husband to know. And they bought his story. Our Russian friends look with sympathy on your – plight.'

Nina rattled her head quickly from side to side like a dog shaking off water. For a minute she really couldn't think. Did Wentz know these were the true facts? Or was he relying on her sense of order, a need she might have for clarity, that would now make her leap in and explain?

Obviously, he had some privileged relationship with the KGB. But then, why should that be so surprising? There were worlds and networks, she knew, hidden, proliferating, behind every appearance, no matter where you looked. Nothing was simple. Nothing was as it seemed.

Finally, she decided to say, 'You're pretty friendly with the other side, aren't you?'

Wentz smiled. 'We have to be – hand in glove. Is that a good phrase?' And then he paused for a moment, studying Nina, measuring her. 'Which is what makes me confident I can arrange for you to be able to visit the doctor again – if you want to. Or if you need to.'

This remark scared Nina. Suddenly she was certain that Wentz knew the truth and that he was using his knowledge to trap her. She ought to protest, to insist that she had no desire, no need to see Felix again. But she held her tongue.

Wentz waited for a whole minute, longer, shifted his feet, rearranged his arms, took a new tack, lolling against the edge of the big table behind him, relaxed, generous.

'We want to help your friends, Nina. We want to get some attention for their – views – in the West. We need more information, though, so we can keep their stories alive in the press. We need news – any change, any event – to bring pressure to bear on the Soviets. Now – with the ballet here, Stravinsky here, the Bolshoi just returning from New York – it's a promising time. Help us out, Nina. Just help us be in touch, better informed. Let us know where your old friends are, what they are encountering. What they are – trying for.'

He pulled out a chair and sat down opposite her, leaning forward, lowering his voice confidentially. 'OK, uh-huh, the Russians say they want the contact between you and the doctor stopped, but on the other hand, the – friendship – gives them the opportunity to find out a little more about us. The Russians are big believers in friendship, love; they know as well as we do who you grew up with here. They understand you were torn from the bosom of your fatherland, from your memories, that maybe you're not entirely happy in your current – circumstances. That you're a bit of a free spirit.'

'Do you mean you're going to tell them that I'm having an affair with the doctor?' Nina's tone was accusing. She sat back a little, lifted her chin as if in disgust at the impropriety of what he seemed to be suggesting. 'Or did you already tell them that?'

He raised his eyebrows in surprise. 'I beg your pardon, ma'am! Don't take offence. It doesn't have to be that specific –'

Nina said firmly, with finality, 'Well, even if it were vague, a suggestion like that would embarrass my husband, to say nothing of how it would make me feel.'

She really didn't like Wentz. Actually, I'm not a prude, Nina thought to herself, but I don't want Wentz to know that. I don't want him to know what I'm like at all, just because of the way he implies that he does know. I'd rather act the part of a prude. It's not just the gross hints about my needing a backstreet abortion; it's the way he wants to use me. He thinks he's discovered some sleazy part of me, some weakness, and that I'll do anything. That I won't even ask him why, what for.

She stood up, as if bringing the interview to an end. She was so close to him that Wentz had to scoot his chair back a few inches. He wasn't able to look her in the eye any more. But she didn't walk away; she couldn't.

And he announced, deadpan, as if he were giving practical instructions, 'Look. We want you to go back and see the doctor, Nina.'

She cast a glazed eye at Phipps, resentful of his presence; every further listener diminished her dignity, she felt. Then she drew herself up elegantly, took her time, spoke resonantly, with majestic disdain. 'Even though I've been told not to by the ambassador?'

Wentz stayed in his chair, spoke casually. 'Don't worry about the ambassador.'

She summoned all her poise to her next statement, saying grandly, 'Mr Wentz, I understand now that you want to use me in some way to further whatever end you are preoccupied with, to follow someone, extract information for you. I won't spy on my friends. For all I know you'll hand it on to the KGB to improve your relationship with them. Tell my husband whatever you think you have found out about me; let the Russians deport me. Will you open the door now, please? I'd like to go home.'

She didn't even pause to consider whether she meant it or what she was chancing; she felt she would do almost anything to defy Wentz, to get away from him. To her amazement, Wentz started to laugh. Nina felt furious, humiliated.

He could see it in her face and he said, 'Good gracious, I'm sorry. I'm doing this all wrong. Let's start again. Let's go back to "Mrs Davenport", OK? Oh, Lord.' He fell silent.

Phipps left his paperwork and came around the table. 'Mrs Davenport,' he said respectfully, 'we don't want you to spy on anyone. But we do want to engage you in a serious and – subtle – endeavour.' He offered the last words slowly, searchingly, as if waiting for her to see that they suited her, matched what she herself was, serious, subtle.

Then he went on, stiffly, hopefully, 'You would need to trust us.' His eyes went to Wentz, then back to her. 'Frankly it's safer for you not to know much about what we're doing,' he reached up and rested his open hand on his shorn head, 'but you've made it pretty clear that you are not going to help us unless you do know.'

He looked at her with pale unwavering eyes from his smooth pink face, neat, washed, uncomplicated, and she felt he was simply being straight with her. She didn't say anything. She was too dumbfounded.

Then Phipps dropped his hand, went on, 'Would you like me to tell you more, Mrs Davenport? Bearing in mind that it would be strictly – confidential?'

Nina sighed. 'I don't know what to say. I feel worked over. It seems like you must be reporting to the KGB and that somehow nobody else in the embassy has noticed. But how could that be possible? How would I be the only person to discover it? And anyway, wouldn't I now be shot if that were so?'

Phipps exchanged another glance with Wentz. And then he said in a voice so soft, so reassuring, that it was almost apologetic, 'We're not reporting to the KGB, Mrs Davenport. Not in the way that you mean.'

There was a silence. Nina reached behind her for her chair and carefully sat back down in it, holding herself upright, perching. 'Look,' she said unequivocally, 'of course I'll listen. You don't even want my husband to know what you're going to tell me?'

She felt herself start to tremble; she was so close to whatever was coming next that she couldn't turn back from it; there wasn't time. And yet she knew that she was wilfully overlooking the distinct opportunity to say, Don't tell me anything more.

'Not even your husband,' said Phipps as plainly as a schoolboy.

'So where do I get some guarantee of something?'

'OK. You will.' He nodded.

Wentz started talking again, slow-paced, unblinking. 'This is about – the intelligentsia,' he said. 'About finding them, identifying them, and ultimately restoring them to – public esteem. We think that's in the interest of the West, of the United States. Quite apart from – sounds pompous – but I personally think it's in the interest of mankind.'

Nina pressed her lips together, impatient, sceptical.

'Look,' said Wentz, as if he were conceding something, 'we're aware that you've been reading that story Tvardovsky wants to print in *Novy Mir*, about the camp inmate, *One Day in the Life of Ivan Denisovich*. That's the sort of thing I mean. If Khrushchev gives permission for that to be published, then we see the labour camps exposed, and it's a beautiful piece of writing. But if there's a bad reaction, Khrushchev can just lock up the author. It's nothing to him. The news will be out, is the point, more bad news about Stalin. It's obvious to Khrushchev that his countrymen find it hard to love the man who took Stalin away from them, the Stalin they imagined he was before they had the truth forced on them. But Khrushchev can let this poor bastard Solzhenitsyn do that work and take any blame. Maybe intellectuals scare Khrushchev, but he thinks he has a use for them.'

Wentz stood up and felt his pockets for cigarettes, shook one free from the pack, Winstons, and rolled it backwards and forwards between his thumb and his first two fingers. 'Besides,' he mumbled, 'I wouldn't be surprised if Khrushchev saw himself portrayed in that book – himself if he'd been sent to the camps, if he'd been forced to lay bricks in the Arctic. Because he would have fought it out, worked like a dog.' Then he sat down again, crossed one leg up flat over the other, and flipped the cigarette end to end on the inside of his raised knee. Finally he tucked the cigarette behind his right ear. Nina heard Phipps sit down behind her just out of sight; she kept her eyes on Wentz.

'Anyhow —' Wentz went on, 'it's not at all clear how secure Khrushchev's grip on power is. He's got awful economic problems, and he's put a lot of soldiers out of work — the biggest cuts since the 1920s, we think — his generals can't be happy to have their pay reduced, to lose their pensions and their servants. Maybe he's duking it out with hardliners inside the Presidium. We just don't know. But if there's going to be a regime change or, God forbid, a nuclear war, we want to be in contact with any group, any outsiders, capable of seizing power or of influencing the outcome in a struggle for power. We have to look everywhere — the prisons, the camps, the hospitals. We have people who trust us with *samizdat* magazines and poems and memoirs, people who've hung around the readings in Mayakovsky Square, who've tried to go to the art exhibitions. We have contacts with scientists, doctors, psychiatrists, lawyers. There is growing opposition, a movement maybe.'

Wentz uncrossed his legs, splayed his hands on his knees, rubbed them backwards and forwards with contained energy. 'We even know of connections between some of these dissident types and their agemates in the Communist Youth League, Komsomol. You'd think they'd hate each other, but the truth is they grew up together, were maybe in the Pioneers together as kids. They knew each other at school, even at university, before the anti-Soviet ones got thrown out. There's mutual respect, a little ongoing communication. I am talking about people much younger than anyone in the Kremlin; practically kids — who have their youth in common, too. They are still idealistic about how things ought to be in Russia, but they are hard-headed enough to recognize how things actually are.'

He slapped his hands on his knees, then demanded, 'What do you think, Mrs Davenport?'

Nina nodded, impressed, a little moved. 'So far you haven't told me anything that makes me feel in danger — at least not so long as I'm in this room, which I guess really must be soundproof.'

Her laugh was only a cough, a click in her throat. She dropped her eyes self-consciously, hesitated. 'Also, you haven't told me anything I didn't already know. Of course, I wonder how you know these things, and I – and how you can articulate them so freely . . .'

Wentz broke in on her with an ardour she found surprising. 'We think it would be possible to make things move in a positive direction more quickly if we could get at the heart of this network of relationships – among the young. If we could identify some sort of leader, someone who should naturally come to the fore, and who maybe just needs assistance.' He snatched the cigarette from behind his ear, held it aloft.

Nina looked up at the cigarette, but she scoffed. Her mouth grew narrow, her eyes dour. 'This atmosphere you're describing, of change, of communication – that's exactly what it is, you know, atmosphere. Just atmosphere. There is no movement. There can't be. I don't really believe that part of your inspirational speech, actually. Much as I'd like to. This isn't America, Mr Wentz. There's nothing organized behind whatever new atmosphere there may be here. Organizations are dangerous. Anyone who comes to the fore in any movement in this country gets arrested and probably shot. You must realize that?'

'We'd pick our moment, Mrs Davenport. It might be a long way off. But we want to be ready when – a turning point comes. For now, it's just a question of gathering information.'

Nina sat very still, very erect. 'Just gathering information?'

Wentz nodded.

'And you seriously think I can visit Felix again – without endangering him?' She was unconvinced, dismissive.

Wentz nodded again, nonplussed, inconceivably relaxed.

'And then what?' Nina demanded.

'Then the Russians will have accepted it's an ongoing friendship, or they'll tell us it has to stop. In that case, you stop.'

'What if they don't come to you to complain?'

'They won't arrest a diplomat's wife without warning. Nowadays they take diplomatic immunity very seriously. We'd have time to get you out of the country safely.'

Nina raised her eyebrows. She felt herself being pulled into the chain of events as they talked about it. It was a less daunting task than she had feared; Wentz's easy demeanour made it seem strangely normal, interesting. Why not?

She was acquiescing only in theory, but already she was thinking with excitement of her next visit to Felix. Was it reckless towards his fate? Or could she regain his respect, at least a little? If she came visiting for reasons apart from her own predicament, unselfishly, could she rid herself of the guilt she had felt when she had seen him? It would be a mission. She didn't for a second imagine she would succeed in changing the world, but she did feel in her heart that she would have a noble aim. Somehow that seemed good enough: to have a role in something with a noble aim. It was why she had wanted to assist the New York City Ballet. This new task, in its privacy, anonymity, unshowiness, felt to her more authentic, more like the person she really was, the person underneath the expensive clothes her mother had made her buy and which she had self-consciously been wearing ever since leaving Paris, acting the part of embassy wife.

In her posture, Nina began to relent. She stopped thinking about whether or not she liked Wentz, she stopped struggling to hold sway in the conversation. She was thinking hard about what she would do next, about John waiting for her outside the bubble, worrying.

'I'm not at all eager to leave the country without my husband,' she remarked noncommittally.

Phipps made a series of marks on his pad, as if ticking things off, dotting an 'i', crossing a 't', then muttered without looking up, 'We'd get him out, too.'

'Oh, great. So that's not a big deal. He'll be just thrilled.' Her tone was caustic. 'And what about Felix?'

'As long as the Russians continue to feel they can get some

information out of your friendship, there won't be a problem. The sentimental attachment gives them a little leverage over the doctor. We've got things we can let them find out without jeopardizing anyone. We just have to ensure that the friendship doesn't produce any particular result. Belov will be fine.'

Then Wentz added unexpectedly, 'Anyway, if they do arrest you, Nina, you know what to say?' He stooped his face down and caught her eye, seemed to be teasing her again.

Nina's haughtiness was suddenly abandoned in a little surge of excitement; she engaged almost recklessly with his twinkle, flung her thin arms about boyishly. 'I'm an American citizen! I have diplomatic immunity. Take me to the consul!'

'And what will you say to the consul?'

She laughed, jerking her head back in mock disbelief. 'It's all about an old love affair? *And* – u-mm – I'm expecting his child?'

'I knew you'd be good.' Wentz grinned.

'So why are you doing this now?' she asked.

'We've just been waiting for you. Your best cover is – your natural inclination. When you got the assignment with the dancers, we thought we'd be waiting for ever; you've been with them every goddamned day!'

At last Wentz produced a box of matches from the flap pocket of his jacket, lit his cigarette, dragged on it, and added in a thick exhalation, 'By the way, there's one guy in particular that we want you to find out about.'

'OK.' Her voice was clear, with an upward lilt, as if she were waiting to hear what she could pick up for him the next time she went out shopping.

'Viktor Derzhavin.'

This was followed by a long silence and, for Nina, a sensation that she was drowning. The smoke from Wentz's cigarette burned her nostrils, hit her stomach hard. She felt she had misunderstood everything that had happened up to now. How could it be chance that Wentz was asking her about Viktor? She felt blindsided, made a fool of, and the smoke hurt, made her dizzy. She began to grow angry, building towards passion. But at the same time she was overcome with weakness, lassitude, breathlessness, stayed limp in her chair, trying to find oxygen, to inhale, to exhale, to steady herself.

Wentz continued unperturbed, as if it were nothing, pulling again on his cigarette. 'You knew him pretty well at one time, yeah?'

Nina remained silent, white-faced.

'By all accounts, Derzhavin is a very brilliant guy. A physicist by training?'

Still she didn't respond.

Wentz pressed on. 'And quite a reputation as a poet – popular even though he got banned after his arrest. Son of two Kremlin doctors – silver spoon and so on. We know his mother disappeared in '52 when Stalin went after the doctors. And evidently there was a completely separate episode involving his father, in '55, a committee to review psychiatric care? A committee that was suppressed and whose work has evidently disappeared?'

He paused, swung around and reached for an ashtray on the table top behind him, tapped his cigarette on it again and again on his knee, long after the ash fell. 'Ever since then, Derzhavin's been in trouble, huh? Despite all that privilege growing up. Cars, holidays in the south, plenty of good food. Seems like a lot to throw away, doesn't it? And the entrée, too – university, the Communist Party, a career slot at one of these research institutes – whatever he might have wanted?'

Nina fixed her eyes on an empty swivel chair pulled up to a typewriter across the room; the four legs of dark brown wood curved down and away from the central pillar holding up the chair seat, and the legs ended in shiny metal castors sitting on a heavily worn patch of the dull grey carpet. It's almost square, she told herself studying the patch. It must be about eight or ten inches square, where the wheels move repeatedly, rolling back and forth, side to side, back and forth, side to side, as if they can't get out, as if they're trapped.

'So tell me if this sounds right, Mrs Davenport: Derzhavin was arrested after the Hungarian Revolution? Because he had achieved too much – notoriety? He's a very charismatic figure; is that right?'

Nina shrugged; she didn't dare say anything, didn't dare look at Wentz.

'And that was just around the time you left Russia, wasn't it?' Wentz stooped his face down again, tilted his head to one side to try to see into her eyes. But Nina dropped her head into her hands, rubbed her face with her flattened palms, then ran fingertips along the bottom edge of each eye; there was moisture there, a tear welling, smudged mascara.

'He was sent to prison but got out after four years? Why'd they ever let him out?'

She was surprised by the question; the answer was so obvious. 'Things like that are completely mysterious in Russia; that's the method of the State, of the KGB. To keep everyone on the edge of their seat, malleable. It's not as if they have any legitimacy; they don't work by logic or by the law; the absurdity makes it much harder for anyone to resist, to even know they should resist, *what* they should resist.' And she looked at him, open-faced, questioning, then turned and looked at Phipps. What they knew and what they didn't know was hard to figure; there were gaps that made no sense to her.

'Right. Well, we feel we're familiar with that.' Wentz moved on, and she couldn't tell whether he was glossing over this bit of ignorance to avoid admitting it, or whether the question had been some trap, some test for her. 'And how'd you ever get out – out of Russia, I mean, Mrs Davenport?'

Again she shrugged. 'That's all on record. After my father's death, my mother applied for an exit visa, begged for the assistance of this embassy, and eventually we were allowed to go. It took about three years.'

'You do know that you and your mother were just about the

very first Americans to be allowed out after the war? Our consular officers are petitioned all the time by these poor idealistic fools who came over here during the Depression and got stuck in some menial engineering job in the sticks. Why'd the Soviets let you out?'

'Poor idealistic fools like my father, you mean?' Nina's eyes were hard, dark.

'I'm sorry. That was a thoughtless remark, but your father worked right here in Moscow, didn't he? Quite a prestigious job, engineering the subway system?'

'It was a lot of digging, as far as I know, and then he was in an accident. They worked non-stop and nobody thought about safety; they hardly even slept. My father was crushed under a temporary elevator; somebody set off a blast without signalling a warning, timbers collapsed. I don't really know more than that. Afterwards we were allowed to stay in Moscow because – because he was – had been – friendly with his bosses – Kaganovich, Bulganin. And really, well, Khrushchev, too. Khrushchev was just Kaganovich's deputy then, but he ran the project. My father was too crippled for anyone to bother over after that. Maybe they felt sorry for his widow, his orphan. Besides, both my parents did translating work, for the Foreign Ministry. So they knew people there – my mother knew people.'

'And you don't know anything more about Derzhavin's arrest?'

'Oh, Christ.' She took a deep breath, let it out loudly, angrily. 'I was nineteen years old, totally naïve. I had spent my childhood taking ballet lessons. I was completely – square. These were my friends, my idols, I worshipped them.'

Nina stumbled, thought to herself, *them*. And then she thought, No. I worshipped *him*. It was entirely personal. She made a little sniffing noise, cleared her throat trying to prepare herself to say something about Viktor's poems. But what could she say?

'Nineteen, Mrs Davenport?'

Nina froze, heart flopping in fear. Then, slowly, she nodded, closing her eyes, thinking, What difference can it possibly make if he knows how old I really am? Even if he reveals it to the Soviets?

'Listen here, Mrs Davenport, I was in the Moscow embassy myself at the time that you left. I've seen all your files, your interview with the consular officer, everything here, everything back in the States. Your mother's file was the place where I first came across Derzhavin's name, also Felix Belov. She was mighty worried about you, wasn't she, your mother? Desperate to get you away from their influence, these dangerous friends you had. She pleaded with the consular officer, told him you were young, impressionable. *Really* young.'

How could she get free of this? This story she repeatedly had to tell? No matter how many times she told it, she was asked again, and she was never at ease telling it, she never achieved any sense of release from it, from this coil of the past which would not give her up, would not let her go.

Phipps was writing. Why? Nina wondered. Doesn't he already know everything Wentz knows? Wentz sat loosely on his chair, waiting, seeming somehow sympathetic.

When she remained silent, he said, 'Of course, it was up to the Soviets, whether they were going to give you that exit visa, but we certainly made it a priority to get you out. Nobody even realized at first that you were missing a birth certificate. Lord, there were still refugees from the war who had no papers at all.'

Wentz was all sunny welcome. Then after a pause, he said, 'I haven't discovered a single instance of a Soviet-born child being allowed out to the USA during that period. But that story your mother's sister told – about the snowy winter night in Buffalo, the aged family doctor – that was obviously nonsense. Worthy of a Victorian novel. Did you buy that? Did your husband?'

Nina touched her forehead with the fingertips of her right hand, then pressed the base of her palm against it, rubbed it heavily from side to side, wishing she could somehow erase what was inside her head, make her memory a blank. She could hear Aunt

Josephine's voice, softer than Mother's, just as determined, canny, persuasive. And she thought, So, if he can establish that we deliberately lied in our interviews last spring, I guess he'll deport us both. And ruin John's career once and for all.

Wentz was at her again. 'Obviously, your grandparents weren't angry with your mother, leaving her all that money, those trust funds. One in your name, as I discovered when I went to the bank to look into it – established, funnily enough, in 1939. And the bank holds a marriage certificate for your parents dated 1935. A woman of your intelligence, I can't believe you didn't know these details, too? And your husband?'

After all this time, Nina thought, everything unravelling. And she saw the packing cartons stacked around the apartment in Leninsky Prospekt, the suitcases out on the beds again, imagined folding the clothes, pushing them all back inside. John would have been so much better off without me, she thought. The bridge of her nose, something in the back of her mouth, were ready to dissolve in tears of regret. She couldn't reply.

'I saw to it no real questions were raised about you last spring – on our side. Of course, we didn't know whether the Soviets would let you back in; we knew they'd subject you to intense pressure on the security side. I reckon you and your husband have a hell of a lot of nerve. Just staggering. Frankly, I'm very impressed.'

Nina realized that she was simply exhausted. She shook her head, bewildered, feeling the nausea pooling again in her gut, making her sag. 'So what are you saying, Mr Wentz? What's going to happen?'

'Tell me what you think turned Derzhavin against the State.'

'Everything.' She spread her hands in the air in expostulation, heaved a sigh, forged on, completely unguarded. 'He was told his mother died of heart paralysis in Lubyanka. But he knew there was nothing wrong with her health. It meant she was tortured to death – his *mother*. After that he just – he had the nerve to say what we all knew. He had always seen things – the leadership –

up close. He had a good brain. And he was confident. Reckless even. He took it to heart that anyone else should tell him how to live his life, should try to control his actions, his thoughts, his writing. He was outraged by his lack of freedom – to think, to speak, to choose. He held those things dear – just as you've said you do, Mr Wentz. Honestly, I can't believe that you need to ask me this stuff. You're an American. This is what you're supposed to be raised on. Isn't it why you – we – are fighting this god-damned Cold War?'

Wentz stubbed out his cigarette, clicked the ashtray down on the table behind him. 'We think that someone may have been in a position to intercede for Derzhavin. That someone close to Khrushchev may have wanted Derzhavin out of prison – maybe even someone Khrushchev himself is unwise to trust. Derzhavin is Jewish?'

Nina tossed her head, as if to say, So what? But she knew it mattered. 'Actually, his mother.' Her heart went cold with it.

'He got arrested again last fall and sent back to prison earlier this year. He wasn't the only one. Anyway, Mrs Davenport, Derzhavin certainly knows a lot of things we would like to know, and despite his rotten luck in being in prison, he almost certainly does have influential friends following his case. Everything tells us that he could take a central role in any move to overthrow the existing style of government in this country. For instance, he's the type who could turn the Komsomol – which, if you don't mind my saying so, *is* an organization – and he's the type who could capture the allegiance of the next generation. Building the communist state is no longer at the top of every Russian's agenda. There are the calls for a return to Leninism, but we don't think the revolution can be done all over again. We are looking for a sea change.'

Nina looked him in the eye. 'Viktor better not be your only hope; life is fragile in this country. The prisons are overflowing with talented people, and they just disappear. It's cheaper to kill them than to feed them.'

'Felix Belov and Viktor Derzhavin trust you. If you carry any message to them – obviously at some risk to yourself – they'll listen. And we believe they'll speak to you honestly. So go back to your doctor friend and find out where Derzhavin is.'

'Can't you do that more easily than me? Through your KGB connections?'

'Oh, Lord. We don't want the KGB to know we're looking for him. Dangerous for him, dangerous for our plans.'

Nina looked solemn for a moment. Off the hook, she mused, is this how John and I get off the hook? By going deeper in? Then she swallowed, began to nod, considered. 'The dancers have tomorrow off, so I'll need to be with them. But I could go on Tuesday?'

'Do it in your own way. It has to be as if we never talked about this. Just rely on your natural inclination.'

'But what do I say?'

'Find out whether Derzhavin is still alive, and find out where he is.'

'What if Felix doesn't know?'

'He knows.'

October 22. The next day Colonel Oleg Penkovsky was arrested by the KGB. A man in a dark blue overcoat approached him quietly as Penkovsky and a colleague were leaving their office at the State Committee for the Coordination of Scientific Research Work at number 11 Gorky Street.

'Your passport is now available to be collected,' the man said, leaning towards Penkovsky in front of the great stone doorway with its classical pediment, 'for your next trip abroad.'

Penkovsky was talking to his colleague, looked up, blinked nervously, wiped at the corners of his eyes with the back of one hand, squinted through the scum lately always gathering there at the unfamiliar face. 'Yes?'

The man had both hands in his overcoat pockets; he removed them, took Penkovsky's arm easily, gestured towards a brown car beside the kerb twenty yards down the hill under a tree. 'I offer you a lift,' the man said, 'and your colleague, too.'

Penkovsky felt a pressure of excitement in his chest. His passport! At last he would be allowed to go abroad again. After so many months of anxiety. He settled into the back of the car, tired, comfortable, closed his eyes in relief, just for a moment. The car eased forward silently. Then, he didn't know why, he felt an earthquake in the cavity of his ribs, his heart bolting. He looked sharply out of the rear window and saw another car following; it had four men inside.

Oh, my God, he thought. A brown Volga. And we are travelling too fast. That's how I know.

They drove him to the KGB prison at Dzerzhinsky Square,

Building Number 2, muscled him inside with his colleague. Then they locked him up alone in a cell.

Penkovsky thought of his Minox cameras locked into the secret drawer in his desk at home, the thousands of tiny photographs he had taken, up close, rapidly, of files spread on open drawers, pages left out on desktops, military intelligence library copies of nuclear missile operation manuals, giving descriptions, measurements, capabilities, procedures, whole articles from the top-secret version of the Soviet publication, *Military Thought*. He thought of the trunk larger than a grown man in which Rodney Carlson had proposed to smuggle him out of Russia. And he thought of his beautiful young wife, Vera, his two daughters.

In his little apartment on Maxim Gorky Embankment, Penkovsky's fine dark suits, his carefully laundered silk shirts, his plain narrow neckties were strewn about the floor. Vera was crying, Penkovsky's mother was crying, Penkovsky's daughters were crying. The drawers in his desk were splintered, his spy loot pillaged.

The longed-for meeting with Queen Elizabeth at Buckingham Palace was not to be. Nor the meeting with President Kennedy. But Penkovsky had served his purpose.

Nina slipped away from the dancers in the middle of the afternoon, caught a tram and then walked to the embassy.

'How'd you know I was leaving early?' John asked, putting a hand on her shoulder, bending down to kiss her on the cheek.

'I just – I wanted to see you,' she answered. She couldn't explain it really, her fear that he might not be there at the embassy, that she needed to see him in the flesh. 'I thought you might like to take a look at where I grew up. I've never shown you.'

'Jesus, Nina, you don't think that's kind of pig-headed right now? After what happened to you yesterday?' He smiled at her, impressed by her tenacity, her refusal to be cowed.

'Don't you believe Mr Wentz – that everything will be fine? He was so reassuring, John. I believe him.' Off the hook, she thought. I have to go through with it.

John didn't reply, thinking about Cuba; he tried to look convinced, but his smile half faded.

'It's a perfectly normal part of town for us to go to,' she added breezily. Then with less confidence, testing her lower lip with her teeth, gnawing, 'And it seems easier than trying to tell you what's going on – inside me.'

Despite everything, Nina still trusted John to understand her. This is the nearest I can get, for now, to opening my heart to you, she was thinking. Showing rather than telling. If I set the scene, maybe the story will begin to unfold inside you, my true history. She imagined that somehow John would follow her, in his instinctive way, would eventually catch up to her, to the immense difficulties at which she had now arrived.

'Well, I'd like to go,' he said. 'But I don't have the car.'

'I know.'

They went by tram to Pushkinskaya Square, and she took his hand to lead the way across the boulevard.

'We never had that,' she said, gesturing towards the new Rossia movie theatre built clumsily right across the front of the offices of *Novy Mir* and *Izvestia* at the end of the square. They passed the state-run Armenian restaurant with its pale stone ballerina in front and started along Gorky Street. In the ornate windows of Gastronom Number 1, Yeliseevsky, there were translucent pyramids of vodka bottles, Belgian chocolates wrapped in gold paper and clear plastic, heavily decorated and beribboned boxes of Krasny Oktyabr chocolates.

As they approached the Central Hotel she grunted, 'We need to cross.'

The little street opposite was hers.

'I used to love that bakery over there,' she paused as they reached the far sidewalk and pointed back across the street at Filippov, 'when I could afford a roll on the way home from ballet school.' Her voice went dull, but she lingered there in the wide, busy avenue, as if she were savouring some moment of satisfaction, a simple pleasure. She considered the occasions in her harangued youth when any public place had been a sanctuary – not school, not home, nowhere, out among strangers. Outside of time, in fact, because no one knew where she was. Gorky Street, the bakery.

Even in childhood, she realized, there had been episodes of evading, dropping out of the routine, the demands, just wandering, her mind undirected. She could remember it distinctly. She thought of how Viktor used to say that he and she were accustomed to feeling alone in the universe because they were both only children, spoiled; how he liked to ignore everything visible – in order to be alone inside his head. But I wasn't spoiled, Nina thought, not in those days. And so she wondered, now, how much of what Viktor had seen in her was really there. Maybe he just saw youth, innocence, a blank. He taught me things, though; he answered my questions. The ones I was brave enough to ask.

The big, nineteenth-century apartment buildings on either side of Maly Gnezdnikovsky Lane seemed taller than she remembered, the lane no more than a passageway, a crack between two imposing, dingy frontages, one grey, one pale pink. She threw her head back, craning at the sky and she could see the join in the stucco where floors had been added in the 1930s, and then, atop the pink building, maybe she saw a newer fourth and fifth storey.

'We can – just look,' she said, throwing her uncertain eyes back towards John.

'Whatever you want.' He let her draw him on by the hand.

The street was narrow, still. The light filtered thinly down between the buildings from high above their heads. The backs of the apartment blocks were a patchwork of plywood and fibreglass, laundry drooping in the lonely air. Voices ricocheted, remote, bodiless, from windows they couldn't see.

'Pretty ramshackle compared to the front,' John remarked, looking up, around.

'This neighbourhood is a nice one,' Nina answered grittily. 'Parts of Moscow really are just a façade hiding poverty and chaos. Makes you realize that the villages Potemkin threw up for Catherine the Great were not at all romantic the way people pretend. Now the word is *Khrushchoba*, you know, like slum – *trushchova*? Such are the sacrifices the State makes on behalf of the people.'

On their left was a vaulted stone archway. Her blood rose a little as she stared, surprised at how exposed it looked. How did we even kiss there, let alone lie down? She felt simply embarrassed.

'I used to meet my boyfriend there,' she said baldly, determined that John should know. And she gave a belittling laugh, not wanting it to seem serious, to hurt him. I ought to tell him more, she thought, but then she realized that she didn't need to. There was no shadow, no ghost. Nothing lingering for John to sense, to guess at. Nothing more to tell. What were they about, those embraces, those tender, heaving abasements? she wondered. Were they just what I believed was supposed to come next? And she had an explicit recollection, like a physical sensation, of disappointment, of failing to get to the bottom of something.

'And the archway leads to a little place to – not really a park, just – open – where I liked to go all by myself when I was much younger. Play hopscotch, leap about in the air, I guess dance.' She said it prosaically and pointed right through the vault of bricks, the thin air. 'We never used to have all the garbage.' Then she stopped, smelling its sourness, heaped on the paving under the arch, and she said, 'Maybe we did, though.'

Further along the street stood older houses, three, four storeys high, stucco. A few bedraggled trees along the fronts. Nina gestured towards them. 'There,' she said, 'on the corner, the blue one.'

John could tell that, suddenly, she didn't want to go closer. 'Blue?' he asked.

'Too hopeful, calling that blue?' Her tone was comical, resigned. 'It's just that I know it was supposed to be blue, or that once it was blue. Or anyway, once we wanted it to be blue. Maybe that's the truest.'

She turned away from the house, eyes down. 'I don't know who's still there,' she said. 'I'd like to show you the inside, introduce you to the Szabos. But it would cause trouble. It could be – total strangers, every room – and they might not let us in. Besides, it might seem depressing, you know, run down, compared to – what we're used to now. There isn't really much plumbing. None at all in the basement apartments; they have to go out into the back garden. And those apartments all share one kitchen; they even take their own light bulb in with them.'

Her voice halted, dwindled, and she was thinking, What did I hope I would find here? She made herself turn around again and look back at the house, its staring windows, blank, dark. How it leaned towards her, with its hidden, dreary quiet, its collapsing staircase.

'It was built as a profit house,' she explained. 'You know, by some landowner or merchant to rent out. Maybe a hundred years ago, more. It was never meant to last this long, to house so many. We always hoped it would last long enough for us – until we could – get out.'

Yet there it is still, she thought, even though we abandoned it, gave up hope. Left it for dead. She could remember what it had felt like to depend on it, to nest there, believe in its dilapidated embrace. It had felt fine. Sometimes entirely happy. Somebody else must be doing that now. For me, it's empty, she thought. There's nothing there that has anything to do with me.

'The Szabos were at the front,' she said aloud, 'just above the front door. See the window sill where the pigeon just landed? We were at the back, where it was wider, without the stairs.'

But now, unexpectedly, it flung around inside her, fear like a stone, battering her, and such a bitter longing – for what? She pictured her old bed on the sloping floor, pushed against the thin wall where the wind shook it, in whacking, unexpected gusts, and she felt as if she were being sucked back towards it, the maelstrom, the night. 'Oh, God, I used to be so afraid –' she let out reluctantly, 'and I was always just trying for – a way to not be afraid. The thing is, you aren't allowed to know what you're afraid *of*. You aren't allowed to talk about it. Everyone behaves as though things are totally normal; everyone has hopes, insane hopes. In the beginning I was maybe just afraid of my own parents . . .'

'I'll take you to the bakery,' John said lovingly, 'and buy you everything you ever wanted. Come on.'

She went with him back out into the clang and bustle of Gorky Street. As they walked she was telling herself, No life. There's no life of mine in that house. Nothing. It's in my head, the fear. Like a hard black knot. Or in my gut. Sucking memories. And the longing? For what?

'Actually, I don't want to go to the bakery, John,' she said plaintively. 'Sorry. It's – enough for now, all this. Our whole life, the way that you and I live, is what that bakery used to be to me. And thinking about my father, I realize – there are things – I need to work out. I never meant to kill it all off – the past. Maybe I've – I don't know. I never had a chance to decide. My father really believed in it – the communist state, the sacrifices. And the way he put it to me, as a girl, it was just – sharing. That's why we were here instead of America. The bakery was – sneaking off. I never shared my roll; I never admitted to having it at all. What would my father say about what I'm doing now? I can't just ignore it.'

'Home, then?'

'Yeah.'

They decided to walk from the Metro at Park Kultury. They

were still holding hands as they made their way towards the river.

Once or twice, John looked back along the street behind them. 'Do you think that's my tail or yours back there?' he asked quietly, inclining his head down to Nina.

She gave a little snort of laughter. 'If you really wanted to know, we should have split up a long time ago to see who got followed.'

'Not worth it. Bugs me that somebody got the afternoon off, though, if they covered us with only one man.'

'Well, we're not exactly working, are we?' And she turned towards him with a generous, sweet smile, so that he looked at her, missed a step, felt air move around him, and his heart lift in an old, warm way that took him by surprise.

'No, I guess not.' He felt the familiar, poignant smallness of her hand. 'I better tell you what's going on,' he said. His voice was sober, apologetic.

Right away, her hand curled with tension, a tight grip, weightless. Now she looked back for the KGB man following them, but she didn't say anything.

'He can't hear. He's too far behind, and too busy trying to blend in. Listen, Nina, the military build-up, you know, in Cuba?'

'I'm listening.'

'It's nuclear missiles. The president is broadcasting tonight, on TV, radio. The missiles can reach Washington and maybe even as far north as Canada. He'll ask the Russians to take them out; otherwise we take them out ourselves. And he's setting up a naval blockade around Cuba.'

For a few seconds, she was silent, and then she said, 'Oh, God.' She saw it all right away. The possibility, the magnitude.

John realized that it was exactly what he had expected of her.

She drew his hand and his arm close, wrapped them inside her elbow, pressed them against her, leaned into him as they walked along in step.

He could feel her ribs moving against his forearm, delicate frets, slipping and catching, right through the taffeta-lined stiffness of her camel hair trapeze overcoat. Even her heart, he thought, I can feel the fluttering pulse of it.

The wind caught them hard as they walked over the bridge, and she fell closer against him, bending, buffeted. Already the black haze of twilight was thickening the air, blowing in across the forbidding stretch of sliding water underneath them.

She was thinking, with each silent, effortful stride, of what she was still holding back from him. And she was wondering what the circumstances would be in which she could assume that all the rules would be understood to have changed. If she had secrets, when could she spill them? Did a near threat of nuclear war change things?

Crossing the Moscow River, she asked herself, in all seriousness, what relationship would she like to be in with her husband if the world was going to come to an end.

Do I need to ask Wentz about panic? she thought. Or do I already know what he would say? He would say that I must act without concern for the short-term outcome. In absolute calm. And then she thought, No, I don't know if that's what Wentz would say. It's what Viktor would say. I'm confusing them because – And she knew it was because Wentz was asking extremely difficult things which had to be answered from the same place in herself which had once tried to answer Viktor.

She remembered, suddenly, that Wentz had said, Or God forbid, if there's a nuclear war, and she realized that she had missed his point. She had thought he meant, in general. But he meant nuclear war *now*, because he had already known about the missiles in Cuba. Did he think I knew, too?

And she thought, So the struggle for power – what is Wentz picturing? Is he picturing that the struggle will take place over rubble and dead bodies? Will anybody survive to care about it? She was awed by the coldheartedness of such planning.

Will there even *be* rubble? Bodies? She saw ash, flaking, drifting, everything burned. And the wind still blowing. Maybe the river, too, still moving. Or maybe only a stream falling away into the earth, some gash in the earth, some shifted chunk of broken, blackened ground.

Out loud she asked, 'Would Moscow survive a nuclear strike from – home?'

'I guess not,' John said solemnly. He looked at her tenderly, moved by her lack of sentiment, her clear voice.

But she was not thinking, as he was, of her brittle efforts to keep house, to start a marriage in Moscow. Where *is* Viktor? she was wondering. A camp in Siberia? Are they thinking *he* would survive?

John withdrew his arm from the light clamp in which she still held him, and he put it around her shoulders, pulling her to him. Nina liked it, fell close against him, felt the chemistry of him radiating, hauling her into a kind of private wholeness. This was the embrace which had always felt right to her; even now, it felt unassailable. And she thought, If it were the end of the world, our world, anyway, Moscow, Washington, that's the embrace I want, the sensation.

I can't tell him about Wentz, about Viktor. I can't even tell him about the baby. Not now. What difference would it make? Worse only. It could make it worse. No world at all to bring a baby into. I was right about that, more than I realized.

'At least you know where I grew up.' And she thought, That was the start. Of wanting to tell you – everything.

She felt a slow, harsh twist of sorrow. It started with an ache of pity towards her husband, a wish to protect him from something, and then it grew into a massive physical recollection of how much she loved him and was bonded to him. She saw she had been resisting the bond. Like a madwoman, like someone split in two, rigidly denying she loved anything or anyone because she was bent on accomplishing certain tasks – having no baby, finding out about Viktor.

The trees in Gorky Park, with their crooked, supplicating

boughs, scared her. Black-boned, naked-fingered. She had been hoping for things. She had been hoping for an outcome from her life, from the past, from all the suffering she had sensed around her growing up. In her American years, she had come to hope for it more than ever, to believe in it. To believe that more could come about in the future, more than what she could already see around her – happiness, something she didn't know yet, couldn't guess. But the trees showed her an intolerable bleakness. What could ever come of anything? Winter, the dark. And she hurried to pass them, hurrying John towards the faint warm lights of their building. He fell in with her sense of urgency, swept her along, practically carried her over the threshold.

As they rose to the eighth floor, the elevator lady scrutinized them to no avail. They didn't speak and she couldn't see inside them. They didn't feel her presence at all, maybe for the first time ever. They might as well have been alone. She clicked her tongue at them when she let them out, frustrated, beside the point.

And then inside the apartment, they went straight through the dark hallway, without switching the lights on, without hanging up their hats. They shed their clothes blindly, making for the bed, as if to continue with something they had left off suddenly, had left unfinished.

There was no moment of calculation or inquiry, there was no courting or playfulness. To Nina it seemed odd when she pulled the covers back from the bed. Why was the bed made up? When had they ever left it?

And when John lifted her onto the white sheets, the soft pillows, kissing her, entirely accepted, invited, there was nothing to talk about, nothing for anyone to overhear.

They dived into the subliminal marriage of their flesh which no one else could be privy to. From a hidden camera, through a peephole, a hand might have been seen to rest taut-fingered on a splayed, helpless thigh, a fingertip to move across a lip, at the mouth, at the groin. What they exchanged might have been identified as love: skins interlacing with smudges of sweat, tawny, alabaster; breasts dallied with; a torso rising, turning; hairs prickling at their ends and tangled with eagerness. Even the mewing pant of joy might have been recognized, labelled. But it could not have been felt, understood – passion with its greed, its insistent appetite, its quake of world-obliterating satisfaction.

Both of them were starved of sleep, and eventually they fell into an enchanted doze under the spell of twilight, blank, peaceful, knotted together. They woke up only through hunger around six.

'Do you want something?' Nina whispered.

'Kind of,' John said. He lifted her hand and tasted the tip of each finger.

'There'll be nothing left once you've eaten it all,' she said, laughing in her chest.

'What should I save it for?' The joke was out before he could stop himself, and they both regretted it. It seemed to bring their little idyll to an end, a black jolt.

They didn't feel tough or defiant at all; they felt vulnerable, frightened. A pair of young lovers wishing to be left alone, wishing for more time, wishing for the rest of the world to end without them.

She hid her face under his chin, kissed his unshaved neck, and he put his long arms around her, running one hand over the delicate cage of her back, the curve of waist and hip. They lay in the fragrant bed in the dark; still, silent, sad. A tremble passed between them, love and fear, equally shared. There was nothing to say. They both felt the same, borne on the floodtide of someone else's intentions, someone else's actions, someone as remote to them as the moon, the planets.

John flailed at the lamp, switched it on.

'I'll make some scrambled eggs,' Nina said, still holding him, dragged across the bed as he sat up.

'Why don't I make them?' He stretched his long fingers around the crown of her head, scrunched her hair, stroked it smooth

179

again. 'You've got to get to the ballet, haven't you? Get changed and everything?'

'There's no performance tonight; it's Monday.'

'Oh, God,' he said tragically, exaggerating to hide his dismay, 'I have to go back to the office.'

'Why should that catch me by surprise?' She wiped away an unexpected tear with the knuckle of her index finger. 'I'll make the eggs.'

At that very moment, Nikita Sergeyevich Khrushchev came inside from the falling night. He had been strolling around his little house in the Lenin Hills with his grown son Sergei, the rocket engineer.

There was an urgent telephone call. In the mellow light of the vestibule, Khrushchev twitched off his flat wool cap, an old *kepka*, a workman's cap, such as he never wore in public any more since the death of Stalin, preferring high-crowned fedoras, Homburgs, fur *shapkas*, panamas, straws. He held the cap in one strong, fat hand, slapping it against his other hand, both arms still bound as if by muscles inside the bulk of his overcoat sleeves, and trundled into the big, formal dining room, where he tossed the cap on a chair, glanced with satisfaction at the places laid for supper, doilies of white lace, baskets of sliced brown bread, and accepted the receiver of one of the telephones ranked there.

Sergei waited outside in the vestibule, shifting his feet on the thick, earthy carpet in the centre of the oak floor, keeping his mind empty, attentive, ready.

Nikita Sergeyevich soon returned and led his son back outside into the dark. President Kennedy had announced that he was going to address the United States tonight. Among the loosely scattered groves of trees, they could see the lights of the neighbouring houses; home to some of Khrushchev's closest colleagues in the Presidium. Comfortable, individual establishments, modest enough, certainly not luxurious, designed on the orders of Georgy Malenkov and built with Khrushchev's approval. The houses shared pathways weaving through grassy, open spaces and a high perimeter fence closed by an iron gate, but they shared no party walls, no hiding places for eavesdroppers, spies, assassins. The KGB held no sway here on anyone's behalf. Still, though he and Sergei walked outdoors alone, Khrushchev felt his colleagues pressing around him in the night, making demands, poking fingers in his face, blaming. His head stirred and throbbed; flashes, darts, discontinuous, unsettled. He found it hard to form a sentence.

But to Sergei, in the dark, he could say anything. Almost anything. Like thinking aloud. 'They must have found out about our rockets.' And once he had said it, it seemed the more certainly obvious. 'It's the only explanation. It's quiet in Berlin. And naturally they would not announce it to us if they were about to invade Cuba.'

'Then what will happen?' Sergei asked. 'After the speech?'

Khrushchev felt irritated, impatient, as if with a child who asks questions that can't be answered, about the meaning of infinity, the end of the universe, the end of time. When he looked up at the dark profile of his son, tall, intelligent, educated and skilled beyond his own proudest imaginings, he felt startled by Sergei's manhood. But he did not feel threatened. 'I wish I knew,' he admitted. Then, like the air going out of him, a drone of resignation, 'The missiles aren't operational yet. They can be wiped out from the air in one swipe.'

Now Sergei pressed him with optimistic objections. 'But surely the Americans would be quiet if they were going to make a bombing raid? They wouldn't announce an air strike any more than they would announce an invasion. The address must indicate that Kennedy wants to start a negotiation, Father.'

And it wore at his father, Sergei's reasonable energy, his separate bright train of thought. How should I know? How should I know? Khrushchev thought. So that he was inclined to retreat back into himself, to draw in his thoughts, hide out, where he could brood and plot.

It would be hours before the address, he thought. What to do? I cannot sit waiting. Steal a march – on my comrades at least, if not on the enemy. But I have only hunches. And if I am wrong?

His strongest instinct was to take action, some action. He was not a man who could do nothing. Nothing was, for him, a form of suffering. Nothing could only invite others to turn their knives on him.

He turned suddenly from the tight little circle they were tensely inscribing among the trees, and started back to the house. 'You'll find out what will happen tomorrow morning.' He lorded it over Sergei, sternly. He knew by instinct and experience that he must take command, although just then he knew practically nothing else. 'Don't bother me,' he snapped, 'I've got to think.'

Patiently, Sergei followed his father inside. Khrushchev surged into the dining room, snatched up the Kremlin phone, demanded that the members of the Presidium be summoned at once with representatives from the Foreign Ministry and the Defence Ministry. His voice was surly, powerful, filled with chastisement.

Malinovsky was the one who had blown it, he was thinking, as they yes-sirred him at the other end. Defence Minister Marshal Rodion Malinovsky. First of all, I will make that very clear. They are all in the wrong. We were never going to unleash war. We wanted only to intimidate them. It's tragic. The United States is ready to attack us, and then we'll have to respond. This may end up in a big war. He was hot in his overcoat, his forehead wet, his mouth dry.

Maybe I'll announce that all the equipment belongs to the Cubans, he thought. Castro can even threaten to use them, just the small ones, the short-range ones.

But we must send some kind of order to avoid any accident. We'll order them not to use the nuclear weapons in any circumstances. No matter what.

Down went the phone with a slam.

No, he thought, we'll order them to use only the tactical nuclear weapons but not to strike the United States without my express command.

No. No. He was changing his mind again. Not to use them at all.

Then he snatched up another phone, shouted into it for his car.

He glanced at the supper table, clucked like a housewife at the waste of good food, and went forcefully about his business.

'Don't wait up for me,' he tossed at Sergei as he swept through the vestibule, 'I'll be back late.'

Around midnight, President Kennedy's address to the nation began to arrive by coded cable at the American Embassy. With it came a personal letter from Kennedy to Khrushchev.

Davenport scraped a stool across the floor, and half leaned, half sat in front of the Teletype machine, reading. A square of pain between his shoulder blades tightened. He lifted his chin, wobbled it to ease his neck, then stretched one foot down to the floor, balancing against it, pushing his spine up a little straighter.

'We have to get this over to the Foreign Ministry as soon as possible, before they can start picking up something by radio.'

A political staff member and a code clerk hanging over the table stopped whispering, stubbed out their cigarettes. 'Yup, we're here, John.'

'The code card's already in the machine.'

The three of them huddled in their shirtsleeves, shoulders wedged one against another, sharp knees pressing grey-trousered thighs. The printing ball surged noisily across the unspooling roll of paper like a black, darting wave, spinning one way, then the other, dancing up and down, whacking out the boxy black letters in the machine's extra-urgent-looking capitals, and the coded tape snaked down on the left onto the floor beside them:

. . . EACH OF THESE MISSILES, IN SHORT, IS CAPABLE OF STRIK-
ING WASHINGTON, DC, THE PANAMA CANAL, CAPE CANAVERAL, MEXICO
CITY . . .

'. . . INTERMEDIATE RANGE BALLISTIC MISSILES . . . CAPABLE OF
STRIKING MOST OF THE MAJOR CITIES IN THE WESTERN HEMISPHERE,
RANGING AS FAR NORTH AS HUDSON BAY, CANADA, AND AS FAR SOUTH
AS LIMA, PERU . . .

There was a pause at the end of the first page of text. Davenport's
eyes followed the tape down to the code clerk's big black shoes
facing him, flat on the floor, duck-footed, scuffed. There were pale,
dried white watermarks showing on the leather, wavy, spreading
from the balls of the feet where they'd walked in the rain.

Then the racket, like the clickety-clack of a fast-moving train,
began again:

THE SIZE OF THIS UNDERTAKING MAKES CLEAR THAT IT HAS BEEN
PLANNED FOR SOME MONTHS . . . THE SOVIET GOVERNMENT PUBLICLY
STATED ON SEPTEMBER 11 THAT . . . "THE ARMAMENTS AND MILITARY
EQUIPMENT SENT TO CUBA ARE DESIGNED EXCLUSIVELY FOR DEFENSIVE
PURPOSES" . . .

NEITHER THE UNITED STATES OF AMERICA NOR THE WORLD COM-
MUNITY OF NATIONS CAN TOLERATE DELIBERATE DECEPTION AND
OFFENSIVE THREATS ON THE PART OF ANY NATION, LARGE OR
SMALL . . .

'OUR OWN STRATEGIC MISSILES HAVE NEVER BEEN TRANSFERRED
TO THE TERRITORY OF ANY OTHER NATION, UNDER A CLOAK OF SECRECY
AND DECEPTION . . .

'THE 1930S TAUGHT US A CLEAR LESSON: AGGRESSIVE CONDUCT,
IF ALLOWED TO GROW UNCHECKED AND UNCHALLENGED, ULTIMATELY
LEADS TO WAR. THIS NATION IS OPPOSED TO WAR. WE ARE ALSO TRUE
TO OUR WORD . . .

The door to the bubble opened from time to time, people

came in, went out. When the ambassador appeared, Davenport was pacing up and down the room reading the text of the president's speech out loud over the noise of a typewriter:

"'First: To halt this offensive build-up, a strict quarantine on all offensive military equipment under shipment to Cuba is being initiated. All ships of any kind bound for Cuba from whatever nation or port will, if found to contain cargoes of offensive weapons, be turned back . . . '"

The ambassador slipped two fingers backwards and forwards inside the leather belt and waistband of his pleated-front trousers, as if he were still tucking his shirt tail in, as if he had been sleeping.

'The car's at the door,' he said. 'How's the speech coming?'

Davenport shrugged. 'The speech is ready. We're just typing out the president's letter. It's all going in English. As is.'

The ambassador yawned, bowed his head over the pages lying on the table. He glanced at the opening of the speech, silently turned over to the next page, rubbed the tip of his index finger against the tip of his thumb gingerly, as he read. Davenport leaned forward and pushed the president's letter towards him.

'It all comes down to whether we can actually talk to each other,' the ambassador murmured, his eyes moving, scanning the letter. 'Have a reasonable conversation. Understand the words. That's especially hard after deliberate lies have been told. Lies make diplomacy impossible; they destroy everything we've done.'

He frowned, jabbed his fingers at the page. 'The president states his fear, right here, "the one thing that has most concerned me has been the possibility that your Government would not correctly understand the will and determination of the United States . . . since I have not assumed that you or any other sane man would, in this nuclear age, deliberately plunge the world into war which it is crystal clear no country could win and which could only result in catastrophic consequences to the whole world, including the aggressor." I'd say his tone is absolutely sane. Measured, firm. Absolutely firm and absolutely clear.'

And then he read out slowly, "'I must tell you that the United States is determined that this threat to the security of this hemisphere be removed . . . The action we are taking is the minimum necessary to remove the threat . . . this minimum response should not be taken as a basis, however, for any misjudgement on your part.'" He looked up at the others, wary.

Davenport repeated, 'Determined.'

'Jeez,' heaved out the code clerk from his stool, arms crossed.

The man who had been typing pushed back his chair, stood up, opened a free-standing cupboard in the corner, rummaged. He walked towards the ambassador with a manilla envelope, a string hanging from the seal, began to shake the pages and tap them against the table top to square them.

'OK?' he asked, workmanlike, waiting, before he wrestled the pages into the envelope.

And the word came from the ambassador, 'Yup.' Then, apologetically, 'It makes for a long day, the time difference, doesn't it?'

Davenport said, 'Look, we'd all prefer to be down here all night with something to do rather than going nuts worrying.'

The ambassador put an arm across Davenport's shoulders, reaching up to his height, then dropped the arm and gave him a slap on the back. 'Well, that's what I need to hear. You're going to have to be on hand when we get an answer back, you or the others who have strong enough Russian. We'll do preliminary translations here. Washington fusses over this stuff and it takes them too long. You guys know the Russian language in real life. We're all better off in your hands. John, I want you to stay put and supervise this thing. Don't go home to sleep, because of course the Russians will take note of any phone calls in the small hours. You can sleep on the couch in my office – if it's available.' He chuckled; nobody joined in.

The typist asked, 'Who's delivering the documents, sir?'

Davenport said, 'Give that to Dick Davies; he's taking it to the Foreign Ministry.'

Then, as the typist went out, the ambassador sighed, 'I don't know if you've seen some of the latest messages from Washington?'

'I thought you were asleep,' Davenport answered.

'They've been bringing me all kinds of telegrams.' The ambassador reached into his pocket, pulled out several unevenly folded sheets, then, running a finger over the pages, glancing up at Davenport, down again, pausing and hurrying by turns, recited, 'There are troops in Florida now. The navy has about 180 ships in the Caribbean. The president has increased low-altitude recon-naissance flights over Cuba. And Strategic Air Command has been dispersed all over the country – to make sure our planes can't be hit all at once like they were at Pearl Harbor. All our own planes have got nuclear weapons on board, and they're keeping one-eighth of our B-52s up airborne. Every time one lands, another's already taking off.'

He puffed out his cheeks, spat air. 'The president has been meeting with the European ambassadors. Our ambassadors have had a "go" message from State to brief heads of state – Macmillan, Adenauer, de Gaulle, they're all on board and ready for a blockade of Berlin, too. The military is going to DEFCON 3, not in Europe, though, and not NATO.

'Let's see.' He looked at the other top-secret pages, blinked, read on. 'They've put up interceptor aircraft for the president's address, in case the Cubans react right away. The chiefs of staff want to take out the missile silos – just bomb them.' Then he looked up at Davenport and said, as if to explain, but sounding puzzled, 'Apparently there's Russian and Cuban military equip-ment all over the place, right out in the open, lined up in tidy rows, as if they were asking us to bomb it, tempting us. None of it is even camouflaged. But the president's restraining the chiefs of staff, trying to give Khrushchev time to back down.'

Flapping his pages in the air, still amazed, his eyes wide and lit with concern, the ambassador murmured, 'We are a hair's breadth away from the biggest thing anyone has ever seen.'

October 23. 'I've heard there's a bomb shelter under Spaso House – put in during the war. But it's not very big. These basements here in the embassy wouldn't protect you from a thing.'

'The Metro's the place to go; some stations and also some tunnels are very, very deep. They were constructed like that on purpose, before the war, to serve as bomb shelters. Comrade Chairman Khrushchev himself built them. He knows all about them.'

It was almost dawn, and the windows were haggard with it. By the water cooler in the ground-floor hallway of the American Embassy, the Russian switchboard operator was talking in a low voice to the American code clerk, who was about to go home. They were having the same conversation that pretty much everyone in the embassy had been having on and off all night. Was there anything they could do to make themselves safe? It seemed clear there was nothing, and that it was far too late to try. Still, the conversation served a purpose; it offered the comfort of consensus. As long as everybody agreed that there was nothing anybody could do, and that nobody was going to try to do anything, the panic stayed small.

Away from the water cooler, away from the conversation, it was almost impossible not to start imagining flight. How to take flight. Where to go. Should I take food? Should I leave now? Because if I wait until I'm sure, then it will certainly be too late. Dry-throated, with the pulsing buzz of fear in the mouth, wondering, How fast, how far can I run? And the legs, light with adrenaline, going feeble, dizzy. Can I even stand up?

In the privacy of each imagination lingered the pathetic conviction that there was some wall, some roof, some door, that was strong enough, some secret hiding place. Everyone had the public vision, The certain death of millions; and everyone had the private fantasy, How I will escape the bomb. By crawling under a desk, under a bed, into the store cupboard beneath the basement stairs where there's plenty of canned food already.

'No place is safe,' said the code clerk.

And the operator nodded. 'What would we save ourselves for anyway?'

Their voices were low, almost complacent, and yet while they talked, while they tried to concentrate on having a conversation with one another, through the backs of their minds flipped and laboured still the tumult of escape, the thought, far more distressing than resignation, that there might be some way out. She, for instance, was thinking of two rooms in a village boarding house outside Moscow where she had spent a few weeks last summer; would that be far enough away? She imagined flashes of light in the distance, the sky shuddering. How far did the poison reach? Could you see it coming? Was it like cinders in the air, the fallout? Was it even true what these Americans said, about the power of the blast?

And he was thinking of cars, trains, travel permits. Would it be possible to buy food anywhere? Would he need all the cash he could lay his hands on? Dollars? Could he use dollars? East would be safest, as far away as possible from NATO. But maybe there would be no help for outsiders in the East, no help for the enemy.

Aloud, they soothed themselves. 'Certainly there is no advantage in worrying,' she said.

'It'll all be over so fast, that's the thing,' he replied. 'Worse to survive.'

And so the day wore on until around three o'clock in the afternoon, when there was a scramble of steps, a flurry in the sinking light.

Someone called out, 'A car's here. From the Foreign Ministry!'

Another voice said quietly, 'It's the deputy foreign minister, Kusnetzov. He has a letter for the ambassador.'

The Marine guard, resolute in his khaki shirt, his red-striped blue trousers, flashed his white-gloved hand to his forehead. The pure white circle of his cap, with its polished black visor, shone like an anonymous certainty and seemed to promise that his dogged attentiveness could secure them all.

There were barking formal tones, Russian courtesies, heavy clicking footsteps slow along the floors, and faster ones, a swirl of cold air sucking through the corridor as chairs scraped, office doors opened and closed.

Then the car drove away.

Now, the whole building was springing to attention.

Upstairs, the bubble suddenly teemed with personnel, expertise, commitment.

Davenport hovered over the ambassador, leaning in, advising. He read out key sentences, mouthing the Russian to himself, then translating in a stage whisper.

'U-u-mm . . . "must say frankly that the measures indicated in your statement constitute a serious threat to peace and to the security of nations. The United States has openly taken the path of grossly violating the United Nations Charter, the path of violating international norms of freedom of navigation on the high seas, the path of aggressive actions both against Cuba and against the Soviet Union."'

The ambassador snorted in anger and surprise, then said, 'Go on. What else?'

'Just . . . "We reaffirm that the armaments which are in Cuba, regardless of the, um, classification to which they may belong, are intended solely for defensive purposes –"'

'My ass. Does he take us for complete fools?' said the ambassador under his breath.

'"I hope that the United States Government will display wisdom and renounce the actions pursued by you which may lead to cat-astrophic consequences for world peace."'

'This is not good. Not at all what we might have hoped for. There really has been no communication here at all,' said the ambassador.

In a low voice Davenport replied, 'It's – a stand-off. Premier Khrushchev certainly doesn't care for the blockade. And he seems to think he's got some kind of advantage here; he's just going for broke.'

In the lobby of the Ukraina Hotel, Alice and Danny had both their heads jammed against one receiver as they waited for their telephone call to go through.

At the Davenports' apartment, Yelena Petrovna, the cleaning lady, was nosing through Nina's underwear drawer when she heard the phone ringing in the hall. She picked up another pair of cream silk, lace-edged French drawers, gave them a snap and a shake to unfold them, held them up and gazed at them, nodded her head in satisfaction. She turned them carefully around in her work-chafed fingers and held them against her broad hips where they hung like a shiny loincloth. Dreamily she admired the effect. Then she turned, laid them on the bed with the ones she had already examined, and scrounged for something more.

The phone stopped ringing. She clucked to herself and held up a pale grey camisole with spaghetti straps and an elaborate lace décolletage. The tiny size made the workmanship all the more delicate, all the more attractive. There were grey silk drawers to match, and she assembled them as a set on the bed, like a shop-girl dressing a window, smoothing them with flat fingers, stepping back for a better view.

She cast her eyes over the bureau, New England cherry, warm, lustrous, with plain brass fittings. Each drawer was lined with blue-flowered paper, scented with lumpy muslin bagfuls of dried blossoms, and held unopened parcels in stiff, rustling tissue. The stockings were in the second drawer, gossamer, shapely.

The phone started ringing again, and it puzzled her. She'd never heard it ring much. She would report that.

Lovingly, she began to fold the dainty articles on the bed, patting them into the drawers one at a time in neat rows. She liked the lace insets to show at the edges and especially on the front. She folded each item to its best advantage.

The phone went on ringing.

'The operator can't have dialled it wrong twice in a row,' Alice said anxiously. 'Nina's not there. Or at least she's not answering.'

'God, do you think people are leaving town?' Danny stood away from the phone, looking at Alice with his inscrutably crisp grey-blue eyes, then pulled out the turtleneck of his tightly fitting black sweater and snugged his chin down inside it thoughtfully. 'Wouldn't they tell us if they were leaving? Why hasn't anyone told us what's going on?'

'Nina wouldn't run off and leave us. I really don't think she's like that.' Alice's neck and shoulder muscles crawled with tension and her fawn-like limbs, swaddled in baby-blue mohair, trembled ever so slightly with the chill of no lunch, of fear. 'God, I want to see my baby. If it's that bad, I have to get on an airplane. Do you think Mr B. will let me go by myself? I can't stay here if something might keep me from my baby.'

'They have to do something about the whole company, Ali. There has to be a plan.' He pulled his chin free from his sweater, dropped it in one hand, his jaw flexing with the paralysis of crisis. 'Or maybe we shouldn't rely on anyone else. Maybe we should figure out what to do, you know, just by ourselves.' His voice was noncommittal, as if only his mind were engaging with the idea of individual effort, as if he thought Alice or someone would talk him out of it.

'We don't even speak Russian,' Alice said dismissively. Then, with a surge of conviction, 'Let's try the embassy. Maybe she's there, or John, you know, her husband. How do we phone the embassy?' She was excited with this new idea.

They waited a minute or two for the hotel switchboard operator. Then it was almost impossible, all over again, to explain what they wanted. And the line was engaged. They could both hear it.

'We'll try again in a few minutes,' Alice said.

They leaned back against the cold stone wall and scanned the lobby – shadowy, pillared, faced with dimly glinting mauve granite, hung with wrought metal chandeliers, echoing and humming like a busy railway station, cavernous and mysterious as a cathedral. A group of dancers was coming up the stairs from the dining room to the left of the revolving doors; the doors were oak, massive, three or four times the height of a man. The dancers were talking intently among themselves, in little clutches of two and three, pale-eyed, taut-cheeked, wan with fretting.

Patrice appeared through the revolving doors, walking fast, still in last night's black stilettos, her arms tightly laced around her lynx coat, her blonde hair loose around her face. She gave the other dancers a stiff nod as she overtook them, making for the elevators. Then she spotted Alice and Danny and rushed over to them instead, as if she had been looking for them.

'Does everyone know about the president's speech? About the missiles?' she asked urgently.

Danny tossed a thumb towards the dancers crossing the lobby. 'We have gossip. There have been calls from New York, starting in the middle of the night, but Ali couldn't get through to her husband. It's just about 8 a.m. there now. So, did you find out something real from your new boyfriend?'

Patrice looked embarrassed, then tossed her head. 'I can't tell you anything that's supposed to be a secret. I'd just get us all in trouble.'

'Oh, come on, Patrice,' Alice said, 'do you really think that guy would tell you something that was supposed to be a secret? He works for the government for Christ's sake.'

'Yes, he might tell me,' Patrice said imperiously. 'We're pretty – involved.'

'Well, you decide, Patrice,' Danny said gently, reaching out to grasp the top of her right arm, then letting it go and taking both her hands in his. 'We just want to know what we should do.'

'Or – what are *you* going to do?' asked Alice. 'Then you don't have to tell us anything Fred Wentz said.'

Patrice took back her hands from Danny, unhooked the top of her coat, then reached up behind her head and grabbed her long hair from both sides, smoothing it hand over hand and flopping it back down on her neck in a single shining hank of blonde. 'I know it's really scary,' she said, 'but if the missiles are aimed at New York and Washington, we're just as safe here. The president isn't starting anything. He's not attacking Cuba and he's not attacking here. I mean – he's trying to wait until the Russians stop.' She paused and looked around behind her, then said in a quieter voice, leaning towards them, 'He just wants to give them time to take the missiles down.'

Alice said, 'The missiles are aimed at New York, too?'

Patrice nodded, barely moving her head.

'Christ, I thought it was just Washington.' Alice's voice faded and cracked. 'I should never have come. It's just too damned far away.' She dashed at her eyes with quivering fingers, flinging tears so that Patrice and Danny both felt them on their own cheeks. 'He's so – little.'

Patrice and Danny looked at her, silent. It seemed to them a poignant observation, true, obvious, somehow irrelevant. They had no feelings at all about the baby. They couldn't get further than caring about Alice.

'If the Cubans fire off any missiles, obviously the president's going to fire back,' Danny said cautiously, 'and if the missiles in Cuba are Russian ones, he'll fire at Moscow. I'm really sorry, but I've read plenty in the newspapers about how much better our missiles are than theirs, or how many more we have anyway.'

There was another silence and then Alice asked softly, solemnly, 'What if the president decided to fire first, and the Russians couldn't fire at all?'

'He's not doing that,' said Patrice in a steely voice, as if she knew. Then more tentatively, 'At least, I don't think so. Anyway, he knows we're here, doesn't he?'

Alice said caustically, 'Patrice, you're talking about the end of the world – what difference does the New York City Ballet make?'

There was anger in her voice, and they stood looking at each other, stunned by the boldness of the remark. None of them wanted to believe it; none of them wanted to address it. Alice felt a little afraid, a little bad, about what she had said. Patrice turned away, looked behind them, gazed longingly around the lobby, wondering what the other company members were doing, what they thought, whether she'd be more comfortable with them than with Alice, with Danny.

Slowly, eyes glazed, Alice chanted, 'You'd need to get some-where in the middle of nowhere, really nowhere, to be safe, and even then, the radioactive fallout would come eventually. And there'd be nothing to eat, no sunlight.'

'Have you been talking to everyone else all day?' asked Patrice energetically. She wasn't listening to Alice. But neither Danny nor Alice answered Patrice. They were somehow cut off from one another, isolated in their thoughts, by the gigantic uncertainty hanging over them.

'At least at home we could find out what the hell is going on. You can't get any information in this country.' Danny was impa-tient now, kicking at it all. 'There's nothing in the fucking news-papers, even if I could read fucking Russian. I can't stand the way everything is kept secret here. And all the time they're spying on *us!*'

'Do you suppose they would take us prisoner,' ventured Alice, 'if there was a war?'

Now the others did hear her, looked startled.

'Well, obviously they're not going to invite us into their bomb shelters,' said Danny. 'But I mean – would they have time to arrest us?'

'I'm trying the embassy again,' said Alice, picking up the phone.

When she finally did get through, it didn't really calm them down at all.

At the embassy, the switchboard operator was battling with her Siemens machine as if it were a pit of serpents. Every light was flashing, every circuit jammed, the maximum number holding all the time. As soon as one call ended and she could put another through, the circuits lit up again. It had been like that for hours. The frantic questions hurtling down the wires at her seemed to be raising the temperature inside her head. The voices were raw-edged, uncontrolled, and she felt that if she couldn't connect the calls quickly enough, her brain would melt.

Alice felt it, and a shrillness crept into her own voice; when John Davenport came on the line, she practically shrieked, 'Where's Nina?'

This rattled John just a little. 'Isn't Nina with you?'

'We haven't seen her all day.'

'She's been so tired,' John said, 'maybe she's home resting.'

'We called her at home. She didn't answer. Has she left Moscow? Is there going to be a nuclear war? Should we all leave? Nobody's telling us anything!'

The tone of hysteria, the rapid firing, automatically produced a professional calm in John; he began to talk in a soothing, managing voice, very sure of himself, relaxed. He knew exactly how to handle this conversation. 'Of course Nina hasn't left Moscow. Why would she do that? Let's all calm down now. Maybe Nina's . . . I don't know, taking a walk. Or . . . out buying beets. But I'm absolutely sure she's just fine. I didn't go home last night myself because I was here working.

'There will maybe be a little anti-American feeling, since Radio Moscow has just broadcast that we're setting up a blockade and building up troops in the Caribbean. Of course they haven't announced *why* we're building up troops – that they've put nuclear missiles in.

'But my advice is, don't leave. Just stick with your programme. Nobody really knows where this is going, and there's not a lot you could do no matter what happens. You all should have had a bulletin from the embassy. When I find Nina, I'll make sure you see that. There'll be one every day. Just sit tight.'

Danny and Patrice, leaning in to the receiver, couldn't quite hear what John was saying, but they could feel the tone; they were nothing if not sensitive to instructions. They began to take themselves in hand. So did Alice.

By the time the dancers were called together for the evening performance, they were already distancing themselves from the outside world, from the concerns of the international balance of power.

They were told, as a company, that panic serves nobody. We take advice from the embassy when they give it, and otherwise we dance – that's why we are here.

The usual information was issued, about the programme, about changes in personnel to cover injuries. Discipline took over. Whatever crisis was at hand, they would measure it out in music, step by practised step.

And they all saw on Mr Balanchine's face the familiar expression of fierce concentration, his sublime focus on the dance. It made them calm; it hypnotized them.

John Davenport, despite his manner to Alice on the telephone, was far from calm. He was racing from office to office looking for Wentz, and when he found him coming out of the bubble, he collared him ferociously. 'Where's my wife? I don't want her sent home in the middle of all this. I want her here with me.'

Wentz played at quizzical, nonchalant. 'Sent home? Why?'

It enraged Davenport, who could feel the tease underneath the surface, the arrogance. But he reined himself in.

'She didn't tell me anything, Wentz. She has been entirely circumspect. But let's not kid around. Of course I assumed after you warned her again on Sunday that she was on the edge . . .'

In mid-sentence, he stopped talking; he could see from Wentz's eyes that he had something wrong. The look wasn't a tease, it was more like a warning. It was about as serious a look as he'd ever seen on Wentz's face. He couldn't fathom it. He frowned.

'Where's my wife?' he asked blankly, flatly. He felt his heart knock lightly in his throat.

Wentz put his arm through Davenport's with a sort of aggressive collegiality, manhandling him back towards the bubble. Davenport let him.

Under his breath Wentz said, 'I was hoping *you* might know where your wife was, John. I've asked her to do something for me, and I want you to get in touch with her and tell her not to bother.'

'What?' Davenport felt the knock of his heart again, a banging flutter against his chest, the back of his Adam's apple, rising almost to his jaw. And then his blood surged right over it. 'What the hell do you mean? Does Kohler know about this?'

Wentz became stolid, spoke very slowly. 'Concentrate on what I'm saying, John. Call Nina at home, tell her whatever you have to tell her to get her to stay in the apartment. Tell her that you're coming home to see her about something important.'

Davenport was white with rage; he clung to his poise; he wouldn't let Wentz best him. 'I already know she's not there,' he remarked coldly.

'I was afraid of that,' said Wentz, still warm, still confidential, as if they were buddies. 'But try anyway. Would you?' His voice was humble, casual.

Davenport looked at him for a good minute, burning with fight, but Wentz offered no spark of confrontation. Finally, as if out of boredom, Davenport picked up a phone at a nearby desk and dialled the apartment.

Yelena Petrovna was just leaving; she paused to listen as she was going out of the front door. Then she shook her head, clucking and tutting, and pulled the door to behind her. She could still hear the ringing as she lifted the rubbish into the elevator.

Davenport held the receiver out towards Wentz; they could both hear it ringing.

'I guess she's already on her way,' Wentz said. He took the receiver and put it back on the hook.

There was another long, loaded silence.

Davenport took a big breath, then heaved it out. 'I need some information here, as a – friend, if nothing else.'

Wentz nodded, resigned. It was true. 'OK, John.' He drew him inside the bubble, right past the security officer, closed the door. 'We think we may have had a friend picked up by the Russians. It might be better for Nina – Mrs Davenport – not to go see the doctor for a day or two.'

'The doctor? What – you mean her – but she's agreed not to . . .' He clammed up because he suddenly thought he might be giving something away, either about Nina or about what Nina had told him. Why had Nina been in with Wentz for so *long* on Sunday? I was so sure that I knew what that interview was all about, didn't want to embarrass her. On the way home, Nina had volunteered, They just asked me all the same old questions all over again, urged me to try to forget about it. John had a dazed sense that he was fighting with Wentz for jurisdiction over his wife, darkened by a kind of uxorious indignation, jealousy even, and there was something blacker, something unnerving, which he really couldn't identify but which was scaring the hell out of him. It had to do with the watchful, savage Soviet machine, the grey, monumental, faceless bureaucracy backed by hidden monstrosity, which he knew he had exposed her to but which he had thought he could protect her from. And the word 'doctor' absurdly panicked him. He couldn't associate it with medicine or health; it tapped into some nightmare fantasy all his own, about mechanized destruction, human slavery, war factories, part Hollywood depictions of totalitarianism, part fearful real knowledge.

Wentz's reply sounded impossibly cosy and sane, almost condescending. 'Look, don't worry. It doesn't make it unsafe for your wife. At least not any more unsafe than it already was. She's just pursuing cultural activities for us. Trust me, John.'

Davenport wanted to trust Wentz; what other choice did he have? But he equivocated. 'Even if I trusted you, would I trust the Soviets? What exactly is my wife doing? Who the hell is this friend?'

'The friend is – is military. It's entirely unrelated. We haven't seen him for a while, and we haven't been able to contact him. We're concerned about him. But there have been no repercussions; it's just that we – don't want any. That's all.'

'So the friend is Russian? A Russian – agent? A spy?'

Wentz smiled, almost laughed, spoke with placating benevolence. 'John, what's needed right now is a dignified way for Khrushchev to get himself out of this mess he's made in Cuba. The president knows that. We have to avoid panic and overreaction. Avoid any incidents that could be embarrassing, or be viewed as provocative. That's why I wanted to stop your wife, that's all. No big deal.'

'I still don't see what this has to do with Nina.'

John thought Wentz looked uncomfortable, passing it off, 'I guess she may have met this guy – at Spaso, for instance. A lot of people did.'

Their eyes locked. John knew exactly whom Wentz meant – Oleg Penkovsky.

'Opening night,' he breathed.

Finally Wentz conceded, 'We certainly didn't have her making any contact with him. I give you my word on that, John.' Then he tipped his head to one side dismissively. 'But Nina's got her own friends – old friends – hasn't she.' It was a statement, not a question.

And now Davenport started thinking again about – what was the doctor called? Felix Belov? Why did Wentz think Nina was going to see him at all? Ever again? Hadn't she promised not to?

'What kind of errand did you give Nina? What did you ask her to do?'

'Honestly.' Wentz chuckled. 'I haven't taught her trade craft, if that's what's bugging you. She's doing something she would do anyway, and she really doesn't need to know much about how it helps us. She's safer that way.'

Davenport felt terrified, but he tried not to show it. 'How could it be safe for my wife not to know what she's doing?' he demanded. 'Why wasn't I consulted about this?'

Wentz, deadpan, said, 'But you were consulted. You said you would be delighted for her to work with me. You said she needed something to do.'

'That's not what I mean,' John growled. 'You're using her – for something else – without telling her.'

'I wouldn't let yourself think of your wife as my dupe,' Wentz remarked drily. 'She knows exactly what she's up to; she's a subtle creature as you know. I told you what the French advise – why *don't* you give her some scope?'

John received this as an insult; and yet, at the same time, he recognized that he had been telling himself exactly the same thing on Sunday morning when Nina went into the bubble with Wentz. He wanted to get away from Wentz, to collect his thoughts, to reflect on what was really going on here. He could sense a certain tension in Wentz, irritation. Neither of them spoke for a few seconds.

Then Davenport asked, 'Is my wife having an affair with this doctor guy?'

Wentz laughed, incredulous. 'How should I know?'

So Davenport challenged him personally. 'Or is she having an affair with you?'

'Oh, come on, John. Now you're just getting paranoid. I don't think your wife finds me attractive at all. I am surely not her type.'

'Are you really sleeping with that ballerina?'

'That's none of your goddamn business, my friend. Let me know as soon as you hear from your wife.' And Wentz walked out.

Nina felt afraid as she pushed open the door to his office, and when she saw Felix's face, blank, spooked, she realized that he was just as amazed to see her now as he had been six days ago. It must be true, she thought, that he had been visited by the KGB. And he assumed I would stay away.

Then, like a creature of stone coming to life, he began to move towards her, began to speak in a crisp professional voice, directing the situation boldly. 'I have the analysis. You definitely are pregnant, Nina.'

He suddenly broke out in a smile of pleasure as he made this announcement, and Nina had a wild impulse to smile back. A feeling of satisfaction burbled up inside her, a giggle, until she thought, What is he smiling about?

But she could feel it in her body, a kind of radiating excitement, a consciousness of a transforming state of affairs. She was intensely self-aware. Her hands turned over in her lap, thumbs up, palms towards herself, as if to touch her stomach, and she looked down, stopping them. What she thought was, My body is dense, opaque; she felt surprised not to be able to see inside it, a glass vessel.

By the time she looked up again, she felt embarrassed, wrong-footed by Felix's smile. He had tricked her into experiencing some other set of emotions than the ones she had intended to have. She clenched her teeth bitterly.

Felix watched her sympathetically, leaning back against his work table, and then he said, 'I'm sorry, Nina. I suppose I fell into remembering you as a – child. As you were when you came here originally. This – development – took me by surprise.' He tipped his head, quickly, in emphasis. 'And it has its own beauty. I've watched you grow; seen quite a lot happen to you. I used to be – fond – of you.'

It upset Nina, his admission. She knew it was true. And she knew how much she had once relied on it, needily at first, carelessly later. For a long time, Felix had simply stood by, aloof, gentle, reticent. She could remember that his presence had invariably felt like praise. It had encouraged her. She had trusted him entirely from the very first time she had seen him. It was as if he had said, Get on with your adolescence; I'm watching.

Once her ankle had begun to heal, she used to come to Felix with more intangible injuries: the failure of her parents' marriage; her father's extravagant convictions, his meaningless life, meaningless death; her mother's rage; the soul-shrivelling realization that ballet was to have been their means of escape and that she, Nina, had let her mother down, that she wasn't entitled to escape, didn't deserve it, was herself the cause of the misery and despair she lived with. Soon, when Felix had introduced her to Viktor – even more idealistic than her father, more gifted, more unbending – she had adopted the habit of confiding to Felix, and hiding from Viktor, the continuous dissatisfaction in her lovelorn heart, until they both knew that she was now injuring Felix, though they never said so aloud. Viktor had been like a piece of broken glass squeezed in their clasped hands, cutting them both until they bled. Finally, on the bleak, blue morning when Felix had come to tell her Viktor had been arrested, that they would not be setting off for the dacha after all, she had announced she was leaving Russia with her mother. There was no solace for that.

Now, as Felix sat across from her, familiar, strange, she squared up to these girlish cruelties. There was her victim, still ignoring the pain as he smiled upon her. And suddenly she felt as though she was committing the same crimes all over again and Felix was letting her, applauding her.

If he forgave her now, would she be absolved? And for what she was about to do – get rid of an unborn baby without telling the father? Uncanny, Nina thought, how Felix, with his smile, has laid claim to the baby. *His* baby because he approves of it, loves it. What she saw in Felix's eyes was not pleasure in what she was trying to do, but pleasure in what she was. He still loves me, she thought. And so he loves the fact that I am now expecting a child. This was intoxicating to Nina. She wanted more of this sensation of unstinted approval. But wanting more was utterly bewildering. It seemed for a moment as if it might be easier to follow Felix's inclination, to give way to the excitement, the sense of natural joy that did not want to be repressed. Why go against Felix, whom she so admired, so believed in? But after all, his inclination was not her own inclination.

She felt a blight steal over her, a blankness inside her head. Her heart kept beating somewhere else, reminding her that she was alive, that time was passing. It was like being in a room with no door, no windows, urgency building, and thinking, What do I –? How do I –?

'Why are you fighting this, Nina? It *is* a beautiful thing, a child. You never used to fear life, and you shouldn't fear it now. You should go towards it. Look to the future. Believe in it.'

Believe in the future? Do I? She didn't try to explain how she felt. It was too hard. If there were aspects of her situation that Felix might be better able than anyone else to understand, there were aspects genuinely outside his ken. And she recognized now a certain depravity in trying to draw upon Felix for her own strength. She kept still, silent. She would cope without his approval.

Felix became impatient. He had offered her something and she seemed to be rejecting it. 'You must do as you wish,' he said brusquely, lifting his glasses from the bridge of his nose and set-tling them again, higher. 'I've made arrangements for you through others. But you will hardly conceal this from anyone now. Everything is transparent; in my opinion, it's totally crazy, Nina.'

He picked up a slip of paper that was lying among his files and held it out. Nina stood up to take it; she kept her eyes on his hand. She couldn't look straight at him.

'See this woman,' Felix went on. 'I believe you can trust her. Take roubles, as many as you can lay your hands on. She risks arrest just as we all do. Afterwards, don't come back here, no matter what.'

'Yes,' Nina said contritely.

'I suppose you know that you will have to rest, at least for a day? You must find some excuse if you are to keep it from your husband.'

'I've thought of all that, I can promise you.'

Then they both stood there, the air heavy with the deliberate thwarting of love. With disappointment. And again it was Felix who gave Nina an opening.

'What is it, Nina?' His voice was tender, probing. 'You are so unsure? Don't do this if you are unsure.' He reached out as if for her hand, but she clutched the slip of paper closely to her, in both fists, and so he let his arm fall to his side.

Very softly and evenly she said, 'I want to know about Viktor.' And then she looked up, looked Felix in the eye, and saw the light drain from his face, the energy.

He sighed. 'Is that why you have come?'

'I haven't lied.' She felt the piece of glass rake and cut at whatever bond remained between them, a twist of agony in the old wound. But she had a new cause. It wasn't personal now. It wasn't for herself. How could she convey that? How could she make him see? Her voice went husky with inadequacy, with embarrassment. She tried to clear her throat, uselessly. 'I came to you for help about the baby – you've seen for yourself that the baby is real.'

Felix took a half-step away from her. 'Nina, don't do this to yourself, and don't do it to Viktor. When you went to the West, it was as if we had attended your funeral.'

There was a long silence. My funeral? She realized at this how completely she had failed to be able to imagine their experience. To them, she was among the missing. But then, she had been missing in heaven while Viktor was missing in hell.

All at once, she could feel the black desolation of six years before, her breath sucked away in lamentations, the wind howling, battering, as she lay on her bed in the endless twilight of the apartment in Maly Gnezdnikovsky Lane. Again and again through the night, she had crept down the weeping stairs, pushed through the dull, wet door, out into the dark. The archway was empty. Still empty. And as she had gone on waiting for him, certain, uncertain, tasting the grit of tears and snot and rage, her mother's frenzy had rippled towards her as if through deep water, muffled, incomprehensible, persistent. Her mother's different need, echoing, unanswered. They had exit visas. They must leave immediately. Forget about that man, he's done nothing but expose you to risks.

Nina gulped a little, reminding herself, Viktor didn't care the way I cared. But at the back of her throat she felt panic rising, a pulse of dread, Is that what I persuaded myself of afterwards? Is that what my mother persuaded me of? That he didn't care the way I cared? So I wouldn't ruin everything just at the moment Mother finally succeeded in orchestrating our escape? Her throat burned because she refused to sob.

At last she said, 'I'm not asking for myself, Felix.'

'Who sent you?' Suddenly Felix was urgent, electric with fear.

'A colleague of my husband.' And she found herself whispering, 'He wants to know where Viktor is. He wants to know what Viktor – *knows* – what he is trying for. He wants to help him – and you. People like you.'

'They've turned you into an agent?' Light moved through his eyes, the muscles in his face shifted, his forehead seemed to expand, as he puzzled it through – surprised, impressed, afraid.

Nina felt him look her up and down; again his eyes changed, darkening with intensity, furtive, sizing her up. Then he went around the work table to the bookcase along the wall and turned on a little radio there. It made her throat go dry.

When he came back towards her, picking up a stethoscope from the table, rubbing it to warm it and reaching with it towards her chest, she wondered how he would hear any heartbeat above the noise of the radio, through her thick clothes. But in fact her heart was pounding loud enough, and she realized, He isn't trying to hear; he's trying to speak.

Felix tilted his head down to her, as if he were listening to her chest, and spoke quickly into her ear. 'Vladimir Prison, maybe one hundred miles outside Moscow. He is about to be moved – it may alarm your friends – to the Serbsky Institute of Forensic Psychiatry, close by in Kropotkinsky Lane, off Prechistenka. Where the KGB sends people to be declared insane. If they are not insane, there are ways of making them insane. Then they can bury them in a Special Psychiatric Hospital. I know this. I am a doctor. My colleagues tell me of such things.

'If your friends really want to see Viktor, they should get him out. Viktor's father is unwell; I think Viktor doesn't know. He could soon be alone – without even leverage. He thinks of spending his life in prison or in the camps. If he is released, he will find a way to get back in; then he will protest – he will complain, he will write letters, he will try to make use of the law which has been forgotten by nearly everyone in Russia. But the authorities get tired of men like him. Last year they issued a new *Instruction on Urgent Hospitalization of the Socially Dangerous Mentally Ill*, which gives them bigger powers, the possibility for systematization, compulsory treatment.'

There was anger building in Felix's voice; Nina felt spit in her ear, could see his pulse throbbing along his neck, the blood blooming there like a bruise under his pale skin. The stethoscope hurt against her breastbone.

'What are the criteria for mental illness?' he hissed. 'Lack of social adaptation! You can be committed if you have a mania for seeking justice, if you cannot accept official lies, if you are crazy enough to struggle regardless of arrest, of physical punishment. Because such things would stop normal people, would make them conform. And they have invented their own Soviet form of schizophrenia which develops especially slowly and which has no observable symptom apart from the constant impulse to protest against the system and perhaps to dissimulate.'

He paused, took his lips from her ear, looked down into her eyes with flashing pain, then afterwards spoke quietly, hardly more than mouthing the words, so that Nina felt herself cleaved open and slowly, solemnly filled with horror, with terrifying information. 'Madmen can't be tried, Nina. They can only be shut away, controlled with punitive measures. Denied books, fresh air, exercise. Beaten when necessary, or wrapped inside a wet bed sheet that shrinks around them as it dries, cracks their bones until they scream. Madmen have no recourse to the law. Why should they need it?

'For schizophrenia a psychiatrist can prescribe, for instance, Sulfazine injections, which cause fever, intense pain, leave sores that last for months. They give this even though nobody knows whether it cures schizophrenia. Or there is Haloperidol to calm the patient and make him obey rules. Never mind that it also gives the patient rashes on the skin, keeps him awake, anxious, makes him shake, makes his muscles harden so there is no position in which he can find comfort, neither sitting still nor moving about, perhaps even brings on convulsions.'

Slowly Felix tapped the stethoscope against his hand, stared down at it, the instrument of any doctor, and Nina sensed the disgust he felt at the difference between what a doctor could do, what he would do.

'A madman's sentence has no length,' he went on. 'Perhaps he will be cured of his madness, perhaps he will repent, perhaps he will die. Viktor is strong. Can he outwit such practices? He is well aware of them, you know, because Viktor's own father was involved with a committee to investigate and reform them. This was assembled at the insistence of one Sergei Pisarev, an old party member and a camp survivor, after he himself was released from the Leningrad Psychiatric Prison Hospital. It was not so long after Stalin's death, 1955 and 1956, at the time when things appeared to be changing for the better. Just at the time you left Russia, in fact. But that committee was broken up; one of its members, Professor Alexandrovsky, was murdered; all the paperwork –' Felix paused, waved his stethoscope at his mountains of files '– disappeared. All the evidence of blame. Maybe that's why Viktor was picked up in the beginning, to control his father; maybe that's why he is still held. In any case, my dear,' he reached a hand towards Nina's face, as if to touch her cheek, paused, drew the hand back, fingered his own pale thin lips instead, 'Viktor has no intention of avoiding this – punishment. On the contrary, he looks upon it as his destiny. But so grave a challenge? Go and tell *that* to your bosses. Put that in your Western newspapers; tell your government to object.'

Nina was sickened, silenced. She couldn't respond. She felt the familiar nausea again woozing through her gut, feared she would retch, choked on the swelling of her throat, the disgust.

At last she managed to ask, 'How could they?'

'How could they,' Felix assented.

She said it again. 'No. How could they – I mean – how could they get him out?' But she thought as she said it that Felix must not have meant that they could really get Viktor out. Of course it was impossible to get Viktor out. Felix had only been railing against the barbarous Soviet state, against the uselessness of foreign powers, against the stubbornness of Viktor's own determination to spend his life fighting this inconceivable, man-crushing battle.

Felix stood very still, leaned close to her; his breath rushed against her neck, hot, loud. She heard him swallow.

Then in a voice whose urgency frightened her, he said, 'While he is in transit. Possibly an accident. An ambulance van travels tomorrow from Yaroslavsky Station.'

He spun on his heel and went to his work table, lifted a stack of brown files, opened them one after another, leafing through and taking a page from this one, a page from that one, until he had collected about ten sheets. They were grubby, wispy and crumpled, as if they had been discarded and then rehabilitated from the rubbish, all different colours, white, light brown, yellow, grey. He held them out to Nina. 'Perhaps you will find a way to publish these in the West. In case Viktor refuses – well it's certain – he will refuse to go.'

Nina felt she couldn't catch her breath; her ears were ringing with the rush of blood to her head. She reached out for the papers, felt them like heat against her fingers, glanced down at them. Right away, she recognized the handwriting, square, hurried, insistent, even in wobbly pencil. He wrote as if his meaning were already known, as if the notation were only incidental, dashed off to stand for the poem that hung vivid, indelible in the mind. It filled her with awe, with excitement, to see his writing here. Viktor *must* be alive, she thought. She realized she hadn't entirely believed it before.

She began to wilt down onto the floor as it came over her, and she felt Felix grip her hard by both arms, to hold her up. He gave her a little shake, pressed his cheek against hers, kissed her three times, left, right, left, then looked her fiercely in the eyes.

'Go now,' he said. 'Go carefully.'

October 24. In the downstairs dining room at the Hotel Ukraina, Balanchine quickly despatched his spartan lunch, then sat over his empty plate. He had his elbows on the table and his hands folded under his chin as he perched forward, thinking. The light from the uncurtained upper half of the huge plate-glass window struck his face full-on, blanching all his features except his dark, flickering bird's eyes which darted around the bright, high-ceilinged room, resting on this dancer, that dancer, Allegra Kent, Edward Villella, Arthur Mitchell, Danny, Patrice.

Nina was sitting beside Alice at Balanchine's table. When Balanchine's eyes fell for an instant on Alice, on herself, Nina felt his restless energy, his subtle, compelling discernment as if he were taking possession of her, making her part of his intention.

It's overwhelming once he sees you, Nina thought, like an insistent lover. And she felt as if he could see right inside her, see her pregnancy, how it disabled her, how she feared it. She wanted to jump up and tell him that she was getting rid of the baby, that she wouldn't let him down. She knew this was absurd even as she thought it.

But already he had realized who she was, not one of his dancers at all; he half-inclined his head in acknowledgement, then continued to look over his resources until the ballet master approached his chair. They exchanged a few words, quick, absolute. Then Balanchine stood up abruptly.

He walked around to Alice, bent down to her from the waist, and whispered, 'When we go to observe class at Bolshoi, bring practice clothes. In just a small bag. Better yet, wear them underneath your street clothes. Perhaps you will join in. No one is to know, my dear.'

Alice nodded, silent.

He turned to Nina, still bending gallantly, flashed a smile. 'They've been filming my company class day upon day, for "future study"! What's wrong with now? Why not study *now* what we do? Work with me *now*?' And rolling his eyes towards one of the official guides sitting nearby, he added acerbically, 'You know, I feel as though even my clothes are bugged!'

Then he stood up, moved away on his silent cat feet, spoke quietly to a few of the other dancers, and left the room.

At the American Embassy that day, some people didn't arrive until after lunch; others had never left the night before. Through the small hours, they had stooped like rangy midwives urging round upon round of messages from the labouring machines, feeding others in. Now Washington was just waking up again, and Ambassador Kohler was reviewing the latest information with a handful of his staff.

They sat inside the bubble over a spill of telegrams marked Priority, Confidential, Secret, Elite – Eyes Only, American Embassy, Moscow.

As several hands fished through the pile, Davenport, sitting on the edge of a desk with his arms linked across his chest, tried to summarize what the messages told them about the world from which they were so strangely closeted. It was one thing to follow explicit instructions from Washington, deliver letters, proclamations, but they couldn't help wanting to understand what was happening, what might be happening, to themselves. And they had to give out bulletins, advice.

'Navy and air force have started low-level air reconnaissance over Cuba, and so the Soviets are suddenly trying to camouflage everything,' Davenport droned quietly. 'But even so, there are new U-2 shots showing that the missile silos are going up faster and faster all the time; they're building nuclear storage facilities and also nuclear bunkers for their own troops to shelter in. You knew Castro was on Cuban TV last night? An hour and a half. Put his military on full mobilization, highest alert.'

The ambassador grunted. Around the table, heads hung low, tired, concentrating.

'Evidently, he denied the presence there of any offensive weapons, but in the same speech sounded off that Cuba is entitled to acquire whatever weapons she wants and that anyone daring to inspect what they have better come ready to fight.'

The ambassador interrupted, clearing his throat, addressing the little group. 'The official quarantine proclamation which the president signed last night has already technically gone into effect. Yes?' He glanced at Davenport; Davenport didn't move. He just lifted his eyebrows, waiting for the ambassador to continue. 'The Organization of American States has met and agreed to support it, and the point is that the quarantine will be enforced by our military from 1400 Greenwich time today, October 24. So – 5 p.m. for us?'

The first secretary spoke up, hollow-eyed, quizzical. 'When I delivered that quarantine order to the Foreign Ministry at six o'clock this morning, I spotted one guy already working away at his desk in a gas mask. I swear the thing was left over from World War II.'

Wentz laughed out loud. 'He may as well have been wearing a Halloween costume, for all the good that'll do him. Maybe they were trying to make an impression – scare you a little?'

'But, you know, they welcomed me as if I were a guest at a party. Asked after my family. Whether we're happy here.'

'The atmosphere seems pretty damned uncertain,' said Wentz, 'pretty confused.'

'Well,' observed the ambassador, 'Moscow put Warsaw Pact forces on alert yesterday. And Premier Khrushchev spent this morning with William Knox, the Westinghouse Electric president, making damn sure Knox understood that Khrushchev would sink our vessels if we tried to stop any of his ships crossing the blockade. If that's not back channel, what is?' He looked around as if for a laugh; only Wentz gave him a thin-lipped smile.

Kohler took a big breath. 'So —' he let the breath out, 'the US military has now gone to DEFCON 2. Everyone will be counting down the miles today as these Russian ships approach that blockade. Five hundred miles from Cuba. Obviously, our forces are going to be all over that line. Ships, airplanes, subs. If the Russian ships don't stop and make clear what they're carrying, we're going to see shots fired. That's it, my friends. The brink of nuclear war.' He paused, red-faced, gazed around at them. 'Now — we wait.'

In the heavy silence which followed, the naval attaché leaning over the Teletype machine startled everyone by saying out loud with sudden intensity, 'Sir, we're getting word that the Russian ships approaching the line have been receiving heavily increased radio communication. Urgent coded messages. And the messages aren't going out from Odessa any more; they're going direct from Moscow. They could be battle instructions. Washington doesn't know; we don't know. And naval intelligence says the ships approaching the line are now being joined by Russian submarines.'

They all sat up, hearts sprinting, pores flushing, tightening. The unstudied announcement made their doom seem intimate, as if they were now in the time of its action, here in this very room, not cut off, not waiting at all.

When he heard the guards coming for him, Viktor wondered if he had lost count of the days. Wednesday October 17 to Wednesday October 24; it was more than five, less than ten. There were his marks scratched on the wall; he counted them again, stroking each frail line with the broad, filth-caked tip of his finger. Then he thought that, of course, they must be able to guess that by now he had made the wrenching, impossible adjustment to endure the ten days. So this was just another attack on his self-reliance, his sense of order, his effort to study and to understand his enemy.

He held his tin bowl up to his chin, tipping it back, trying to glug it down. But he was too slow. There were still the tiny fish bones, a little broth, when the bowl was knocked from his hand. He stood up, and in the same movement, managed to slip the remainder of his hard brown half-loaf into his pocket before his arms were shoved into the coarse canvas sleeves of a stiff white garment. He thought, This feels all wrong. These sleeves are far too long; I can find no end to them. But, ah-ha, it's a straitjacket. I'll never reach my bread now, he thought, as his arms were yanked forward, interlaced across one another, hard around behind him, bound. And he saw the advantage they got by their trickery; he had been dallying over his meal, trying to make it last as long as possible. So it was sacrificed. Diabolical.

Take an interest in this, he told himself. Forget the food. What are they up to? What will come next?

What came next was a blindfold. And then, to his genuine surprise and enormous interest, Viktor was marched along endless passageways, not to his cell but to the prison yard. A motor was idling there; he could hear it, smell the exhilarating fumes. He was bundled up some shaky steps into a van, pushed backwards into a tiny cell box inside, too low to stand, too narrow to sit, and he heard the big steel prison gates sliding back, the wince-making rasp of the metal.

For a while, he tried to guess where he was going.

In fact, it wasn't hard because the van didn't travel far before he was made to get out and lumber, hogtied, up into a train. The destination must be Moscow, he thought. They wouldn't ship me to a camp in a straitjacket. It's too much work for them.

The sense of possibility distressed him. His mind floated up, like a balloon filled with gas, with hope. From on high, the view was unlimited. Who was aware, just now, of his relocation? He thought of his father, of Felix, just for a moment. And then he began to try to weigh down his mind, to ballast it, pull it back to where he actually was.

He had a lot more room in the train than in the van, but he had nothing to lean against, no way to keep himself upright on the hard wooden shelf where he had been left. The train picked up speed, swayed, racketed, and he was slammed around the empty box car as if by invisible hooligans, until he wedged himself flat on the floor against one wall that he struck and pressed his hips against it with the puny might of both his half-bent legs, his back and neck twisted to the side. And so he lay, his very spine clicking and jolting along the rusted rails, once in a while dislodged by a whomping explosion of air when another train passed in the opposite direction.

Mind and body both uncloistered, rolling about, he thought, in mock freedom, and both at risk of injury. Have a care. He thought of Sochi, on the Black Sea, the excited summer train journeys there with his mother, how the heat closed in on them in the carriage as they drew nearer, the sudden moist scent as they climbed down blinking, stretching, at twilight – oleander, cedar, sweet gum, eucalyptus. On holidays like that, we felt entirely free, skipping stones over the lapping depths of the water, climbing in the vine-rampant forest beneath the snow-capped mountains. I was curious, in the gardens, about palm trees, the arid, scaly incline of their trunks, and about the dense, thumping fall of peaches, pomegranates, quince. Grapes with their misted lustre, I could pull from the arbour while I stood on the grass, one at a time, and suck their sweetness as I pressed them with my tongue, burst them with my teeth.

He had felt it was not really work to her, the beck and call of the dachas, but simply who she was – the sure, still hand on the brow, the confident fingers on the pulse, her watch held up, counting. Outside, the humid air moved softly. In Sochi, I never noticed when she had come or gone because there she seemed omnipresent. It was all pleasure. And we would continue with the same questions, my juvenile investigations; I was altogether unaware

216

of invalids, sick children. Perhaps she worried about death, their deaths. It didn't touch me. Freedom comes from within. Of course she had to teach me that. Mother Russia teaches that. But what did my own mother really mean? It's true and it's not true at all. This idea also keeps people in chains. With these thoughts, Viktor refreshed the bottomless reservoir of his rage, the vision of his businesslike, white-coated mother attending her torturers, healing them, healing their children.

His discomfort increased as the journey grew longer. He wriggled his fingers which pricked from the tight binding. He shifted the pressure of his weight from one leg to the other until eventually both cramped. His forearms grew numb; his biceps burned and ached; his shoulders were bruised by the beating he had taken from the walls. And still the train plunged on.

They must be planning to haul me up in front of a medical tribunal, a psychiatrist. Why else the straitjacket? he conceded. Maybe a good thing, Viktor proposed to himself. Safer, better for my health. A hospital, an asylum. More food. But he knew it was false comfort. He could remember the disgust, the anger of his father on discovering what happened in such places. My father gathered the evidence, Viktor thought, which was too monstrous to be aired, and now, how perverse, how excruciatingly apt, that I will be the one to test its veracity. He felt a rare sensation, noxious, gritty, like a smell – of the unknown, the unforeseen, a whiff of fear.

In his mind's eye, he pressed no further towards his fate. He was travelling with his mother to Sochi, rocking southward in her efficient care, in her loving company.

Nina couldn't take her eyes off the youngest girls in their floppy white hairbows, rapt, wide-eyed, pale-faced. Their skinny stork legs trembled with ardour below their floating, short, white skirts, their silky, thin-strapped tops. *Plié, tendu, rond de jambe, grand battement, fondu.* Four in first, four in second, four, four, four.

217

Nothing has changed, Nina thought, since I stood at that barre. Does Elizaveta Pavlovna Gerdt make them face the barre through the whole first course, when they are longing to spring about on the floor, to jump, to turn, to dance?

And the little boys, barrel-torsoed, manly, in buttonless, open-necked white shirts that, inexplicably for the Soviet Moscow Choreographic School, recalled the sailor-suit of the long-dead Romanov Tsarevich Alexis. They look as if they might be preparing to dance for the Imperial Court, Nina thought.

Silently, efficiently, the children gave way to their seniors in plain black leotards, cream tights. It was as if they'd spun through adolescence between bars in the music. The tempo quickened; the combinations became more difficult, more striking. Twenty right hands draped the barre, twenty straight left legs swooped through the air, twenty sinuous backs arched down to the floor, fantastically low and fast, while the free arms floated up, up, like feathers, like down, on magic, invisible strings raised by snake charmers.

Balanchine looked on beside Elizaveta Pavlovna and once or twice spoke softly to her in Russian, but Nina couldn't hear what he said above the piano. She knew that Gerdt had been his favourite Maryinsky ballerina, even above Kschessinska. He had admired her ethereal lightness, her purity. Gerdt was the daughter of the greatest classical dancer ever on the Imperial stage, Pavel Gerdt, and the widow of Balanchine's teacher Samuil Konstantinovich Andrianov, dead of tuberculosis at thirty-three; later she married someone else. She was a bent old thing now. Did she seem to Balanchine another creature altogether? Nina wondered. Lashed to the floor as she was, flat-footed, heavy-ankled? Her voice was a girl's still, babbling, insistent, high-pitched.

When at last she released her class from the barre, yet a higher flight of dancers took up their places on the floor. Mature men and women all in black, the ballerinas with flounced practice skirts, toe shoes. Nina hadn't noticed them come in. They were already warmed up, with a gleam of sweat on their necks and brows and most of the men damp across the chest and in the small of the back; the familiar bitterness burned Nina's nose, the smell of their bodies, their rank practice clothes.

The pianist began to play the folk dances from Prokofiev's *The Stone Flower*, and the room instantly blurred with the enormity of synchronized movement. Nina fell back closer to the wall she was leaning against, reminding herself of the fabled size of the Bolshoi stage that these dancers were trained to fill. As she tried to stand up straight again, she felt as if the dancers were lurching down upon her from a great height, might crush her, and she saw that they held their bodies inclined on a diagonal all the time, so that it seemed as if they must move, right away, all at once, or fall on their faces.

Balanchine had risen to his toes, was leaning towards the dancers, with the same dangerous posture, the posture of inexorable, necessary movement. No one could stand like that, ready, inclined, Nina thought, and not launch full-out into the space before them. She felt the risk and the thrill of it, the controlled energy, waiting. Her feet stirred, as if with an excited memory, her spine unfurled towards the nape of her neck, her chin went up, shoulders back.

She saw Balanchine lift one arm, elbow softly bent, open palm upwards, and speak again to Gerdt. His head was bowed as if with humility. Gerdt fluttered and flushed, then swiftly buried her smile, turned back, poker-faced, oblivious, to her class, while Balanchine looked towards his own dancers, putting his hands together as if he might clap, but making no sound. Yet they knew. He nodded, smiled.

Nina imagined he might have said to Gerdt, It will give them great benefit to have your instruction. And then, all innocence, to his dancers, something like, Have you brought clothes? Shoes? Join the class if you like.

Alice had already taken off her baby-blue mohair cardigan; she rubbed her thin white shoulders and upper arms. The room was hot with effort, with physical possibility. As the American dancers hurriedly disrobed in full view, they seemed for a few moments awkward, exposed; but when they took up their positions, their noble postures, on the floor, they were, clearly enough, dancers, like the others.

Nina couldn't help feeling that she, too, was a ballerina in disguise. She longed to join the class. She felt her soul lean towards the music. She had often danced in this very room.

Just then at sea north-east of Cuba, the Soviet freighters *Kimovsk*, with its seven-foot hatches, and about forty miles behind, *Gagarin*, with its vaguely announced cargo of technical materials, were closing on the quarantine line. Their massive, implacable hulls rode heavily through the grey-green swell. Between them, thirty miles clear, a Soviet submarine slid through the depths like a big slow-moving bullet, plainly discernible to US naval sonar.

Aboard the towering US aircraft carrier *Essex,* a prickle of fear, of coming insult was building, as the enemy ships bore on towards the imaginary line. Every man from the captain downward brooded on his orders – received, given – like a mantra, like a prayer. Prepare to intercept, use horns, flares. A small depth charge to signal the sub to surface and identify itself. Use sonar signals, but don't rely on them in case the Russians can't understand.

The *Essex* carried anti-submarine-equipped Sikorsky helicopters whose task was to harass, damage, drive off the sub so the cargo ships could be safely intercepted. As if the sub were just an eel, the captain thought. He pictured an eel, startled, in flight. But the sub was no timid wild creature, and, while the captain deliberately permitted the sub to draw closer, it offered an almost intolerable menace to his floating acres of runway stacked with snub-nosed attack jets, to his fuel tanks, his electronic circuit boards, his mess halls teeming with skilled and steadfast youth.

In the wide surrounding solitude of radio silence, the captain cooled himself, thinking, There are any number of miles still, any number of steps, between us and real trouble. It ran through the back of his mind again, If the ship doesn't stop, fire a shot over her bows; if she still doesn't stop, a shot over her stern. Last of all a shot to disable her propeller. Call for her crew on deck so they can't get hurt. Then a boarding party. At each stage, use the minimum amount of force.

And all the time, he was wondering, What could be aboard those ships? Armed men? How many? How tough? Are they guarding weaponry they will fight to the death to conceal? Or an innocent cargo, farming equipment, fertilizer, medicine, baby food? Will they defy us on principle, regardless of what lies below their decks? Are they offering themselves as provocation, inviting a firefight, so they can tell the world we burned up a cargo of wheat, shot nurses? One thing he was certain of, that no captain of any ship wants to be boarded by a hostile crew.

Helicopters, dwarfed by the scale of the *Essex* and the ocean panorama, hung staunch overhead, their blades whipping through the skies like the arms *en haut* of a ballerina in *pirouette*. Scattered on the brimming waters, in the chop and the wind, US Navy destroyers and cruisers stood by. Once in a while, a US surveillance plane fizzed across the wind-scraped horizon, and US submarines, riding surfaced, vulnerable, threw thin white spray from their grey, mysterious flanks.

Viktor was asleep, rigid with half-conscious effort, when the train finally stopped. They had to lift him like a log, drag him off, bouncing against the stairs, and he nearly collapsed when his feet hit the platform, both knees buckling. But the guards held him, hefted him upright, commanded him to stand up and walk, as if he somehow was refusing on purpose, or simply hadn't realized what was expected of him. They loosened the straitjacket when they took him to the toilet, and they gave him a drink of water, but the momentary relief made the pain seem greater when they bound him again, pushed him into the back of another van, another half-man-size transport cell where his great limbs had to telescope impossibly, muscles cracking like snapped kindling.

As the light faded around him, Viktor tried hard to think about trees, about leaves in their millions. He reminded himself that he had as much time as he liked before he arrived at the little dacha, before he returned to his poem, unfinished, on the desk. It helped him to bear the pain in his straitjacketed arms, to ignore the intense aggravation of his blindfold, tight at the nose and the temples, suffocating. What did it matter when he reached his destination? He could drive on for ever.

Sometimes he thought he could hear talking in the front of the van, the driver and the guard. But their voices hardly penetrated his thoughts. Then he smelled cigarette smoke, the intoxicating cloud from newly lit Russian tobacco. It triggered a craving that caught him unprepared. He worked on the craving like this: he pictured in his father's car his own newly opened pack of cigarettes, Kazbecks, on the shiny dashboard. He imagined that he had just finished one, his first from the pack. He had plenty left. He mustn't smoke them all at once. It was indulgent and bad for his chest. He'd wait. He'd have the next one at the dacha. So he began to look forward to lighting his next cigarette on the porch, smoking it there in the dark with a girl he loved, before they went inside. She'd have a cigarette, too, he decided, lit from the same rich-sour sulphurous match.

The tendons rolled along Viktor's jaw line. His lips worked backwards and forwards over his teeth, without spit. He stared at his pack of cigarettes. Not yet. Soon.

Suddenly, the van swerved from its course, tyres screaming. Viktor was thrown sideways, one cheek and shoulder hitting hard against the side of his transport cell, his bound arms useless to save him. There was an aroma of blood in his nose, but no trickle, nothing flowing. Nowadays he could easily tell when he'd been struck too hard. He knew he was dazed, bewildered, OK.

Nearby, he heard cursing, a motorcycle revving again and again, as if it could get no traction, and in the distance, police sirens blaring.

I just want the blindfold off, he thought. He couldn't help wanting to see where he was. Even after years in prison, with his strict self-taught diffidence, his determination to abide in the flow of events, he was intensely agitated now by the feeling that he was trapped inside a crashed vehicle, that it might start to burn. He wanted out. The accident made him uncontrollably want out. He was breathing fast with excitement, with outrage, impatience, he wanted his freedom in the instinctive, physical way a trapped creature wants to wriggle out of a hole, out of a corner, out of a cul-de-sac. His image for freedom, his black dot, his full stop, blew apart inside him; liberation, chaos, death to his captors – he couldn't stop himself wanting them all.

He worked at his blindfold with his head against the side of the van, and, in a few minutes, he pushed it askew so that he could see. What he saw was a dim, small space, his arms wrapped across his stomach in the white canvas straitjacket, his dirty blue prison trousers. The sirens had come near, stopped; he could see a pulsing glow of red in the wired gap at the top of his cell.

He realized that the van hadn't turned over at all. And now he heard voices, smelled more tobacco. The passenger door opened, and the van shifted with the weight of bodies getting out, getting in. Then the engine started, the van backed, turned, set off.

Nina was amazed by the overt competition breaking out in Elizaveta Pavlovna Gerdt's class. Elizaveta Pavlovna did nothing to stop it. In fact, although there were many more of her own Russian dancers in the class than there were Americans, she fell into a pattern of asking for a combination now from a Russian, now from an American, now from a Russian, now from an American, as if to egg them on.

I suppose it's a form of courtesy, taking turns, Nina thought.

The combinations were becoming more complex, the dancers

on both sides seemed to be taking them faster and faster, and they were adding sauce of their own, at every opportunity, doubling the *rond de jambes* called for, adding one more *fouetté*, two more *pirouettes*. The women were just as macho as the men. There were outbursts of applause.

Nina began to feel that despite the extreme refinement of their cosmopolitan ballet vocabulary, the dancers were engaged in a primitive folk tradition, grouped around the age-old tribal fire like gypsies and hurling themselves with primordial energy at ever more devilish, ever more daring, more ingenious, more risky feats, leaping higher and higher like flames against the night.

Balanchine looked on in silence, expressionless. As she studied his quiet face, Nina considered his Georgian background, how his father had collected and recorded folk music. It had been Balanchine's own idea, she thought, for his dancers to come to this demonstration class ready to dance. There's no way he didn't foresee exactly what would happen. He wanted to kick his heels in the air. To show them off! What a chance he's taking. Of course he knows how good his dancers are, but they're so – outnumbered was what Nina settled on, as if dancers could take strength from numbers like an army. And they have to perform tonight. She looked at her watch. God, less than two hours. She wondered if she should remind someone of the time. When will they eat? When will they *rest*?

Despite the din, Nina was sure she heard Elizaveta Pavlovna ask Balanchine, in Russian, 'Would you like to teach mine something of yours?'

And Balanchine, pressing his lips together so that Nina thought he might be restraining a smile, replied, 'If you will teach mine something of yours.'

'I have nothing of my own,' said Elizaveta Pavlovna with a shrug which implied that it was of no consequence, that surely he knew. Then she gestured grandly, imperiously, for him to go ahead, as if whatever he now taught was hers anyway.

Nina persuaded herself that if Balanchine loved and admired Elizaveta Pavlovna and the husband who had once been his own teacher, then perhaps he now wished to honour them by demonstrating what he had been able to add to the great tradition they had passed on to him. Perhaps it was not a simple wish to show off, so much as a wish to bring the past forward into the present, the present where he lived, now, and in which he professed he always worked.

With a soft clap of his hands, he called for demonstrators. Some of the Bolshoi dancers looked around, coolly glancing over their shoulders, eyes down, then lined up behind his own, ready to copy. They all seemed to grow taller, flexing their muscles, on their mettle. How fast could they learn a new combination? What would he show them?

Balanchine spoke to the pianist, turned to the class, gently swayed onto his toes, his body coiling with energy. 'Aaand one,' he said.

The contest began anew. Nina began to feel anxious as well as excited. The conflict was fraught with pride, with ambition. When eventually the dancers were sailing in pairs, boy, girl, through a series of high, flat split *jetés*, she could not stop herself from thinking about the day she had fallen. Landing from a split *jeté*, the right foot turning over, the ligaments exploding, the muscles tearing, the heap she had made on the floor, wind knocked out, tear-soaked, remorseful, as if somehow it had been her own fault, as if she had wanted it to happen. To break the tension, the unbearable pressure that had built up in her at that time.

What if somebody fell now? she thought. What if there's some kind of accident, some kind of injury? She pictured Balanchine's wife in her wheelchair, paralysed, trapped. But that was polio, Nina reminded herself. Still, she couldn't get the image out of her head.

And then she saw Masha, waiting to try Balanchine's rapid, unforgiving steps. Stockier, more sinewy than Nina recalled; her colourless hair bound severely close against her head, her blue eyes narrowed, glittering in concentration as she watched the pair of dancers before her cross the floor.

How could I have missed her, Nina wondered, all this time? And as the pair finished right in front of Nina, Masha's eyes, following them, met her own. Masha's eyebrows lifted almost imperceptibly; Nina was certain.

She's known all along that I was here, Nina realized.

A moment passed as they stared at one another, eyeball to eyeball, across the open floor.

Then it was Masha's turn. She balanced her lilting fingertips on her partner's manly, outstretched hand, and they stepped forward quickly, flew with ruthless grace through the fearful combination.

It knocked Nina's breath away. How many of them recognize me? Should I have greeted them right at the start?

At the American Embassy, the naval attaché was still hanging over the Teletype machine. Nobody had moved. Their muscles were rock hard with prolonged stillness, prolonged attention, intense anxiety.

And now the attaché read out in a monotone, a little hoarse, '*Gagarin* and *Kimovsk* are approaching the line. There's a Russian sub with them. But – now they've – stopped. Washington says – they've stopped dead in the water. And behind them, others. About – six – of the Russian ships have stopped.'

The ambassador flinched a little, then sat very still. 'Holy cow. They've stopped?'

'What the hell does that mean?' demanded Wentz.

They were all so surprised that they couldn't make sense of it.

Davenport was the first to get it. Very quietly, he said, 'That's easy. It means they're observing the quarantine.'

There were looks of incredulity all around the room, as if the Russians had pulled some outrageous stunt. Then everyone began to breathe again, just a little.

Absolutely nothing had happened.

At least not yet. Chairs creaked with shifting weight; Wentz took out a pack of Winstons, reached for his lighter.

'Now – wait – it's more than that,' said the naval attaché haltingly, as if he couldn't quite get his breath. Then in a burst of understanding, 'About a dozen Russian ships have stopped dead in the water and some are turning around. They are heading back towards Russia. There are other ships still underway, but they are hundreds of miles off. They won't reach the line until tomorrow or even later.'

'So that's what all the coded messages were about,' said Wentz, nodding a little. 'Go right up to the line, guys. Look them up and down, scare them good. But don't cross.' He exhaled a long smooth cloud of smoke. 'Our guys better not let off any firecrackers, because if we make a mistake now, with those ships showing us their tails, the end of the world will definitely be our own fault.'

Somebody laughed, a barking shout of exploded tension, then stifled it.

Davenport said thoughtfully, half to himself, half to the ambassador, 'The Soviets are certainly making a point here. They're accepting the quarantine, but they're not submitting to inspection – a subtle gesture. Subtle, but entirely clear.'

'Thank God,' the ambassador replied. 'It looks like a break in the game. Some kind of compromise.'

By the end of the class, Elizaveta Pavlovna Gerdt conceded, 'You have done so many more different kinds of things. Your dancers learn faster and dance faster. More makes possible more again.'

Balanchine simply nodded.

It was clear enough to everyone in the room that, on this engagement, the American dancers had 'won'. They got the most applause.

Nina thought to herself about the applause, Maybe it's just that there are so many more Russians in the room. Every single Russian clapped devotedly, open-heartedly.

The leaps from both companies went through the ceiling. Nobody fell; nobody was hurt. And the Americans made it to the Palace of Congresses in time for their performance.

They danced that night on adrenaline, on air. They were adored and applauded beyond anything they might previously have thought possible, and it lifted them above their exhaustion, feeding off the enthusiasm of six thousand ravished fans. The evening proved to be an unquellable riot of mutual appreciation.

Viktor arrived by night at a nineteenth-century yellow stucco building surrounded by lawns and by high concrete walls mounted with barbed wire. He had a good look at the inside of the steel gates, the soldiers guarding them, the watchtowers among the gaunt, leafless trees, before it was noticed that he had slipped free from his blindfold. It was tied on again, roughly, tightly.

He felt exhausted, beaten by the journey and by the unexpected effect on him of the accident. Already he was telling himself that the authorities had planned it in order to throw him off, to upset him, to remind him that he was at their mercy. That he could never master his situation. If the accident had been intended to kill him, surely he would be dead by now? They could have shot him at the scene, burned the vehicle and all it contained. Easy. In fact, it seemed impossible to understand why they hadn't.

He hadn't eaten for hours. He had no idea where he was. But he was determined to throw down his marker.

As he stood in a shadowed entryway, he could smell bleach, carbolic acid, floor polish; he heard keys rattle, papers rustle. He said in a jovial voice to his new jailers as he was handed over, 'Don't sweat it, boys. It's perfectly obvious to all of us that the accident was planned. But here I am, entirely unharmed. Don't let it worry you. I don't even need to be checked by a doctor. We'll be friends, eh?' And he smiled broadly, blindly.

Nobody answered him.

He was taken by both arms, hustled along a corridor. Into an elevator. The elevator door screeched and clanged; they swayed upwards sharply. He tried to calculate how high, two floors, more likely three. Nothing like the levels in Lubyanka. Then back along the corridor, through a bright doorway. Everything around him seemed white, brilliantly lit. He could feel the glare right through his blindfold. He was placed in a stiff-backed chair, still straitjacketed. He had not yet heard the voice of any of his new jailers. He was left alone, waiting.

October 25. Nina didn't see Wentz again until the next morning. He looked at her face as she came towards him through his office door and stood up so fast that he knocked his chair over backwards.

'Not here,' he said abruptly, grabbing both her arms, spinning her around and pushing her back out the door.

Inside the bubble, he knocked all the animation out of her.

'Don't come looking for me all the time, Nina. People will think something's up between us.'

She reddened at this, then said, 'Creep.'

'Even though your husband works here, it will get reported. There are Soviet eyes and ears all over the embassy.' His voice was matter-of-fact, not chastising; he knew that Nina knew what he was talking about.

'OK. OK. But you've got me in here in the zone of silence. So tell me. Where is he?'

'We think he's in the Serbsky Institute,' he said.

'You *think*?'

Wentz looked directly at her. Nina saw his pupils tremble and swell in the blue blankness of his eye. She reeled back a little, seeing something unmasked there that she hadn't seen before. She didn't know what it was, but she knew that for once he was being straight with her. It was frightening, a sensation like swimming deep underwater, putting your foot down for the bottom when you need to get back up quickly for air, and not finding the bottom there, pushing hard against only water, against bottom-lessness, realizing you have to swim up without the push-off, starved for breath.

Quietly, evenly, he said, 'We didn't try to – intervene, Nina. We couldn't. It would have been impossible, totally crazy.' There was no defensiveness and no consolation in his voice. He wasn't protecting her from anything.

After a long silence, she said, 'What if they – do something to him?'

'They will do something to him.'

'But – the drugs. Or – what if they use electric shock therapy, or lobotomize him for Christ's sake? You don't know what could happen. He won't be the same man. Felix said to get him out *now*.'

'I do know what could happen, Nina. I'm sure he knows, too. Unfortunately, we all know. But that doesn't mean we can do anything about it.'

He looked away, seemed to be shrugging, but with only a barely perceptible tilt of his chin, a lift of his thumbs.

This made Nina angry, this tiny gesture signalling his diffidence, his lack of urgent concern. It occurred to her that he had never intended to try to get Viktor out at all, that it had never really been possible. She leaped at him, hitting with both hands, furious, out of control.

He stood and took it for a few seconds, then he fought back a little, casually, striking upwards against her arms to make her blows glance off. His strength made Nina even angrier. It was like smacking at a stone wall. She could make no impression, and it hurt to go on hitting him. Finally, he caught both her arms in his hands. She wrestled him, outraged that this man for whom she had so little respect, who was not a worthy man in her judgement, should prevail so easily over her just because he was physically bigger, physically stronger. This was not a man she was prepared to give in to, but she felt stunned by the imperturbability of his strength. He was a massive immoveable block. There was nothing she could do. She struggled for a while, until the skin on her arms burned in his grip, then she gave up, tears in her eyes.

'*How* could you do this? You can't just leave him there! You have to do something!'

'Oh, Lord, Nina. Don't be silly. Naturally, you're upset. But that's just personal; that's how *you* feel. The whole goddamned planet was balanced on a pinhead yesterday; it wasn't the day to break a Jewish anti-Soviet poet out of prison. We had to let the opportunity go by. We've been ordered from on high not to do anything that could anger Khrushchev or embarrass him even a little. The president doesn't want him backed into a corner. You're a very smart woman; why am I explaining this to you? I don't want you down at Lubyanka. Nor the doctor either, frankly. I don't think you have any goddamn idea how valuable that doctor is to us.'

Nina was chastened by this remark; she calmed down a little. But she felt herself harden inside. She recognized the sensation: powerless rage. She used to live with it long-term; it had been the story of her father's life in Russia, her mother's life in Russia, her own. It had been the agony of her adolescence, not being able to get what you want, not even being allowed to express what you want. I thought I was done with this, she found herself thinking. It's why I gave Viktor up in the first place, to be set free from this feeling. She remembered her mother hounding her, insisting: America was where you could do something, complain, change things. Nina believed in that. But now here was her fellow American telling her to forget it. Forget speaking out against the powers that be; they do what they do. Forget about your personal point of view, your feelings. She found it almost unbearable, being dragged back to emotions so agitating, so wearing, so inescapable. She didn't think she had the strength to cope with it again, to bottle herself up, to accept things that were unacceptable, that were unjust. She already knew how it was going to eat at her gut in the night, how she was going to lie awake consumed with defiance, with passionate frustration, with the impossible task of burying the continual sense of moral emergency, of crisis.

Even as she fell silent, assumed an air of repose, Nina was already thinking, I will find a way to see Viktor. She hadn't taken the time yet to reflect on what she hoped for from seeing him, but she knew she couldn't let this be decided by others. She had to exercise her own will, as she had somehow failed to exercise it before. The feeling had to do with her precious sense of what it meant to be American. Or maybe it was her sense of what it meant to be an adult. She couldn't just quietly lie down and take it.

She kept her eyes on Wentz, backing away a half-step. She didn't say anything to him. She didn't try to excuse her frenzy. But he saw that she was collecting herself a little.

Wentz smiled. 'We've been thinking about it for a long time, Nina. If you were an intelligence professional, you'd know that the message you brought back from the doctor about the transfer to Serbsky wasn't entirely news to us. For one thing, we don't rely on information unless we can confirm it in two or three separate ways. You brought us a date, actually. We already knew Viktor Derzhavin was in for a very bad time.'

This statement made Nina angry in an entirely new way. It wasn't just Viktor who had been betrayed; she'd been taken for a fool personally. She felt insulted by Wentz's condescension, seething.

Wentz knew it right away. 'Don't get mad,' he said. 'It's a waste of everything.' He didn't smile; his tone was gentle, with no hint of a tease; there was something in it more like an apology. 'We go to a lot of trouble to set things up.' He leaned towards her, confiding, offering something to show his respect, to draw her back in. 'For instance, I know you're aware of the going over the Poles and Czechs gave to the scenery and costumes coming in from Austria. It took weeks and weeks to circulate the kind of rumours we thought would make them suspicious enough to spend all that time inspecting things. We know for sure that the Soviets were embarrassed by it, and so they won't let anything like that happen again on the way out. That's one place we can hide a man, you see. In one of those costume trunks, which will go out by air instead of by truck because they have to be rushed through to meet the announced schedule of the New York City Ballet at the other end. Maybe it could be Derzhavin. The tour still goes to Leningrad, Kiev, Tbilisi, Baku. We have a few more weeks. If I had burdened you with knowledge like that, it would certainly have made your visit to Felix Belov a lot more dangerous, and for all the risk you took, you might anyhow have ended up just accidentally informing him of what we were hoping he would tell us. Now you know, so watch yourself. You have a man's life in your hands. More than that.'

Nina was dumbfounded. 'Why the hell did you involve me in any of this? You don't need my help at all. Why couldn't you leave me alone?'

Wentz didn't really answer her question. 'I can understand that you feel used, Nina. You have been used. We Americans like to be in charge of our own destiny. But you really *are* serving a greater good. So dump your pride, because otherwise we risk that none of us will be in charge of any of our destinies – and maybe there won't be anything to be in charge of anyway.' He rolled his eyes with exaggerated cynicism, then said with resolve, 'On the other hand, now that the Cuban naval blockade has gone into effect and the Russians have sort of accepted it, Washington will calm down. We may get another chance with Derzhavin. In the meantime, we'll maybe try to get a message to him.'

Now Nina saw her way, and she pounced on it. 'I want to take the message.'

Wentz snorted, half laughing. 'I don't think so.'

She rushed on, pressing him with practical points. 'I speak Russian well enough to go as a Russian. An old girlfriend or a fan from the poetry readings. I'll bribe my way into the hospital. I know how to do it. There'll be cleaners there, cooks.'

'That's not how we would do it. It's way too dangerous. No disguise would hold up. Plus, your husband would probably run down the road and tell the Russians what we were up to just to spite me for putting you out there.' Wentz turned away, fishing for a cigarette.

Nina waited for him to look up, and as he clicked at his lighter, inhaling, she started in again, 'Listen to me,' her face was white with tension, 'right now, during this Cuban crisis, is probably the safest time. Don't you think Washington has that wrong? People have their minds on other things. Who's going to be worrying about one prison inmate?'

'Nope. Forget it, Nina. First of all, the Russian man-in-the-street hardly knows there's a problem. Troops have had their leave cancelled; that's about it. There's been no announcement in this country that there's anything going on with nuclear missiles. It's all about the threat to Cuba, thousands of miles away. US imperialism on the high seas, and the possibility that we'll invade, try to overthrow Castro. Maybe there's a little gossip out of the Defence Ministry or the Foreign Ministry, but I can assure you that nobody here *is* distracted. Unless you told him, your doctor friend doesn't know much about Cuba either. Derzhavin certainly doesn't know.'

'Gossip in this country works harder than you think,' Nina said. 'Anyone in charge of anything knows about the missiles. And they've told everyone they know. The Moscow grapevine is as good as any newspaper, and it's free, that kind of hardworking gossip. Maybe this was the perfect day to go after Viktor – when everybody was busy talking.'

But they were off at a tangent now, arguing for the sake of arguing. She didn't try to emphasize to Wentz how painful all of this was for her personally; it never occurred to her that Wentz was capable of understanding. And she felt glad that she had never told him about the little sheaf of Viktor's poems that she was carrying, even now, in her handbag.

Later that day, the American ambassador gave a lunch for the New York City Ballet at Spaso House. It was a lavish affair, dancers, diplomats, embassy staff seated at small round tables in the big, low-ceilinged ballroom that had been added to the Russian palace as a single-storey wing. Afternoon light flooded in from the garden through the glass panes of the French doors on three sides of the room. The tables were draped in heavy, freshly ironed white cloths, piled high at the centres with autumn fruits and flowers, ornately laid with glistening china and crystal. The room was lively with chatter, with grace, with enthusiasm; the Moscow visit had proved worthy of celebration.

Towards the end of the second course, as the plates were being cleared, and the desserts prepared on trolleys at one end of the room, the deputy chief of mission stood up and tapped his wine-glass with a spoon. Heads swivelled expectantly, glasses were quickly refilled by those who could reach a bottle, talk faded to a burble.

But there was no toast. The deputy chief of mission scowled and curtly announced, 'I'm afraid I must ask you all to leave the building quickly now. Thank you for coming. It's been a privilege to have you here.'

That was all.

Hardly anyone in the room understood him. At his own table, there were expostulations of surprise, and then, when he himself didn't sit down again, one or two of the men stood up, brushing off the lapels of their jackets, looking around, eyebrows raised, puzzled. The deputy chief of mission pressed a hand against the nearest back, pushing it towards the door, nodding vigorously, gathering his neighbours.

After a little silence, everyone started talking at once, with a sudden roar of inquiry. Chairs scraped and rattled.

'What's happening now?' Danny craned across towards John Davenport, holding one hand over his lavender silk tie to keep it inside his suit, away from the cream sauce pooling beside his uneaten piece of veal.

Davenport was already out of his chair, circling the table. He stopped, leaned down, reassuring, friendly, but oddly alert. 'It's nothing to worry about. There's going to be a student demonstration at two thirty. The schools have been let go early. Just make your way out.' He gestured airily towards the state dining room, the grand salon visible on the other side, and began to walk away.

Danny, ever-polite, stood up uncertainly. 'A demonstration of what?' he called to John. 'What do you mean? Is this to do with the Cuban thing? I thought the Russians didn't know about it? Why would they demonstrate?'

John stopped, contained his impatience. 'No. Well, yes. It's just – anti-American. You could say they're protesting the naval blockade, although I doubt the protesters themselves even know about that. They are reminding us in general that they don't like the way we're handling things.' Then he said again, 'It's nothing to worry about. It's a propaganda exercise. Not so much for us as for the press.'

John made a beeline for Nina who was sitting wanly with Alice and Patrice, watching in disbelief as the lunch broke up. He took her arm and said intently, under his breath, 'The thing is just to get everyone clear of the area as quickly as possible. Go with them. Walk if you have to, or take a bus.'

She didn't answer; she didn't move.

'Nina?'

When at last she looked up at him, she seemed empty-eyed, sad. He wanted to comfort her, but there wasn't time, and he thought there wasn't really any need. Why was she so upset just now, about a student demonstration, when he needed to rely on her sharpness, her efficiency? Why wasn't she getting it, why wasn't she reacting?

He thought with chagrin that he had hardly seen her these last few days. They had each been continually on the move, following separate schedules. Whenever he had thought about her, worried about her, he had been somewhere else and he hadn't even known where she physically was; by the time he was with her again, for some brief little respite, the worry had already abated, or had been replaced by something newer, more urgent. He couldn't explain all this now, in a roomful of bewildered people. Still, he whispered, pulling her up from her chair, 'Don't be frightened Nina, this is just a local disturbance. Really. It's all staged. I'll see you at home. I'll call you.'

He gave her arm a little shake, to reassure her, or, as he thought afterwards, because she seemed almost to be sleepwalking and he wanted to wake her.

Vaguely she nodded, turned back to Alice, to Patrice, to the others at her table, urging them to come. Danny was the one who had snapped to, caught up with them, hung on John's words, helped Nina to rouse them, move them.

There were nervous questions on all sides as the half-fed group stuttered and flowed out through the grand salon, down the red-carpeted stairs to the coat room, snatched outer layers off hangers. It was like a fire drill, hushed, self-consciously unpanicky.

They walked up the driveway to the little square, Spasopeskovskaya, the wine clearing from their heads in the fresh air.

'I don't see the buses,' Nina said to Alice loudly, 'and the drivers weren't expecting us to come out for another hour at least. Let's walk this way.' She turned sharply at the entrance.

In the square, in front of the Russian Orthodox Church called Tserkov' Spasa na Peskakh, Church of the Salvation on the Sands, students were milling around. They were young, Nina thought, teenagers. That's about the age I was when I used to go hear Viktor read. But she couldn't recognize anything else about these students. Where was the burning intensity? Where was the defiance, the animal look that hollowed the eyes and cheeks when you were ready for the KGB, to dare them to take you? These students looked strangely unconcerned, as if they were waiting for the start of something perfectly ordinary, something that had nothing to do with them, a school assembly or a trip. They were talking among themselves, engaging in a bit of tomfoolery, giggles, rough play.

Nina scurried along the pavement, dancers fanning out behind her in bunches, heads lowered, clutching their coats around them. Yellow leaves floated down, slid around their feet. The gold dome on the church softly gleamed.

As they approached the stop for the public bus, she looked around again at the loose-knit crowd of demonstrators, gormless kids, moving closer to Spaso House. She could see that, inside, the shutters had been closed over all the windows; it looked deserted, as if the occupants had shut it up and gone away on holiday. And that's just how it will look if nuclear war comes and everyone flees or hides in the cellars, Nina thought.

She felt shut out, excluded. The sudden end to the lunch, the abrupt withdrawal of hospitality, the hurried departure, made her feel unwanted. John is inside with all the American staff, and I'm out in the street with the Russians. She swung around and took in the American dancers; but she didn't feel close to any of them. She felt alone, empty, cold, inexplicably sorrowful, as if Spaso House itself were fortified against her. And she thought it was something she had done wrong, some destiny she had chosen, or that anyway she couldn't escape.

There was nothing to do but wait at the bus stop. Mechanically, the students began to chant; at first it was just two or three of them, in time with the agitators; gradually the others took it up, so that the volume built and resonated around the small square, guttural, patterned. The crowd seemed to take shape now; it was becoming a mob, energized, lit.

'What are they saying?' Danny asked her. 'What are they shouting about?'

'Down with US bourgeois imperialism,' Nina said flatly; she didn't try to explain. Somehow it seemed depressing to try. Then they started again with, 'Hands off Cuba.'

Patrice was alarmed. 'Don't you think we should get away from here? Obviously they noticed where we came from.'

Then the rocks started. At first, Nina caught with the corner

239

of her eye just a quick, sharp movement in the depth of the mob, the curve of an arm, physical, sudden. But there was no sound until someone managed to hit a window. The smash of glass. Then more rocks, well-aimed, raining onto the same broken window, splintering the wooden shutter inside. Rocks thumped now on the stucco all around it.

The shouting grew rougher, irregular and sharp, as the mob became excited, fed off the damage. Nina heard more glass breaking, high up on the walls, little popping explosions, and when she looked up to the second and third storey, she saw enormous blue-black splatters spreading downwards, like creeping Rorschach blots.

'They're throwing bottles of ink,' she said, as she suddenly re-alized what she was seeing.

'Bottles of ink?' The dancers craned to see, shuffling closer.

'Because it leaves the stain, the mark of the disapproval of hard-working Soviet youth,' Nina said.

She felt the eyes on her of one of the official guides, hot, watchful; this wasn't something he would be explaining, Nina thought, or certainly not explaining away. The dancers were sup-posed to bear witness; they were supposed to be frightened and take away the impression that Russia wouldn't stand for it, being bossed around, the impression that Russians would protest, maybe even fight, man, woman, and child.

She watched another ink pot smash against the wall, and she looked at the students. She knew only too well how hard they worked in school, those children; how everything depended on it, not just advancement, but food, warmth, personal safety. Whatever learning or self-improvement they might have aspired to is just smudged and splotched by this kind of thing, she thought, by organized violence. And she decided that the ink pot missiles were like state propaganda in a bottle, an empty threat the stu-dents were being made to hurl at an enemy they didn't under-stand. Do they really want to stick up for poor, defenceless Cuba?

Those missiles don't mean anything to anyone; they just spoil the façade of Spaso House.

Danny, standing slack-shouldered, nonplussed, said, 'Forgive my vanity, but when the audience shouted for us last night, that's not how it sounded. Sure, those kids are throwing things, but, on the other hand, it seems like they would stop if you asked them to. The audience last night – nothing could stop them.' He lifted his hands in emphasis.

Nina said, 'They're only doing it because they've been told to. There are some of the leaders – there,' and she pointed with just a flick of her finger, holding her hand low, near her hip. 'You see those two who look so much older? How lean their faces are? The faint shadow where they've shaved, because they're old enough to need to? And they do it professionally. It's a job you can have – to be an agitator. In the Party, it's an honour. To be chosen to get people into whatever froth the Party requires. And look, over there, you see those photographers?' She flicked her finger again.

Two men in dark, unbuttoned overcoats, box cameras slung around their necks, unwieldy flash attachments, were idling against the railings on the far side of the square. One dropped a cigarette on the pavement, crushed it out with his shoe.

'Oh, yes,' said Danny slowly, with dawning understanding.

'Recognize anyone from the airport?' Nina asked. Her voice was sarcastic, bitter.

'I hate this, I hate this!' Patrice was grabbing their arms, pulling them backwards, her hair flying. 'What if they start throwing rocks at us? Can we please get out of here before something awful happens!'

'It's OK, Patrice. Really. The bus is coming now.' Nina pointed towards it. Danny put an arm around Patrice's shoulders, pulled her around in front of him towards the bus.

But Nina felt it, too, the suppressed hysteria, the cataclysmic anxiety which would loose itself at any trigger, in any direction, unreasonably, because it was there all the time just underneath the surface of consciousness and of activity, the feeling that something awful was about to happen, the end of the world, a broken bottle of ink. The fear was like an illness, Nina thought, like a form of madness barely kept at bay. And she wondered how long she could keep control of herself; she was standing by the door of the bus, calmly motioning everyone to board, looking sane, she assumed, properly dressed, looking like a guide, a leader, but she felt waves of bewildered pain washing around inside her, overlaid by the thinnest membrane of calm, something easily ruptured. She felt that she wasn't sure who she was, which side she was on. Who are all these dancers, these Americans? Why are they listening to me, relying on me? She thought to herself, Am I going to pieces? Will I scream? Take flight? And she remembered how she had run from Viktor after the agents burst into the lecture hall to break up his reading. How she had told herself, There's nothing to be afraid of. Nothing to run from. And yet her feet had moved underneath her, her unreliable, uncontrollable, betraying feet.

Inside Spaso House, the afternoon light was doused by the shutters, the atmosphere melancholy like a child's bedroom at nap time, play suspended. In the ballroom, the ornaments were being dismantled, the cloths whipped away and bundled down to the laundry, the unvarnished round tables exposed as charmless and cheap. Safe in the basement, the kitchen help was working full out in the warren of small, white-tiled rooms. They stored flower arrangements and fruit back in the cooler, washed fork upon fork, knife upon knife in scalding water, dried and polished the crystal with threadless white rags, elbows knocking against one another, water sloshing over the floors and steam hanging around their heads as they chatted and hustled. Cupboard doors creaked open, slammed shut; the shelves moaned with reloading as the stacks of dishes were rattled into place, still hot, still sudsy. The kitchen help, a mixture of Russians and Chinese, couldn't hear the chanting, the thuds of rocks and bottles on the masonry. They were mightily content with their employment.

Upstairs, the atmosphere was more brittle. About a dozen members of the embassy staff, most of the political section, had stayed behind. They uniformly adopted a pose of nonchalance. It was forced, thin. They felt trapped; they had nothing to occupy themselves with; they weren't about to admit it. The crisis was wearing on everyone.

'Don't try to get out now,' the ambassador remarked to nobody in particular. 'This won't last long.' He had said it a few times, in a friendly voice, as if advising them to wait for the rain to stop. 'Have a seat. Make yourselves comfortable.'

They were gathered in the warmly upholstered, heavily curtained downstairs library, collapsed on the sofa, in a few chairs, on the arms of chairs. Every now and again, someone would get up, pace around the room in a fit of restlessness, and the ambassador would again invite them to stay, to relax.

He took a couple of decks of cards from the drawer of a side table, held them out silently. Nobody moved. So he snapped the cards down on the coffee table, then took up his place leaning against his desk in the window bay, arms akimbo, surveying his team. Suddenly his cat appeared from the sill behind the window curtains, padded across the desk, shoved and rubbed against the back of his suit; the ambassador picked up the cat, buried his fingertips deep in the white fur of its neck, ruffling, stroking, until the cat began to purr.

Conversations started and stopped again after a sentence or two. 'Too bad about the lunch.'

'I'll say.'

'The veal was pretty good.'

'M-hmm.'

Then after a silence, the ambassador asked, 'What about the president's reply to Mr Khrushchev's last communication? We're dealing with that?'

Davenport looked up and nodded, locking eyes with him.

'We got that out before lunch,' Davenport said. 'Less than a page, repeating things that have already been said; it didn't take us long. You know I wouldn't have come otherwise, sir.' And he gave a little smile. 'Mr Khrushchev should have it by now.'

He realized that Wentz was watching him, warning him to shut up, to watch his back. Davenport knew perfectly well that the CIA sweep could never reliably clear all the Russian bugs in Spaso House. Even if Mr Khrushchev already had President Kennedy's latest message, there were other Russians who didn't have it, and who might like to know what the message said. It was never simply a case of us against them; each side had many factions, all listening, all collecting information, all struggling for an increment of power. Davenport felt Wentz's look as part of the infighting that went on all the time between the State Department and the CIA, between the diplomats and the spies. Davenport was a diplomat by inclination and by choice; he liked conversation in which a common aim was being strived for without trickery, without opacity; he liked plentiful and direct explanation, fair play, candour, trust; he liked his job right out in the open. But on the other hand, he was a man of insight, of intuition; he couldn't help sensing what was going on under the surface of a look, a gesture, a word. He knew that he had gifts which might have suited a spy.

Right now, Wentz's attention confused him, not because he couldn't understand it, but because he couldn't decide what to do about it. He wasn't able to discount it, and it made him uneasy. He wanted to disapprove of Wentz, to have nothing to do with him, but he kept feeling that he liked Wentz. Or at least that Wentz was the man in the room of whose intellect, whose breadth of knowledge, whose powerful calm, he was constantly aware. And he knew that Wentz could read people, too. The feeling of sympathy with Wentz wouldn't go away. It was as if Davenport recognized Wentz as being somehow like himself – or himself as being somehow like Wentz. Wentz was wary of him; they might easily become rivals; yet Wentz seemed to be available to be on his side.

Maybe Wentz has been trying to make a friend of me, Davenport admitted to himself as they sat on in the library. And I just haven't let him because I know that I'm a little attracted to his way of doing things. I might find it hard to resist getting drawn in. Nina's too fragile for me to try that; her circumstances are too complicated, too weird. It wouldn't be fair to her.

Wentz picked up a deck of cards and started to deal himself a hand of solitaire, slouching over the coffee table. The room fell into deep silence, broken only by the slow, rich ticking of the grandfather clock and the occasional slap of the cards. Outside, the noise of the crowd and the pelting hits against the walls gradually died away as the twilight drew on.

At last the door opened and the housekeeper announced that there were two cars here to take everyone to the embassy. They perked up their ears, bestirred themselves, stretched, ambled out into the hall.

Davenport made a point of sitting beside Wentz, four of them crushed into the back seat of the big Ford. They were silent on the short ride to the embassy, but he felt easy against the warmth of Wentz's leg, against his elbow, the bulge of his shoulder; he didn't resist their pressure.

Wentz knew it; he knew Davenport was perfectly content to be involved with him.

Wentz and Davenport were only a minute behind, but inside the bubble a political officer was already updating the ambassador in an earnest undertone.

The ambassador nodded, listening, then swung around with papers in his hand, shaking them at the assembling group.

'How about this? There's just been a Soviet tanker across the quarantine line, the *Bucharest*. Evidently we hailed it, and they identified themselves and their cargo, but didn't stop. We're shadowing it, but it looks like we're not going to try to board it. A tanker obviously can't carry weapons and we haven't got petroleum, oil, and lubricants on the prohibited list. So the navy's still out there looking for the right ship to board, to establish this thing, this quarantine.'

There were quiet nods around the table.

'We still have absolutely no acknowledgement from the Russians that these missiles are even there,' continued the ambassador, pulling a chair back and sitting on the front edge of it with his knees bent back underneath him, thighs bouncing, fretful, 'and yet today, Washington again has new spy photos showing the missile silos nearing completion. Some of the damn things are going to be operational any time now. So this is crazy, this pretence.'

Clearly the ambassador was feeling fed up, as if he were dealing with an intractable child. He could make no sense of it.

'Adlai Stevenson will be speaking at the UN tonight and he is going to introduce intelligence photos of the missiles and missile sites in the General Assembly. It's going to embarrass the hell out of the Soviet delegation, since Ambassador Zorin continues to insist there are no missiles. Maybe, just maybe, Zorin still doesn't know himself that the missiles are there.'

This produced laughter all around the table. The ambassador looked dazzled by it. Then he indulged his family with a smile. 'I'm glad you all haven't lost your sense of humour. There's not a lot in this situation that's funny.'

His stern face returned. How could he relish the public humiliation of the country to which he held a mission he looked upon with solemnity and respect? He sighed. 'So now once again we wait for Mr Khrushchev's reply.'

The meeting broke up slowly. Nobody had anywhere to go.

Davenport was called to the phone, and he found himself yet again reassuring a dancer. 'No, don't leave the country. There's no reason to leave. The demonstration was a set-up. Watch the Soviet papers tomorrow, how they present it, and you can make up your own mind. You'll see exactly what I mean.' Then, as he put the phone down, he thought with chagrin, But of course the poor kids don't read Russian. He wondered where Nina was, what she had told them. Whether she could do more in that vein in the morning, be more reassuring. As Davenport started to dial home, Wentz came to his elbow with a tumbler of whisky.

'We all need one of these, I think.' Wentz lifted his own glass to Davenport then threw his drink back firmly, smacking his lips as it went down. So Davenport joined him.

Then Davenport sat down and put his feet up on the desk in front of him. It wasn't his desk, but it didn't matter. Wentz stood leaning back against it, swirling his empty glass in one hand, building up to proposing another drink.

Their colleagues were dispersing to other desks, other offices; lights were being switched on up and down the hallway. A type-writer started up nearby, a rattling chirp of effort.

Everyone was tired, nobody was quitting. Here they would sit, through the night. The atmosphere of vigil had gelled around them. The student demonstration had somehow sealed the effect. They were in this together, Americans, embattled.

Davenport and Wentz talked about nothing in particular, repeating their thoughts out loud to one another. What's this guy Khrushchev up to? When's he going to answer? What will he say next?

After a while, their faces sagged with tiredness, their suits rumpled, their shirts grew limp and sour. They shared half a pack of Winstons, though Davenport wasn't much of a smoker, switched from whisky to coffee, back to whisky, back to coffee.

At the Serbsky Institute, Viktor still sat alone on the chair in the middle of the big, brightly lit room. He felt certain someone was watching him, although he couldn't hear them or smell them. Once he had been given a drink of water from a thick-rimmed glass; once he had been taken to the toilet. He tried to remain alert to a presence, to foresee what was going to happen. But he was almost delirious from hunger, and his head was thick with sleep. His mouth grew slack; he moved his eyelids inside the blindfold, trying to keep his eyes from closing. Then he slumped to one side, a drooping jerk, bent-necked. He dozed.

He didn't know how much time had passed when he felt fingers moving against the back of his neck, intermittent, fumbling pressure as the blindfold was untied. The touch of the fingertips delighted him. He realized the delight was in fact induced by the smell of food, the savour of sautéed meat. There before his eyes as the blindfold fell away was a small piece of, he thought, veal, on a white china plate, with pale brown sauce skimmed over it. Steam rose from the sauce. He could see translucent circles of melted yellow butter speckling the sauce like so many tiny eyes in a peacock's tail. And there were little, veined, white chunks of onion in the sauce, too.

'Sip the tea before you start on that,' advised a deep, gentle voice by his ear. Viktor's neck was so stiff he couldn't look around. The glass mug was raised to his lips. 'Careful. It's hot.'

Viktor contained himself. He allowed a dribble of tea to pass between his lips; it was potent, sweet, and it spread like a sensation of heaven over his tongue. He felt the muscles inside his nose, on the front of his face, lift and sigh with yielding, with relief, right up through his forehead, around to his temples. He rolled the tea about inside his mouth to make it his own before he swallowed it. And he chided himself, Eating out of their hands. The pain of the straitjacket now became worse as his body began to come to.

'I'd better help you stand up.' Viktor felt the soft pressure of a hand under his shoulder blades. 'Take a little more tea first.'

Two more slow swallows. It was easy not to look at the meat, but it was impossible not to smell it.

'Now, stand up as slowly as you like. Get your balance.' One hand lifted him from the centre of his back, the other grasped his wrists where they were crossed and tied over his belly. The pain in his arms was indescribable; he held back a groan. Maybe he grimaced. He wasn't sure.

'I'm so sorry. Of course your arms are terribly uncomfortable, aren't they?' The voice was warm with concern.

But he was up now. And the straitjacket was being untied. Viktor held his breath, kept his biceps pulled in close to his body, let his arms go free of the sleeves only slowly. He felt as if his bones were cracking. As he lifted his hands to rub his upper arms, he felt another pair of hands there first.

'Once the blood flows more freely, the pain will go,' and he was subjected to a gentle, probing massage. He hung his head, waiting.

'Just walk around the room once or twice, then come sit and eat this meal before it's cold.' The voice was friendly, casual, somehow familiar.

Viktor did as he was told. Slowly, thoughtfully, he strolled around the very outside edge of the room, eyes down.

Then as he made his way back to the chair, he studied his companion. It was natural to do so at this point; the man was in front of him, directly in his path.

Viktor knew right away he was a doctor – slim, tall, perhaps forty-five or fifty, neatly groomed, distinctly handsome, with a fine-angled plane of bone glinting, pale-skinned, under his clear grey, intelligent eyes. His waving hair was almost pure white. Underneath his knee-length white coat, he wore grey wool trousers with a sharp crease down the front, a crisp white shirt, a thin blue-black tie with the dim sheen of silk.

Viktor thought, This is the sort of man I once knew. Dressed like my own father. Eyes the colour of my own. And what am I to him? A prisoner, a patient, a file. Someone to subdue.

Like the most solicitous of hosts, the doctor said, 'Do sit down. Please start right away.'

He held out cutlery, a fork, a knife.

Now he gives me weapons, thought Viktor, and shows he has no fear.

Viktor sat down and ate. He needed food. He needed much more food than this tiny piece of veal. And it was the most exquisite piece of veal he could ever remember eating.

It's not just that I'm ravenous, he thought to himself, they must have a special chef for this. Worthy of the Kremlin, of the finest home, the finest restaurant. This is all part of it, part of their method.

He cleaned his plate as well as he could without picking it up and licking it. He longed to pull yesterday's bread from his pocket to wipe up the last traces of sauce; he needed every calory, the vitamins, the fats. But he decided not to. He didn't ask for more food, nor was he offered any. The meal was over.

'So, Viktor Nikolaievich Derzhavin, let's get to your case.'

'My case?'

Carefully, the doctor put Viktor's plate on the floor underneath the little table that had been brought in for the meal. He laid a file on the table in its place, then pulled up another chair just like Viktor's and sat across from him, close.

Without looking up, he opened the file and announced quietly, 'It is my task to arrive at the correct diagnosis so that we may begin the treatment. Tell me, Viktor Nikolaievich,' he continued amiably, 'have you always felt this need in yourself to object to everything?' He looked up, catching Viktor's eye.

Viktor sat still, held the doctor's eye, a tumult inside him, burning in his chest, in his face. He said nothing. He knew that any comment at all would imply some acceptance of the question. He knew it would be noted down, turned against him. Already he recognized that it was the same as when they tried to force you to confess in Lubyanka to things you hadn't done, meetings with foreigners, acts of espionage. Although there, in Lubyanka, they thought nothing of beating it out of you. Here, Viktor thought, they are more sly, more subtle. But of course, he saw the pattern; it was the same beginning – sleep deprivation, hunger, thirst. Now, though, something new.

Stillness, quietness, kindness. And they are prepared to wait, Viktor admonished himself, maybe for ever.

'Your obsession with protesting against the State. It's an interesting pattern,' the doctor said in a tone of slight interest. 'We see this sometimes. The compulsion to write – I have here some letters. You have feelings of persecution, Viktor Nikolaievich. You feel uniquely singled out?' He held up a piece of yellow paper, much folded, written over in pencil. 'This is yours, isn't it? This handwriting?' And he laid it on the little table under Viktor's eyes.

There was more silence. Viktor pretended to study the letter. He felt glad to see that his letter had made it out of the prison. That proved something. That proved that the guards didn't throw them out, light their cigarettes with them, wipe their arses on them.

The doctor took out a pen and removed the cap. It was a fountain pen, shining, substantial, foreign-made. He held it poised above a blank sheet of paper in his folder.

Viktor thought, He has the will and the means, but this man cannot write. He cannot write anything true, anything accurate. He has sold his soul to the devil. He is more a victim of the State than I am.

At last Viktor said, 'This is my handwriting on this piece of paper.' What was the point in denying the obvious? That could only mark him as unreasonable, uncommunicative, antisocial. But he said nothing more.

The doctor put the nib of his pen to the page, tilted the nib forward a fraction in preparation. The paper drew the ink downwards, and Viktor could see the black liquid bridge the space, a filament of connection joining paper and pen. Then the doctor pulled the nib away. A tiny fleck of black leaped onto the page by itself. A dot. A round black dot. Nothing more. Viktor stared at the dot of ink. It seemed to be there of its own choosing, free. He liked thinking about the black dot, and so he let himself.

The doctor laid the pen down, put his hands in his lap, looked at Viktor as if assessing him. The pen rolled away from the piece of paper and from the file towards the edge of the table. Viktor reached for it, picked it up just as it was about to fall to the floor. He held it out.

'That's a fine pen, doctor. Take care with it.'

'Thank you, Viktor Nikolaievich.' But he didn't reach out to receive it from Viktor's hand.

Viktor hesitated. If he were to put the pen down on the table, it would probably roll off again.

'Would you like to have the pen, Viktor Nikolaievich? You like to write.'

After another long silence, Viktor leaned forward, held the pen closer to the doctor. 'I couldn't accept such a generous gift, however much I might cherish it,' he said evenly. 'A man in my position cannot afford to be seen to value goods manufactured abroad. But I am grateful for the gesture, doctor. Anyway, I have no ink. Such a pen would soon feel the lack of it. Indeed, such a pen is of no use at all without a bottle of ink.'

'I understand.' And now the doctor accepted the pen from Viktor's outstretched hand. He replaced the cap, put it into his inside jacket pocket, sat back from the folder.

All this made Viktor feel that whatever his professional intentions, there remained in the doctor the shadow of a man who, even half consciously, could not help wanting Viktor's respect. Viktor felt oddly certain that the doctor hadn't offered the pen as a way of savouring and supplementing his power over Viktor, to show he could give or withhold the pen, make Viktor beg; he had offered it for the simple reasons that he had stated, that he saw Viktor had no pen and would like one to write with. It was even possible that he had offered it to Viktor because he liked him. And that everything happening between them was spontaneous, unplanned, authentic.

But Viktor also knew that none of these things would ever become clear, and that they would darken and make more difficult any moments he passed in the doctor's presence. For Viktor recognized that the doctor had long since allowed to collapse inside himself any distinctions between his private motives and the motives of the State; the doctor was no longer able to act in accordance with any ideals or principles he might once personally have held. He was the sort of man who was in the habit of using his good impulses along with his bad impulses to serve whatever needed serving; he couldn't separate them, he didn't bother to try. However odd the circumstances, he might like to make a friend of Viktor for all the right reasons: mutual respect and interest, attraction even, between cultivated men of high intelligence, broad reading. But obviously the doctor would never be able to keep such a friendship safe, uncorrupted. It wouldn't even seem important to such a man to try.

Now the doctor said, 'I will see to it that you are allowed a pencil, paper. Perhaps some books to read?'

Viktor inclined his head. 'That's very kind.'

'We must get on with your clinical diagnosis.'

Viktor said nothing.

'I can't keep you here for ever.' This came in a tone of self-justification. It felt like a warning to Viktor; it chilled him.

'Of course not.'

'Well, then. Perhaps we'll start tomorrow?'

Again, Viktor did not reply, and he sensed it could only be exasperation which finally drove the doctor to say, 'The Leningrad Psychiatric Prison Hospital is the obvious place for you; you could spend a whole life there. It's filled with schizophrenics. Though, of course, not many of your variety, the slow-developing kind whose symptoms are imperceptible to many psychiatrists. Although they are perfectly clear to me.'

Then, as if to finish Viktor off, the doctor added in a contained, sociable voice, 'I was sorry to hear of your father's illness.' He gave a nod of respect. 'I know him of course. He's very fond of you.'

Viktor's heart flexed rage, then went cold, hard. He remained perfectly still. Such blows, he thought, carefully orchestrated, may not even be true. He allowed himself this hope.

After the doctor went out, two orderlies came in and took Viktor to the toilet again. They allowed him to wash and then walked him back to the same room. On the little table between the two chairs lay a thick tablet of paper, three new pencils, a stack of books in faded covers. Viktor couldn't make out the titles of the books; he leaned down to them eagerly. He was surprised when the orderlies suddenly tightened their grip, holding him back. Then he felt the hard jab of a needle in his right thigh; he couldn't help flinching in pain and in anger. He felt the hot poison spread over the leg, the limpness, the fizzing sensation in the muscles. The orderlies snapped him upright, shoved his arms into the straitjacket, even though he protested.

'Surely this isn't necessary?'

As they put the blindfold back over his eyes, Viktor thought of the paper and the pencils and the books. But he couldn't see them now. His leg began to throb. He felt overwhelmed in his limbs and in his thoughts, flooded.

They left him in the chair in the brilliant white room.

He thought he could hear birds somewhere, dawn coming at the windows. In prison, he had never heard birdsong. He trained his ears on it now, imagined the spreading light, a bed of leaves in the woods where he was going to lie down. Still he hungered for the paper and the pencils on the table, the books. He wondered again about the titles; had he already forgotten them? Or had he not yet read them? Surely not a narcotic, he thought, administered in the leg. What books had they given him? Leningrad? He wanted to make a journey. He couldn't think where.

October 26–October 27. Nikita Sergeyevich Khrushchev woke early on Friday. He'd had a good sleep, took only a small breakfast in the little house in the Lenin Hills estate, and went at his day with bounce, with gusto. Problems to solve, people to persuade, an air of crisis to make his blood keen. How now, America, he was thinking, as he strolled to his waiting car, kicking up a few leaves along the path to the gates on Vorobyev Highway, if the UN requires that you call off your quarantine? At the very least I'll get my promise that you won't invade Cuba! Then we shall see.

He swooped down across the Moscow River, the sputtering traffic peeling away on either side to let him pass, and barrelled in through the high gates of the Kremlin, benevolently touching the brim of his mighty Homburg as he nodded at the ramrod Kremlin guards tensely ornamenting the walls and arches with their portable arms, their teal-blue, red-starred caps.

But the new intelligence from America was not at all what Khrushchev had expected. In his office, he sat over the file, trying to make sense of it.

Now the Americans were launching an invasion of Cuba? He was absolutely amazed.

He turned over one page, another; the pages fluttered in his hands as if of their own accord, slipped about like eels, slid to the floor. Did it matter what order he read them in? He fumbled them back into the grey-blue folder, tried to smooth them down, pressing them heavily, creasing them, in his impatience, in his bewilderment. How he hated papers and words. How he distrusted them. Action was what he liked, practicality, work.

According to this latest report, American journalists were already setting off to cover the invasion, and they were speaking of it freely enough to be overheard in Washington. US troops were massed in Florida, Georgia, Texas; hospitals were preparing to take in the wounded. The Soviet Embassy in Washington and the KGB there both confirmed it.

It must be true.

Had he fallen into a trap, tiptoeing around the quarantine? Before the eyes of the whole world? At the hands of a boy, this Kennedy, younger than his own son? Did Kennedy think he was so smart, so clever, so cultivated? Holding me in check, warning me, threatening me with a great show of force in the Atlantic, all the while intending to invade as soon as I showed any sign of compromising?

Khrushchev's blood boiled and raged. He sent for a stenographer. He would send Kennedy another message, a personal letter.

Then, while he waited, he was seized by uncertainty. Khrushchev was no good at waiting; he needed to move forward. He preferred not to reflect on things too much. Waiting even five minutes was, for him, a kind of torture.

He began to fidget and ferment, his thoughts churning: I can't fight this man; I don't know how. I can't do it. I can't blow up the whole world. I must stop this whole business now. I will plead with him, go down on my knees, beg. He has to understand, man to man. I will admit my faults, my mistakes. I will be honest with him. It's the Party way, to concede one's errors, to search one's soul. This I can do. Nobody's perfect. Why should anyone think I am better than the next man?

In torment, overwhelmed, Khrushchev even thought, for a childish instant, about God. He experienced a brief sensation of awe at the enormity of his circumstances, and he thought, not very clearly, not very hopefully, of his mother, who had taught him to pray. As a communist, Khrushchev had long since ceased to believe in God; nevertheless, he feared Him.

By the time the stenographer arrived, Khrushchev was pacing up and down the room, sweating profusely. It occurred to the stenographer that she had hardly seen him sit down for days; evidently, his emotion was too great. And the torrent of words that now began to rush from his broad, gap-toothed mouth seemed unstoppable. She wasn't even seated yet, hadn't opened her pad.

'I have participated in two wars,' he roared, one finger in the air, 'and know that war ends only when it has rolled through cities and villages, everywhere sowing death and destruction!'

She raced to keep up with him, her pen dashing across the page as he explained with vociferous awkwardness that the weapons in Cuba were not there for attacking the United States but only to defend Cuba.

'From what you have written me it is obvious that . . . we have different definitions for one type of military means or another . . . Let us take a simple cannon for instance. What kind of weapon is it – offensive or defensive?'

'. . . those who destroy are barbarians, people who have lost their sanity . . .

'. . . you can at any rate rest assured that we are of sound mind and understand perfectly well that if we attack you, you will respond in the same way. But you too will receive the same that you hurl at us . . .

'. . . we are sane people . . . we correctly understand and correctly evaluate the situation. Consequently, how can we permit the incorrect actions which you ascribe to us? Only lunatics or suicides, who themselves want to perish and to destroy the whole world before they die, could do this.'

She soon felt her fingers sting with cramp, her back burn in its long-held posture.

'We want . . . to compete peacefully . . . not by military means.'

Eyes down, she saw the thick, short legs as they stomped past in the baggy fawn trousers, the stout brown shoes.

At times, Khrushchev's voice became so insistent that she was distracted by its tone. She felt as if the American president might even be there in the room with them, as if Khrushchev were trying to persuade Kennedy not with words, but with the urgency of his delivery – shouting, imploring, heckling by turns. How was she to record that? The symbols couldn't hold such feeling.

Again and again he repeated that death, destruction and anarchy would result from nuclear war and must be avoided. Again and again he raged against the quarantine. 'Anyway,' he puffed, 'there is no point in attacking my ships now bound for Cuba. There are no weapons on those ships. All the weapons are already there!'

He reminded the American president of their meeting in Vienna when Kennedy had admitted that the American invasion at the Bay of Pigs had been a mistake. Russians, too, can make mistakes.

'Remember that we too have acknowledged mistakes committed during the history of our state,' Khrushchev intoned grandly. 'We not only acknowledged but sharply condemned them.'

In his excitement, he neglected to put forward any mistakes of his own; he bragged about the mistakes of others, of greater men, his predecessors. Their mistakes were more important, after all; besides it took a courageous man to point out a mistake made by Stalin.

So much for mistakes, thought Khrushchev. Bigger men than me have made mistakes. Big mistakes.

The stenographer looked up just for a moment, in fear and astonishment, at the short, fat man in his white Ukrainian peasant blouse tucked tightly into his trousers, the trousers belted high over his round belly, his jowly half-a-neck bursting from the collar, his thinning white hair cropped to mere prickles over his round, pink baby scalp. And she thought, He's afraid. Afraid of what? He's afraid of disaster. He's trying to avert disaster.

He gestured passionately with one arm, flinging the bell of his embroidered cuff through the air, and then he put his stubby fingers to his shiny, flesh-swamped face to wipe away tears.

Now Khrushchev reminded himself that the Americans had tried to overthrow the Soviet government during the revolution.

They can't bear our revolutionary regime! Cuba is so small, a poor, puny country; the great Soviet Union must protect the revolution in Cuba.

On he went with the letter in his complicated, confusing way. Loyal, committed, the stenographer made no attempt to understand him; she simply wrote down what he said.

'If assurances were given that the President of the United States would not participate in an attack on Cuba and the blockade would be lifted, then the question of the removal or the destruction of the missiles sited in Cuba would be an entirely different question . . .

'Armaments only bring disasters. When one accumulates them, this damages the economy, and if one puts them to use, then they destroy people on both sides. Consequently, only a madman can believe that armaments are the principal means in the life of society. No, they are an enforced loss of human energy, and, what is more, are for the destruction of man himself. If people do not show wisdom, then in the final analysis they will come to a clash, like blind moles, and then reciprocal extermination will begin.'

There, he thought with satisfaction, I've demonstrated that there is no economic argument in favour of using the missiles. He had struggled towards this conclusion as if through a swamp, a mist, almost sinking in the darkness and difficulty of it; the effort it cost him was so great as to make him feel that this moment of illumination was entirely his own, that he was the first man ever to realize that there is no economic benefit from war. Let the American president consider that!

All I want, he was thinking, is a fair bargain. I will not send any more weapons to Cuba, and I will take out my missiles, if he will agree to stop his blockade and not to invade. Not to invade!

He ran at his argument yet again, thinking now that he would illustrate it with an image, a picture from real life, which would make it even easier for Kennedy to understand him, which would make his thoughts as clear as clean water.

'If you have not lost your self-control and sensibly conceive what this might lead to, then, Mr President, we and you ought not to pull on the ends of the rope in which you have tied the knot of war, because the more the two of us pull, the tighter the knot will be tied. And a moment may come when that knot will be tied so tight that even he who has tied it will not have the strength to untie it, and then it will be necessary to cut that knot, and what that would mean is not for me to explain to you, because you yourself understand perfectly of what terrible forces our countries dispose.

'Consequently, if there is no intention to tighten that knot, and thereby to doom the world to the catastrophe of thermonuclear war, then let us not only relax the forces pulling on the ends of the rope, let us take measures to untie that knot. We are ready for this.'

When at last the stenographer moved to the typewriter, Khrushchev called for tea for them both. He didn't retire to a chair or leave the room to meet with the Presidium, but stood over her as she typed, studying her work.

'You aren't changing anything?' His voice was pettish as a boy's. He placed his trust in the woman, not in the words on the page.

Gently she assured him, 'It's as you have spoken it, unless I have made an error.'

'Uh,' he grunted in approval. And as he stared at the machine, her fingers whacking at the keys, the curled white page filling with the black code of language, he considered how what she was doing had the power to convey, as if by a kind of magic, his most ardent wish to be understood, to be accepted, to be in the right. He had always worked hard; he was willing to do anything. No one was helping him; he had no one to consult. No one he could trust.

And the urge now came over him to make his points again, more forcefully, to supply them with further energy, to bring them home more completely. No effort was too great.

The door opened behind them; immediately shut. He thought

he could hear voices in the hall, shuffling footsteps. He would have to break off, to chair the Presidium. His comrades were assembled, waiting, restless.

But he stood his ground. As the pages came from the typewriter, he took them one by one to his desk and laid them in a pile. After a while, he sat down in his chair and began to puzzle over them.

He opened his desk drawer and took out a fountain pen, unscrewing it slowly. Here and there he made a mark indicating a change. The ink in his pen was purple, as purple and as opaque as his wildly moody prose, which beseeched and bullied by turns.

When the last page was typed, and the stenographer stood up and pulled it from the machine, she resisted the urge to stretch. Inside her shoes, she lifted her toes and wriggled them; inside her dull grey suit she stretched her spine, settled her shoulders back invisibly.

She came and stood respectfully by Khrushchev's desk, laying the page near his hand. Immediately her eye fell on his alterations. 'Shall I retype those pages now, Comrade Chairman?'

He didn't answer. He reached for the last page, and she saw his head wag almost imperceptibly left and right as his eyes ran backwards and forwards over the words.

'No,' he pronounced at last. And he signed the letter with a firm careful signature: N. Khrushchev. 'I want you to send it directly to the American Embassy.'

She thought he seemed nervous, this demiurge, this untutored force of nature. It must be the meeting starting; there must be more important business coming, she told herself.

It didn't occur to her that the apex of Khrushchev's power had passed from him this morning, alone in this room, with her. He sensed it. He knew that he had hatched something which he could not control; just now, before the world, he had chosen to back down. He had put his signature to the letter, as if signing a confession, an *akt*, revealing his weakness, acknowledging his error.

Before long his colleagues would savage him, a year or two. When they came for him, he wouldn't even fight them. It was incredible that he had survived until now, risen so high. All five feet one inch of him. He was the only one of Stalin's close colleagues whom Stalin, at five feet six inches, had towered over. And Stalin had liked him.

But I will point out to them, Khrushchev thought, that by criticizing Stalin I have made it possible for them to criticize me. I will tell them, That's my contribution. I won't deny my own mistakes; bigger men than me have made mistakes.

'This didn't come in the Foreign Ministry car,' Davenport said, as he leaned across Kohler's desk and handed him the envelope late on Friday afternoon. 'It was a private car.'

It was twilight; they were both stale, dazed.

Kohler scissored open the envelope and the pages spewed out all over his desk. 'By God, it's a monster,' he said.

Davenport was already leafing through it. He came around the desk and stood next to Kohler's chair.

'It's nine – ten – eleven pages – geesh, even more.' There was a long silence as he scanned the text. 'And it's . . . Well, he admits the missiles are there. But . . . he . . . It's very detailed. Maybe conciliatory. It makes an offer to remove the missiles, if we call off the quarantine and promise not to invade Cuba . . . although it changes tone . . . or repeats . . . I don't think this came from the Presidium, actually, sir.'

'OK,' said Kohler, standing up. 'Let's take this in the bubble and divide it up and you'll all get to work on it at once.'

An entourage gathered around them as they hurried through the building, and Kohler was soon giving orders.

'There's only one copy of this thing, so pull up close and share. We'll start transmitting to Washington as soon as we have the first few pages translated.

'Get the nuances,' urged the ambassador softly, 'the folksiness in the language and so forth. The president needs to feel like he's in the room with Mr Khrushchev and like he speaks Russian himself. Fully inside the man's head. Everything's riding on these communications now. Everything.'

He paced alongside the big table, the envelope and its contents clutched in his left hand, laying each of the pages on a separate desk, a separate surface. His officers barrelled towards the paperwork on wheeled chairs, packing in side by side, lifting stools, whipping out sharp pencils. And then they all froze practically in mid-air, poised above the text like surgeons with scalpels ready to make a first incision.

For a few seconds, nothing happened. Silently, they read, looked for a way in, a thread of sense, a significant word. Until, now like students taking an exam, they bent as if with one motion closer over the pages, began to dab at their notebooks, and then to write in earnest, fast, pressing down hard. A pencil lead snapped and flew through the air, falling lightly nowhere in particular. The writer cursed, was handed another pencil. Concentration settled. Somebody reached for a dictionary. There was a question out loud about a verb tense, another about a Russian idiom. Then the silence broke up, shimmered, rattled, cohered, a mosaic of steady endeavour.

Davenport didn't feel surprised that Wentz had taken the seat next to him.

'Who do you think wrote this thing?' Wentz asked under his breath. 'It sure is a corker. Not just the mistakes. It hardly makes any sense.'

'I know.' Davenport squinted hard at the page in front of him, then wrote furiously for a few seconds.

Wentz peered over onto Davenport's piece of text. Then he reached into his shirt pocket and took out his Winstons. 'It's got to be raw Khrushchev,' he said, lighting his cigarette.

Davenport turned and looked at him, Wentz's smoke coming into his nostrils, clearing his head, and said, 'Which we are usually well shielded from.'

'It's just that if he's writing his own letters now, and not sending them through the Foreign Ministry, it means there could maybe be a split in the leadership – if his colleagues haven't even seen this?'

'And you want to know which group has its finger on the trigger?'

'Don't you?'

Wentz took another drag on his cigarette, leaned forward, propped it in the ashtray, and began to write in silence.

Then, head down, he said, 'The guy's definitely obsessed with the idea that we are about to invade Cuba.'

Davenport kept writing. The ambassador came up behind them and said, 'John, I want you to check everything over before it goes. Read it all out loud to me and then we'll cable it.'

'Yes, sir.'

'So why does he think we are about to invade Cuba?' Wentz mumbled, half to himself, half to Davenport. 'Is he just over-reacting? Or has he got some bum intelligence? Somebody who maybe thinks they are on to some top-secret plans?'

The room was gradually filling with cigarette smoke.

Davenport erased something with the pink tip of his pencil, wrote in something else, then tore the page from his pad and laid it on the table. Eventually he replied, 'I'd say he's backing down, really. But he's so full of anger and resentment, it's hard to tell. He realizes he's made a mistake, that's for sure. He didn't foresee having the missiles spotted before the elections in November, and I'd say he didn't expect such a quick, definite response from the White House. He's got no choice, but he's mad as hell. He's convinced he's being bullied and that he's sticking up for his underdog of a country.'

'Do you think he's stable?' Wentz asked.

'What do you mean, "stable"? His hold on power? Or his mental condition?'

Wentz laughed. 'Both. Of course both. You think he could be having some kind of a breakdown, emotionally?'

The ambassador, repeatedly circling the table like a worried dog, had come up behind them again and overheard this last remark.

'Jeez. What do you think, John?' he asked.

'Well, he's upset. I'll grant you that. But he's an excitable man. I don't really know how you tell about emotional breakdowns. I wouldn't say these are the rantings of a lunatic. Although . . . there's some repetition and a real lack of focus. On the other hand, what quality of debate can there be? I mean, who does he test out his scenarios on, his what-if-we-do-this-what-if-they-do-that? Obviously, he thinks open debate is too risky, and maybe he's even afraid he'll be humiliated. But in a situation like this, what's to gain from secrecy and paranoia? Nothing but more fear and a bad decision, I tell you.'

Wentz laughed bitterly and said, 'I make him the Caliban of the Soviet Union. He knows somebody's going to force him back down into his cave. It's just a question of when.'

'You certainly are a Special Cultural Officer,' said Davenport archly, 'Shakespeare no less.' He stood up, slapping Wentz lightly on the back. 'Let me see what you've written there, young fellow. I'll bet your translating is mighty fine, too.'

'Nowhere near finished yet. Go check someone else's work, teach.'

Davenport and Kohler began to sidle around the table, looking over shoulders, assessing the time.

About 2 a.m., when they were huddled around the Teletype machine, Wentz finally brought his paragraphs over. He dropped the pad on a high, grey-green metal stool beside them, and the stool trembled and fizzed with the thin sound of a snare drum.

'I'm going home to get some rest,' he said.

Slowly the others drifted away, too, or fell asleep on chairs, on office floors. They dozed fitfully, well into the next morning.

Davenport dreamed about Nina. He saw her walking about a block ahead of him along a busy street, maybe Gorky Street. She was wearing her old duffle coat, a colourless scarf tied over her head. She walked fast, darted across a side street through traffic, almost as if she were trying to lose him. Did she think he was a KGB tail, spying on her? Was it Nina at all? Or was it maybe a Russian woman who looked like Nina? Someone he didn't even know, who was afraid to be approached by a foreigner, to whom he offered only risk. Suddenly the clothes seemed to be anybody's clothes, nobody's clothes.

In his dream, he thought, What if Nina were a Russian woman? And he felt reluctance, tried to push away a pain this caused him, because, of course, Nina might have been Russian, living here still. She easily might have been. But there would be nothing I could do about that, he told himself, sleeping. It wouldn't be my business to care. I wouldn't even know her.

And all the other Russian women? What about them? he wondered with passive dream-desperation. Wait, he thought. That's crazy. This just isn't my country.

Nevertheless, he cared. He couldn't help it. I should have gone home, he muttered half aloud. Even if Nina was asleep.

Just then, a smelly, unshaven political officer rushed into the ambassador's office announcing excitedly, 'The Foreign Ministry car has brought another letter – from the Kremlin. They say it's urgent.'

Davenport sat up with his eyes still closed, alarmed, thinking, It's broad daylight already; I would have seen her this morning.

He heard the ambassador saying somewhere above him, 'Jeez. Washington's still reading the last one.' Then, as the envelope crackled and tore, 'At least it's shorter this time. My officers are getting writer's cramp.'

He dragged himself to his feet, slitty-eyed, stiff.

The ambassador spread the letter on his desk and the three of them stared at it together.

At last the ambassador said, 'Well? What do you think?'

Davenport tried to shake off his stupor. 'Well . . . it seems to me that it's a lot more clear and – but it's tougher, sir.'

'Oh, for crying out loud,' said the ambassador in exasperation.

'Yeah.' Davenport dug the heels of his hands in below his eyes, dragged them out across his cheekbones, pressed his temples with them, rubbing. 'Now he's proposing to remove the weapons in Cuba in exchange for our removing the weapons in Turkey. He didn't mention Turkey in that last letter. Um . . . he promises not to invade Turkey if we promise not to invade Cuba – just to strengthen the comparison. It looks like he's trying to squeeze out a deal at the last minute.'

The officer who had brought in the letter snorted and said, 'Don't *they* know those Jupiter missiles are obsolete?'

'Obsolete or not, they're dangerous as hell if anybody fires them off.' Davenport shrugged. 'Don't expect the Soviets to be reasonable. Not now.'

The ambassador said sternly, 'The Turks don't want those Jupiter missiles removed. They've been asked and they said no. They don't care if our Polaris subs can do better from the Mediterranean. They believe in what they can see, and those missiles make them believe we are prepared to go atomic against the Soviets if we have to. The Turkish Air Force has only just been given the control of those missiles this week. Besides, it's a NATO decision. The US can't just pull NATO weapons out whenever we feel like it. Going through NATO would take months.'

'Maybe Wentz is right,' said Davenport thoughtfully, 'about a split, you know, in the leadership, and we have hardliners talking now. How could Khrushchev change his mind like that, overnight?'

'He's a man of many moods,' said the ambassador, 'changeable as all get out. And he likes to cover himself. But it maybe does seem like someone's reining him in.'

'And, jeez, will you look at this, sir,' Davenport exploded, 'they've sent the letter out already over Radio Moscow. Before even informing us.'

The ambassador froze, then said briskly, 'Christ. OK. Have everyone get started on translating this. I'm sending a message to

Washington to let them know we have another letter. A different letter, more formal, a harder deal.'

As they entered the bubble, a communications officer approached clutching a bundle of cables. 'A few new items of information, sir. The FBI says that the Soviets have been shredding documents in New York. Washington has new photos showing those Soviet bombers, the Il-28s, being uncrated and assembled in Cuba. So they are not slowing preparations for war, sir, and the build-up is being reported on the news at home. They're broadcasting that the missiles are being put on operational status. And the president is adding even more flights over Cuba.'

Nina attended the ballet alone again on Friday night. The company was back at the Bolshoi presenting a new programme: *La Valse*, *Pas de Deux*, *Episodes*, *Western Symphony*. She left as soon as the performance was over, arrived home tired and low, gave a trembly sigh as she let herself into the apartment, listened, looked around, hoping for John.

Maybe I should have stayed out with the dancers, she thought. But she knew she was barely clinging to these last few perform-ances. The company had taken her on; she was accepted, more than accepted by Alice and Danny; but she wasn't part of anything real. She had to apply herself so hard to her role to make it exist at all. Whenever she didn't arrive to support and guide the dancers, somebody else did, and somebody else would do the same during the next part of the tour, and thereafter. Maybe they didn't really need help anyway. Her energy was dwindling, moving off at so many tangents, breaking up. When she watched the company perform, she felt their discipline, their focus, their strength; they were dancers and they were dancing. But who was she? What was she doing? She was trapped in an empty identity, in pretence.

She put her handbag on the spindly-legged table in the hall, went to the fridge for milk, drank it straight from the bottle, three swallows, thinking, What you need is a stiff drink, girl, whisky, and to stop all this forlorn nonsense. She winced. She didn't really want whisky.

Of course it was Wentz who asked for me to help with the dancers, she realized, looking back. John told me the truth; he didn't beg for the job. And what did Wentz actually want from me? Why did he draw me on to make another visit to Felix? Why did he get me all crazed and excited – that fantasy that I could somehow help to rehabilitate the intelligentsia, oppose the State, play some part in Russia's destiny?

She sneered at herself. It's absurd. I'll never find out anything more about Viktor, she thought. Nobody can penetrate this massive goddamned system, this fortress he's buried in.

And if the whole world's coming to an end, what difference can it possibly make anyway? Poking through the kitchen shelves, she had trouble believing in the missile crisis; what was around her was so much more solid, so much more convincing. Yet the extremity of the crisis dwarfed her own predicament. And the continual taxing fear that there might be a nuclear finale brought on a fretful, perverse impatience for it to hurry up and happen, for something to happen, for some kind of punctuation to the desolate, nervous hours that would begin again in earnest when the ballet left town. The reality might be that she would soon be marking time again with meaningless activities – rearranging the apartment to avoid superficial, effortful friendships, or scouring the city for ingredients to cook for a man who never came home to eat.

She stalked out of the kitchen, frustrated, unsettled.

Where was John? Where was John ever? Nina had fended off self-pity for a long time, but she had to admit to herself that she felt hurt by his continual absence. She couldn't help it. Even though she knew where he was, what he was trying to do, she minded. If we are all going to die, I'd like to see him, to be with him. Is that what he wants any more?

Moscow has simply cut us adrift from one another, divided us more and more each day. We came to be together; I came to be with him. Nina thought that she couldn't keep on indefinitely, so much alone, with nothing to do. John had no idea at all what had happened to her during the last week, the few days of inspiration, zeal, and now her life more diffuse, more aimless than ever. He couldn't have even a clue how painful it was for her, waiting for time to pass, time which she had once thought was so precious, which could never be had again. She had stopped living.

It didn't feel like love, this slow etiolation, this prison of waiting. She was making herself numb on purpose. Avoiding – everything. Is it all because of what I've done, lying to him?

But no, she thought, it started before I knew about the baby, before I got pregnant. And the loss of conviction, of absolute commitment, when did that start? She wasn't exactly sure. There had been fear, already, as she had shopped in Paris. Even before that, as she had packed boxes in Washington. She could remember the fear, even though she had tried not to admit it to herself at the time. I was hiding it from us both, and hiding it from my mother. Because Mother had begun to attack John so ferociously behind his back.

Nina undressed, hung up her suit, put on a taupe satin nightgown with a plunging neck edged with lace and silk cord. It was the first nightgown her hand fell on in the drawer, and she thought, What is the point of a nightgown like this? I'm here alone. Who is this nightgown *for*? And then she thought, grimacing, It's for my mother. Because she wanted me to be dressed like this when I arrived back in Moscow.

Not that John doesn't like it. But he doesn't require it. Mother requires it, as proof of who I am, what I am, an American heiress, a Yankee, here only on a tour of duty from another world, another planet, a fairy princess who can come and go from the Soviet Union as she likes. Who is condescending to help out her husband by appearing at his side, an empress compared even to the wife of the American ambassador.

She slipped into bed and lay on her back in the dark, stiff with resentment.

It'll be better after I see the doctor tomorrow. A visit to the clinic. A day in bed. That's all it is. Dealt with. Then I can move on. If we're all still here.

Then she remembered how Felix had smiled at her when he told her she was pregnant. She ran her hands along the smooth satin of her nightgown, felt her waist, the flat of her stomach. Her waist hadn't changed at all, but towards the very bottom of her stomach, just above the pubic bone, she could feel a hard little lump, and she knew it was there, already growing. It pricked her, a pleasure she couldn't afford, refused to long for, even to think about.

And she thought, How odd it would be if I died pregnant. If that were my destiny, to be annihilated with my unborn child. Not that anyone would ever know.

That was Mother's fear, she thought, to be annihilated with me. Lost for ever, forgotten, in the Soviet Union – the war, the winter, the never enough to eat. I'm really not afraid of that, though. That is not my own fear. And Nina had one of her little moments of clarity about herself and her mother: I suppose Mother's fears used to be so big that I thought they were mine; I was enveloped by them, lived inside them.

But what was I afraid of, if that was her fear?

Afraid of their being afraid, yes, Mother and Dad. Afraid of them fighting. All children must hate that, she thought, grown-ups fighting. That's nothing to do with Russia – except I was afraid of how Mother always threatened to leave. And Dad would say, You can't leave; they'll never let you. He would yell at her. Or not yell, cry out. That's an empty ridiculous threat, he would cry. You should stop making it. It's beneath your dignity. But she never did stop. Mother insisted on it until the day he died. And afterwards, too.

Then Nina considered with surprise how she had sometimes

sensed that her father had not been entirely content, that he had wanted to leave Russia just as much as her mother had wanted to. How did I know? Did he tell me? Whisper it to me when I sat on the arm of his chair? That chair that was so difficult for him to get out of, that smelled of his leaking pee? She could remember the purply-yellow plush, marked, faded, crusted over with spilled soup, drink, cigarette ash, caresses.

She stroked the pillow by her cheek, turned her face into it, rolling onto her side. On and on her thoughts turned and pressed, dredging the dark, the elusive, insoluble past.

I guess he couldn't bring himself to take that line, because it was Mother's tireless line – that she would leave and that she would take me with her. So, of course, Dad wanted me to stay. I was the thing they could fight over, the thing they could exercise some power over. Everything else in their lives was entirely beyond their control.

They must have loved me, though, she reassured herself. In whatever crippled way they were capable of. I always felt that Dad loved me. Mother must have loved me, too. Just – she never let on. To her, I was a tool, or a weapon, or a burden. Would she have left me with Dad if she could have gotten out alone? Did she threaten to take me just to be cruel to him? Did she actually want me? I wonder if she even knew?

In fact, Dad was the one who couldn't leave. It was only Dad.

It seemed like a revelation to Nina. She sat up in the dark, as if she would get out of bed, as if she must do something about this. She had a sense of impatience, of hurry. Because of his crushed legs. Because he couldn't walk, if we had needed to walk on the journey, if there had been difficulties, challenges. It was Dad whom Mother hated, for keeping her here. For persuading her to come in the first place.

I was the way out. An American child. Not the burden, not the problem at all. Why did Mother berate me with how she'd never meant to have a child? With how I'd kept her here that year before Dad was hurt, until it was too late to leave? Had there been some moment, some flickering passage through which Mother might have slipped? A child was the proof of her weakness for Dad, weakness to the point of folly.

And Dad had a weakness, too – he couldn't face being alone. If he had admitted the error he had dragged Mother into, it might have set her free. Instead, he always boosted his communist ideals. But he must have lived on the hope that we would never have a choice, that we would be forced to stay with him. He was that vulnerable – inviting Mother's rage to bond her to him, to hold her attention.

And Nina thought of it again, as she had often done for as long as she could remember, trying to imagine it, the flashing, black chance in the dark, the elevator screeching down to the wet dirt floor of the shaft where her father was standing – the last time he would casually stand, checking a drawing, alone. The flying, invincible weight. But he must have cried out, she thought. Somebody found him, pried him loose. Splintered bone and bloody shreds of trouser. Maybe fallen timbers. It might have been his grave.

By the time he came home from the hospital, I had learned to walk. I don't remember him walking, ever. I only think I do. I never saw it. Mother gave me false memories, to bolster the lie about my age.

Slowly, Nina lay down again, conjuring her father's face. It was hard to do now, remember Dad's face.

Dad always favoured my independence. Let the child be, he would say. But maybe he was just giving in. Or trying to get Mother to give in. We have been living with these people for years now, sharing the most basic facilities, our john, for Christ's sake! And we will probably always live with them. Why not be friends? Why not let them give the child candy?

Insights, recollections fluttered at her, swarmed.

Mother spoke to me in English because she wanted a private life. If the Szabos joined in, in English, Mother didn't speak at all.

Dad wasn't afraid of becoming Russian. He was afraid of getting arrested for not being Russian.

The only thing they agreed about was ballet. Dad was proud of me. For Mother, it was a way of building up the separation from everyone else, training in something to do with the wider world, with European culture, another life.

Until I hurt myself.

Oh, Christ. Why did I hurt myself?

She flopped around in the bed, fighting the sheets, wild with a sudden sweat, a panic. I did it on purpose. Out of love for Dad. Out of guilt over Masha, to share her downfall. There were so many reasons. To oppose my mother. To punish her.

Nina opened her eyes wide in the dark. Now she could see her father's face, tilted back against the hardened plush of the chair where his grey threads of hair always rubbed. His upper lip was thin, stretched high over his gums; his jaw fell away too low, all wrong; his breathing was loud, rattling with spit. His eyes, mostly closed, were only papery lids over glass, no irises showing, not moving with her, following her, around the room. He was the same colour as the chair.

At ballet school, they kept me to sleep with the children from outside Moscow. Mother must have gone to a lot of trouble to persuade them I needed those few nights away. And when I finally got home again, even Dad's chair was gone. Dad's own chair, not saved for me to crouch in, to smell.

I blamed Mother for everything. Or blamed myself.

It wasn't such a shock, Nina thought, America. All my life, I had been half expecting it. It seemed strangely normal. The warm, enormous house in Buffalo. The beauty of the lake on the drive to town, the glittering drifts of snow, different in America, American snow. The reliable plumes of factory smoke. It wasn't so unlike Moscow, apart from the comfort and the plenty, the fresh coats of paint everywhere, the clear air, the scenery brought into crisp, new-edged focus.

Yet the welcome of that first winter was a blur, really. At first, my rowdy, shambling boy cousins all seemed the same. Maybe they were too young to interest me individually, but they helped me to feel strong when I was allowed, eventually, to go out to parties. They carried me along with their energy, like some kind of team. Family. I had never had that before. It was easy to feel safe and happy with them; they had no sisters, no girlfriends, took me in. With them, I was a tomboy, unselfconscious.

And she thought, I was really younger at seventeen than I had been at sixteen, fifteen, fourteen. That was when my childhood began, that first dazzling, pell-mell Christmas; that's why I always feel that I grew up in America. I lost the rest, threw it all away, what I had already experienced, licking my wounds, healing. Working on the new sensation, freedom. Everyone kept telling me about it. What did it mean? How did it feel?

She could remember solitude. Even when she and her mother were still staying with her cousins, Aunt Josephine, Uncle Bill. The spreading rooms, decorated and twinkling, had been crowded with beautiful furniture and objects, but not crowded with people. And when they moved into their own house, it had been full of bright, snow-reflected air, sunbeams, dark wood. Full of nothing at all. Just her and her mother and the tutors who came to help her catch up, to prepare her. She was kept under wraps for her own good, no schooling, nothing that might allow her to fail or to reveal herself before she was ready. In the quiet, there were flowers blooming indoors all winter. Hyacinths, orange trees fresh with sweet-smelling white stars, little moons of gold fruit, orchids on their looped, snake-neck stems.

But in some other, personal, inward sense, the rupture – Moscow, Buffalo – might as well have been a bomb blast. Sudden, total. I didn't know for such a long time what had happened, what was lost and gained. The absoluteness, the finality. In fact, maybe not until I came back here again with John. Not until now. Tonight.

And so at last her thoughts turned to Viktor. What about when Mother took me away from Viktor? Because I was old enough to stay if I had insisted on it. I lost my nerve. I let her take me. She was so afraid of trouble, of arrest. Dad had had the same fear, every single day. Everyone in Russia lived with it. Everyone had felt it loom over them, shadow them. It made us sick in our core, doom-illness, rot, abject fear. A stranger asking directions in the street, footsteps on the stairs in the evening, or worse, in the small hours, a car engine throbbing down below. You didn't dare look. Nothing monumental like bombs or the end of the world, but the torturers, lopping us off, one at a time, catching us out, breaking our hearts, our bones, our spirits – until the numbers added up. And no one ever spoke of it, what lay under the surface.

The change that came with Khrushchev was perfectly real. There was an atmosphere of freedom; maybe I craved it more than I knew? If Dad hadn't died when he did, if I hadn't gotten hurt, I might have just been a dancer. But Nina reflected that those years of the so-called thaw had come to seem to her in hindsight like the beginning of going to America, first the freedom at home, then the absolute liberation: America. Otherwise, maybe America would have overwhelmed me.

But what if I hadn't left Russia? How often she had asked herself this question; she had never been able to imagine any answer. Like a horse baulking at a jump, her mind fell back from the enormity, the darkness. Blankly, wanly, without any real effort of penetration, she wondered if she could have stood it, like Viktor, like Felix. It's not as if there was an easy way in Russia. Not an easy way and be in the right.

She dozed for a while, but all night she never slept deeply. She didn't toss and turn. On the contrary, she grew calm, settled. She hardly moved at all any more, so absorbed did she become by the images in her mind. At last, when the dark began to glow with the nearness of dawn, she fell asleep.

Then at mid-morning, she started up wide awake all at once. She had forgotten something. Or perhaps she had been afraid of it.

She got up and ran to the hall, groped in her handbag for the little bundle of Viktor's poems that Felix had given her. She brought the poems back to bed with her and read by the weak light of the silk-hooded lamp on the little bedside table. Her hands shook, so she laid the pages on a pillow and leaned back beside them on one bent arm.

The subjects were not personal. There was one about stones: the sizes and shapes of different kinds of stones, hewable, some less so; the adhesive power of lime mortar, merest grindings of crumble and dust, layered between them when stones are formed into a wall; the porous cold of their surfaces, differing from stone to stone; their lack of heart. If you have a tool and cut away at a stone, flakes fly off, but you find no centre, nothing inside. You end with broken chips.

She could hear Viktor in that, the accuracy, the didacticism, writing about something before his very eyes, a prison wall, infusing it with passion, yet cold, marmoreal.

There wasn't any poem that made her cry. They were bold, absolute, abstract, inspiring. Like her boy cousins, they made her feel strong.

These poems aren't about Viktor any more than they are about me, Nina thought. I would never find clues in them to his well-being, his state of mind. The poems are about truth. They are about what's plainly the case under a truthless regime. It's not grandiose to say that. Viktor was never interested in himself, nor in me really. Not much. He was only ever interested in truth, in justice.

She read them all: poems about sheets of paper, about pencils, water, bread, nail parings. How deeply, searchingly each subject was noticed, in what abundant, excruciating detail it was assessed, valued.

He's a sage now of the closeted, starved life, Nina thought. A monk. And she realized that her feelings about the poems were altering her feelings about Viktor. It was a cumulative effect, reading them all; there's no story, she thought, and yet it's a biography of his spirit, of his soul.

Then suddenly, like an inward flood of tears, her admiration for him washed up inside her throat. If he can make this with nothing, she wondered, what could he make with freedom?

Or is it because he has so little that he truly sees it?

Up she got from the bed, with the poems in one hand, a little queasy with lack of sleep, reaching for the doorjamb to hold herself upright as she lurched unexpectedly. It's the baby, she thought, making me sick like this. She picked up her open handbag in her other hand, pushed the poems gently back inside it, and went to the kitchen for bread to staunch the nausea. She ate a lot of bread, standing at the sink staring out into the morning as it spread up the eight-storeyed sky, and she felt better; she felt illuminated by morning.

Now she made coffee. She put water on to boil, struggled with the canister, spilling a few grounds. When the coffee was dripping into the little glass jug she'd brought from Paris, she went into the hall and called the embassy. John wasn't available, neither was Wentz. She knew that meant they were in the bubble. I give up, she thought to herself bitterly.

Then, to guard against her sense that something might go wrong that day, she wrote John a note, sitting at the table sipping the coffee, not especially liking the taste. I don't like the taste of anything any more, she thought, except bread and water.

'Dear John, You are a lover of the Russian language. These are some of its masterworks. Read them. Get them out. Get them published. Love always. N.'

Just in case we somehow don't meet here tonight, she thought.

She reached into her handbag, pulled out the fragile sheaf of poems and laid her note on top. Next she unrolled a piece of wax paper from its long thin cardboard box, folded it back, creased it hard, and tore it carefully along the sharp-toothed edge. She slid the wax paper under the poems, rolled all the papers up together, and put them inside the coffee can. Then she slid the tight-fitting lid back on the coffee and put the canister back on the shelf.

Yelena Petrovna knew better than to nose around in the food. That was one thing Nina wouldn't allow because it made her feel too guilty. And besides, Yelena Petrovna wouldn't come again until Monday afternoon.

But Nina was only half thinking about Yelena Petrovna. She was picturing John finding the poems, and she was picturing her cousins in Buffalo, who had introduced her to John, one summer, during college. John whom they'd grown up with at home before he went off to Exeter. There were many close links there, blood brotherhood – capillaries, veins, arteries. Lifelong friendship. There was strength, conviction. They would all get it – John, her cousins. The team. They would all read Viktor's poems. John would translate them. She knew she could count on them, believe in them. Six thousand miles away, the poems would come to light. Viktor's story, everything. The words would get out, would get through. Was this what Felix had wanted?

And she recalled that first staggering instant when she had seen the ocean. With her mother, crossing to America from France, in 1956. As they had steamed out from Cherbourg, the plain of water around them had grown bigger and bigger. Wide beyond imagining, so that her eyes had been free to see the entire distance that the water stretched, until they wore out with looking. There had been no barriers, no shadows.

Freedom or courage, she thought as she sat at the kitchen table, what is it? Having the chance to choose? Or having the nerve? She could almost taste the bright, frozen air of the winter ocean on her tongue, now, inviting her. As if to swim, to fly. She thought, Why do I hold back? What am I waiting for, what am I saving myself for? And she thought, They'll read the poems. They'll want to know. They will understand.

Nina took out a stylish short-sleeved light blue A-line coat dress with a broad navy-blue panel concealing the buttons down the front, and packed it into her canvas shopping satchel. Then she got dressed in her old, grey-brown Shetland cardigan, her long wool skirt, her brown tights, her boots, as if she were expecting bad weather, snow even. She rifled her stocking drawer, taking out the last four unopened packages of stockings and slipping them underneath the dress already in the satchel. She checked in her handbag for money, counted her roubles.

It wasn't long after she had put on her duffle coat that the phone began to ring. But she didn't hear it. She was in the elevator already, halfway down to the ground floor.

Felix had made up his mind before he fell asleep, and he felt no differently when he woke the next morning. They would all three take this chance together. Nothing could ever be right for any of them otherwise; it would probably never be right in any case. He owed Nina something, some scope of action.

Lying on his back in his narrow, familiar bed, he could see a dripping line of soot on the raised white sash of the window. A wet wind snatched at the flimsy, yellowed curtain which he had pulled back for fresh air, and beyond the blotched glass, the crooked tree branch shuddered with it. From time to time, he could hear a hiss of traffic on the street below. All night long, in the never-dark, never-light of his dreary room, the past had run before his half-closed, shivering eyes. He felt as if he could remember everything Nina had ever done, ever said. It moved him painfully to think of her, how fast she always walked as if to show that she could keep up with anyone, how she would stand tilted onto her toes as if she wanted to be taller, wanted to join in something going on just over her head, to engage with the next experience, to find out what else there was in life, some connection, some mutual understanding.

At Novodevichy Cemetery one summer afternoon she had seemed to dance among the monuments in thick-strapped sandals, slim-waisted cotton dress, bare-armed, bare-legged, bending and inquiring of each departed life, like a butterfly presence, flickering, What about death? The convent had been the destination of sultry urban desperation: trees, water, grounds and groves to walk in within the sweating, white-washed walls; Viktor had joined them and drawn them away from the shouldering clutch of domes and spires out to the graves, where they had strolled, talking, smoking. What was the point of doing away with God, Viktor had demanded grandly, of allowing no nuns, few priests at the seminary inside, if we were only going to return to ancestor worship, more prim-itive, more divisive? Then, circling an arm to show them, The shrines crowd around us right here on the grass, busts, photo-graphs, mementoes, a pantheon for idolators. Why should *these* be our heroes? Where, he had asked, are the memorials for those who have been ground underfoot? The tortured, the terrified, the slave labourers? Have they no right to be remembered?

She had been shocked by his talk, gripped. Felix had seen it right away; neither of them seemed even to hear him when he pointed out the grave of a Decembrist, worked to death in Siberia by the Tsar. Some swaggering need was launched in Nina by Viktor's presence, so that she, too, had taken a cigarette, her first ever, and then chucked it in distaste after one drag. And that was how she met Viktor, crushing Felix's cherished, unsmoked tobacco under her strong, playful foot. She had never tried smoking again.

Felix knew all too clearly that he had made no effort to resist the absurd danger of becoming newly involved with Nina over the last week. After all, he had never expected to see her again. But how could he account to himself for the fact that he still lived in this doctors' dormitory, with no wife, no family, no intention. He had friends, colleagues, patients, a web around him of those he trusted and mistrusted, those he could help and not help. He lost himself successfully in their needs. He owed caution and concern to each one of them, love, counsel, care. And there was his own family – mother, father, little brothers and sisters – miles and miles away in the dusty outskirts of Rostov-on-Don, practically forgotten. But something in him would not lie down in his cell, this small, undecorated room with its one window, its hard, dishevelled bed.

I, myself, want to see Viktor, he thought. Who can blame *her*? He reflected again upon the night of Viktor's first arrest. She was the only one who had not expected it.

'My father has been taken three nights in a row now, around ten o'clock,' Viktor had told him. 'They bring him back at dawn. He doesn't refer to it. Yesterday he walked with pain, though he tried to disguise it. Forget the thaw. Hell is freezing over before our eyes.'

He had reached inside his coat, pulled out the fat, dilapidated brown folder. 'Today, he let me have this file of papers – I insisted. He told me not to read them; he said only, Keep them safe, then, until I ask for them again. Well, of course, I have read them. They are committee papers. Take them, Felix, and bring them to the dacha tomorrow. I'll get my father's car and pick you up on the way. The woods are bare, the leaves already down; still, we can hide them in one of my old places. As long as we're not followed. For me, this is uncertain. There are eyes on me now almost constantly. I won't come if I'm followed.'

'If you don't come?'

'Hide them yourself. You'll think of something. The hospital must be full of files just like this one.'

'What shall I tell Nina?'

Viktor had looked impatient, tired.

And Felix had pleaded, 'She expects to come with us. You've promised her so often.'

'Tell her – the same. The woods are bare, the leaves are already down. It would be cold at the dacha. Too cold. Maybe in the spring I can take her. We'll try in the spring.'

'She couldn't care less about the cold.'

'You know her best, Felix. Tell her whatever you think is right. She's young. What does she really believe? She hasn't even found out yet. She should – play it safe. Reserve her energy.'

Later, when Felix had noticed how many men were watching – obviously, lumpenly – outside the lecture hall, he had felt as if the file inside his coat was giving off heat, giving off light. I have nowhere to leave it, he had thought, and it's not safe to bring the papers inside. He had turned around on the staircase, deciding he would simply walk the streets until the end of the reading. But there was Nina running up, just behind him, pulling off her fur hat so that the loose strands of her fine, bright hair, which she had swept up high with pins underneath, crackled with static and clung around her square white face, snagged in the damp between her lips. She had embraced him, confiding, 'I had to lie to my mother to get permission to go out; I might have to leave before the end, depending how long it goes. Otherwise I'll never manage to get away tomorrow to drive to the country. She'll walk with me all the way to school if she suspects!'

And Felix had thought, I shouldn't let them see her with Viktor, observe her being intimate with him. That could prove dangerous for her. He had helped her off with her coat, folded it over his own arm, gently kept hold of her hand, hoping she wouldn't object.

She joked brazenly to Viktor about her lie, and Viktor had teased her: 'You tell me you are a grown woman, you put up your hair, and yet you are afraid of your own mother's prohibitions. Do as you are inclined! Decide what you believe!' He had smiled from his overwhelming height, in his dramatic nearly black wool suit, stiff-collared white shirt, thin black tie, and then he had tousled the elegant knot she had made of her hair so that a hank fell loose down the side of her face, splayed onto her shoulder.

'You have so much energy, beautiful energy. You ought to go back to your dancing if you like to take instructions from others so much! And that way you'd be safe. Or go away to America, with your mother. That'd keep her quiet, wouldn't it? So, let's talk afterwards if we can.'

Then Viktor had turned away to greet a former teacher, quietly, respectfully, dipping his head, brushing back his swathe of brown forelock with one hand, bending his great shoulders, chivalrous, attentive, humble. And before he walked to the lectern at the front of the hall, he had grabbed Felix's arm and whispered to him, 'Look after Nina. Don't let her feel sorry.'

Felix had thought, Why are you going ahead with this reading? It will only enrage them the more. It's obvious what's going to happen. They'll find you later, in the night, when the crowd is dispersed, somewhere private, your own house even, in front of your father. They will want your father to know. Maybe this time, they will take you both.

I sat beside Nina near the back, upright, ready to fly, the file burning a hole in my chest. I checked the time constantly, as if there were some moment that would be the moment to go. As if a clock could tell me. The room was crowded, hot; I had to keep my coat on to conceal the file, and perspiration drenched me. Each time Viktor announced a title for his poems, the applause in the small space went out of control, deafening, so that I felt sure it could be heard from the street. People leaped to their feet, stamped, shouted. It made me unbearably anxious.

I caught Nina's eye, lit with excitement. 'Your mother,' I mouthed. Nina made a face, as if to say, Who cares? And she fumbled at her hair, trying to restore it.

I put an arm around her, pulled her from her chair, whispering in her ear, You'll have the whole day tomorrow. If you don't get caught tonight. She pouted, tried to pull away, but couldn't struggle much without disturbing everyone else, without attracting attention. At the back of the hall, the crowd was thick around the doors, more people entering, pressing upon us. And then there was a sudden movement, the doors thwacked wide open, the crowd was shoved harshly forward, people fell over, the leather-coated men came in six, eight strong, to break up the meeting, to scare everyone. I had to get the file out of the building; I couldn't risk being questioned or searched while I was carrying it.

I gathered Nina up altogether, lifting her feet from the floor along with the coat I was already holding, and walked out, signalling vaguely that she was ill, that she needed fresh air. And they looked through us; to them, we didn't exist, just a girl student, sick, irrelevant. Why involve her? Anyway, I was practically a full-fledged doctor, and I was prepared to show my papers to prove it. She protested, looking back over my shoulder towards Viktor at the front of the hall, encircled, protected, as he would then have been by his many admirers.

'Stop, Felix, please stop. I can't see Viktor. Something's wrong, something's going wrong.' She cursed me under her breath, murmured angrily as I carried her down the stairs. Eventually, she collapsed against me in tears, tugging her skirt down over the backs of her humiliated thighs.

It was incredible that nobody stopped us, nobody asked us anything. Completely incredible. Outside, I made her put her coat back on and we walked for twenty minutes, nowhere in particular, before we spoke at all. She was still sobbing.

'He'll come find you later, at your mother's,' I said. 'He's not afraid of your mother.' She didn't laugh at this. 'Otherwise, tomorrow; where is he picking you up?'

But Nina was blaming herself. 'I shouldn't have run out on him like that.'

'Don't be silly, Nina. How could you have helped?'

'At least I could share in what – whatever was going on.'

'He wouldn't want that.'

'What would he want?'

'For you not to feel sorry,' Felix answered. And then he embellished it: 'I mean, if anything – does – go wrong, he would want you to get on with your life, as he just told you, go back to your dancing, go to America.' He felt cruel as he said it, felt he was telling her that Viktor didn't care for her. The truth was, he didn't know. Certainly, Viktor had turned a calloused heart to Nina that night. But Viktor had his reasons, Felix thought. He had to survive.

And then, when Felix had walked Nina upstairs to her apartment, there had been a disgusting scene. Nina's mother roaring, uncontrolled.

'You think I don't know what you're doing with your boyfriends?' Nina's mother had shouted hysterically, in front of him, in front of the Szabos, as if to affirm that they all disapproved of Nina's appalling, irresponsible behaviour, her depravity.

'You are going to get yourself into a mess, and I will never be able to get you out of here! Don't think you are so goddamned smart, young lady. I know exactly what you are doing, skipping school to sneak off with them. My father tried to warn me. I didn't listen; I've paid enough for it now. What kind of men are they to be mixed up with anyway? They should be ashamed of themselves! They tell you it's ideals; I tell you it's sex! You'll get plenty of that when you are old enough, when you are married!'

Nina's mother had never even looked at Felix, not one withering glance, and it had dawned on him only slowly exactly what she was implying – about himself. Then he had been too startled, too repulsed, to object.

'Don't you dare wind up pregnant! The last thing you want in this country is a baby or a boyfriend in trouble. What are you going to eat if the father of your child gets arrested? Who's going to look after you? Because I will be gone. And if you have a grain of sense, you will come with me. We can leave next week. It's taken years, Nina. Don't blow this chance.'

One thing Nina told me before she left, Felix recalled as he lay watching the wettest, heaviest drip of soot break from the line and slide to the bottom edge of his open window sash, was how much she had wanted to say goodbye to Viktor.

It's my fault because I carried her from the hall.

Slowly, deliberately, he got up from his bed, dragged yesterday's clothes back on over the underwear he had slept in. He walked to the stairs at the end of the corridor, down to the street, along the cold morning pavement, and up the staircase two doors away. Two flights up, part way along the corridor, he knocked at a door exactly like his own. A bearded young man opened the door, sleepy, rubbing his thin, singlet-clad chest with both palms, stretching his blueish face. He nodded at Felix, neutral, familiar, reached behind for a shirt, shrugged it on, stepped out into the empty corridor, looking sidelong right and left.

'Your friend is still there,' the young man said very quietly. 'We drove no ambulance service at all last night.'

'And tonight?'

'Well, anyway I'm on duty again. Medical Assistant at least.'

'Can you get his pregnant girlfriend in to see him?'

The young man raised his eyebrows in amazement. He was silent, staring, thinking. Then he shrugged, tipped his head to one side, dropping his eyelids over his yellow eyes. 'It's possible. Maybe it's possible. I think she has to bribe the driver, possibly the soldier at the gate and then – maybe. Tell her ten o'clock, Kropotkinsky Lane, where it meets Prechistenka, on the southwest side, but away from the corner, she must wait out of sight. The best bribe she can manage, a whole block of cigarettes, foreign ones if she can get them, or money.' He paused. 'Can she still move fast enough – with the pregnancy?'

Felix nodded.

'And keep her mouth shut?'

'Of course.'

As Felix walked back to the stairs, he thought with a rush of strange excitement, I can send a message to her at the clinic.

Nina didn't take her seat at the Bolshoi that night, but stayed with the dancers backstage. She had seen everything in tonight's programme several times – *Scotch Symphony, Concerto Barocco, Donizetti*

Variations, La Sonnambula – and she drew back from it. There was a great deal of excitement and anxiety among the dancers; she thought perhaps her presence was reassuring, that she could fulfil in some way her duty to her country, to her husband, by this little piece of hand-holding. But her mind wasn't on it; she hardly spoke to Alice, to Danny. She was afraid they might notice she was hardly herself. Instead, she hung around Patrice.

There were things she could learn from Patrice; Nina felt she ought to have realized it much sooner. She watched Patrice with care – her eyes, her gestures, her style of dress, her sense of herself. Where did Patrice get her nerve? Nina wondered. Because she's really not brave like Alice. And yet, she pulls it off. She gets what she wants. A coldness, an impenetrable glass surface, a fix on details, impressions, rather than on anything big. A resistance, Nina concluded, to feelings, to depths.

As the dancers began to go onstage for the last ballet of the evening, *La Sonnambula*, Nina wandered away to an empty dressing room at the end of the hallway. There she changed her clothes for the second time that day. She took off the blue dress which she had put on mid-morning and pulled her old clothes out of the satchel which she had been carrying since then. From time to time, crouched over, she looked around the room furtively, but she saw no one. And she heard nothing but distant music, and eventually, she thought, a burst of applause.

Quickly, she folded up the blue dress and put it back into the satchel. The four packages of stockings she removed and folded into her coat pocket. She took the roubles from her handbag and put them in her other coat pocket. Again she looked around, then she pushed her handbag and the satchel underneath a plain wooden chair, the satchel, nondescript, in front. It wasn't well hidden, but what difference did it make?

At the door to the dressing room, she checked up and down the hall before making her way silently out of the theatre. She nodded to the guard, curt, tough; walked fast through the swing door to the Metro at Ploshchad' Sverdlova where she scurried through the long, echoing underground passageway to the station at Prospekt Marksa and boarded a train for Smolenskaya Square.

Once in a while, Nina wondered if anyone could be following her, but the train seemed deserted. They've become used to me staying through the whole performance, she thought, and accompanying the dancers back to the hotel. She checked her watch; it was already ten. When she came out of the Metro, the wind was blowing hard. She felt it against her legs and thought how tender she'd become, always so well and warmly dressed. The feeling of real cold was a lost sensation, the hard goose bumps rising now on her thighs. Or was it nerves?

It was only a few blocks to the Serbsky Institute. She took the precaution of keeping away from Smolensky Boulevard, coming through the edge of the Arbat among the old wooden houses and nineteenth-century mansions.

Was there a footstep behind her? She turned, limp, breathless, but the street was empty. There was only a distant lamp; she couldn't see well in the dark. As she approached Prechistenka, she slowed her pace, hung back from the kerb, clinging to the walls of the houses, trying to blend into them, to disappear behind the trees. She didn't want to stand still, she was far too excited, and she thought she might be noticed. A car passed, making her shudder; she crossed to the south side of the road.

And suddenly, there was the ambulance van, swishing to a stop, moon white, looming, with its red stripes that promised professional help, rescue. A slight, fair-haired man with a beard jumped from the front, opened the back, lifted and shoved her inside, and slammed the doors on her. She opened her mouth in astonishment, gasping. In the dark she could see nothing. She heard breathing, smelled tobacco, human sweat, the intense stench of penned creatures. She was jammed in a tight space, right up against the doors. Nobody spoke. They jolted into gear, rounded the corner, stopped in bright light which seeped inside but illuminated nothing at all, and then she heard metal gates rushing open before the van leaped through.

The doors were opened again by the fair-haired man with the beard; she saw that his eyes were tawny yellow, unblinking, scenting her mood like a dog. And behind his head she saw high walls, barbed wire coiling along the top, the peaked roof of a watch-tower, a young soldier staring right into her own eyes from under-neath it, twenty-five feet in the air.

'Quickly, quickly,' muttered the bearded man, and he hurried her around the van, into a building, up three flights of stairs.

Nina was breathless now with fear, with anticipation, a pleasure, longed for, dreaded, something intimate, personal, that seemed to be lodged deep inside her. It felt to her almost like an object, or like an explosion, something much bigger than her, welling up in her body, and it seemed inexplicable, the size and energy of it. How could she even climb these stairs? Walk up to a room where she might again see Viktor? An ill-lit corridor, deserted, silent?

The bearded man said, 'Wait here. When they take him to the toilet, you will see.'

Nina waited an hour, she thought, maybe more. For a long time, she continued to be so gripped by emotion that she had no thoughts at all, she simply experienced the heat of fear, of expec-tation, of hopefulness, of longing for meeting. The nearest thing she had to a thought was a silent inward chant, I want to see him. Inchoate. But then as the time grew longer, she worried that someone would pass along the corridor, notice her. What could she say for herself, stranded here? But there was never so much as a sound in the lengthening night.

She began to doubt that Viktor would come, to doubt that she would see him after all. She felt bitter at the repetition of the dis-appointment she had already experienced so harshly. All over again, she thought. He will not come, all over again. And I must find the resources in myself to cope with knowing nothing. Into her mind trudged the line of relatives and friends, bundled, tense, that she had used to see in Kuznetsky Most, not far from the Bolshoi training school, waiting hour upon hour for the window to be opened by the KGB staff there who could accept packages for prisoners in Lubyanka. If they took your package, you could feel as good as it was possible to feel because it meant the prisoner was still alive. If they turned your package away, you had to accept that the prisoner had died or been shot. That was the nearest you could get to saying goodbye. You couldn't expect anything else; you had to live without a farewell. Or maybe you could satisfy yourself by trying to imagine what you might have said to one another in such a final exchange.

As Nina slouched against the wall, hypnotized by sorrow, a skin-headed giant lumbered towards her along the corridor, held at the elbows by the bearded man and by someone else. She was seized with horror. Blindfolded, emaciated, straitjacketed, ungainly.

Oh, my God, she thought. Viktor. What do I do? How can I . . . ? But she went straight up to him, reaching out towards him.

The bearded man said, 'She needed to see you. She's pregnant.'

Nina shook her head as if to deny it, to ask him not to say it. And she saw Viktor move his mouth. He made no sound at all.

She looked down, put her hand over her own mouth, clutching at her lips, gathering her strength.

Then she said, looking back up at Viktor, putting her hands on his forearms which were bound across his ribs, 'It's Nina.'

She had intended to tell him, I've come to say goodbye. But now that she had the chance, it was the last thing she wanted to do. It was intolerable, the idea of saying goodbye. Cruel to him, cruel to herself. Never say goodbye, she thought, until it's over. Until it's actually – too late. Then she thought that maybe Viktor had known this all along.

So she only said, 'I've come to see you.' The most obvious, most desultory remark.

Viktor smiled. Not just a flicker, a whole grin. 'I must see you as well, then.'

He gestured clumsily at the blindfold with his shoulder. 'Come now, fellows. I can take my punishment straight.' He leaned down to the bearded man, spoke confidentially. 'If this is what my torturers are serving me today, I like it even more than the veal Stroganoff. Perhaps this will make me pliable? Make me putty in their hands at the next session? You must let me see my pregnant girlfriend. Please let me suffer.'

And the bearded man reached up, trembling, fumbling. When the blindfold fell away, Viktor kept his eyes closed, so that Nina was frightened that it had concealed a wound, some irreparable damage. As she stood watching, waiting, tears starting, Viktor sighed deeply, a tranquil look on his face. At last he opened his great grey eyes – at the moment of his own choosing. Silently he stared at her.

'What joy to see you, dearest Nina.' His voice was majestic, commanding, his cadences slow and formal. 'You are well, whole, beautiful. A feast for me. Your image will fill many hours. And the pain of parting cannot possibly last as long.'

They looked at each other for a long time, absorbing what they could. It was a rickety hope, that memory might later yield up this experience again.

Then Viktor said wryly, 'I like the pregnancy, too.'

'It's true, Viktor.'

'Yes, I believe it. Not just a trick. I believe it.'

Nina looked down at the floor, tearful, in silent, self-conscious apology – sorry to have thrived, to have succeeded, to have been so happy while Viktor was not.

'It's not something to feel sorry about, Nina. This is who we are fighting for, the next generations. And now I can be sure of them in my thoughts, something new to conjure.' After a pause, he said more quietly, 'I've often hoped you would find what you wanted – that you would come to know what you wanted. You have so much energy, pure energy, which I love.'

Suddenly the yellow-eyed, bearded man was pulling Viktor's arm, yanking him away, and he said harshly to his colleague, 'Get her out of here.'

There was a clanking at the far end of the corridor and Nina realized an elevator was rising, someone was coming. She was hurled into the stairwell, one arm brutishly viced, her light frame snapped like a whip, painfully. She kept silent, stumbling down the stairs, running, half dragged, trying not to fall.

At the bottom, the orderly muttered, 'The people in here are all crazy. You don't want your boyfriend if he's in here. He can't do anything at all for you. He told you so himself. And they make sure, with the crazies, that they can't do a thing. Not to you or for you. You can have me. Then maybe you can have my friend upstairs. We'll do a fine job. You can have us both.'

Nina felt angry, disgusted. I don't know how to get out of here, she thought. How the hell do I get out? She put her hand in her pocket, felt the packages of stockings.

'Maybe your girlfriend would like these?' Her voice wavered just a little. She pulled out one of the packages, tipping it back and forth in her hand so that the Cellophane wrapping gleamed in the light.

'Maybe you'd be my girlfriend, eh? Just for tonight? So pretty as you are?' He grinned, revealing tobacco-stained teeth, the spreading puce of chapped, thick lips.

Nina began to feel ill with the beating of her heart, with bile rising. The blood pounded in her face so that she thought she could taste it, smell it in her nose.

He reached for her breast, put his dirty, hardened hand on it. 'Not so bad,' he guffawed.

She didn't allow herself to recoil, to feel disgust, or to feel anything at all. This isn't about my body, she told herself. It's not personal. Because I don't know this man and he's nothing to me apart from the fact that he can get me out of here. He's a key, a piece of metal I have to pick up and use. It's a transaction, and I will complete it.

'If you get me out, maybe I'll see you afterwards,' she crooned at him. 'Would you like that?'

He didn't answer her, but she could see the leap of darkness in his eye, the venal eagerness.

He looked around, hard-groined, craven, and she sensed with dismay that he was looking for some shadowed corner, even here beneath the stairs.

Her mind was heavy with confusion, with bursting sweat. 'Not now,' she said, half-heartedly. 'We could meet tomorrow.'

There was a pause, then a change in his face. He didn't believe her. 'You must have something besides these stockings?'

'Maybe.'

And he lifted his palm towards her, curling his fingers in and out, quickly, greedily, as if to signal, Gimme, gimme.

So she said, 'I have roubles.'

At this his face brightened so intensely that she feared she had made a terrible mistake. But he just stared at her, waiting. She reached into her pocket and pulled out a handful of small rouble notes, crumpling them into his half-open fist.

He nodded, satisfied, grabbed her arm again, walked her out of the building across the bright, exposed driveway towards the young soldier at the gate. 'Give him the same.'

'Can't you share?'

The attendant laughed at her.

The soldier demanded, 'Share what?'

Then the orderly reached into Nina's coat pockets with both his own hands, but as he stepped close to her, he stood on her foot at the same time, and sent her sprawling hard on the wet ground. She cried out with the blow, to her hip, to her head.

The soldier began to heckle him. 'Let me have my share, you bastard.'

The watchtower light swung around onto the three of them.

'Put her outside!' The orderly was snarling, urgent. 'I'll give you what you deserve.'

In the few seconds that the soldier took to open his small door, Nina struggled to her feet. She wondered if she would lose control of herself, if she would suddenly be ill. Then the soldier pushed her, reeling, out into the street.

She stumbled along in her boots, her coat hem unravelling, one whole side of her wet with muck, leaves clinging to her, and suddenly a hand came from nowhere in the darkness behind her, clamped over her mouth, taking her breath away, and her arms were pressed so hard against her that she felt weak, light, a feather, at the mercy of whatever was happening now. Her surprise was total.

'What the hell are you doing?'

She recognized the voice right away, despite the whisper, the hiss of contained rage. It was Wentz.

She went floppy in his arms and tears choked her. Her self-control was finished.

He felt her give way, softened his grip, held her up. 'Don't make any noise. We can't be seen together. Not here. Go back via the Metro.'

'I don't have any money.'

'Oh, Lord, Nina. Not even five kopecks for a fare?' He let go of her, reached into his pocket and gave her the coin. Then he walked off and left her there.

Nina did as she was told. She didn't spot him in the station, but Wentz materialized in the bright, rumbling train in a dark blue overcoat, brown fedora, well-shined black shoes, and sat down beside her.

'You look like you've had a bad time.' He spoke very quietly, with a lilt of interrogation.

'I don't want to talk about it,' she mumbled. Her hands trembled a little in her lap, and she picked them up and wrung them, slowly, as if to wring strength into them, as if to reassure herself. She didn't look at him.

'I saw what happened, Nina.' His voice was gentle, sympathetic.

'I mean, I saw them pick you up in the ambulance and I saw that goon throw you out.' He put a hand on her knee, patted it, almost absentmindedly, then said in a frank, familiar tone, 'What the hell are you doing? You're more nuts than anyone realizes. You're lucky they didn't lock you in with the others.'

Nina swatted at his hand by her knee, even though he had already taken it away. She began to cry. She tried to keep it to herself, peering around them at the almost empty train. A lumpy, wrapped-up woman near them dropped her eyes ostentatiously and fiddled with the handles of the string shopping bag that hung loose and half empty across her lap. Nina could almost feel the woman's ears straining towards them.

'I'm pregnant,' she finally said, her eyes still on her hands. She offered it as an explanation for her behaviour, an excuse, and she said it neatly, crisply, as if a woman being pregnant accounted for simply anything. But she felt it as a confession, hard to make, and her heart was silently imploring Wentz, someone, anyone, to understand this, to understand her, to help her. Too many things were happening at once; she was feeling too much, she was feeling more than she could bear.

'Congratulations,' Wentz said with his know-it-all smile. 'I'm glad to hear it's true. Who's the lucky father?'

He might as well have hit her. 'How dare you! You cruel, cynical bastard. Get away from me. Get away once and for all.' It came between her clenched jaws, toothed rage. The woman with the string shopping bag flinched in excitement. Nina saw her.

'Forgive me, ma'am.' Wentz stood up, suddenly formal. 'Honestly – I'm sorry. It seems I always misunderstand you. I really did not mean to hurt your feelings.' He touched the brim of his hat, bowing a little. Then after an instant's pause, he started in again, cautiously. 'Naturally, I'll move away if you want me to, but first I think you'd better listen to what I have to say.'

She was silent, weeping, her chin on her chest.

Wentz stood over her, hanging from a pole, and unbuttoned his coat so that it spread in front of her like a curtain and blocked out the other passengers in the train. He watched her as if to see whether she would object, then leaned very close.

'An unarmed American spy plane was shot down over Cuba today. It's brought things to a head. Washington can't even monitor the situation there any more unless they take out the Cuban surface-to-air missile sites first. So there may be a bombing raid tomorrow morning. You can't be pulling these crazy stunts at a time like this, Nina. I realize now that I should never have asked you about Derzhavin. That you feel too strongly about him.'

'How is it possible to feel too strongly about someone?' Her chin snapped up at him, her mottled face flushed with rage and sorrow, her eyes blazed bitterly.

'God, you really did grow up in Russia, didn't you?' He couldn't resist another wisecrack, and he regretted it right away, feeling the heat of her stare. He put his hand up as if it could shield him.

'Nina, please! Wait. If there's chaos tomorrow, then maybe we can get to Viktor somehow. I don't know. But you have just got to realize this is not a ballet. The men are not all here to hold you up so you can dance and look dramatic. OK, you can wrap any one of us around your little finger, that's obvious. But there's work to do, and we can't always be there to catch you if you fall. You have to get control of yourself. You can't just jump with your eyes closed.'

She was silent for a moment, and then she said, rigidly, evenly, 'That's not fair. And you know it. You sent me to do something pretty dangerous and you didn't really tell me anything about it. You encouraged me to deceive my husband, tried to pry me loose from him somehow. And you don't know what you are doing any better than I do; you just make it up as you go along. What is an intelligence professional, anyway? Of course this isn't a ballet; and you're not a choreographer. You think you've researched me, but you know nothing about me, what it feels like to be me, what it was really like for me growing up in this city.'

She felt the train stop, looked about with a sense of uncertainty, alarm, felt the curtain of Wentz's coat brush against her face. The doors closed, kissed the air behind his lifting heel. For the second time that night, he was gone.

Nina couldn't bear the way Wentz had manipulated her; how easily she had let him. But she had listened to what he said, and she brooded on it as she walked home.

The elevator lady was agog as she took Nina upstairs. Her face revealed by turns shock, disapproval, outrage, concern. None of these expressions got a rise out of Nina. Nina nodded as she got in, got out of the elevator, and kept silent, as though it were perfectly normal to come home looking as if she'd rolled in the gutter.

But inside the apartment, she tore off her clothes, thinking with disgust of the orderly, of the soldier. She started scouring her skin with a washcloth at the sink. She couldn't bear to bring their filth into the bathtub and sit in it. As the steaming water roared into the bath, she squatted over it, with the plug out, thinking about the abortion she hadn't had. And about Viktor, about his terrible vulnerability. Felix warned me. But I was thinking of what Viktor wrote, about what's inside his mind. He only shows strength, but even his mind is threatened.

Suddenly her guts began to heave. She clenched her teeth in fury and revulsion, held onto the side of the bath as sickness overwhelmed her, vomit and tears. Wave after wave spewed out of her into the running water. She clung there, helpless, giving in. Afterwards, she rinsed her face, the inside of her mouth, swooshed the water over herself, over the bath, trying to wash it all away.

Everything except the baby. She lay in the thin stream of water, weeping in exhaustion and dismay. What had she done, exposing the baby to such danger? She considered, with urgent, desperate anxiety, that the baby was her link to everything that had for a time been right in her life. The baby had been conceived in joy, in conviction, in ecstasy. It mustn't die. It connected her to John, to their brief, perfect past, to something that could not be defiled. It connected her to what they had hoped for.

She thought of the plane that had been shot down. The pilot falling through the air. Alone. Did he know what was coming? The lurid, fantastic explosion? The lurch? The black bursting mushroom of fire, rushing emptiness. On the ground, they must have heard the whistling roar, the target plummeting towards them like a bomb, and seen, high above them, debris fanning out on the air, flakes of fallout spreading on updraughts, silent, weightless, rising heavenward like smoke from a sacrifice.

Nothing more, nothing worse can happen to me, she thought. There would be dying, and that might come tomorrow for everyone. But what is the good of acting from fear?

She dragged herself from the bath, wrapped up in a towel, went looking for clean clothes. Every drawer was full of satin and silk from Paris; the cupboard was crammed, hangers draped with extravagant dresses and suits. She hated them all, felt disgusted by them, thinking of Viktor, of his evident starvation, of how he had nothing at all. She thought of what Wentz had said and of how much it had hurt her, that the men are not all here to hold you up so you can dance and look dramatic.

'Oh *what* is all this for?' she cried aloud. 'What does it mean?' And she thought, How much easier to be a man! This is my mother's idea – a trousseau, to set me apart from the world, to make men get me what I want because that never happened for her. Because she chose the wrong thing. Then she shouted out again, 'I hate these goddamn clothes! I want them out. I want them gone.'

She began emptying the drawers, throwing everything inside them onto the bed, onto the floor. She threw things right out the bedroom door into the hallway. Kicking them in the air, kicking them away. Nightgowns and underclothes fell in heaps, shining, delicate, gossamer, limp on the floor; shell pink, champagne, dove grey. Carefully stitched, unworn.

Her towel fell away and she whirled through the rooms naked, crazy with energy and distress. She ran back to the bedroom, pulled one hanger after another from the cupboard, hurled them across the room: jewel-coloured cocktail dresses; tight-fitting wool skirts, A-line or with kick pleats at the back, clamped in heavy wooden skirt hangers that thumped loudly against the floor when they hit; little, short-fitting jackets cut from matching lengths of cloth. No more costumes, she was thinking, no more acting, no more pretence, no more lies. She pulled cardigans and hats from the shelves. The hallway was ankle deep in cashmere, fur.

She danced through the living room, opened the window, and began to pitch the clothes out into the night. Down they swirled, spread-eagled, glorious, a strapless black chiffon evening gown, the shoulder-length black suede gloves that made it wearable on a cold Russian night. Her white bouclé Balenciaga suit. She felt relieved, exhilarated, watching them disappear in the roaring wind, the dark.

Then she heard the elevator rising. The sound startled her, quenched her mania.

Oh my God. Someone's coming. The clothes must be landing in Leninsky Prospekt. They'll think I'm nuts. And she looked down at her nakedness, thin-legged, grey-pink, chilled and trembling. They'll think I'm really insane.

She took John's bathrobe from the hook on the back of the bathroom door, wrapped it deep under her arms, tied the belt tightly, and crept along the hallway. Carefully, she opened the door, peeked out. There was the elevator lady, glittering-eyed, ferocious. She held out the white bouclé jacket, scowled, shrugged, forced the jacket closer to the door, shaking it a little to push her way in.

Nina opened the door, raking her chaotic hair back from her

face, and the elevator lady came in scolding. 'Where is Mr Davenport? Where is he all the time now? Maybe we should phone him?' She looked at Nina closely, squinting at her, grumpy.

Nina took the jacket and made a show of finding a hanger to put it on, smoothing it, brushing off a bit of dirt from the street. The elevator lady followed her along the hall into the bedroom, trawling up a chemise, a pearly blouse, a mauve cocktail dress along the way, then brandishing them accusingly.

Nina's feet had become swaddled in her mink coat. She picked it up in both hands and held it out, heavy, lank, prickly-smooth, smelling of Chanel N° 5. 'Here, you have this.'

The elevator lady backed away, shaking her head.

'And those,' said Nina, inclining her head to indicate the things the elevator lady was already holding. 'I don't want them. I don't need them. Just take them away. Take anything you like.'

'Yelena Petrovna will die over this mess,' said the elevator lady.

'I'll save her something,' Nina said sweetly. 'What would she like?'

The practicality of this question caught the elevator lady off guard, or it addressed her uncertainty about accepting things from the crazy American, things she knew Yelena Petrovna admired and jealously guarded. She relaxed her arms around the loot she had already collected, stopped trying to push it towards Nina, held it in a bundle, close against her stomach. Then, lifting her eyebrows, she looked around, considering. 'Well,' she said, 'Yelena Petrovna is a bigger woman than you. Bigger even than me. But she has daughters, and daughters-in-law, too. Maybe some skirts for them, blouses, jackets.'

Nina began picking things up, folding them hurriedly, making little stacks on the bed, of pieces that belonged together. She took down a new leather handbag from the cupboard shelf, her mink pillbox hat, held them up, saying, 'She could use these herself, couldn't she?'

Then they both heard the elevator bell ringing from the down-stairs hall, insistently.

'I must do my job,' said the elevator lady. She lifted her bundle poignantly, reluctant to let go, wondering what to do with it.

So Nina now found herself offering to take it back. 'I'll keep these things safe until you go off duty. And the rest I'll set aside for Yelena Petrovna.'

Nina was collapsed on the sofa in staring bewilderment when John came through the open apartment door and along the hallway carrying her black chiffon evening gown, a glove, the white bouclé skirt that went with the jacket.

She couldn't lift her face to his. She couldn't speak. She needed a sign from him.

He said nothing.

She could feel his eyes on her, and she wondered how much he could see of her regret, her sorrow.

It didn't occur to her that he was blaming himself for what he saw on the sofa. That his joints had gone liquid with dread, hot and loose, as if his limbs might let go of his body. That he could barely stand up, hold onto her clothes. The woman he idolized appeared to him to be rejecting her life, her very identity, throwing it away, right out the window.

It seemed all too plain to John now that he had destroyed Nina by bringing her back to Moscow. It shocked him to recognize it, to admit it. He felt his mind emptying of hopes, dreams, shreds of illusion; he felt he had wilfully deceived himself and her. Suddenly, he was facing a bleak reality. Cold, dry, unarguable fact.

I never accepted that she had fled; I somehow let myself imagine that it had been a journey of choice. And I never saw how dark the background was behind her, either. He clenched his teeth in self-hatred, in rage at his folly, his immaturity, his over-confidence. It was a fantasy I had about Russia, I let myself be enchanted – so that I even confused her intelligence and her passion with something that would be here still, something she could return to. I forced it on her, the idea that she could come back, return to some element she had sprung from. Live half in it, half out. As if she were a nymph, a mythical creature, swathed in a blizzard of light, in furs, swept by romantic winds. It all deserted him now, the power to picture things as right, bright, wonderful; it had all been false magic, like Nina's clothes.

He was afraid to go to her; he was afraid of what he had done, and of whatever he might do next.

She was crying silently by the time he finally said, 'Wentz told me —' He stopped and started again. 'Wentz was concerned about you, darling. So I came as quickly as I could. I should have come sooner. I'm sorry. This has all been too much for you.' He corrected himself, feeling that what he had said was condescending, but he was vague, cautious. 'It's all been too much for everyone. For me. Cuba getting scarier and scarier.'

She didn't answer. He couldn't feel in himself what to do, what to say. He couldn't read her, and he began to panic. 'Should I call the doctor?'

'No, no,' Nina said tensely, and then in a low, sad voice, 'Let's not involve anyone else in this.'

She stood up, gathering his robe around her, her eyes downcast. All she wanted was to tell him everything from the beginning, but she was tired and unsure. She was anxious that she had previously kept too much back and thereby strayed from what they knew and understood about each other; maybe he would turn from her altogether. If he did, she had no idea what she would do; she didn't even know how to think about it. It seemed too much like the end of life. She realized that until now, despite the fact that she had deceived him, she had never really considered it possible that he *would* turn from her. But if she didn't tell him all the truth now, when would she? And how would they move on? It seemed clear she had to risk it.

She took a step towards him, looked up to his face at last, lean and wary above her, saw the fear in his eye and was surprised by it. What had she expected? Anger? Hatred? Retribution?

And she found herself telling him first, because she thought it would alleviate his fear and because she wanted to offer him something good, something that had the kind of feeling she wished for between them, 'It's just maybe I can't wear the clothes anyway, because I might be pregnant. I mean – I hope so. I'm not sure.'

'What?' He smiled in puzzlement, confusion. 'You can't wear the clothes? You might be pregnant? So – the clothes would be – you mean, just too small?'

Suddenly John saw everything completely differently. He had walked in on a tableau of breakdown, a young wife ruined by her husband's career, but now it seemed that the tableau represented some altogether different set of circumstances. The change in understanding came about in an instant; he began to laugh.

'You said, "I hope so",' he blurted out, still laughing. 'Does that mean that you –'

'It means that I'm pretty certain and that I want it to happen.' She smiled. 'I mean – if you want it to happen.' There was still a space of three or four steps between them.

'And the clothes,' she went on, 'are just – they are something my mother wanted for me. The truth is that I don't know what I want for myself. I mean – I want to move on – with you, with our lives. I realize it now; I don't have to live by her fears, her desires.' Nina felt happiness between them, trying to well up.

Not crazy, John thought. Pregnant. Herself, but pregnant. He looked at her in a rapture of recognition. A woman who would throw thousands of dollars' worth of clothes out an eighth-floor window in Moscow to defy her mother back in Buffalo, to express her wish to have a child – this was the creature of conviction and abandon who had first bowled him off his feet.

He took the last steps towards her, wrapped her in his arms, felt her as brittle, surprisingly frail. She barely responded to his embrace. And he thought, But she is not robust. It occurred to him that maybe she never had been robust, except in her spirit. She was now perhaps more delicate, with the pregnancy, with the child.

Moscow has cost her a lot. I haven't been able to protect her from pain, and there's more to come, worse. I can never really protect her enough. He thought he would drown in the difficulty of it, his helplessness, his bittersweet joy at her revelation.

To his surprise, she was the one who said, vigorously, 'There's a lot to talk about, John.' She was thinking, Wentz hasn't told him much, maybe nothing. It's for me to do. And she wondered how John would bear it. She wanted more of his physical reassurance, but she couldn't allow herself to need it, to go to sleep in his arms, to forget herself. She held back from his warmth, barely managing to.

He sensed the resistance in her, and he couldn't understand it; he felt impatient.

'Nina, I'm wrecked. I've hardly slept this week. But if you want to talk, let's do it now and be square with each other by morning. Darling, let me be clear. Khrushchev, Kennedy, their generals, they may blow us all sky high in a matter of hours. We can't spend another day drifting, misunderstood. We have tonight – maybe it has to be for everything.'

He led her by the hand into the kitchen, saying, 'Let's eat something. You sit down.'

He put water on to boil, opened a can of creamed chipped beef and emptied it into a saucepan, started making toast. When the water boiled, he took down the canister of coffee and opened it. There inside were the papers Nina had hidden for him that very morning.

He dropped them on the table, paying no attention, put a filter in the little glass jug, filled it with ground coffee, poured the boiling water on top, ladled the chipped beef onto the toast on two plates and put the plates on the table. All the while, Nina stared at the little roll of wax paper, wondering whether to draw his attention to it. She couldn't breathe, it was so present, so evident.

John sat down, lifted his slopping toast to his mouth, took a huge bite, poured out coffee while he chewed, and then said, his mouth full, 'What is that? That little package inside the coffee can?'

Nina hadn't eaten anything. She unrolled the papers, removing the note she'd written, spread them in front of John, right way up for him, and held down the curled sides with shaking hands.

John read, chewing. He furrowed his brow in concentration. Then he put his food down, swivelled around, grabbed the dish towel hanging over the back of his chair, wiped his hands carefully on it, and pulled the papers towards him, slowly reading through them all.

After a few minutes he said, 'Where the hell did you get these?'

Nina didn't speak. She wasn't sure if she could, and anyway she knew that in the apartment it wasn't wise. So now she laid her own note on the table, and let him read it to himself: Dear John, You are a lover of the Russian language. These are some of its masterworks. Read them. Get them out. Get them published. Love always. N.

'"Love always. N."? Why so valedictory? When was I supposed to find these, Nina? What is this all about?'

There was trouble in his voice, Nina thought, suspicion.

'The poems are Viktor Derzhavin's,' she said quickly, under her breath. 'I thought you'd know that right away.'

'But isn't he the one – didn't you tell me that he was in prison? That you – had lost touch with him? This makes it seem as if – as if you're about to run off with him or something.'

'Oh, don't be ridiculous. That's not it at all,' Nina cried out. 'Keep your voice down for God's sake.' She stood up wearily, walked to the counter, turned on the radio, the water in the sink, and picked up her shopping pad and pencil. She came back and stood beside John, leaned down and wrote on the pad in front of him, 'The poems have been smuggled out of prison and passed to me.' Then she whispered, 'I – I thought – I *knew* that you would see how good they are, how important, how revealing.' She scribbled on the pad, 'Dangerous, but worth whatever it would take to get them out to the West.'

'I didn't want to give them to Wentz,' Nina went on by John's ear. 'Maybe I should have, but I couldn't bear it. I wanted you to see them. I wanted you to be the one to do this – for Viktor.'

'But why not just give them to me yourself? Where were you planning to be? And what's Wentz got to do with all this anyway?'

She froze involuntarily, then eked out, 'Well, this morning I – I wasn't sure when I would see you. And the feeling we've been living with, that everything we do is maybe for the last time . . . I guess it doesn't make sense, that you would be alive to find the poems if I couldn't be here to give them to you, but –'

'No, Nina, it doesn't make sense at all.' He was angry. 'And I want to know exactly how you got these, why you would have given them to Wentz, and what the hell is going on with this doctor.'

Nina grew even more tense. 'We need to be careful, John. I'll tell you everything you want to know, but think hard about what I say, believe in me, understand me. I have to choose my words carefully. Maybe we can be overheard.'

And so she sat down again in her chair and began to try to explain what Wentz had asked her to do. She scratched out the most telling phrases on the pad, terse, hurried, and they pushed the pad back and forth, big-eyed, watchful, like mistrustful card players. The writing couldn't hold it all, and words spilled over out loud in frightening bursts. But still, for Nina, the pad was like a discipline, helping her to control the awful tale as she told it – how Wentz claimed to have brought John to Moscow in order to get her to Moscow, how Wentz had waited until she made contact with her old friends so he could locate Viktor, because of the people Viktor knew, because of what Viktor was like, because there might be a power struggle coming. How he had forbidden her to tell John.

John was rigid, chewing his lip, his green eyes more stunned each time she pushed the pad back to him, the pupils like points of onyx, shining and hard, then at last he announced in a strident, assertive voice, as if he were trying to convince himself, 'Wentz is a good man; I respect him. Whatever he's trying to do, it's for a good reason.'

He didn't want to believe that Wentz and Nina had been in league to deceive him. The business of why he and Nina had been brought to Moscow was almost impossible to take in. He hardly knew where to direct his confusion, his sense of betrayal. So he directed it at his wife, challenging her harshly. 'For days I wondered whether you were in love with that doctor; now I discover the doctor's a goddamn woman? That's not how you described it to me, Nina.' And he picked up from the table and held out a paper with the name Eva Simonova on it, followed by an address and the date Saturday, October 27. 'Your lover can't be a woman?'

'My lover?' Nina stared at the paper, swallowed uncomfortably, then said, looking John in the eye, 'I was going to have an abortion. But I didn't. I put that in by mistake, her address; it was with the poems in my purse.'

There was a long silence.

'OK,' John said, 'I think I understand.' His voice was forbidding.

'I'm sorry, John, about the abortion. About not telling you. I was — terrified about having a baby. I tried to tell you. At first I was afraid that you could never understand, and then once I had agreed to do what Wentz asked, and agreed to keep my mouth shut — well — then I couldn't tell you.'

Tears appeared in his eyes, at the loss of trust between them, at the thought of all that had gone wrong.

'It gets worse, John.' She couldn't look at him, at his tears. 'I went to see him. Last night. I went to the — hospital — where

308

they're holding Viktor. Wentz told me which one. And Felix arranged –' She began to cry.

'What, darling, what happened?' His concern was painful to her. He reached for her hand, across the table; she pulled it back, then made herself lay it on the table underneath his, fluttering, unsettled.

'He – I – it was so frightening. Unbearable. I don't know how he can survive it. It was so hard to leave him. And then I – I realized that actually I *wanted* to get away, I couldn't stop thinking about – about being free of it all . . . That's the thing you need to know.'

'What on earth are you saying?' John's voice was hoarse, derisory. 'That you saw this guy Derzhavin last night . . . ?'

She went cold with it, stopped crying, stared at him emptily. Nodded. Then her stomach began to heave again, and she wrapped her arms around herself, trying to stay in her chair, trying to calm herself.

He got up and stormed around the table. Stopped on the brink of something. Stood still. Then leaned down to her, ever so gently put his arms around her shoulders, rocked her. 'Oh, God in heaven, how has this all happened? To my wife. To my precious, only Nina.'

But on top of his sweet, instinctive forgiveness came more rage. 'What has Wentz got you into? What has he done? I'll kill him.'

'It's not Wentz,' Nina lamented. 'He told me not to do it. He warned me. But I *had* to see Viktor; Felix understood. I thought you would understand, too.'

'Why, Nina?' John wasn't in control of himself, of his voice, which got suddenly loud, louder. 'Why should I be able to understand this? I'm flesh and blood! What is it that you feel for this man? Why did you come back to Russia, Nina? Why did you agree to it – when we both knew it was so dangerous? Was it to see this man? Is that why you married me for Christ's sake? Am

I just a passport to your old life, your true love? The man you are straight with? Why do you lie to me so much? I can't deal with lying. I don't get it. I don't get the point. Why would anyone lie unless they had things to hide?'

Then he fell quiet, struggling to make some calculation about how Americans were so straight, such suckers, that they couldn't deal with Europeans, Russians, foreigners; that he'd been made a fool of; that he didn't understand women, or how the world worked, the Byzantine intricacies of some other language of behaviour, some other system of love, not strictly monogamous; how he had wanted to understand, to be cosmopolitan; how he had never really been interested by anything else apart from understanding what was going on inside other people, the more mysterious and difficult, the more intriguing; how he had thought, believed, that he had special gifts of empathy; how he now felt at bottom that the reason he didn't get all these things was that he simply wasn't sufficiently depraved and didn't want to believe in the depravity of others.

'Whose baby is it, Nina? If you want me to get the poems out for Viktor, I'll do it, but I want to know whether it's his baby.'

This wrung an astonished cry from her. 'How could it be his baby? Please don't doubt me now when I need you to – to bring me back to the side of life where you are, where our future lies. Just let go of – your – well, it's a delusion, John.' She dropped her voice to an urgent, horrified murmur. 'Viktor is in prison for Christ's sake. I haven't seen him since 1956 – apart from last night. The baby is yours. If there is a baby.'

Oh, please, she moaned silently in her head, please let there be a baby. Don't let it be harmed. And she thought of how hard she had fallen, the vomiting afterwards.

She forged on: 'I know from the way I feel about you, have always felt about you, from the way we – are together – that I never would have been happy with Viktor even if we could have been together. He's for the whole world; he's not just for me.

How can I explain it to you if you don't already see? What he loves are ideas, principles, justice. He is given to history – I mean it. He could never love me – not as I actually am. Not in the way that you love me. And that love affair, such as it was – well, I was just a kind of disciple, a passive observer. At eighteen, nineteen – I was much younger than that, in fact, wasn't I? – I wanted experience, knowledge, in any form. I rode along on his certainty. I don't think I had any will or any beliefs of my own because nobody had ever let me. And the feelings were really all his, too, I think, even the love. Maybe I hid something of myself from him, or acted a part; that's what teenagers are like, tough-shelled, idealistic, proud. I guess I was even using him to fight my mother, because my father wasn't there any more to help me do that. Anyway, Viktor was focused on other things: his writing, the atmosphere he was trying to create – of opposition, of dissent. He didn't know how to look inside me. He was looking up, looking away, looking at the State, looking out for trouble.'

Suddenly John lost patience, demanded angrily, 'How the hell do I compete with this, with heroes, moral demigods?'

'What?' Nina was panic-stricken, white.

'I can't stay here, Nina. I have to go back to the office.'

'You think Dobrynin trusts you, Bobby?' asked the president.

Bobby Kennedy still had his hand on the doorknob, halfway out of the Oval Office on his way to the Justice Department. The light slanted through the door into the dim hallway, pooling around his shiny, big black brogues, the bottoms of his short uncuffed trousers, his boyish ankles in their thin black socks. He looked back towards the president, but he couldn't see his face because the president was sitting in his rocking chair, and the others – McNamara, Rusk, George Ball, Ros Gilpatric, Tommy Thompson, Sorenson, Bundy – were mostly already standing now, rustling papers, getting ready to leave, to have supper.

Bobby let go of the doorknob, shrugged his grey flannel suit jacket up around his square, skinny shoulders, buttoned the top button of the jacket with one hand, his Adam's apple wobbling and jumping. He looked down at his shoes in the puddle of light, nervous, rolled his lips around his mouthful of big white teeth, grimaced. Then he said, 'I think we have an understanding. But, it's what *he's* up against. Don't we all wish we really understood that?'

'Anyhow, I trust Dobrynin if you do, Bobby,' said the president from the depths of the room.

Rusk ran a hand over his baldness, spoke from his lumbering height. 'Ambassador Dobrynin is a smart man; the Soviets have never before sent us an ambassador who didn't need his hand held the whole time. He doesn't rely on a minder or any interpreter. He's his own man, and he knows what he's talking about. You two are speaking English, alone, Bobby. I think the relationship sounds the best you can hope for.'

'Look, Bobby,' said the president, 'you and Ball have persuaded everyone to ignore Khrushchev's new letter and accept the informal terms he offered in the long one. So I'm confident you can get this message through for us now: I *will* take those Jupiter missiles out of Turkey as long as the Russians keep quiet about it. There's no way we're going to go to war over obsolete missiles. Just make sure Ambassador Dobrynin understands that Khrushchev's going to have to trust me. No public announcement whatsoever and nothing at all on paper. No written assurances. We'll get it through NATO if he waits – four or five months. I am not issuing an ultimatum. I am just trying to give Mr Khrushchev what I think he wants. Though it's been damn hard to figure that out.'

Now Bobby laughed, his wide lips gummy with phlegm, with

anxiety. 'I may be jumpy as hell, but I know the deal, Jack.'

'Good luck, then, kiddo. Give him your telephone number here, in the White House.'

McNamara pressed his glasses against the bridge of his nose with a long, bony finger. His pupils were swollen, magnified by the lenses, intense. 'We have to get his answer by tomorrow – we can't hold off the joint chiefs any longer. They want to go in with these air strikes Monday morning at the latest.'

'Sure, sure, sure. I know that, too.' Bobby was impatient, chafing.

As he made off down the deserted hall, he could hear Rusk's Georgian drawl continuing carefully, quietly to his brother, but he didn't take it in.

'If Khrushchev doesn't accept this deal, Mr President, we could call my friend Andrew Cordier, the Under Secretary General at the UN. I'll pass him a statement for the Secretary General, U Thant, to publish over his own signature, proposing that the USA and the USSR both withdraw missiles – from Cuba and from Turkey. Then it doesn't come from us, and NATO and the Turks can't complain.'

The president replied calmly, 'OK. We could do that. Good idea. But first let's see whether Bobby can persuade Ambassador Dobrynin and Mr Khrushchev to do this deal on the quiet.'

He made a deep backwards rock in his chair, then stood up as the chair came forward again, a hand moving to his lower back. 'Let's give this thing some time to work, give it a real chance. I'm going to take a swim.'

October 28. Alone in the eighth row at the Bolshoi, in her white bouclé Balenciaga suit, Nina continued to cry on and off throughout the performance. Her hands were so wet with wiped tears that she had to balance Viktor's poems on her lap; she had been afraid to leave them in the apartment, and she was afraid even to touch them now in order to slide them back into her skirt pockets. The poems had become for her like a stone, sinking her marriage. But she would hold on to the stone.

When she had woken that morning, John had not returned and the poems were still lying on the kitchen table; she had tried to accept it as his response to everything that had happened between them. Or not happened. He hadn't taken the poems into his care, hadn't taken them to the embassy for safekeeping until he could get them out.

Maybe none of this matters anyway, she thought bitterly. Everyone is hunkered down, ready for the end, the firestorm, the looming, spinning dust. The poems are just a flourish of defiance, like what's in front of me on the stage.

She stared at the dancers, still hardly seeing them, and thought about Wentz, his hurtful remark about her expecting men to be there to hold her up, to catch her if she fell. And she wondered, Do I expect men to do that? Do I want a partner with no desires but my desires, to help me fulfil some dream about myself? Did I think that Wentz was choreographing a ballet, a drama, just for me to star in?

Felix is the only one who has the right to say such a thing, she thought indignantly; it's true that I've always expected too

314

much of Felix. And she knew that was why Wentz's comment had hurt her so much. It's almost as if Felix and I had been in love with Viktor together. I wasn't strong enough to try that by myself; or anyway, I would never have had the nerve. But with Felix looking on, I thought – I thought I could.

She remembered the way Balanchine had looked at her in the dining room of the Ukraina at lunchtime just a few days ago, how she had felt him notice her, look right inside her and take possession of her. Like a lover, was what I thought at the time, she reflected. But in that way, I am so easily misled. It was only because he thought I was a dancer, a tool through which he might express his inward vision. His energy dropped away in an instant when he recognized me. Here in the theatre, she thought, is where he is at his most intimate. She felt it with uncomfortable intensity: that his sensibility was laid bare utterly in his ballets, so that what she now saw before her eyes, right out there in public in front of so many people, was the flagrant display of something private – and infinitely complicated. There is something essential, personal in what he has the dancers do with their bodies, she thought, and because it's bodies, it is undeniably erotic. She felt a little shocked.

So what about *his* marriages, *his* wives? she wondered. Why don't *his* marriages ever last? Does he have sex with his wives? Maybe he would rather make dances for them. They none of them have babies. None. Ever. Birth control or not. Is that why they leave him? It seemed to her at once controlling and abject, this attitude towards women that she saw reflected in the ballets. If there was ever a pedestal, she thought, a ballerina's on it. And if she dances for Balanchine, all the more so. The men in his ballets are almost prissy in their restraint, subdued, emasculated.

Why is Felix still alone? Why has he never married? Why, when we both knew he loved me, did he never – express it, act on it? He only – protected me, at great cost to himself. And I became used to it, didn't value it enough, his strength, like an indulgence.

Maybe my mother was right – how I might have been safe as

a ballerina. Or was it Viktor who advised me of that? But I didn't want safety. Was it just that I didn't think I deserved it? How would I get off the pedestal, get into the bed? How touch one another directly, with nothing mediating, without art, without transformation, without translation?

And then she thought, eyes fixed on the stage, moving with the movements she saw there, that there is a pathos in the mere physicality of the dancers. Balanchine's choreography perfectly reveals his understanding of the music, but even the greatest dancer cannot move as precisely, as perfectly as music. Only heartbreakingly near perfection. On the other hand, Nina considered, what the body lacks in perfection, it makes up for in erotic power – and that power is extra, a boon. It's something like – a grace of mortality, she thought. The idea wrung her heart. She thought of Viktor's mind, the music and perfection of it, in contrast to the woeful circumstances of his body. As if he were in chains. The contrast was too great to bear.

Balanchine's after something transcendent. He sees it in the ballerinas, or sees he can express it through their bodies, but after a while, the ballerinas must realize that he isn't looking at them for themselves. He has his eyes fixed on something else, something in the distance, just above their heads, over their shoulders. Some phantom. They are only human bodies, human beings.

That's how it was with Viktor, she thought. Everything he ever felt had to be changed into a form of words, a point of view, a principle to suffer for. It could never be just a feeling, a sensation – for instance, a feeling about us. Which is why I would never have stayed with him. And it ran through her head again, I would never have stayed with him.

It wasn't just fear, however natural, however blameless it might be to fear arrest, torture, death. The truth is I knew he was looking somewhere else, over my shoulder, just above my head.

What is it that a shy young woman does? Nina wondered with pain. Offers her body like a gift to someone she thinks she loves, lets him use it, but takes no delight in it for herself, fails to insist upon satisfaction because it seems somehow selfish in the heat of love to make demands. And so sexual passion dies, or is never ignited at all. The relationship dissolves, the collaboration ends. However much I thought I adored him, there was no sexual passion at the heart of it. Maybe it was his very worthiness, his greatness, which prevented it.

I suppose I never went back to the Bolshoi school for the same reason – because I wanted my body for something else. For myself. It was hard for Nina to admit this, but she knew it was true. It seemed lowbrow, animal, lazy, lacking in artistic commitment, or in the effort of sublimation. Viktor seemed to be just as unrelenting as my father, and I responded to that at first. But why would I want that all over again, someone who leaves you in the middle of things, with a puzzle you can't solve?

And John. Well, John had looked directly at Nina, saw her and nothing else. She chewed her lip, trying to drive off regret.

He saw exactly how I was made, what I wanted, she thought. To John my body was – private. Its delights, beauties – also private. What was between us sufficed. Carnival energies, festival nights. Her mind bubbled perversely with rich terms. None of it would ever be articulated for public display, as a form of art. That's why the KGB, the eavesdropping, she thought, set me on toxic edge, corrupted our pleasure. Privacy. Privacy which initiates and which guarantees freedom.

Except that maybe now, Nina realized, there would be a child. A work of the flesh. A public token.

And she heaved a sigh, a tincture of blood rising in the fine pale skin of her face, as she sat beside John's empty chair, slight, tired, forlorn. I've wanted to be in partnership with someone, in a marriage. Centred over a deep involvement, an unbreakable join. I don't want to be pushed aside for something else, something more important than me, a belief. That's what's wrong with my mother, what my father did to her.

My mother was pushed aside, not even on purpose. She started out with everything and threw it all away, for love, without knowing. Panicked when she couldn't get anything back. Didn't want me to make the same mistake. But after all, it isn't *things* I want.

She felt an unexpected throb of sympathy with her mother. It obviously wasn't *things* Mother wanted either, Nina conceded. Not at first, or she never would have left home with Dad to begin with. Things are what she ended up with, her only power. Things she could push on me. Tried to. I have to get rid of things. It's not because I'm a communist. It's just that things don't move me. People move me.

Men like Viktor, like Balanchine, like Dad, can't partner ordinary people, mere pedestrians. Because they won't spend themselves on the gestures of ordinary life. They want a partnership in their chosen medium − in dance, in words, in ideals. These last two weeks, when John seemed to be devoting his best self to the office, to translating Russian, maybe I began to be afraid that he was like them. But he isn't.

Oh, God, he isn't. Down went her head into her hands. Because she had known perfectly well for plenty long enough that John had a genius for ordinary life, for human understanding. That should have been my fate; it was within my grasp. There is another fate for other kinds of people. There is no end to the kinds of fates there can be − artists, great men, ordinary men, ordinary women, all the spectrum in between. But now, we all are being handed one fate, one premature cataclysmic end. Forget finding out who we are, how we should live. We're locked in. By misunderstanding, by inarticulate posturing, bullying. By some past individual hurt that was never redressed.

She should have delighted in the row upon row of white tutus *bourréeing* magically over the stage, the lithe men in black tights and fitted black velvet tunics slicing through the air above them. On other evenings, she had smiled with helpless pleasure throughout *Symphony in C*, the vast stage thronging with synchronized legs, pale, silk-beribboned insteps, bouncing, glitter-studded tulle, Bizet's signature motif whimsically regenerating itself faster and faster.

When the dancers and the music stopped, the applause rolled around the Bolshoi like thunder, shaking Nina in her chair, out of her deep thoughts. On and on it went, unlike any applause she had ever heard before, and she felt in it sorrow and dismay that this new expression of the great Russian art form, ballet, was now finished in Moscow, was leaving the ballet lovers, the life lovers, to their bleak, permitted offering of Soviet dance, Soviet life. She also felt in it the pent-up hysteria of the Caribbean crisis, now stretching, for the public, through its sixth day. Everyone in this audience knew by now that the danger had reached a maximum.

In the tumult, Nina didn't notice John in the aisle almost beside her. When he sat down in his empty chair, her heart turned over in fear and longing.

He put his arm around her shoulders, held her close, and said in the most ordinary voice, 'I'm sorry I missed the performance again, darling. I thought I would make it this time, especially when Khrushchev's message went out at five. But there are always so many additional details to be sent back and forth. The communiqués are endless.'

She turned her face to him, teary, questioning, and his eyes went dark with confusion.

After a moment, he realized what had happened. 'You didn't hear about Khrushchev's message, did you?'

She shook her head.

'Oh, jeez, I'm sorry. I asked someone to call you and tell you to listen, Radio Moscow, at five. He's agreed to remove the missiles.' He smiled and tilted his head left then right. 'The crowd seems to know? Everyone's wild with joy.' He rattled her shoulders a little within the circle of his arm. 'Everything will be OK, Nina.'

She buried her face on his chest, sobbing; so he let her, patting her back, murmuring again and again as he bent over her, 'You can stop crying now, Nina, everything will be OK. We have all the time in the world. Everything will be OK with us, too. We've been reprieved. We can leave Moscow tomorrow if you want to. I've already talked to the ambassador about it. You need – fresh air. There are a lot of things we need to get straight between us. I lost my temper last night – I'm sorry. I don't doubt you, Nina; that's not what I feel, not real doubt, despite the – lies. Maybe I don't know you as well as I thought, but there's nothing I care about more than I care about you.'

She hung on him, reached up to kiss his cheek, relieved, overwhelmed. And still she cried. And still the applause roared around them. On the stage the dancers took bow after bow. Balanchine himself at last appeared from the wings, slim, light-footed, soberly dressed, head bowed, eyes down. He held out his arms to the audience, to the orchestra, to the dancers. He nodded but didn't smile. Nina thought his expression seemed reserved, preoccupied, as if he was already thinking of something else, somewhere else. As if he found the present enthusiasm charming, unimportant.

John stroked Nina's hair. At last she stopped crying.

'What about Viktor?' she asked. 'And Felix?'

'I know. I spoke to Wentz. I didn't think he would tell me any-thing. But he was pretty forthcoming. Obviously, he can't tell what's going to happen. It's a tight network. You can only hope that Felix won't be exposed any further than he already has been. I guess he knew what he was up to; it's not as if he was coerced. What we can do is take Viktor's poems out with us.' John sighed, spoke with less certainty: 'But, darling, you know that if the poems are published in the West, it could trigger Felix's arrest?'

Nina was silent. Then she said, 'He knew that when he gave them to me, John.' After another silence, she went on solemnly, nearly choked by her own heartbeat, 'He chose to take the chance. It's not up to us to choose differently – to save him – try to stop him. We have to go through with it. Give him the freedom, give Viktor a voice.'

'If we could save him,' John said drily.

Nina caught his eye, and he responded without much energy to her questioning look. 'There might be another – initiative. Maybe Leningrad. But there might not be, darling. This is a big, big thing, it's – still to come. Viktor's role could be significant or nothing at all. Nobody can control it, and it's painful thinking about what can happen to just one individual or two – worse if you care for them.' He paused, watching her.

She made no effort to conceal her distress, the falling away sensation inside her, something she wanted to reach for, to see again and again in her mind, a look she could still vividly behold in Viktor's clear grey eyes, shrugging at the thing which tried to stare him down, hold him down. Look, you can see what they do to me, to anyone, he might say. The loneliness, the hunger, the boredom. Obviously true. And the rest also true: plenty of pain, and so much worse besides, you can't imagine. The melancholy emptiness seemed to drop down deep inside her, making her weak, and she felt tears that lay and waited, collecting, unwept. Felix standing at her bedside, diagnosing grief, confusion.

'How can we leave them? How can *I* leave them?'

John thought, You've done it before. But he didn't say it aloud. It was plain enough.

He was noncommittal. There was a new way, he was thinking, which he wanted to be with his wife. Doing nothing at all, remaining neutral beside her experience.

'We'll see. Why don't we wait and see?' he said. 'You have to believe there can be a future, Nina. Viktor anyway chose his life. They both believe in what they are doing. These are not people who would easily agree to leave Russia. Why would they? So – if it's not too corny, maybe think of Viktor –' John waved a hand towards the dancers, 'in the wings, waiting to come on. He has a presence, however shadowy. He has a voice which is very powerful, even in his hidden life, even offstage. His time will come.'

Nina saw that Felix had given her a role. It gave her no comfort, but it was an important role.

Just then, Patrice, with a beige nylon robe over her glittering white tutu, was talking to Wentz backstage about how the scenery and costumes travelled with the company on tour. She opened one of the enormous aluminium containers that would go by truck to Leningrad, Kiev, Tbilisi, Baku, and then by truck and by air back to New York. Laughing, she climbed inside, lay down on her back in a cloud of white phantom layers, net bodice and filmy skirt, closed her eyes, and with one extravagant gesture of her wraithlike arm, covered herself with the coquette's red and black gown from *La Sonnambula*.

'It's pretty comfortable for me,' she giggled, 'but you're so much bigger. Why don't you get in here yourself? Get in with me.'

In a van travelling nearby, Viktor was thinking about trees.

I could not have written this book without the generous help of Anna Blinova and of her husband, Craig Kennedy, nor without the first idea for it given to me over dinner by Peter Semler. I am deeply grateful to them and also to Stephanie Cabot, Michael Stuart Cassidy, Melanie Essex, John Fuller, A. J. Heath, Bob Maguire, Robert McCrum, Roger Pasquier, Jamison Stoltz, Erik Tarloff, Susan Watt.